Siren Song

Siren Song

by

A.C. Warneke

ISBN: 1477407944

ISBN-13: 978-1477407943

To friends and family both near and far; for those still here and those that have passed on. Words cannot express how much each of you means to me.

ଓଃ

To my sons who keep me humble by telling me I am like one of the seven dwarves only shorter and my daughter who tells me it is okay to be short, mainly because she'll always be shorter than me.. And 5' 3 3/4" is not that short.

I love the three of you so much!

Chapter 1 (Friday)

Glancing around the bar, Lexi Darling made note of the small camera crew setting up for the reality series of some up and coming young starlet. Lexi was hoping to be out of there before the chaos began, and with just a few more things to finish up, she was well on her way. Her scalp was starting to itch like mad beneath the long, platinum blond wig she was wearing but she refused to scratch; scratching would have ruined the effect. Instead she continued to smile widely as the bartender with sandy blond hair and warm brown eyes handed her the shot of tequila then held out his hand with the salt. With a heated look, he placed the lime wedge in his mouth and set the shot of tequila in front of her, smiling his familiar, devilish smile.

With only the slightest hesitation, she licked the fleshy mound of skin between his thumb and forefinger than slammed the tequila. As soon as her mouth was empty, she leaned over the bar and sucked the lime into her mouth, getting a touch of bartender lips in the process.

The crowd cheered as she sat back on the stool and laughed, "I need a chaser."

"Here ya go, my love," the bartender grinned, setting a glass of lemon-lime soda down in front of her. His pectoral muscles flexed as he did so and nearly all of the females in the bar squealed their approval. "I'll give you a moment before I take my shot."

"Thanks, Dima," she smiled, her hazel-green eyes sparkling with amusement as she drained the sparkling soda. Glancing around the most popular bar in Minneapolis, she made a mental note of the cliental *Skin* attracted: lots of twenty-somethings, flashy, upper-middle class. Her own hooker-chic outfit, which had seemed a little bit on the risqué side when she put it on earlier, blended very nicely. In fact, with a short, leather skirt; sheer black, thigh-high nylons; three-inch, platform-soled, leather knee-high boots; and a black bustier pushing up her breasts and baring her slender midriff, her outfit was almost tame. She might have to work on that a bit, maybe skipping the sheer black thigh highs next time.

When she turned back, there was another shot of tequila in front of her and Dima was holding up a lime wedge. "You ready?"

She smiled sultrily, parted her lips and leaned towards him. He put the lime between her lips, then returned her smile, upping the sex-quotient tenfold. Leaning forward, he licked her throat and as she took a sharp breath, he sprinkled salt on the wet spot. Tilting her head to the side, she studied him, the glimmer in his eyes as she took the lime out for a moment and asked him, "The cameras aren't rolling yet, are they?"

"Nah; they're just setting up," he grinned, pushing the lime back between her lips. Licking the salt from her skin, he took the tequila shot and then claimed her mouth. Oh, yeah – and the lime. The flavor of tequila was overwhelming, though she could still taste the sour lime. She almost smiled from the heat of Dima's mouth as his tongue swirled around the citrus fruit. Once more, the crowd cheered the antics of the author of their favorite monthly column in *lavish* magazine, 'The Scene.'

Lexi laughed and pushed away from his hard body. "Dima, you're too much."

"You know you love me, Lexi," he grinned, taking a drink of water from his own glass. Leaving the rest of his customers in the very capable hands of the other bartenders, he leaned across the bar and spoke softly so only she could hear, "Is there anything else I can do for you, love?"

"I think I got everything I need," she answered, winking at him as she reached into her small purse and turned the microphone off. "I'll be sure to give your bar a glowing review."

"Make sure you emphasize how hot the bartenders are," he grinned, flexing his biceps to highlight his point. And once again, the female patrons squealed in delight. "By the way, I like how you look as a blond; have you ever considered something more permanent than a wig?"

"Oh, please," she scoffed. "Do you know how expensive upkeep is on blond? I much prefer going this route."

"Well, I appreciate the effort," he shrugged, taking her glass and refilling it.

"You know, Dima, it looks like business is already amazing," she said, glancing around at the exuberant crowd once more. The music was thumping in the background and there were plenty of people on the dance floor, as well as crowding around the tables, just hanging out. Add in the extra exposure from the reality show, and *Skin* was going to be the hottest place to be for a very long time. "You really don't need me to mention you or your club in my column."

"Don't even say that," he rumbled. "Besides, you owe me – all of those nights I helped you cram for finals, the myriad number of pizzas I helped you eat; Cancun…."

"Nyuh uh," she interrupted, holding up her hand and forestalling any further grievances. "I seem to recall a fair number of mutual cramming sessions. As for the pizzas and Cancun," her lips curved upwards in a smile at the memory. "Well…."

"Fine," he conceded. Crossing his arms on the counter, he leaned in and offered her his heart breaking smile that she adored, no matter how many times she was on the receiving end. Dima was a very good-looking man with his warm brown eyes and sandy blond hair and perfect swimmer's body. But when he smiled he was almost too attractive and he knew it. He used his looks to his advantage, hiding his intelligence with his dimples and charm, preferring to be underestimated by women and rivals alike. "Then do it because I'm your best friend."

"Low blow, Dima," she paused only a moment before she shook her head and smiled, standing up to leave. "It's not like you need my little blurb – these cameras are going to give you all of the media attention you could ask for."

"That's in like two hours, when her entourage finally arrives," he said. Lowering his voice, he added, "If the cast arrives; I'm not holding my breath."

"They would be fools not to show up – your club is awesome; and the bartenders are sexy as hell," she grinned. As he continued to frown, she exhaled dramatically, her eyes dancing, "You know I will include your club."

"Thank you," he beamed, looking out over the crowd, obviously pleased with the turn out. He should be; he worked like the very devil to make *Skin* the place to see and be seen.

"I've got to get going so I can catch a cab."

"Stay and we'll go home together when I get off," he offered, mixing drinks as their chatter turned to more mundane topics.

"I need to get home sometime this evening so I can start on my article; with the show being shot, it's going to be forever before you can get out and give me a ride," she smiled at her friend, while gathering up her stuff. "And if you plan on bringing someone home, please keep it down; I want to get up early tomorrow and maybe head in to the office for a few hours before meeting the family at the club in the afternoon."

"It's Saturday tomorrow; why would you want to waste any of it at the office?" Dima asked with a disgruntled expression, letting her know exactly how he felt about her going into work on a Saturday.

Lexi shrugged, "Jeffrey sold the paper and I want to get all of my stuff in order to impress the new boss. Or to update my resume so I can find another magazine to work at."

"If the bastard fires you should come work here."

Lexi made a face, "You know that will never happen; *Skin* is where I go if I want to escape my sisters' attempts to pry into my life; if I worked here...."

Feeling a change in the air, Lexi abruptly stopped talking and twisted around to see what could have caused it. She very nearly spontaneously combusted when she saw Him. It was an unfamiliar, and slightly terrifying, reaction for her to have towards anyone, especially a stranger. Usually she enjoyed admiring from afar with a cool detachment; that wasn't possible in this case.

One thought crowded out all of the others: this man was a warrior, sleek, strong, powerful and a little bit dangerous. And virile. Definitely virile. His mere presence was playing havoc with her hormones from across the room; there was no telling what he would do to her up close and personal. A delicious shiver went down her spine at the thought.

From where she stood, she appreciated the way he wore his clothes, wondering how he would look out of them. He was very well-dressed; very expensively dressed, in a dark, Italian suit, with a white shirt; the whiteness emphasizing his golden skin. Her fingers curled into her palm at the thought of touching that carved jaw, those lush lips. And she saw that those lips were set in a firm line as he surveyed the room with piercing eyes, not missing a thing. He looked like he was checking the space out for danger except he was the most dangerous thing there.

The wool-clad warrior was a devastatingly handsome man, with a sculpted face: a strong jaw, high cheek bones and a straight nose, softened only by lips that were made for sin, lush and wicked. His raven black hair was short but long enough to drag her fingers through. It was also perfect without a single strand out of place. She had the strangest urge to walk up to him and just muss it up a bit. She could imagine him with tousled hair, looking down at her with that intense gaze as he moved over her.... Whoa, too far; she told herself to rein in the lustful thoughts and just admire.

"You're drooling, Lexi," Dima whispered in her ear.

"I am not," she shot back, surreptitiously wiping at the corners of her mouth making Dima laugh. Leaning back, keeping her eyes on the new-comer, she asked, "Who do you think he is?"

"I don't care who he is," Dima breathed into her ear, his attention diverted as well. "Who's the red head he's with?"

Lexi turned her head slightly and saw the pretty, little red head hanging on the god's arm, a sultry smile playing about her lips as she looked around the crowded bar. She said something and the dark warrior bent his head to hear her and a rush of desire crashed through Lexi's body at the move. "Do you think they're together?"

"God I hope not," Dima murmured.

"Look at them, Dima; they are so very comfortable with one another," Lexi said, holding out her arm in the man's direction. "They're probably together; their bodies move together as if they are intimately familiar. And they both reek of wealth and prestige, like they belong at the country club and not in a bar like this; she should be drinking a Manhattan and I think his preferred drink would be a martini...."

"Shaken, not stirred," Dima finished in a quasi-British accent, causing them both to laugh.

"Stop that," Lexi grinned, swatting at his arm and hitting air, her eyes never leaving the man. She tilted her head to the side in thoughtful contemplation; he was magnetic and she was mesmerized. Her lips curled upwards in an appreciative smile as he helped the red head out of her coat, setting it on the back of her chair as he held it out for her. "Nice. Do you think he might like blond?"

"I like blond," Dima countered absently. "Brunette, black... but I think tonight I prefer red."

After a moment of silence, he leaned across the bar and asked, "So, do we take a divide and conquer approach so I can have the red head and you can have the man she's with?"

Lexi frowned, "I don't think so; he's for looking and not touching."

"But she's for touching," Dima purred, his breath moving across Lexi's bare shoulder. "Snag his attention so I can make a move on the girl."

"You're a sick bastard," Lexi teased, enjoying the view as the man remained standing, looking around the bar with a certain arrogance she found appealing. The man was very much a 'look but don't touch' and Lexi needed to leave before she gave in to the impulse to touch, knowing she'd want so much more if she touched; she'd want it all. Tearing her gaze away from the perfection-incarnate, she faced Dima with a frown, "I've really got to go."

"Here," he said, pulling out two fresh shot glasses and filling them with the foul-tasting tequila. "Do one more shot with me before you go."

"Why? I'm already a little buzzed; one more and I'll be worthless."

"I need the courage so I can steal Red away from the big bad wolf."

She took a deep breath and let it out, a low, painful groan emanating from the back of her throat as she narrowed her eyes and glared at the two glasses. "Fine."

"That's my girl," he grinned, sprinkling salt on his hand once again and holding it to her mouth.

She held his gaze as she slid her tongue over his flesh, seeing the flash of dark humor in his eyes as she did so. She really hated tequila and if she was smart, she'd have refused the last shot. But she needed something to fortify her resolve to not touch. With a little whimper, she took the tequila and slammed it, quickly taking the lime from Dima's mouth. With a shudder, she wiped the back of her hand against her mouth, "God, that's disgusting."

Dima laughed, "My turn."

Grumbling under her breath, Lexi took the salt and sprinkled it on her hand and held it in front of Dima's mouth. He simply smiled at her and shook his head, "Nyuh uh."

"Dima," she protested, though it was ignored as he leaned forward and licked the curve of her neck and poured the salt there. With another sigh, she put the lime in her mouth then tilted her head to the side as he nibbled her skin before drinking his tequila. This time when he captured the lime, he took his time, grabbing her shoulders and holding her in place as he moved his mouth over hers, as he prolonged the kiss. Lexi twisted her head away and chuckled, "Dima."

"Pardon me," a luscious, utterly masculine voice murmured from behind her.

Lexi flattened her hands against Dima's chest and pushed, breaking the lime-kiss and stumbling backwards into a solid wall of muscle belonging to the man standing behind her. Heat enveloped her body and her flesh started to hum. Without seeing him, she knew that it was the warrior-stranger and the laughter quickly faded away, replaced by sexual awareness. Her eyes slid shut until she became aware of Dima softly chuckling and she came crashing back to reality. Narrowing her eyes, she glared at her friend, though her smile softened the look, "Dickhead."

But then warm hands wrapped around her bare arms to steady her and the rest of the world simply vanished. She felt like a cat, needing to rub her body against his, wanting to have him stroke her. Relishing in the strength of the stranger, his scent filled her nostrils, clean and male with no artificial odors. There was something wild about his scent, as if he spent his nights running naked through the woods. Heat burned through her as she pictured him in her head, standing beneath the bright moon in all of his naked magnificence, his piercing eyes holding her in place as she....

"Pardon me," the masculine voice came again and the solid wall rumbled against her back. She realized that she was still pressed up against him, that his hands were still holding her. And she didn't want to move; she just wanted to stay there and continue experiencing the loveliest sensation she'd ever known.

Lexi returned from her brief sojourn to fantasy world and jumped, turning around as she did so. The gorgeous man truly was standing there, looking down at her with the most intense silver eyes she had ever seen. Her tongue lost its ability to move and she was unable to articulate a single thought as her knees decided to disappear and she fell against the bar. Even wearing three inch heels, she only reached his chin, making him 6'2, maybe 6'3; and he was solid; steel and sinew, bone and muscle. And all she could do was stare at the pagan god come to life and try to find her tongue, maybe remember how to speak.

He was even more striking up close and personal; and having been pressed up against him, she knew his body was honed to absolute perfection. And whatever he was doing, her body was definitely responding. The reactions that were strong when her back was towards him became nearly unbearable. His eyes seemed to burn right into her, sending chills along her skin and making her stomach flip over. Even her nipples tightened into two hard buds and her belly began to buzz in anticipation. She wasn't even going to consider the dampness between her thighs. No one ever elicited that type of response from her; and never a stranger. Maybe it was the tequila: yeah, that's what she was going to tell herself anyway even if she knew it for the lie it was.

If she stayed there any longer, she wouldn't be held accountable for her actions, and that thought scared the hell out of her. Attraction was one thing; this all-consuming, all-compelling force was something else entirely. With her pulse racing, she knew she had to get out of there. Unfortunately, she had no desire to leave.

His silver eyes melted her bones as he spoke in a husky tenor, "I saw you standing over here and I was wondering if I could I buy you a drink?"

She needed to get out of there because touching him was everything she had hoped and dreaded. But then she found her voice coming out in a low and velvety rasp, "One drink."

He smiled, revealing perfect white teeth and her stomach dropped to her feet; he was even more dangerous to her well-being when he smiled. Holding up two fingers, he ordered a couple of shots and Lexi almost groaned, already tipsy from her earlier shots. But then he looked at her with those silver eyes and his voice caressed her as he murmured, "If you don't mind?"

She looked at him as he held out his hand towards her. Not knowing what else to do, she put her hand in his, catching her breath at the electric sensation that shot up her arm. His fingers wrapped around her wrist and pulled her against his hard body. His eyes glittered as he held her gaze, bringing her wrist up to his mouth; he ran his tongue along the delicate skin and then sprinkled salt on the damp spot. Unaware of anything other than his beguiling eyes, she was startled when a wedge of lime was placed in her mouth.

"Thank you," the gorgeous stranger murmured as he licked the salt from her skin and then slammed the glass of tequila. Lexi was transfixed by the way his throat worked as he swallowed, how the tendons moved and his Adam's apple bobbed. She didn't get to spend enough time studying the lines of his neck before his mouth was on hers and he cursed beneath his breath.

Pulling back slightly, he squeezed the bitter juice into her mouth and pulled the lime out before continuing with the kiss, his tongue stroked along hers and she lost herself in his lips, receiving the full impact of his kiss, feeling it in her belly and lower still. Her arms slid around his trim waist and she pressed herself harder against his solid body, luxuriating in the heat that wrapped itself around her. Her head was spinning and she wasn't sure if it was from the tequila or the kiss; probably a bit of both. She wanted the kiss to go on forever, which was ridiculous since she didn't know the man at all. But, oh! he could kiss!

Reluctantly pulling her lips from his, she took a wobbly step backwards and looked up at him, a siren's smile curving her lips, "My turn."

As much as she despised tequila, she was looking forward to doing the shot, if only to taste the scrumptious man once more. With one hand on his arm to steady herself, she glanced at Dima, ignoring the cynical humor blazing in his eyes as he poured the tequila into a second shot glass. With a wince, she took a deep breath and turned back to the gorgeous stranger. "Ready?"

"Always," he rumbled, his molten silver eyes caressing her face and making her burn even hotter.

Leaning against him and going up onto her toes, she slowly slid her tongue along the exposed skin of his neck, tasting his woodsy, masculine flavor and closing her eyes at the sheer pleasure of it. A stifled groan came from the back of his throat and his fingers wrapped around her elbows, as if he was as unsteady as she was. She pulled away just enough to squeeze the juice of lime into his mouth, running her finger over the ripe fullness of his bottom lip. His eyes flared even brighter as she grabbed the shot and, pausing but a moment, slammed it down her throat with a shudder. Her throat burned and her eyes watered but it was worth it; even the hangover she knew to expect in the morning was going to be worth it.

Wrapping a hand around the back of his neck, she pulled him down as she rose up, their lips meeting somewhere in the middle. Citrus and man erased the vile taste of the alcohol and she took her time exploring the wet heat of his mouth, a hum of approval coming from her own throat. Suddenly, she wanted this man more than her next breath, more than she ever wanted anything; she wanted to explore the defined ridges of his hard body, the heavy weight of his thick erection. She wanted to tear off his clothes and touch him everywhere.

She wanted to fuck him until the world ended and she was left standing among the ruins.

With their lips still connected, she blindly set the shot glass down on the table as they stumbled a few feet away from the bar, lost in a haze of unexpected and overwhelming lust. Her fingers slid into the black silk of his hair and she pressed herself until she was flush against him, the hard planes of his chest and stomach hot and unyielding; the stony ridge of his erection tantalizing. His palms were blistering her skin and she knew that she was going to have hand prints on her back everywhere he touched her, stroked her.

"Let's go somewhere," he rasped against her lips, giving her a chance to catch her breath and let a smidgen of rationality return.

She licked her lips, still tasting him against her tongue and wanting to give into impulse and throw all caution to the wind. This insane rashness wasn't like her but at that moment she didn't care, even if he didn't arrive alone. "But your date?"

"We're just friends," he said, brushing his thumb over her lower lip, the silver gaze tracking the movement. The intensity of his expression made her stomach tighten in awareness and a little bit of trepidation; was she really going to do this? Did she even have a choice? Well, of course she had a choice; it just wasn't one she wanted to make because she wanted him. "I was only going to stay long enough until her friends showed up. And look, they're here."

How could he possible tell, since he hadn't taken his eyes from her since he captured her in his arms? Intrigued, she looked past him to see the red head surrounded by a pack of equally gorgeous men and women. They were watching her and the man with amused and inquisitive expressions; even the red head was more curious than angry. Lexi's eyes returned to him and he was smiling at her as he said, "See? I'm all yours if you'll have me."

"Oh, hell yeah," she blurted out, blushing slightly at the blunt enthusiasm of her reply. Glancing at Dima, she offered an apologetic shrug, "I guess I have a ride. Um, good luck."

"Be careful, Lexi." His voice came out in a low rumble as he warily eyed the man who was taking her away. "If anything happens to her, I will hunt you down and kill you."

The man simply smiled, dismissing the threat as he turned away from Dima. Putting his arm around Lexi's shoulders, his heat and scent wrapping itself around her, drugging her, he whispered, "Are you ready?"

"Yes." She knew she was an idiot and that she was being reckless and stupid but she couldn't seem to help herself. With one last look at Dima, she followed the stranger out of the bar. If he ended up being a murderer or a rapist, she was going to have to rethink instant lust and impulsiveness. But if he was simply a gorgeous man that had her hormones battling for supremacy over her mind, well then....

*****

Duncan Tremain prowled along in silence as he led the blond from the bar, sparing an apologetic glance towards Ashley, his friend and prospective mate, the only woman his wolf could tolerate for any extended length of time. She gave him a mocking grin and exchanged words with one of the pack members and the two of them laughed. He knew they were talking about his odd behavior but he didn't care; he had a gorgeous blond on his arm.

He liked the feel of the blond's slender body against his, the smooth skin of her arm beneath his palm. He had volunteered to go up to the bar because he had seen her standing there, a thoughtful gleam in her eyes as she checked him out, oblivious of his attention. Her full, ripe lips beckoned him and invited a kiss and he wanted to taste those lips. She was exotic and luscious, to say nothing of her seductress body and come-hither outfit. It was enough to make a pious man sin and he was not especially pious. But it was more than that; a gut-twisting reaction had him walking towards the bar despite being on an outing with Ashley and several of the single members of their pack.

It was an unusual feeling, this powerful, instant attraction and he wasn't sure whether he liked it or not. He could feel his wolf's interest perk up, matching his own interest. He decided that the best course of action would be to get closer to the girl and discover whether or not the instant and raw lust was genuine or an anomaly due to the whole image she presented. So he told Ashley that he would get them a couple of beers while they waited for the others.

He didn't expect he'd be able to touch her until she fell against him; and despite the attraction he wasn't prepared for the intensity of his reaction. Blood rushed to his cock, leaving him slightly light-headed as his body responded instantly and painfully. He knew she would be able to feel his erection pressing against her back but she didn't cringe or leap away in disgust. For the longest moment, she just stood there in his arms, her back pressed against him, taunting him, torturing him with the smell of citrus and tequila. But beneath the citrusy scent she smelled like spring, clean and fresh.

When she had turned around and looked up at him with heavy-lidded eyes, he was momentarily stunned by her prettiness. Even though her hair was light, her lashes were dark, long; and her large eyes were really the most remarkable color, gold and green all swirled together. A smattering of freckles danced across the bridge of her slender nose. But it was her lips that still begged to be kissed, bee-sting and shiny. She was, in a word, breathtaking. For the briefest moment of time, the world disappeared, and all that existed was the girl and him.

Wanting to bask in her presence a while longer, he offered to buy her a drink. It was unexpected and perhaps inevitable when he did a shot off her luscious body and promptly asked to take her somewhere for sex, something that was completely out of character for him. It was foolishness and madness to take a stranger off to his hotel but he couldn't muster up the energy to care. He simply wanted her with a desperation that bordered on the tragic if it weren't so potent and intoxicating.

Really, he knew nothing about her and in relationships, as in business, it was best to know as much as possible about the opposing force. Usually he never reacted on gut-instinct alone; that was something his wolf would do. Instead, it was best to approach any given situation with a cool head; emotions just mucked everything up. And yet he was going to take a gorgeous stranger to his hotel because he could not wait to get the blond naked and spread beneath him.

He glanced back at Ashley as he got to the door and smiled somewhat guiltily even as she gave him another amused smirk. He knew he should be staying with Ash; a nice, companionable relationship with another wolf was exactly what he had wanted, not the tempestuous reactions elicited by the blond sex bomb walking next to him. He needed to find a wolf to mate, even if it wasn't Ashley; he was of an age to do so and it was what was expected. Hell, his pack had joined them tonight in the hopes of enticing him into selecting a mate from amongst their females.

They were probably laughing at him for bailing on them before anything could happen but he didn't care. He was going to have sex with the most tempting woman of his acquaintance and his beast was roaring his approval. He would get the girl and this strange and powerful reaction out of his system.

Chapter 2

"The hotel where I am staying isn't very far from here," the man said as they left the loud nightclub behind. "Would you mind walking?"

"I'm okay with walking, as long as you don't mind me leaning against you for support," she said with wry smile, grateful that she wasn't wearing her stilettos. Lexi knew that she still had time to change her mind; she could offer an apology and run back to Dima with her tail between her legs.

He chuckled, wrapping his strong arm around her waist and hauling her against his hard body and she forgot her objections. "I don't mind in the least."

She sucked in a breath as sexual awareness rushed through her body at the contact. She should have expected it, considering the sparks that had been flying from the moment he had walked into *Skin*, but it still came as a surprise. Now that they were alone, everything seemed more intense somehow, including her reaction to him. She had no desire to turn back and walking through the city in this man's arm was absurdly appealing, even knowing he was taking her back to a hotel to have sex with her. And she didn't even know his name. "Lexi, by the way."

He paused and looked at her, a slight frown crinkling his forehead as he cocked his head. "Hmm?"

"Since we're going back to your place for sex, I figured I should tell you my name." She felt the heat in her cheeks as she explained why she blurted out her name like that. "It's Lexi."

The corners of his mouth turned up in that sexy smile of his, "Duncan."

Her cheeks tightened as her smile grew impossibly wide and she leaned more fully into him. He radiated heat and she could have wrapped herself up in his warmth. Why couldn't they be there already, then she would be that much closer to seeing his naked body, to exploring his naked body. "So, how far away did you say your hotel was?"

"Not far," he grinned, obviously reading her sexually-inundated mind. Bending, he wrapped his other arm around her knees and swooped her up and against his chest. Her breath left in a whoosh as she automatically wrapped her arms around his neck, holding onto the only port in the hormonal storm raging around them.

Breathlessly, she asked, "Did you think I'd change my mind?"

"That never even crossed my mind." His eyes moved over her face and the laughter faded from his silver eyes, leaving only desire behind, "I simply wanted to hold you in my arms and I figured this was the most efficient means of doing so."

"It certainly was," she agreed, absurdly pleased by his display of strength and manliness. If she were sober or had two brain-cells not completely turned on by him, she might have been concerned by his superhuman strength; instead she felt safe, cherished. Resting her head against his broad shoulder, she let her eyes drift shut and simply breathed in his woodsy scent, "I feel so primal right now, a helpless damsel being taken by the big sexy wolf back to his lair to have his wicked way with her."

She felt his jaw tighten against her forehead a moment before he spoke, "I don't normally accost strangers in bars and solicit sex from them."

She chuckled; he sounded almost offended. "I'm not complaining. Besides, I don't normally go home with strangers I just met, hoping to have my brains fucked right out of my head."

A low rumble of hunger vibrated against her breasts and he relaxed the tightened hold he had on her. His words rasped over her skin as he said, "I can't wait to get you naked, Lexi; I want to kiss every inch of your skin until you are begging me to fuck you."

This time she moaned and felt her body loosen; she was already too close to begging and he had barely even begun. Hell, they were still on the sidewalk heading to his hotel! Maybe she should have had sex before so the surge of lust crashing through her body right now wouldn't be so overwhelming. On the other hand, she doubted anything would have prepared her for Duncan; he was different from any of the men in her life, from her best friends Cole and Dima to the men at the office where she worked. He was just so... primal beneath his façade of a civilized man and that very primal-ness called to her.

She also knew that it could only be sex because what woman in her right mind would want to marry a man who could reduce her mind to mush mere moments after meeting him? Her brain would turn into tapioca pudding and she would spend her days counting the moments until they could fuck again. She'd die because she'd forget to eat, spending her days in a fog of arousal. Chuckling to herself, she had to admit that she was a little bit more than buzzed and her thoughts were not making any sense. She knew next to nothing about Duncan, not what kind of husband he'd be or what type of lover he was or what type of man he could be. For all she knew, he was a serial monogamist or a philandering cheater or a virgin like herself.

She laughed out loud at that; there was no way the man that so easily carried her in his arms was a virgin. He practically radiated virility and sex; it oozed out of his pores and left a trail of desire and broken hearts in his wake. He probably started having sex at an early age and hasn't stopped to take a breath since. How many women had he been with? A gazillion and a half....

"What's so funny?" he asked, his lips quirked up in a half smile.

She shook her head as she managed to get her giggles under control, "I was just wondering how many women you've fucked because you probably have women throwing themselves at you all of the time and it would be so easy to give in to temptation when it is so readily available and I don't know why I just said all of that."

He tilted his head to the side, a thoughtful expression descending over his face as he seriously considered her statement. "You will be the... fifth, I believe. No, the fourth; I didn't actually have sex with the first one."

She pulled her lips between her teeth to keep from laughing out loud but tears welled in her eyes and a snort escaped. "I wasn't asking for numbers."

He smiled ruefully, "No, but it emphasizes my earlier point; I don't usually do this."

"Or you could be lying," she offered, noticing that they were entering the lobby of an elegant and exclusive hotel. People were staring at them but she didn't care; let them stare and be envious.

He cocked his head to the side in that adorable way of his as he stepped onto the elevator and somehow managed to push the button to his floor. "Why would I lie?"

"Well, in this day and age of sexual promiscuity, some might be charmed by your lack of experience." Her eyes sparkled with amusement even as her body continued to burn for his possession. And she *was* oddly charmed by his low number of lovers; a man that gorgeous and sexual and dominant could have scores of women. That he didn't said more about him than anything and her heart did a stupid pirouette in her chest that she was to be among those low numbers.

"I didn't say I lack experience," his purred, his eyes darkening once more

"Just numbers."

"Oh, man, you're making me hot," she purred back, a low moan threatening to work its way up from her belly.

"Good, because we're here," he said as the doors slid open and they stepped out onto the top floor. He jiggled her in his arms as he reached into his pocket and pulled out the key – an actual key – to his room. She should have felt as if she was going to fall but he held her firmly and she never felt safer in her life. The only danger would be if he didn't have a condom and that would be easy enough to remedy; the hotel probably had someone on condom-duty who could deliver a condom anytime one of the guests had an urge for sex.

The door opened without a sound but Lexi didn't bother to look around; Duncan held all of her interest and nothing else mattered. Every girl should lose her virginity to such a man. Her voice was guttural as she asked, "Where's the bedroom?"

"Don't you want a drink or something to relax first?" he asked out of politeness. She knew it was out of politeness because his silver eyes gleamed with lust and a muscle ticked in his jaw. His masculine scent was awash in musk and she reveled in it; his wild smell was becoming even more intoxicating.

"I have no desire to relax," she was almost panting. "I want to find a bed and get naked. I don't even need a bed."

He growled as he lowered her legs and let her slowly slide down his hard body. His erection pulsed against her stomach and she had to suck in a breath; she was so aroused right now she was pretty sure she was going to implode violently if she didn't get to touch his skin. Holding his eyes, she started unbuttoning his shirt, desperate to get him naked as quickly as possible.

He put his hands over her wrists, stopping her from undoing more than three buttons. At her questioning look, he smiled ruefully, "I think we should start in the bedroom because I want to see all you, naked and spread out on my bed. If we don't start there, I'll never have my fantasy fulfilled."

"We can't have that," she purred. Her smile was slow and sultry as she slipped her hand into his and followed him into the enormous bedroom. Butterflies were dancing for joy in her stomach as he flipped the switch and low light from several lamps bathed the room. She barely glanced at the massive bed before his mouth was over hers and his lips were possessing hers. Duncan definitely did not lack experience; he was an expert kisser, knowing when to demand and when to cajole, teasing her and then giving her more. She lost herself in his kiss.

As badly as she wanted to press her naked skin against his, she wanted to savor his kisses. His essence wrapped itself around her, invading all of her senses until she was floating on a cloud of desire and hunger and she never wanted it to end. And then his broad palm covered her breast and gave a gentle squeeze and she moaned low in her throat. "Naked. Now."

He stepped back and she missed his heat, even as he held her eyes and started to take off his clothes. Frozen in place, she could only stare as he shrugged out of his jacket and let it fall haphazardly to the floor, unconcerned about ruining the expensive garment. His fingers moved to the fourth button of his shirt and she wanted him to hurry but he stopped, damn it. Arching an eyebrow, he asked, "Aren't you going to undress, too?"

Snapping out of her Duncan-induced daze, she grinned self-consciously, "Of course."

Putting her fingers over the zipper on the side of her bustier, she was about to pull it down when his phone rang and she stopped. He continued to disrobe, ignoring the chirping of his phone, until he noticed she wasn't undressing. He arched that eyebrow again and she had to bite back a groan at how sexy he looked with an arched eyebrow. "Aren't you going to answer that?"

"Why would I do that?' he asked in a low, velvety voice. Abandoning his shirt buttons, he stepped forward and slid his hand into her bustier, curving a palm around her breast. The heat from his skin scalded her, making her even more desperate for him. "When I have you here?"

She moaned when he brushed his thumb over her hard nipple, almost coming on the spot. It took a moment to regain the ability to speak but she managed, "It might be important."

"More important than making love to the most exquisite creature I've ever met?" Lightly, he tweaked her pebbled nipple and a mini orgasm rippled through her body.

Oh, if he kept talking like that and doing things like that she'd throw the damn phone out the window and jump him! But the phone was still ringing; whoever was on the other line was persistent. "Are you expecting any important calls?"

He paused at that and frowned, reluctantly pulling the phone from his pants pocket with his free hand, his thumb still toying with her nipple. Flipping the phone open, he held her eyes as he said in a perfectly composed voice, "Hello?"

A heartbeat later his hand slid from her bustier and he turned his back on her as the person on the other end of the line started talking. Without the distraction of his talented fingers, Lexi was able to breathe once again. She was also feeling the effects from all of the tequila she had earlier; if he didn't act soon, she was either going to take the phone away from him and hang it up or pass out. She hoped the call would be quick; she didn't want time to think; she just wanted Duncan.

"Give me a moment," he told the person on the other end. Turning around and covering the mouthpiece, he looked apologetic, rueful. "I am so sorry but I have to take this."

"Important?" she asked lightly, the room spinning now that he was no longer there to hold her steady.

"Very," he grimaced. "I'll make it quick and we will finish what we began."

"I'm holding you to that." He was heading to the door and a wicked thought grabbed hold of her and wouldn't let go. "Duncan?"

He stopped and turned around, "Hmm?"

With a sultry look, she reached beneath her skirt and hooked her thumbs into her panties. Slowly, she pulled them down her legs and stepped out of them, watching as color flooded his face and he adjusted the front of his pants. With a sway to her step, she closed the distance between them and slid the damp panties into his pocket. Standing up on her toes, she pressed a soft kiss to his cheek,

"Hurry."

His arm slid around her waist and he pulled her against him, taking her lips in a fast, hard kiss. "I will."

Letting her go, he reluctantly turned away and took another step but she didn't want him to go, not yet. "Duncan?"

He took a deep breath before he turned slightly and faced her. Turning around, she flipped the hem of her skirt up and flashed him her bare ass. "Incentive."

His hands squeezed into tight fists as he swallowed thickly. His voice was harsh as he rasped, "That kind of incentive will kill me."

She giggled as he grudgingly left to take the phone call, leaving her to explore the elegant room. The only thing that held her interest was the bed, and not because she was going to have sex in it; that was still in the future. Without Duncan she was feeling the effects of the alcohol; tequila always made her tired. It hadn't hit her before because being in Duncan's presence had been so stimulating; the sexual energy being generated between them was enough to power a small city.

Climbing onto the big, plush bed, she let her eyes slide close; if she took a quick nap, she would be up for an entire night of sexual exploration. She was going to need it so she could enjoy every moment of her night with the delicious Duncan. With a loopy smile, she let the oblivion of sleep claim her; it was only going to be a quick nap….

****

Duncan clicked the phone shut and exhaled, pleased with the outcome. Unfortunately the phone call took much longer than he expected; he wouldn't be surprised if Lexi was furious with him and demanded he take her home immediately. In a way, he was almost grateful for the interruption; he had no business absconding with a human and taking her back to his hotel room. He preferred long term relationships with women who engaged his mind as well as his body, not the insanity and hot burn that Lexi made him feel.

But then the thought of Lexi rekindled the fire that had been banked and lust roared through his body. Screw sensible; he was going to be wild and reckless just this once and then he would go back to being a rational wolf. Tearing the shirt from his body, he stalked towards the bedroom to claim his prize. He was going to wring every drop of pleasure from her body, indulge in every carnal delight he could dream up, let his beast have his fun, and then when Monday came, he would return to normal.

He unbuttoned the top of his slacks and was pulling the zipper down when he burst through the bedroom door. The bed was bathed in the low light and Lexi was in the middle of it, curled up in a ball and sound asleep, her gorgeous ass peeking at him from beneath the hem of her skirt. Taking a breath to put a lid on his raging hormones, he quietly made his way over to the bed and sat down, her body shifting from his weight.

He studied her face and he was surprised to realize how young she was. And how unutterably beautiful. Upon closer inspection, he noticed that her blond hair had shifted and he chuckled softly; she was wearing a wig. Tenderly, he brushed his hand over her smooth cheek, smiling as she smiled in her sleep.

He should have ignored the phone call and lost the multi-million dollar deal; it would have been worth it.

Running his hand over the curve of her body, he reluctantly stood up and finished getting undressed, leaving his boxers on before throwing a blanket over her sleeping form. After turning off the lights, he slid between the covers and stared up at the ceiling, listening to her soft breathing, the occasional snore. His wolf was oddly content simply sleeping next to her; it was almost peaceful.

For the first time in his life he wasn't battling with his beast for dominance. It didn't mean anything, of course; Lexi was simply a sexy woman which his wolf appreciated. That thought made Duncan frown; what was it about Lexi that made his wolf happy? Yes, the chemistry between them was astronomical and had him behaving in a way more suitable to a cub, not the Alpha but there were always exceptions to the rule. Surely Lexi was his exception. But that didn't explain his wolf's silence this past hour.

Closing his eyes, he nudged the wolf within, waking him from his restful slumber. *Who is she to you?*

The wolf mentally yawned, *She's just a girl, oh formidable one. Perhaps I should be asking who she is to* you *since you were unable to keep your paws off her.*

The wolf was mocking him, laughing at him and Duncan flexed his jaw. They had been butting heads since he was fifteen and while Duncan had managed to subdue the beast, the beast never let him forget his presence. *It's a simple chemical reaction.*

The wolf chuckled, *If you say so, my most honorable and noble liege.*

Stop that, Duncan growled, his jaw tightening until it felt like it was going to snap.

Perhaps I wish to claim her, the wolf continued. *She is a tasty morsel and so very eager to please. Do you think she would let me take her?*

Absolutely not, Duncan bit out, surprisingly jealous at the thought of sharing her, even with his beast. *You will not claim her; she's a human.*

Yes, the wolf shuddered, closing his mental eyes in pleasure. *A sinfully delicious human I am very willing to devour.*

Shut it.

Let me keep her.

Hell, no.

No, it would be better if he simply drove her home in the morning and put the madness of this night behind him; anything that made his wolf happy couldn't be good for him. With a sigh, he rolled onto his side away from temptation. If he gave in to desire, his wolf would gloat and hold it over his head for the rest of his life.

He refused to allow the wolf to win.

****

Lexi woke up with a start, disoriented, with a pounding headache and unsure where she was. There was a furnace heating her backside and the bed was not the one she usually slept in. But her mouth didn't taste feel like death; it had the faintly woodsy taste of....

She groaned as memories slowly filtered in to her cotton-stuffed head: the bar, the tequila, the man. Flinging herself at the gorgeous stranger and practically jumping him in the bar. She was never going to drink tequila again.

Slowly, trying to keep her head from falling off her neck while attempting to be as quiet as possible so as not to wake Duncan, she slid out of bed. As the air hit her bare butt, she blushed, remembering the brazen moment when she stripped off her panties and stuffed them into Duncan's pocket. If he hadn't gotten a phone call, she would have been initiated into sex by the most dynamic man she had even encountered.

Oh, well; it was probably better this way. And hopefully, she was never, ever going to see him again. Because she didn't think she'd be able to stop herself from tearing the clothes from his body and having her wicked way with him where he stood, even if it was in the middle of the city square.

With a slight smile, she silently made her way out of the room without sparing a single glance at the gorgeous man on the bed. It was for purely selfless reasons; if she looked, she would have touched, and then she would have stroked, and then....

She shuddered at the possibilities and quickened her pace, the strangest sensation of being watched passing through her. But, no, Duncan was snoring softly, his breaths even; and if he was only pretending to be asleep than he must have also realized the foolishness inherent in their reckless actions and he was letting her go without a fuss.

She should have been grateful for the act but she was disappointed. Which just went to show her how silly she was being. Not bothering to look back, she made her way through the hotel lobby and out the entrance and into the night. Taking a deep breath and filling her lungs with the city air, she sighed in relief and regret.

The night doorman flagged down a cab for her and she slid into the back, determined to get her head screwed on straight and to forget the events of this night. If by some chance she did run into him again she would be able to control herself; she was just going to have to make it a point to stay away from alcohol. And limes. And maybe the woods, especially on a moon-lit night.

Closing her eyes, she leaned her head against the cool glass and smiled to herself. Dima was going to give her hell for failing to seduce the man who had whisked her from the bar for the express purpose of having sex and Cole was going to make fun of her for passing out. She chuckled as she imagined the two of them giving her grief while making her laugh until her stomach ached with the pleasure of it.

"Thirteen seventy-four, miss," the cabbie's voice interrupted her reverie and she realized she must have dozed off for a few minutes.

"Hmm?" she hummed, rubbing the sleep from her eyes and sitting up. Reaching into her purse, she asked, "How much was that again?"

His eyes glazed briefly before he hopped out and ran around the car, opening the door for her. "There's no charge, ma'am. Have a good evening."

With a frown, she handed him a twenty, a little disturbed by the besotted expression he wore; did she accidentally flash him? "Um, thanks."

"If you ever need a ride, call me," he said, hastily writing something on the back of a card and handing it to her with the twenty she had just handed him. "Day or night."

"Um, okay?" she awkwardly accepted the business card but when she tried to give the money back, he adamantly refused to take it. Crossing his arms over his chest, he leaned against the cab until she sighed and put the money back in her purse. "Thanks, I guess."

He smile brightened but he didn't move. "I'll just wait here until you are safely inside, miss."

"Uh huh." She was so confused by his strange behavior but figured it was best to get inside quickly before he changed his mind and decided she'd make the perfect specimen to add to his blond hooker collection. She was happy to discover that she had no desire to jump the cabbie's bones and her rational mind was working once again. But with his graying hair and portly body he was a poor substitute for Duncan in just about any situation.

Glancing over her shoulder, she was dismayed to see that he was still standing there, watching her closely. Only, she didn't get any hostile vibes from him. Turning back, she took another step when the door opened and light spilled out into the darkness. With a smile, Lexi took another step, eager to find comfort in Dima's arms after her foolishness. She froze when the red head from the bar stepped out instead and Dima's naked arm slid around her thin waist.

Jumping into the shadows to give them some privacy, she held her breath as the red head purred huskily, "You have my number?"

She ran a long red nail over Dima's decidedly naked chest while he nodded his answer. Licking her lips, she whispered, "Call me."

"I will," he promised, letting her go. As she turned away from him, he swatted her on the butt, making her squeal. She simply smiled at him and sauntered towards the waiting cab. She stopped next to the shadows where Lexi was hiding and turned her head, looking directly at Lexi, "The blond from the bar."

"The red head with Duncan." Lexi's heart pounded in her chest and she wasn't sure why. There was something elemental about the red head, something dangerous, predatory. Even though Lexi didn't feel threatened she felt as if the red head was studying her, checking for weaknesses.

The red head smiled but didn't say anything more, disappearing into the taxi and waiting until the cab driver got into the car. Startled to realize that the cabbie was still waiting for her to get inside, Lexi hastily sped up the walkway and darted through the door, slamming it with a bit more force than necessary.

Pressing her hand over her racing heart, she leaned against the door and closed her eyes. What a strange, strange night. And if she never ran into Duncan again it would probably be for the best, no matter how much the thought of never being with him hurt.

"Lexi?" Dima's voice interrupted her thoughts. Slowly, she opened her eyes to see him in the kitchen entry eating a sandwich, a pair of boxers hanging low on his waist. "How was your night?"

"I passed out before anything could happen and then I snuck away when I woke up and found him sleeping," she blurted out, pushing herself off the door and drifting over to her best friend. Automatically, he opened his arms and she fell into them, relishing his strength as he hugged her. "It was not one of my best moments. How was your night?"

She felt his smile and heard it in his voice, "Amazing."

"Yeah; it looked amazing," she heaved a sigh. "I guess I am just doomed to virginity."

He chuckled as he kissed the top of her head. "Get some sleep, minx."

"You, too, Dima." Dragging herself from his sheltering arms, she stumbled up the stairs to her bedroom, "I love you, you know."

"I love you, too."

Chapter 3 (Saturday)

The next day, Lexi slept in until ten and she didn't make it to the office. Swallowing a few aspirin, she took a long shower to scour the residual lust from her brain and then got ready for her lunch date with the women of her family. Despite the ridiculous amount of alcohol she drank the night before, she was feeling pretty good, even if she refused to think about a certain man that twisted her up on the inside. He could star in as many of her dreams as he wanted but she was not going to let him conquer her days, at least not often. The occasional day dream of him walking towards her, his naked chest glistening with manly sweat, a smile on his handsome face as he reached out his hand... hmm, that would be all right.

She arrived at the country club just a few minutes late since it had taken her a little longer to dress up in the perfect outfit and put on the perfect makeup, designed to deliberately annoy her two oldest sisters. And when she saw them, all three of her sisters wearing a similar sheath dress, her smile widened. Thea was wearing beige, Agatha was in shell pink, and Penelope wore buttery yellow; all of them wore their thick, dark hair in elegant buns. Of course they each had perfectly manicured fingernails with just the right amount of jewelry. They fit in perfectly amongst the country club set.

As she walked, Lexi jangled from the sheer number of bracelets she wore on both of her wrists. Her hair was tucked up under a mint green, chin length wig and there was enough glitter on her face to make any four-year-old girl squeal in delight. Lexi was particularly fond of the sparkly blue lipstick and sparkly blue false eyelashes that distracted her every time she blinked. Low riding, green leather pants hugged her legs and the cropped baby doll showcased her flat stomach and discrete belly button piercing. The outfit was paired off with a pair of wedge-heeled flip flops that were surprisingly comfortable.

Bending down, she air-kissed her mother's cheek, not wanting to smudge the immaculate make up with her blue lips. She took a moment to inhale the warm, light scent of gardenias her mother favored, a scent that reminded her of childhood and feeling loved. "Mom."

"Alexandra," Charisma, her mother, beamed at her. She was still a beautiful woman at 60, with seven children and several grandchildren. Her dark hair had a few strands of white, making her look distinguished; she definitely didn't look like a grandmother. Still trim, she had the shapely body that all of the Rudnar woman enjoyed. She was dressed casually in white linen pants and a pale blue cardigan set.

Lexi faced her unconventional Aunt Sophie with a warm smile. Sophie was wearing a deep purple dress that flowed around her body. She was younger than Lexi's mother by almost ten years and she could pass for someone even younger. She always had a new boy toy, preferring variety over longevity. Her hair was cropped short in the back, close to her scalp, and longer in the front, in a sexy pixie-influenced cut. Lexi adored her Aunt Sophie, calling her up for advice whenever it was needed. Hugging the older woman, breathing in the familiar magnolia scent, she smiled, "Aunt Sophie."

"I'm glad you decided to join us today," her aunt good-naturedly chastened. It wasn't a secret that Lexi normally disdained the country club and all of the trappings that went with it, despite being born into such privilege. She preferred the casual atmosphere of Cole's gallery or the cutting edge energy of Dima's bar. Or the comfortable warmth of home. "We weren't sure you would."

"Alexandra," Thea murmured in her controlled, dulcet voice. Heaving a sigh, she shook her head even as she pursed her full lips, "Would it have been too much to ask you to tone it down some?

"Yes, it would have," Lexi grinned, sitting down and joining them at the table. Taking the napkin, she snapped it open and spread it over her lap. "Not everyone can pull off mint."

"Well, I think you look fantastic," Penny interjected before the oldest Rudnar daughter came to blows with the youngest. As the very middle child of seven children, she was an expert at keeping the peace. As the mother of two sets of twins, she was learning to let things slide. "Jenny will want that wig when you decide to retire it."

Lexi chuckled, picturing the little girl that already had so many of her cast offs. Out of all of her nieces and nephews, Jenny was the only one who appreciated the artistry involved in Lexi's wardrobe. The other girls were miniature replicas of their perfect mothers. And grandmother. And yet all of them were able to wrap males around their little fingers without so much as batting an eyelash. And in a family that was predominantly female, it was a sight to behold whenever they got together.

Agatha summoned a waiter without saying a word and Lexi wondered once again for the millionth time how she did that. Aggie seemed to smile a secretive smile and suddenly a waiter would appear, eager to take her order and give her whatever she wanted. Lexi tried it once but the wires seemed to cross when a group of men appeared, not a waiter among them. Agatha had the same melodic voice that

Thea had but it was more sensual, less measured and the waiter was practically salivating to do her bidding. "We're ready to order; girls?"

As everyone ordered, Lexi glanced around the table and realized how beautiful they all were, from her mother to her aunt to her sisters. She sighed; without her makeup and wigs, she was rather plain when compared to the rest of her family, with ordinary brown hair and regular hazel eyes. It was true that she had a spectacular pair of breasts but so did the rest of the females in her family; and they were all stunning without the blue lipstick or green wigs or creative outfits.

They were all so elegant, like pretty little butterflies, fluttering about with their smiles and their perfect hair. And Lexi loved them to pieces; she loved watching them primp before the show, or party, and then preform, both on stage and in their social gatherings. They made the complicated dance of social interaction look so easy while Lexi felt more comfortable just barreling right through, spinning and dancing along the way, until she was in the sanctuary of her best friends' circle.

She listened as her sisters chatted about their husbands and their children, smiling with pleasure at the antics of her nieces and nephews. One of the things she loved most about having such a large family was listening to them talk, the companionship amongst them. Even if they didn't always get along she knew that any member of her family would be by her side in a heartbeat if it ever came to that. And yet she was a different person with her sisters than with Dima and Cole; with those two, she was the one doing most of the talking while they happily listened, offering their sage advice whenever it was wanted or needed. She wondered what her life would be like if she hadn't met them and then she shuddered at the thought; it wasn't even worth considering.

"Alexandra, there's something we need to talk to you about," her aunt said, interrupting her pleasant interlude.

Lexi's eyes widened at the thought of suddenly being included in the conversation; she had nothing to add since she was still single and had no immediate plans to have children. And she knew that in spite of how much they loved her they didn't understand her or why she chose to live with a bartender and an artist rather than at the estate. "What did I do now?"

"Well," her aunt hesitated, exchanging a worried glance with her mother.

"It's recently come to our attention that you might be more of a Rudnar than we thought," her mom said carefully.

Lexi frowned at that, her thought process whirling rapidly and taking her to the logical conclusion of that statement: they didn't think her dad was her father. In a hushed voice she asked, "Why would you think daddy wasn't my father?"

"What?" her mother's voice rose an octave while she jerked back in her chair as if Lexi's words were a slap to her face. "Alexandra, no."

"Why would you say I might be more of a Rudnar if that wasn't the case?" Lexi returned, almost as confused and flustered as her mom.

"Why would you even ask that?" her mother continued in a hurt tone, her eyes watering with unshed tears. "I've never even wanted any other man. From the moment I met your father's eyes during home room in ninth grade he has been the only one I have wanted."

"I'm sorry, mom," Lexi apologized, wondering how it as her fault for making an honest assumption based on her mother's strange comment. But then again, it was her mother, who was still hopelessly in love with her father even after almost 40 years of marriage. And however many years of knowing the man "Of course you've been faithful."

"Of course I have." Charisma looked up and to the left to keep the glistening tears from falling, unwilling to mar her makeup by something so messy as emotion. At least, not while she was out in public, especially the country club. Having a daughter wearing a mint green wig had to be embarrassing enough.

Aunt Sophie chuckled, daintily wiping the corners of her eyes with the edge of the napkin. "Oh, Char, you're scaring the poor girl. Just get on with it and tell her."

"I need a moment." Her mother murmured and Lexi wanted to slam her head down on the table in frustration. But her false eyelashes might get stuck and that would have been awkward.

"Do you know who just moved back to town?" Penelope asked into the silence, drawing everyone's attention away from Lexi, for which Lexi was eternally grateful. "Dee Tremain!"

Agatha hummed her approval and Lexi heard glass shatter somewhere close behind her. Glancing over her shoulder, she saw the embarrassed waiter trying to scoop broken glass back onto the tray he had just dropped; water had splashed everywhere and Lexi felt her heart go out to the poor boy.

Her mother's sharp voice chided, "Agatha!"

"Sorry, mother," Agatha said softly, her eyes sparkling as she watched the red-faced waiter rush off to bring them some more water.

"Who's Dee Tremain?" Lexi asked absently, confused by her mother's scolding of her sister. It wasn't Aggie's fault that the waiter dropped the tray, was it? No, that was impossible.

"Really, Alexandra, you should have paid attention to this kind of thing when you were growing up," Thea chided, exchanging a knowing look with Agatha and Penelope. "If you hadn't had your nose buried in a book every time we hosted a party you would know."

It wasn't her fault she preferred reading to the pretentions of the people who attended her parents' parties. She was never sure who was honest and who was lying to get what they wanted; the dynamics of the social circles she was born into eluded her. And so she left that world behind and found happiness in her new world, the world of Lexi Darling. "Well, who is she?"

"*He* is just the most gorgeous powerbroker this side of Mars," Agatha gushed, waving her hand in front of her face as if the merest thought of Dee Tremain was enough to make her blood boil.

"That doesn't tell me much."

"I'm surprised you haven't heard of him," Aggie continued, pleased to show off her knowledge to her uninformed sister. If only Aggie knew how much Lexi didn't care. "He's the head of Tremain Industries and Technology, one of the most deliciously ruthless businessmen in the country. He's ice cold in meetings and red hot in the bedroom. So I've heard."

"What does he have to do with any of this?" Lexi asked, annoyed at her sisters' adoration of the trappings of wealth and privilege. Even though they were married to some pretty influential men themselves, Agatha, Penelope and Thea still enjoyed gossiping about the goings-on within their social circles, especially the men.

"Nothing," Agatha admitted, still wearing a dreamy expression at the thought of the mysterious Dee Tremain. "I just think it's great that he's back. When he went away it was a huge loss for the women of our acquaintance. I think every female hoped to snag him."

"I heard he's still single," Penelope said, leaning in and lowering her voice as if her words were of utmost secrecy. "But he's on the market for a wife."

"Oh, good God," Lexi laughed, rolling her eyes at her sisters. "The three of you are married; I don't think Dee Tremain is interested in another man's wife."

Penelope tilted her head to the side and looked at Lexi, a mischievous smile curling her lips, "Wouldn't Mr. Tremain be a perfect addition to the family?"

"Absolutely not," Thea said rigidly, her lips pressed together in a firm line as she glared at everyone at the table, especially Penelope. "While our families are on very good terms socially we cannot have anything to do with the Tremains or their relatives on a more intimate level; our kinds do not mix."

Lexi snorted at the dramatic words, as if they were two different and incompatible species, like one was a bird and the other a fish. She wondered if the flying fish would be an exception to the rule or did flying fish even fly? She'd have to look that up when she got home. But then she played the words over in her head and she frowned at her sister, "I'm not marrying some guy to add anymore prestige to our family; I think the three of you have that covered."

They had the good nature to blush. Aunt Sophie patted her hand and offered a consoling smile, "We actually wanted to discuss something else with you, dear."

Agatha did that special smile again and a waiter appeared instantly. "My sister would like a glass of red wine, please."

"Aggie, it's barely noon," Lexi reminded her. "And I am just getting over a hangover; wine is not something I want right now."

"Take it, dear," her mother encouraged, her eyes sympathetic as she looked at her. "You're going to need it."

With a low groan, she let her family have their way. But just because the wine was there didn't mean she would have to drink it. "So, what is the big secret? Are one of you pregnant again?"

Agatha blushed as she put her hand over her flat stomach and Lexi couldn't help but chuckle. "Congratulations, Ag; do you think you'll have another girl or are you hoping for a boy?"

Her pregnant sister licked her lips and exchanged another look with the rest of the women at the table. Aunt Sophie cleared her throat, drawing the attention back to her. "Actually, dear, that's something we want to talk to you about."

"Well, *I'm* not pregnant," Lexi said, pressing her fingers to her chest for emphasis. "It's kind of hard to get pregnant when you're not having sex."

Her mother closed her eyes and swallowed thickly, "*Are* you having sex?"

Lexi felt the heat rise into her cheeks and she did not want to be having this conversation with her mother or her aunt or her sisters in the middle of the restaurant. Or anywhere. "Didn't I just say I'm not?"

"Have you ever had sex?" Charisma asked, her eyes still squeezed shut and Lexi wasn't sure which answer her mother would prefer to hear.

"Is this really something we should be discussing in public?" Lexi asked softly. At her mother's nod, she continued, "And is the answer so important?"

"Just answer the damn question, Alexandra," Thea snapped, making Lexi jump at the ruffled sound.

Sitting back in her chair, Lexi let out a breath of air, "Fine, if it's so important, I'm still a virgin. Happy?"

Her mother started swearing under her breath, her hands fluttering uselessly around her head; her sisters started chirping to one another; her aunt simply looked at her with compassion. Crossing her arms beneath her breasts, she addressed the only one who appeared half way lucid, her aunt, "I take it that was the wrong answer."

"Yes... no," her aunt shook her head and smiled ruefully. "I don't know; maybe."

Lexi simply sat there and watched the drama unwind before her; as her mother pulled herself together, smoothing her hands over her perfect chignon; as her sisters gathered their composure and once again sat serenely in their seats. Arching an eyebrow, she asked, "Is there something I should know?"

Annoyingly, the group exchanged another look when her aunt groused, "Fine, I'll tell her because the four of you are being absurd; it's not like it's that big of a deal." Turning to Lexi, she took her niece's hands in her own. "Alexandra, my pet, you're a Siren."

Lexi stared at her aunt for a long moment, waiting for some major, life-changing announcement to fall from her lips and when nothing more came, she bit down on her lips. It didn't help and the laughter rushed out of her; after all of the drama, it was a huge relief to discover they were just pulling a major prank on her. All of that build up for something so utterly crazy... "Only you guys could pull off a joke of this magnitude; I was seriously worried for a moment there...."

When no one joined her in her laughter, she paused and looked at their earnest expressions as they simply stared at her. "You've got to be shitting me; a Siren? And what would make you think something so... so... ridiculous?"

Aunt Sophie took Lexi's hand in hers, gently rubbing her thumb over the tight joints. "Well, we erroneously believed that you hadn't inherited any Siren... gifts because you didn't seem to be the type and we had no reason to believe otherwise until recently."

Lexi's eyes widened impossibly in her face; how could they possibly know about Duncan? She hadn't told anyone other than Dima and Dima didn't gossip with her family. And none of her sisters would be caught dead at Dima's bar, even though it was one of the most popular spots among their friends. And there simply hadn't been enough time between last night and this morning for them to discover anything. "But, how...."

"Aunt Cassandra saw something when she was visiting you last week that worried her," Thea sighed, looking at her nails and obviously bored by the entire conversation. Out of all of her sisters, Thea was the one who most loved to be the center of attention, putting on a glorious smile when surrounded by her adoring sycophants. It had to be killing her to share the spotlight with Lexi.

Lexi glanced at her aunt and mother, wondering what Thea was talking about, "Nothing out of the ordinary happened when she came for lunch." With a reluctant shrug, she added, "Well, she couldn't seem to take her eyes off Cole and Dima but I figured that was because Cole was dressed in a purple poet's shirt opened to the waist and Dima was barely dressed at all. It's hard not to stare when those two are in the same room."

"Yes, but you live with them and yet you're not sleeping with them," Thea's cultured voice was bitter with more than a trace of acid, though she had never expressed any jealousy over Lexi's living arrangements before.

"Thea, that's enough," her mother warned. Turning back to Lexi, her eyes swam with apologies; only, Lexi wasn't sure for what she had to apologize. "It's our fault for not figuring it out sooner but you see you were such a quiet child and when you came back from Cancun ready to take your place in the family lore you had Dima and Cole at your side. Naturally we assumed you were sleeping with one of them."

"Try both of them," Thea snorted.

Lexi was quiet, trying to digest what her family was saying and failing to understand the significance. "And why would that matter?"

"Well, you see, there are varying ways the Siren gene expresses itself, as well as varying... degrees of Siren-ness," her mother said slowly, trying to figure out what to say as she was saying it. "Because I happen to be a Siren, you and all of your sisters are all touched by it, naturally."

"Naturally," Lexi agreed simply because she had no idea what else to say.

"We just assumed you only got a smidgen of Siren blood," Charisma continued, visibly distraught at having to have the conversation. "Since you used to shun the spotlight."

Lexi nodded, remembering how her sisters loved preforming in the school plays, and how adept they were within their social circles. But what did that have to do with her? She'd rather have been caught dead then have to get up on the stage and say her name. Thoughts were raging through her head and her scalp was itching but she ruthlessly ignored it; she had the feeling she needed to concentrate completely on the conversation she was having because it was all very random, what with the talk of her extroverted sisters, her dotty Aunt Cassandra, Sirens, and sex. "All of you are the life of any party."

"It's more than that," her mother said. "People, men especially, are drawn to us and there are certain things we can do that... increase the attraction. It's the allure of the Siren."

"Of course it is because why wouldn't it be?" Lexi couldn't take anything they were saying very seriously because Sirens were a myth, to explain manatees and shipwrecks. Standing up, she started to leave when the waiter appeared with her wine, his puppy dog gaze traveling to Agatha with devotion.

"Thank you," Agatha murmured, dismissing the poor man with a smile.

Lexi could only stare as the man handed her the glass and then blissfully made his way back to the kitchen. Looking at her family, seeing their expectant expressions, she exhaled, "Come on; that doesn't prove anything. He's a waiter; he's doing his job."

"Thea?" her mother said while holding Lexi's eyes.

Thea preened, straightening her shoulders and thrusting out her generous breasts. With a demure smile, she met the eyes of a distinguished older gentleman across the room and with a come-hither glance, she silently invited him over to the table. When he arrived, he stood proudly before them and cleared his throat, "Ah, the lovely Rudnar women and Ms. Beauregard; it is a pleasure to see you looking so well this afternoon."

"Thank you, Mr. Lenao," Thea purred. "That will be all."

Lexi shook her head as the gentleman left, a loopy grin at odds with his dignified mien. "Still doesn't prove anything. Mr. Lenao has always been friendly. Now, if you could make Mrs. Lenao act as graciously I might believe you."

"Oh, sit down, Alexandra," Thea growled.

Lexi sat and then glared at her oldest sister, "You did not make me do that."

Thea looked startled for a moment and then the whole table chuckled softly, the tension of a moment before eased. Reluctantly, Lexi smiled, "So, it's a sort of mind control?"

"No, not at all," Aunt Sophie smiled. "It's simply the Siren's allure; her... influence. We cannot make anyone do something they truly don't want to do; we can only... nudge."

"Until we push them right off the cliff." Lexi shook her head, torn between laughter and pulling her hair out by the roots. Luckily, the green wig prevented the second option. "Say I believe you about being a Siren, or whatever; what does that have to do with me? As you said, I was an awkward child, preferring my books to the limelight."

Aunt Sophie and her mom exchanged looks again and Lexi slammed her hands down on the table, "Would you stop doing that? I'm not a child; I can handle whatever you have to tell me."

"We think you might have a little bit more Siren blood in you than we first realized," Charisma said slowly. At Lexi's blank expression, she caught her lower lip between her teeth and frowned, "You see, the Siren gene is passed from mother to daughter but not every female shares the same... gifts. Those with a higher concentration of the Siren gene tend to be exceptionally monogamous while those with a lesser concentration tend to be... more adventurous."

"Such as sleeping with two men at the same time," Lexi ground out, hating that her relationship with Cole and Dima could be made to sound so base. She wished she had slept with them – at the same damn time – just to piss Thea off if nothing else. "So, you thought it would be better to let me live in ignorance of my Siren heritage while I fucked my way through the city's population of men. Why? Did you think I would use my *allure* to rape an unwilling man?"

Her mother blushed, "Of course not, Alexandra. We thought it would be better to not burden you with what it means to be a Siren if you weren't one. If you had been sleeping with those two boys, then our concerns would have been minimal because you exhibited normal, if not a little bit more adventurous, behavior."

"And what does it mean to be a Siren?" Lexi's head was spinning. "And why do my sisters know about this and I don't?"

The three girls blushed and avoided her gaze as her mom explained, "They were informed of their gift when it was becoming apparent they were unduly influencing members of the opposite gender in their teens. We are informing you now because you seem to be a late bloomer and your bloom is extraordinary."

The side of Lexi's mouth quirked upwards in a half-smile at her mother's description. "So, what difference does it make if I'm a virgin?"

Lexi had to close her eyes and count to ten as her mother and aunt exchanged another look. When her aunt spoke, she spoke slowly, "Well, it has to do with True Love."

"What rot," Lexi scoffed. "Love is not foretold, or fated; it happens."

"For normal people," Charisma said. "For Sirens, it is more. Fate tends to bring love into our lives...."

"So you were all virgins when you found your True Loves, or whatever?" she asked her sisters, looking around the table and seeing the flags of color on all but Penelope's cheeks. "Yeah, that's what I thought."

"Our Siren blood isn't as powerful as yours," Thea sneered, glaring at Lexi with such venom. "Aggie and I could fuck a thousand guys and be fine; you'll be lucky to fuck one."

"Thea!" Charisma scolded her eldest daughter. "Language."

"It's ridiculous to be having this conversation in a public place where anyone could walk by our table and hear what we're talking about." Lexi spoke in a low voice as she slammed her hands down on the table. Leaning in, she lowered her voice even further and hissed, "It's ridiculous to be having this conversation at all; Sirens are a myth."

"They're not and the reason we are having this discussion here is because you're less likely to freak out if other people were about," Penelope said gently. "If we were at the house, you would have retreated to your bedroom by now."

"Or flown back home to your precious Dima and Cole," Thea sneered.

Lexi turned on her oldest sister, "Are you more upset at the thought of me fucking them or the fact that I haven't and now I'm some sort of super Siren?"

"It's not fair that you get any of the Siren's allure let alone the lion's share," Thea seethed, glaring hotly at Lexi. "You've never wanted the attention and now, whenever you walk into the room, hardly anyone pays attention to the rest of us."

Lost, Lexi looked at her mother for confirmation. Charisma sighed, "We started to notice it when you returned from your trip with the boys but we assumed it was the outfits , the persona of 'Lexi Darling.' But now, we believe otherwise."

"Why bring this up now?" Lexi threw her hands up in the air and shook her head that was aching with a headache that kept growing with each word spoken. "What in the world could have possibly have happened that changed your mind?"

"You made coffee for Cassandra," Aunt Sophie said softly.

"Yes, I can see how that would lead one to the conclusion that I was a Siren," Lexi said with heavy sarcasm. Grinning, she rolled her eyes, "Was it my affinity for the water or my ability to pour it into a cup?"

"Oh, do shut up, Alexandra," Thea rebuked.

"Make me," Lexi shot back. It was amazing how quickly she reverted to a teenager whenever she was around her sisters, especially Thea.

"Girls, enough!" Her mother's admonishment quickly silenced them. Several heads turned to see what the commotion was about but not being able to hear what was being said, they quickly lost interest. Unless that was the influence of a table-full of Sirens. Lexi still wasn't sure if she believed their tale or not.

Heaving a sigh, her mother looked at Lexi with pity, "By nature, Sirens are not aquatic creatures no matter what the myths say or however much we enjoy the water. Our ancestors originally came from a small, Grecian island that has long since disappeared. So, no Alexandra, it wasn't your affinity with the water that caused your aunt's alarm; it was your interaction with Dima."

Lexi thought back to that afternoon and could think of nothing out of the ordinary that would have caused such a stir. Sure, Dima and Cole were more affectionate that most people were perhaps comfortable with but she had grown to love their hugs, their friendliness. Some days they were her oxygen and she couldn't breathe without one or the other. Shaking her head, she said, "But nothing happened."

"Exactly," Aunt Sophie said. "You were singing, Dima came into the room and started kissing your neck, and nothing happened."

"Of course nothing happened." Lexi was appalled at the implication. "Aunt Cassandra was sitting right there; I may do some crazy things but I'm not going to have sex with my best friend in front of my aunt."

"But according to Cassandra, and by your own admission, you have never had sex with your best friend," her mother said gently. "Or anyone else."

"Of course not," Lexi scoffed with a little huff of laughter. "No one has interested me in that way until…."

"Until when, Alexandra?" Aunt Sophie asked softly, leaning closer, her eyes wide.

Lexi turned her head and slowly met her aunt's eyes and suddenly she didn't want to be there anymore. Standing abruptly, she grabbed the wine and slammed it down, wiping her mouth off with the back of her hand and wincing as the taste registered. "I've got to go."

"Alexandra, wait," her mother said, standing up as well. She wrapped her slender fingers around Lexi's wrist, holding her daughter in place. "Did you meet someone?"

A slightly hysterical laugh burbled out of Lexi's mouth even as she shook her head, "Of course not. Is the Siren song a myth or is it real, too?"

"It's very real, I'm afraid."

"That would explain what happened in Cancun," Lexi chuckled to herself. She knew she wasn't making any sense but, damn, her entire world had been flipped onto its head in the last hour or so. Here she was nursing a hangover, looking forward to a relaxing luncheon with her family, maybe have a daydream or two of a certain sexy stranger that she was never going to see again and Wham! suddenly she's a Siren.

"What happened in Cancun?" Penelope asked softly, perhaps realizing how close Lexi was to losing it.

"It was an open bar and an open mike," Lexi murmured automatically, the world blurring as tears filled her eyes. "Cole, Dima and I got up on stage to sing and the moment I belted out my part the entire bar went dead silent." She laughed without humor, "I thought it was because I was so horrible that I refused to sing another note and left the bar."

"What happened after you left?"

Lexi huffed a laugh, "Apparently there was an orgy but that doesn't prove anything. There was a lot of alcohol involved and you've seen Cole and Dima.... It doesn't prove anything. I really have to get out of here."

"But, Alexandra, there's so much you need to learn," her mother protested.

Aunt Sophie put a restraining hand on her sister's arm and held Lexi's eyes as she spoke, "Let her go, Char. Alexandra, you know you can call any of us when you're ready or if you have any questions."

Thank you, Lexi mouthed the words and quickly made her way out of the country club, not caring who she bumped into in her haste to leave. She was going to go back to the house, take a long, hot bath, and make Cole take her out for a night on the town. Well, just a movie because she just wanted to escape for a few hours and not think at all.

*****

As they left the theater, Ashley put her hand in the crook of Duncan's arm, leaning against him as they walked. "Where are we going for dinner?"

"I have reservations at the Prague," he answered. "Unfortunately it is just going to be desserts and a drink since I have some work to catch up on."

"What is so important that we can't have a full meal?"

"I bought a magazine," he said. "Since I'm meeting with the staff on Monday I want to go over my notes so I'm prepared."

"I'm sure you're already completely prepared," she sighed. "Let's have dinner than you can come over to my place tonight; maybe spend the rest of the weekend with me?"

"I can't," he said with an apologetic smile. "I have too much to do before Monday."

"Damn it, Duncan," she growled. "It's been almost a month since we've copulated and that was only because there was a full moon; I'm practically a born-again virgin."

He laughed at that statement. "I know for a fact that you didn't go home alone last night."

"What's a mere human when compared to an Alpha?" she pouted, nudging him with her hip as she looked up at him and grinned unrepentantly. "He hardly counts at all; just like your interlude with the blond."

Looking down at her, ignoring the dull ache in his gut when he thought about Lexi, he said, "After my meeting on Monday I'll take you out for lunch and we can see where things go from there."

"Promise?" she asked, the hope apparent in her voice.

"Yes," he nodded. It was counter-productive to think about Lexi; she was completely ill-suited as a prospective mate and he should be focusing on his future, which meant looking for a mate amongst the wolves. Which meant concentrating on Ashley the wolf and not the elusive Lexi the human. Deliberately, he draped his arm around Ashley's shoulder, "And don't worry, Ash; you're still the front runner in my quest to find a mate."

She rested her hand against his chest and sighed, "It does make the most sense, doesn't it? It's just… I don't think I'm ready to settle down just yet. I've finally bonded with my wolf and we are enjoying our freedom."

Duncan bit back his sharp retort regarding his thoughts about the insanity of bonding with their wolves. Forcing a smile, his voice came out rough, "I've noticed."

She threw her head back and laughed, the sound sensual and earthy. And completely wasted on Duncan. Last week, he would have taken her in his arms and covered the saucy sound with his mouth, absorbing it into his body as a prelude to a round of hot and heavy sex. Now, it just amused him. "Surely you remember how sexual you became when you first bonded with your wolf, wanting to hump just about everything in sight and having the ability to do so? The rush of power and the animal sex is exhilarating."

He didn't tell her that he hadn't bonded for that very reason; he wasn't going to be ruled by his hormones like some beast, some wild animal. He learned his lesson when he was fifteen and started the bonding process; his wolf had run wild and nearly brought Duncan to his knees before Duncan ruthlessly got him back under control. And until last night, he had remained perfectly sane and rational.

Some awareness made him lift his head and he stopped dead in his tracks. Lexi was standing not fifteen feet away from him, her eyes closed as she remained blissfully unaware of him. It didn't matter that she was leaning up against another man, his gut tightened and his body went on alert.

Her hair was glossy and light brown, pulled back into a high pony tail, with a few wisps curling around her face, making her appear fresh and wholesome. Instead of leather she was wearing jeans that caressed her body and a simple, white t-shirt, the outfit emphasizing her feminine curves. Intuitively, he knew that this was the real Lexi, the woman beneath the blond wig. While she wasn't as exotically gorgeous as she was before, she was a thousand times more beautiful in her natural state. A million times more appealing.

"Ticket, sir," the valet said, bringing him back to reality.

Reaching into his pocket, he pulled out the stub, never taking his eyes off the girl. He had no business obsessing over the human but that didn't mean he couldn't take a few moments and just admire her.

She opened her eyes and their gazes collided head on; he was lost once more, not caring that he was drowning. In that moment, he could see her spread out beneath him, welcoming him into her body. Then her tongue darted out to moisten her lips.... His erection was instantaneous and painful, causing him to adjust to make room for the unruly organ. Her lips curled upwards into perceptive smile and he almost abandoned Ashley, to walk over to her and claim her, damn the pack.

The spell was broken when the man she was with said something and she turned away. Before he completely lost his sanity, he grabbed Ashley's hand, holding onto her like she was a life line back to reality. With her lineage, her nature as a wolf, Ashley was who he should be thinking about; not some girl who played dress up and kissed like a goddamn dream.

"Isn't that the blond from the bar?" Ashley's serene voice broke into his ruminations.

He looked down at her and smiled at her unassuming face, "I don't know what you're talking about."

"Liar," she laughed good-naturedly, smiling up at him. This companionability was exactly what he needed in a relationship; none of those tempestuous emotions associated with Lexi. He didn't need madness and that is what he would get if he gave into his primitive instincts.

Even if she was a wolf, Lexi, was not the type of girl someone like him married. Hell, she wasn't the type of girl someone like him got involved with. She would twist a man up inside and he would be powerless to stop her. He would even put his finger on the knot so she could make a bow. But she wasn't a wolf; he had absolutely no business thinking about her at all.

The valet pulled his roadster up in front of them and Duncan opened the door for Ashley, his fellow wolf. Looking back one last time, he firmly put the fantasy out of his head. Sighing heavily, he walked around the front of his car and took his position behind the wheel, feeling the loss and knowing that it was the right decision to make. It was the only decision to make.

"So, anyway, what magazine are you buying?" Ashley asked, taking his mind off his melancholy thoughts.

Duncan turned his head and looked across the seat at her, blinking, trying to focus on the present. "Um, *lavish.*"

"Really?" her eyes widened in approval. "I just recently started reading that; it's the one with 'The Scene' in it, isn't it?"

"I wouldn't know," he shrugged, pulling away from the curb. "I bought it because it was a good investment."

"This writer is certifiable and absolutely brilliant. She's a human who does all of these wild things and then writes about them," Ashley continued, oblivious to the fact that Duncan couldn't care less about some fluff writer. "This week she wrote about your brother, Senator Carson. She got an interview with him last month by going wind surfing with him and after she beat him in a race she got him to announce his plans to run for presidency in the next election."

Even though he had discussed some of his half-brother's political ambitions with Philip, Duncan raised his eyebrow at that statement. "Philip would hold a press conference for that type of announcement. I doubt he would casually mention it to a writer of a small, gossip column in an exclusive magazine."

"She challenged him and won," Ashley explained as if that made perfect sense. "Last month she interviewed a wildlife survival guide and ate sautéed earth worms and the month before…."

"That does not sound at all like the type of article one should find in *lavish,*" he lamented, making a mental note to fire whomever it was that wrote that crap. His magazine was not going to have fluff pieces, even if they did yield an occasional news-worthy item.

"Even though she is a mere human I think I would be friends with her if I ever met her in the real world," Ashley said with a half-smile. "She tackles life and wrestles it to the ground, much like a wolf. I would even consider biting her, just to keep her around."

"Most, if not all, humans can't make the transition, Ash; I'm sure your writer is no exception," Duncan said disapprovingly. "And if what you say is true, that she is reckless and daring, I don't want someone like that on my staff. Or in my pack."

"You can't fire her," Ashley said, aghast.

"Watch me," he promised.

Chapter 4 (Monday)

Lexi struggled under the weight of her bags as she ran into the office building, late for the most important meeting of her journalistic career. The new owner had decided he wanted to meet the staff and layout his vision for the future of the magazine, which meant he was going to be going over everyone's contributions and weed out the ones that did not fit his standards. And apparently the new owner had very high, very rigid standards and while Lexi knew she was a good writer she also knew that she was going to have to prove herself, just like all of the other talented writers on the staff.

The only bright spot was the fact that the meeting was being held at 11:00. If it had been any earlier she would have missed it completely and had absolutely no chance of saving her job. As it was, if she managed to make it up there in the next ten minutes, she might still have a career. At the very least, she would know whether or not she still worked for *lavish.* With each second that ticked by, that possibility was growing slimmer and slimmer.

Because her alarm failed to go off, she wasn't as put together as she had hoped to be, missing the small, personal touches that completed her look. She was wearing a pleated, plaid mini skirt with a white blouse and thigh high nylons, held up by the very sexy garter belt she bought last week; it was just visible beneath the short hem of her skirt. She had wanted to wear the auburn wig with pony tails to complete the school girl look but had to settle for a very cute, sleek black bob. In addition to not being able to take the time to put on the right wig, she couldn't find the tie. Instead, she wore the shirt with the top three buttons undone, her already full breasts pressed upwards by the push up bra she wore.

"Hold the elevator!" she called out as the doors were half way shut and she was still ten feet away. A hand shot out to keep the doors open and she sighed in relief as she quickened her pace to keep her savior from waiting. "Thank you so much."

"My God, Lexi," a familiar voice drawled derisively behind the opening door. A sickening thud weighted her stomach down and she dreaded seeing the man who came with that voice. "What look are you going for now? Anime porn?"

The doors opened completely to reveal the guy who had wanted her column, Mason Jones. He was the most vocal detractor when she was hired – and the only one still complaining. With his white blond hair slicked back, he looked almost bald, which only emphasized the icy cold blueness of his eyes. Those eyes narrowed as he looked at Lexi with equal parts disdain and lust and she debated whether or not she should get into the elevator or take the stairs. Since she was running so late, she really had no choice; besides, she really didn't want to try to climb all of those stairs with slip on heels. She was already wobbly enough walking on a flat surface.

"Mason," she said politely, trying to rearrange her bags so she wasn't quite so off-balance. She shouldn't have brought so much work home over the weekend, but she wanted to be prepared for the meeting. Unfortunately, the two days had been spent reeling from her family's revelations, though she still wasn't sure whether or not she believed them, and the nights had been spent twisting in her sheets, thanks to a certain silver-eyed would-be lover.

"You should be illegal," Mason sneered, though he didn't take his eyes off her. If anything, he continued to peruse her like he purchased her in the back room of a comic book store. It was a very disconcerting feeling and she fidgeted slightly under his intense scrutiny, trying her damnedest to ignore him. He let out a low whistle, crossing his arms over his chest and leaning against the wall, "In fact, I'm pretty sure that in some states you are."

"That makes no sense," she said, refusing to give in to the urge to tug her skirt down, maybe button up the undone buttons; there was no way she was going to let the weasel win. Wearily, she watched as he unfolded an arm and moved his hand to the stop button. "I'll have you know that I am wearing five inch stilettos."

"So?" he asked, his hand still moving towards the stop button.

"Have you seen what a five inch stiletto can do to a man's private parts?" she asked, raising a single eyebrow. "Needless to say, you touch that button and you won't have to worry about testicular cancer. Ever."

He quickly – and wisely – pulled his hand back, "Geez, Lexi; you are one cold bitch."

"And don't you forget it," she smiled serenely. She knew that her outfits drew attention, and she knew that it was often sexual in nature; but there was something about Mason that gave her the willies. The vibes he gave off were hostile, menacing.

Trying to tune him out, and ignore the way he was looking at her, she mentally tried to recall which bag she put the information in for that month's column. Crap, she couldn't remember. Getting a little nervous, she glanced at her watch. The meeting started six minutes ago.

"Are you running late, Lexi?" Mason's voice interrupted her silent plea for the elevator to move faster, giving her another reason for wanting it to speed up.

"Of course not," she lied, looking up and seeing there were still three floors to go. If the gods were smiling down at her there would be no one getting on. Of course, being that it was an extremely important meeting, she was running really late and she was stuck in the elevator with a lecherous misogynist, the cart stopped two floors from hers. "Damn."

Two people stepped on and pushed the button for the ground floor. As the doors closed, she closed her eyes and begged the mischievous gods to let them keep going up. As the elevator started moving, she opened her eyes and realized the gods were spiteful, little bastards. Pressing the button for the floor immediately below their current floor, she waited until the cart came to a lurching stop and the doors yawned open. With a lunge, she stepped off the elevator, hearing the cackling of Mason as it started its trek *upwards*. She was going to have to climb three flights of stairs in heels.

Spiteful. Little. Bastards.

With no other choice, she found the stairwell, pushing the door open and stepping into the other-worldly nothingness of concrete. Clutching the bags, she bent down and took off her shoes, knowing she risked grievous injury if she attempted to scale the stairs in the aforementioned weapons. As she started the journey upwards, she realized that she wasn't going to be able to stop at her office to drop off her stuff.

"Hey, Lexi, how many more flights do you have?" Mason's voice echoed through the hollow stairwell, followed by his maniacal laughter and the sound of the door closing. She was so going to get him for that; just not until after her meeting, which could very well be her last meeting at *lavish* magazine. That would satisfy Mason, even if he didn't get her job – 'cause, honestly, who would want to read about the latest stalker techniques or the best places to masturbate in public?

A wry smile parted her lips as she mounted the stairs, not caring that the bottoms of her stockings were going to be filthy. Dima and Cole were going to laugh at her; and after she was done pouring over her horrible morning, she would probably be laughing as well. And then they could make arrangements for a trip to the Caribbean, since it wasn't likely she was going to have a job after, oh, fifteen minutes.

Finally, she reached the top of the stairs and dropped her shoes to the ground, sliding her feet into the sexy heels. She pushed against the door and nothing happened; it didn't budge an inch. Slamming her fist against it, she yelled, "You son of a bitch!"

In frustration, she pulled at it. And felt like a complete idiot when it opened. Rolling her eyes at her stupidity, she couldn't prevent the smile from forming, or the laughter from bubbling up. Dima and Cole were going to give her such grief for that supreme act of idiocy. A laugh escaped just as she stepped through the door of the board room and died almost as quick. Everyone in there was deathly silent; never a good sign.

"Hey, sorry I'm late, but my alarm failed to go off and almost everything else that could go wrong managed to do so," she called out, stumbling over to her spot, oblivious to the other people in the room. Pulling out her chair, she set her bags on the table, determined to find the necessary folder she had prepared for the new owner. Burying her head in one of the bags, she pulled out the folder with her notes and smiled. Finally, success first time out!

Someone cleared his throat and she looked up. Thank God the chair was behind her since she was pretty sure her spirit completely left her body for a moment. And a body without a spirit is unable to stand on its two inanimate legs. Her bottom hit the chair with more force than normal and she hoped she wasn't going to end up bruised.

"Duncan. Wow, I am so glad we didn't have sex the other night," she said without thinking. "Otherwise this meeting would have been really awkward."

Someone snorted and she heard the words she spoke and flushed hotly. "Not that this isn't already awkward."

"I'm glad you could join us, Miss...." he said, arching that expressive eyebrow, acting as if he had never had his hand on her bare breast or his tongue down her throat. Maybe she was still asleep and this was just an elaborate dream because there was no way in hell that the man standing there acting like the new owner of the magazine was the very same man she almost slept with on Friday and who subsequently disturbed her sleep for the rest of the weekend.

If it were a dream, wouldn't he be smiling at her right now instead of glowering? And along those same lines, wouldn't they be getting naked and horizontal? But then, if that were true, why were all of her co-workers there, acting as if it weren't a dream? Someone nudged her and she grimaced; not a dream. Okay, she could deal with this. "Um, Miss Darling; Lexi. But you know that."

"Mmm hm," he murmured in a non-committal manner. His silver eyes looked right through her and she frowned; how could he act as if he had never met her when they had that Moment? "Would you like to share anything else or can we continue with the meeting?"

He was so not how she expected he would be should they ever meet again. Of course, in the many scenarios she imagined, this was never, ever one of them. The room was still silent and she looked up to see everyone watching her. Rolling her hand in the air, she murmured, "Sure, we can continue."

"Thank you," he said. "Now, as I was saying, I plan on working closely with you over the next several weeks to get the feel for the dynamics of this magazine and to determine which writers will be staying and which ones will not." And as those words left his mouth, he looked directly at Lexi, sending a familiar fire through her bones. But he was talking about firing her. That would explain that fire analogy. Damn, this was not how she imagined their reunion would be. Perhaps it was that idiosyncrasy that was making her mouth speak without the benefit of thinking first.

With a frown, she met his gaze. "Are you suggesting that I am one of the writers who will be released?"

"Why are you interrupting me?" Duncan asked, crossing his arms over his broad chest and making her mouth water just a little bit. Reality, Lexi; this is reality. No warm caresses or heart-melting kisses or a simple hello. Just imminent dismissal. Reality sucked.

"You looked at me," she explained. She really needed to separate fantasy from reality because in real life, this guy obviously didn't experience the same earth-shattering connection on Friday night. Or he was furious that she bailed on him after passing out before they ever even had sex. Unfortunately, her body was responding as if he were seducing her with hot words and hotter caresses. "I presume you are going to fire me."

"I haven't made that decision yet," he said, shifting slightly in his seat as he glanced around the room before meeting her gaze once more. If she looked close enough, she could almost make out a flare of desire in his eyes but it was banked beneath opaque silver.

Her eyes narrowed as she studied his straight-faced expression; not a muscle ticked and his jaw was perfectly relaxed as if she didn't affect him at all and it kind of pissed her off because her hormones were fighting one another to get closer to the stoic bastard. Her eyes dropped to the hand that rested on the table and as she watched, he squeezed his fingers into a fist and then relaxed them and she smiled to herself. He wasn't as unaffected as he pretended. "If I sleep with you it won't be just to keep my job."

A few gasps filtered into her rebellious brain but she held Duncan's silver gaze, watching with fascination as it became molten. He spoke through clenched teeth as he bit out, "I don't sleep with my employees."

Her lips tilted upwards in an amused smile, "So you'll fire me just to have the pleasure?"

"I'm not going to fire you," he bit out, his nostrils flaring as he continued to glare at her.

Ignoring the sound of someone, probably her old boss Jeffrey, clearing his throat, her eyes sparkled, "Then eventually you *will* be sleeping with an employee; it's only a matter of time."

"Lexi," Jeffrey murmured next to her. "Stop talking."

She shrugged her shoulders as she continued to hold his silver gaze through lowered lashes, "Forgive me, Duncan; I just never expected to see you again and to have you show up here as my new boss is a somewhat disconcerting."

"You have no idea," he grumbled, exhibiting the first crack in his smooth exterior. Heaving a sigh, the mask slid back into place and he resumed glaring at her. "Everything – everyone – is going to be given one month, even your… fluff."

"Fluff?" she squeaked, offended on behalf of all of the subjects of her articles. Thrusting her shoulders back, prepared to do battle, she asked, "Have you read even one of my articles?"

Working his jaw, he silver eyes flashed, "I don't need to read it in order to know that it won't mesh with what I have planned for the magazine."

"What? Are you going to make it even more pompous and full of itself? The magazine where fun goes to die?" she fired back. Turning to Jeffrey, she smiled a little sheepishly, "No offense, Jeff."

The older man smiled but their moment was interrupted by the clearing of a throat, "Lexi."

"Duncan," Lexi said sweetly, smiling at the gorgeous man sitting at the head of the table. Arguing with the man was almost as exhilarating as kissing him and she could imagine plenty of scenarios that included explosive arguments and then even more explosive sex. Her nipples pebbled at the thought of tearing off his suit and pushing him down as she straddled his hard body and punished him for calling her work fluff. And then having him return the favor. During the past few minutes, his silver eyes grew fierier as he continued watching her with horrified fascination. Waving her hand in the air, she leaned back in her chair, "Please, continue Mister?"

"Tremain," he ground out through clenched teeth. "*D* Tremain."

Her jaw dropped open as he told her his name and she felt her stomach flip over on itself. He was Duncan Tremain and she remembered her sisters raving about him at the lunch, she just hadn't realized that the man they were talking about and the man she had almost had sex with were one and the same. Chewing on her finger tip, she stared at him and tried to remember what they had said but she was coming up blank. It would come to her – eventually. Lowering her hand, she let out a long breath and pasted on a serene smile, even though her heart was pounding furiously in her chest. "Pleased to meet you, *Dee* Tremain; but why do they call you Dee? Isn't that a girl's name?"

"D is short for Duncan," he ground out, his eyes burning. If they made it past the week without fucking she would be surprised. That is, if he was still planning on giving her a month's grace period, which seemed less likely now than a few minutes ago. "And while we are at the office you will call me Mr. Tremain."

"Will you call me Miss Darling?' she asked suggestively, her lips curled in a sultry smile as she batted her lashes at him, ignoring the audience that was watching the interaction with interest. "Or Darling Lexi?"

"God Lexi, you do torment a man!" he bellowed, sitting upright in his chair and pinning her with his silver eyes. "You are making it nearly impossible to let you stay."

"So I should pack up my stuff?" She caught her lower lip between her teeth and looked at him with wide, hazel eyes, knowing she projected the image of wounded innocence. And she thought she didn't want the spotlight; she did, as long as it was Duncan's spot light.

"No." His lips pressed together in a tight line and she was perversely enjoying seeing his civilized veneer crack. She wanted to press harder and watch it shatter, wondering if he would dismiss the other writers before he reached across the table and grabbed her. "Miss Darling. For now. Your job. Is safe. Are there any other questions?"

She bit her lip to keep from speaking but his short, clipped manner nudged her into asking, "Yes. When will I know whether that is a permanent condition or something to shut me up?"

"If it was a ruse to get you to be quiet don't you think it would have worked?" he asked, his eyes luminous as he rose from his seat and planted his palms on the table in front of him. He leaned towards her and she felt his presence wrap itself around her bones, even though there was still four feet of table between them.

"If I thought you were sincere in your offer," she countered, also rising to her feet and flattening her hands against the table, knowing the advantage she had as a well-endowed woman with a gaping shirt. She smiled as his eyes dipped down. "If I thought you weren't just trying to appease me."

"I don't appease my employees, Miss Darling," he ground out, his eyes a liquid silver as they met hers once more. "And I don't make statements that are untrue. If I say your job is safe, it is."

"For now," she said, unable to help herself. She fell back into her seat, crossing her arms beneath her breasts. "My job is safe for now."

"You try my patience, Miss Darling," he bit out, sitting down in his chair, mirroring her gesture by crossing his arms across his chest.

"I get that a lot," she said with a guileless shrug. Adrenaline pulsed through her veins and if she didn't get out of there soon, she would continue to put her foot in her mouth and Duncan was going to have no choice but to fire her. She was so damned turned on by arguing with him she was about to come apart at the seams and if she stayed she would push and push until, well, until she did. "It's part of my charm."

"I don't doubt that," he said, the hint of a smile playing in his silver eyes, glancing down at the fluorescent green folder with hand drawn flowers covering it, taunting him much the same way as its owner. "It's my job to withstand your… charm for the greater good of my magazine."

"Ha!" She shot out, shooting out of her seat before she did and said anything else to provoke him. Bending over the table, she tapped the folder, "Read, and then decide whether or not I belong here. Until then, I'm going back to my office."

"Miss Darling!" he called out.

She held up her hand and turned her back on him. "Unless you have magically read my work in the last two seconds I don't want to hear it. Until you're ready to give me and my column a fair chance, I have nothing further to say to you."

"Miss Darling!" this time it was Jeffrey who spoke as his hand encircled her upper arm, turning her around to face him. "Are you trying to get fired?"

She thought about that for a moment, glancing over the man's shoulder at

Duncan Tremain, seeing the familiar heat in his eyes, only it was mixed with anger. Maybe she was trying to get fired; because God knows it would be easier than working for *him*, if only for a month. "He started it."

Yeah, that was real mature. Jeffrey looked at her as if she had lost her mind; which come to think of it, she probably had. "He's the one who's going to be signing your checks."

She guffawed, "Yeah, if I still have a job."

"Which you're trying awfully hard to ensure that you don't," Jeffrey warned, leading her out of the room. Looking over his shoulder as he opened the door, "Excuse us for a moment, please."

Duncan waved his hand magnanimously and with a final glance, she was ushered out the door by her former boss. "You didn't have to leave with me."

"I'm making sure you don't do – or say – anything else that might jeopardize your position here," he explained as they wove their way through the cubicles to her office, the smell of coffee and printer ink in the air.

She actually shared an office with one other writer, but since he mostly traveled, he was rarely there. While he had been away on an important assignment, she just sort of moved in and when he walked in on her sitting at a secondary desk, he didn't object. Of course, he had continued to stare at her, his face turning red as beads of sweat broke out on his forehead.

His reaction might have been because she had been wearing just her demi-bra; she had spilled coffee on her blouse and had wanted to get the stain out before it set. Asking if it was okay to share an office, since he was hardly there anyway, she looked at him until he managed to mumble something while he palmed the front of his pants. Okay, so maybe there was some truth to her being a Siren but it wasn't like she used her powers for evil; just a little mischief.

Jeffrey opened the door to her office and as soon as she entered, she dropped her bags and flung herself onto the comfortable chair, crossing her arms beneath her breasts and exhaling loudly. "He's judging my work without any knowledge of it; if he read it and thought it was shit, fine, but he hasn't even read it."

He laughed, sitting down in the chair next to her. "Give him a chance; he hardly knew what hit him when you walked through the door." When she glared at him, he patted her leg, "Poor Duncan is going to have his hands full with you."

"I don't understand," she frowned, crossing one leg over the other, not caring that her skirt flipped up revealing the tops of her thigh. Tapping her foot in the air, she raised an eye brow, "I'm very easy to get along with."

"Yes, but you have the ability to make grown men uncomfortable."

"I don't do it on purpose." She scowled at the photographs hanging on her wall, not seeing the beautiful images but instead seeing her mother and sisters sitting around the table talking about being a Siren. If being a Siren made her so unconsciously manipulative, she didn't want anything to do with it.

"You are so passionate, Lexi; so full of life. Mr. Tremain doesn't know what a treasure he has in you," he smiled, leaning forward and patting her on the cheek. Resting a hand on her knee, he shook his head and laughed, "And you are so damn tempting yet you don't even realize it."

She was quiet for a long moment, her family's words echoing in her head and she swallowed painfully. "Um, did I by any chance hum or sing when I applied for this job?"

Taken back, he looked at her as if she had lost her mind, "Hum?"

"Yes, hum," she hummed a few notes to prove her point. And abruptly stopped when she remembered the scene her sisters caused when they hummed. "Or sing?"

Then she realized he was shifting uncomfortably as he swore beneath his breath, covering his awkwardness with a laugh. She felt guilty for causing whatever she caused, even if she wasn't, exactly, sure what she caused or how she caused it. "You didn't hum or sing, Lexi. You simply approached me at a bar and handed me your resume on a napkin. I have no idea why I decided to give you an interview but I sure as hell am glad I did."

"Why did you end up hiring me?" she asked, desperate to know the answer, even if it was one she didn't want to hear.

"I liked your creative thinking and so I hired you to stir things up a bit and you have done a fantastic job of it. You have breathed new life into this old magazine," he assured her. "That's why I asked Mr. Tremain to give you a chance before he axed your column out of hand."

"So I haven't completely screwed the pooch on this one?"

"No but I wouldn't press my luck; Mr. Tremain isn't one to cross." He laughed out loud and shook his head in amusement as he continued, "I have never seen Duncan so prickly. You really got under his skin."

"He got under mine first," she muttered. "It isn't fair that he should appear so unaffected when I was practically squirming in my seat."

"Trust me, Lexi; he wasn't unaffected." Jeffrey smiled wryly. "He is just used to dealing with hostile situations better than you."

"I was not hostile," she protested, feeling the heat rise in her cheeks as she realized that she might have been a little hostile in her attempt to get him to notice her. "Besides, did you see how he was looking at me? All silvery-eyed and antagonistic?"

"That wasn't antagonism, it was awareness; hunger," Jeffrey laughed. "And there was a fair amount of heat coming from your end as well."

"Well, of course there was; have you seen him?" she asked incredulously, throwing her hand out in emphasis. "He's absolutely gorgeous but I didn't expect to see him again and now I have to figure out a way to put my rampaging hormones on the back burner because he's my new boss and he says he refuses to sleep with his employees."

"Hell, Lexi, had I known selling the magazine was going to cause you such hardship I wouldn't have sold it," Jeffrey chuckled.

"Why did you sell?" she asked.

He shrugged his shoulders, "Mr. Tremain offered a lot of money and I figured I could sell it now and enjoy retirement; maybe get a villa in the Tuscan hills where Albert and I could wile away the hours."

"That sounds nice," she smiled gently, not wanting to see her friend leave, but happy for him for the opportunities he had. The door opened and she froze, not expecting to see those silver eyes staring at her with that much hunger so soon after arguing with him. She nearly melted into a puddle and slid right off the chair.

*****

Never before had an employee ever stood up to Duncan in that manner; and if they did, they surely wouldn't continue being in his employ. Lexi Darling was one tempestuous, intoxicating, infuriating, desirable female. The moment she had entered the meeting he nearly had a coronary. But then seeing the color drain from her face and having her fall back into her chair.... He actually winced when she abruptly sat down; she probably bruised her bottom and that would be a shame; she had a very nice ass. It had taken every bit of his willpower to not dismiss everyone else and have her to himself. Hell, his wolf had begun panting the moment she walked through the door, before she said anything.

And then there was the ridiculous, incredibly erotic outfit she had on, making him feel slightly lecherous for lusting after her. The shirt was pulled tight across her amazing breasts, threatening to burst apart under the strain of bound flesh meant to be free. He desperately tried to keep his eyes off of her; but he was unable to do so. She drew him by merely being there; her sauciness and too-tight shirt tempted him further. And having had the briefest taste of her he knew the passion that surrounded her was soul deep.

Despite being in a meeting, he couldn't seem to stop himself from arguing with her just to have another taste of her passion. Seeing her riled up and feisty had him thinking about sex; specifically sex with her. With that fire burning in her blood, she would be incredible in bed. Or against a wall. Or in the woods. Or any of the other thousands of places he imagined taking her.

While they sparred, everything else disappeared. It was just her and him, separated by a mere four feet of table. Had she not sat down, he would have done something incredibly stupid – like reach out and grab her, drag her across the table and into his arms; claim her mouth, her body. And as she left in high-drama, he had no choice but to follow her. Wrapping up the meeting in record time, he excused himself in a move that was everything Duncan Tremain was not. He was right to assume that she would be someone to twist a man all up inside, even if she wasn't a wolf.

Standing outside her door, he overheard her admitting to wanting him and a ridiculously pleased smile crossed his face. But it would do no good to let her know how she affected him; not if he meant to work with her for the next month. He could not get involved with her, an employee. A human.

A temptation.

He could feel his wolf mentally prowling, wanting to steal the girl away from the civilized world and hide her away in his den. He refused to give the beast the satisfaction of having Lexi Darling; if she was to be had it would be by Duncan, not a wild creature.

No, he wasn't going to break his cardinal rules: no sleeping with a human and no sleeping with an employee. He had never been so tempted before, though, and it bothered him that he might be just as uncivilized as his wolf.

Closing his eyes, he took a few deep breaths to bring his raging desire under some semblance of control. Telling himself to imagine freezing water, ice, falling stock prices, his wolf gaining power over him, anything to get his lust quieted, he pushed against the door. And every ounce of control he fanatically fought for disappeared in a split-second. She sat with her leg crossed over the other, exposing the tops of her silky nylons, the bare flesh of her thigh; the flash of silky pink panties.

If Jeffrey weren't sitting there, looking up at him with an amused expression, Duncan would have gone completely primal, putting his wolf to shame with his primitive behavior. He would have closed the door behind him, dragged her to her feet as he unfastened his pants; kissed her as her pushed the scrap of material to the side; buried himself in her and fucked her until he made her scream.

"Mr. Tremain," she breathed, uncrossing her legs and smoothing the skirt down. Slowly, she came to her feet, desire simmering in her hazel-green eyes as she looked at him. Her eyes shifted downwards at the tell-tale bulge, flying back to his when she saw the erection he didn't even bother trying to hide. Fuck civilized behavior; the wolf could win this round.

"Miss Darling," he said, his voice husky and harsh. He nodded towards Jeffrey, who was getting to his feet. "Mr. Holmes. I hope I'm not interrupting anything."

"Of course you're not, Mr. Tremain," the older man smiled. He reached out and squeezed Lexi's arm in a show of support. "I am going to leave the two of you alone...."

"Knowing what I just said are you sure that's such a good idea?" Lexi asked before she could think better of it. Her eyes flew to Duncan's and her cheeks reddened slightly at the obvious intent of her question. The older man just chuckled and left, leaving them alone.

Finally.

Chapter 5

"It's been nearly two and a half days since I've had you in my arms," Duncan said softly, his eyes widening as if he was surprised by the words coming out of his mouth.

"I was perfectly capable of walking, you know," Lexi replied lightly, her voice rough with naked desire.

"But where would the fun have been in that?" His liquid silver eyes and his raw velvet voice caressed her skin and she leaned closer, expecting his lips to brush over hers. But he pulled back, withdrawing back into himself and frowning. "Forgive me; I didn't come in here to pick up where we left off...."

"I wouldn't mind," she interrupted and watched with fascination as he seemed to lose his train of thought for a moment. But only a moment, unfortunately.

Clearing his throat, he continued speaking in a controlled voice as if he wasn't sporting an impressive erection that was pressing against the front of his expensive slacks. "We need to establish rules, Miss Darling; boundaries. You are now my employee and a relationship between us is strictly prohibited."

"It could be our secret," she persisted, her eyes moving over his face, absorbing the exquisite lines of his jaw, his lips. "We could be perfectly professional in the office and after hours…."

"Lexi, I doubt I'd be able to act professionally around you once I've had you in my bed," he admitted, laughing ruefully. Shaking his head, he held his hands out to his sides and huffed, "Look how I charged after you just now; I cannot risk more."

"It'd be worth it." She wanted to touch him, run her hands over the hard planes of his chest, sink her fingers into the black silk of his hair.

"I'm sure it would be but it cannot happen."

Waving her arm through the air, she turned around to try to gather herself together. He was right, of course he was right. But that didn't alter the fact that she wanted him beyond reason. Having him near made everything too tight, too binding; he made her burn. She walked over to her desk, needing to put some distance between them and clear her head. Her heart was pounding in her chest and she wondered if he could hear it. "Of course you're right; still…."

"Why do you wear these things?" he asked directly behind her, his fingers brushing the ends of her wig. She hadn't even heard him move and was startled at his sudden close proximity. The heat from his body was warming her cool skin, melting her insides.

How could she be expected to work in the same building as him when all she wanted to do was rub her body all over his? Her hormones were seriously out of control and if he would just make one tiny little exception to his rule she could have sex with him and then get him out of her system and get on with her life without all of these unruly desires.

"They go with the outfits," she explained absently. Snippets of her sisters' gossip over the years tried to make their way through her befuddled brain and she concentrated on remembering anything about Duncan Tremain. They had been impressed with his accomplishments, saying that he was one of the most powerful men under the age of thirty. But that was several years ago; he had to be in his late twenties, early thirties and he was so damn delicious she was having difficulty thinking straight. Agatha gushed that he didn't take over businesses, he conquered them, that he was a ruthless warrior, surviving in the twenty-first century by decimating his opponents in the fields of business rather that battle.

The image of him in a loin cloth with a shield and a spear made her nearly faint and if he were to turn all of that masculine strength towards seduction.... The thought of him in action made the butterflies in her stomach leap for joy, wanting to be caught in his net. Dear lord that was cheesy. She glanced at him from beneath her lashes and had to bite back a groan; did he have to be so... magnetic?

He wouldn't even have to try very hard to conquer her; it would be over in a heartbeat as she surrendered willingly. Squeezing her eyes shut, trying to rein her inner vixen in, all she could see was Duncan naked and strapped to a bed while she stood over him wearing nothing but heels and a smile. Maybe she'd be doing some conquering of her own, bring him to his knees, and all that. Her breasts swelled at the thought and she had to press her legs together to ease the ache of inappropriate lust.

Taking her by the shoulders, he turned her around and when she opened her eyes she was staring at his chest. Woodsy spice and masculine heat filled her nostrils; the scent of Duncan. Looking up at him, her heart lurched forward and slammed ruthlessly against her ribs, hungry for his embrace. He exuded masculinity, strength, power, ruthlessness, sexuality. And she wanted him like she had never wanted anyone or anything ever before. She should have been terrified.

She wasn't.

She reached up and brushed her fingers over his lips, absorbing the feel of the tender flesh, remembering how expertly he had kissed her. She looked up and met the molten silver of his eyes and her knees disappeared. Falling against the desk, she swallowed at the desire blazing in the silver depths as he gazed at her. But he simply stood there, towering over her and filling the room with his presence as he looked down at her. He held his body stiffly, as if a breeze would shatter his resolve. What she wouldn't give for a breeze at that moment. "Give in, Duncan."

"I'm not sleeping with you," he rasped through dry lips. Her tongue flicked out to moisten her own lips and he sucked in a tortured, ragged breath.

"You can't deny the attraction," she said, her voice velvety with desire, her eyes slowly moving over his handsome face: his chiseled jaw, his harsh cheek bones and straight nose, his beautifully sculpted lips. His raven black hair was still perfect, not a single strand out of place. Not a single strand of hair would dare defy him. And it still made her yearn so badly to mess it up, the urge almost overwhelming now that he stood so close, smelling so tantalizing and hot.

"I can't," he admitted. He reached past her and pressed the palms of his hands to the desk behind her, trapping her between his arms. The solid wall of his chest was not quite touching her breasts and she never knew torment could be so pleasurable.

"You want me," she breathed, as he foolishly kept closing the distance between them. He was so close his breath fanned over her face and she could smell the woods at midnight; she could feel the latent strength of his body as it almost touched hers.

"That was before you worked for me," he whispered. Tentatively, he reached up with his hand, touching her cheek with the tips of his fingers. Her eyes started to roll back before she caught herself and forced her eyes to remain open. "But, Lexi, this can't happen."

"It's just sex," she whispered bluntly. She knew she was going to burn because the fire was too pretty and she wanted to touch.

He laughed without humor, his fingers trailing to her jaw as he continued to caress her without seeming to realize he was touching her. "Somehow I doubt that it would be just sex between us and I cannot offer anything more."

She swallowed as his fingers moved across her skin, her throat, threatening to dip into her shirt. His eyes focused on his hand as he came dangerously close to her cleavage where she wanted him to touch her, to make him burn like she burned. "If it can't happen then why are you still here, torturing me with what I can't have?"

"Hmmm?" he murmured, lost in his own sensual haze. He lifted his gaze, "What?"

"You keep telling me that we can't but you are destroying me with your touch," she said softly, looking up at him with wide eyes. "Couldn't you break your rules for one afternoon, maybe lose yourself in my body for a few hours and then forget me?"

"I can't forget you," he said, his hand moving over her skin to the side of her breast, his thumb separating from his fingers and brushing over her taut nipple. He looked down and she knew he would see that her nipples were hard, aroused. When he looked up again, he bent his head forward, his mouth so close to hers but not touching, not taking. And when he spoke, his air entered her, sliding in with effortless ease, "God knows I've tried but I can't."

"Is there someone else? Maybe the red head?" she asked, feeling her breath mingling with his, mating. His pull was too strong and she wanted to experience this overwhelming lust until she bled

"I told you I'm not seeing anyone." He shook his head in denial, moving his head in imitation of kissing her, but not kissing her. He took the final step, closing the distance between their bodies, pressing his hard muscled body against hers until she could feel the thickness of his erection against her stomach. Pressing his arousal against her, he whispered, "But that doesn't change anything; we cannot give in to this madness."

"Yes, we can but you're being stubborn," she whispered, her eyes dropping to his lips, wondering why they weren't connected to hers. Her eyes closed as his breath heated her skin and she waited for him to finish, to begin. The scent of coffee washed over her skin, teasing her, tempting her. Making her want, making her yearn, for everything.

And then there was nothing. Slowly, she opened her eyes and saw him looking at her, a strained expression on his all-too-handsome face. His nostrils flared as he took deep breaths, a tic working in his jaw as he held himself apart from her. Tilting her head to the side, mystified, she asked, “What is it?”

His brows furrowed together as he swallowed, the movement of his throat emphasizing his golden skin. He shook his head as he dragged his fingers through his hair. His silver eyes were tortured as he looked at her with a hint of desperation, “I have to resist you, Lexi, otherwise I am no better than an animal, a wild beast.”

"What’s that supposed to mean?” she asked as he continued to look at her, anger and confusion and lust warring in his silver eyes. Her eyes narrowed as he straightened his tie, ignoring her question. “Do you think I am a wild animal?”

“Of course not,” he said quickly, adamantly, turning his back towards her as he pressed his hand to the front of his pants, gasping in pain as he did so. The muscles of his back were taut as he admitted, “I usually have much better control and yet denying you is going to kill me.”

“Then don’t deny me,” she asked, softly putting a hand on the middle of his back and feeling him stiffen at her touch. “It’s like I said, no one else need ever know.”

“If I gave into you even once anyone with eyes would be able to take one look at me and know,” he vowed fervently. He turned around to face her so that her hand was over his heart and she felt it thumping rapidly beneath her palm. Putting his hand over hers, his voice was guttural as he pleaded, “Give me back my sanity, Lexi; release me from your spell.”

His words were a slap to her a face and an ocean of cold water to her libido and she stumbled backwards, her desire and fantasies crashing to the floor and shattering into a million pieces. Did she do this to him with her… Siren-ness? Did she turn a sane, rational man into a slavering beast, ready to give up all of his principles to satisfy her whims? Pressing her hand against the vomiting butterflies in her stomach, she turned her back to him and in a voice that lacked emotion, she whispered, “I think you should go.”

"Lexi," he asked, compassion making her heart crumble to dust. "What is it? What's wrong?"

"Out," she repeated with a little more volume, pointing her finger to the door, unable to face him knowing what she did to him, what she was doing to him.

He walked over to the door, pausing with his back towards her, "I didn't expect to see you here and I let my… baser feelings control me. Forgive me, Lexi. Miss Darling.

With that he left, leaving Lexi swimming in doubts and fears that she truly was a Siren and her entire brief relationship with Duncan was false, based upon her own lust and desire. He didn't really want her at all but he somehow couldn't help himself. Thank God they hadn't had sex because it would have been rape on her part; it couldn't be considered consensual if he wasn't in control of his actions. Leaning against the closed door, she slid to the floor, burying her head in her hands and laughing at the tragedy of being a Siren, of lusting after men and never knowing if the lust they offered in return was genuine or manufactured.

But she owed Duncan – Mr. Tremain – an apology; she was going to have to go to his office and offer one.

She was just going to take a few moments to compose herself. She'd ignore the Siren's demand for sex with Duncan – Mr. Tremain – and respect his wishes. And then she'd learn how to suppress the Siren bitch so she'd never put another man into such a compromising situation again.

She groaned, feeling the pressure low in her belly demanding release. Knowing she had to apologize sooner rather than later and knowing that if she went up there while her body was so close to the edge she'd do something unforgiveable. She'd just take a few minutes to herself; the Siren wasn't going to win.

Closing her eyes, she slid her finger beneath the elastic of her panties, touching her swollen sex. She was wet, wetter than she knew possible, and her fingers slid over the folds of her sex. With thoughts of Duncan wreaking havoc on her body it didn't take much to get her off.

*****

Duncan stood in the middle of his personal bathroom, cleaning the sticky mess from his hand and glaring at the image reflected back at him. He was thirty-three years old, what the hell was he doing jerking off in the boys' room like an adolescent getting his first glimpse of a skin magazine? What the hell had he been thinking, chasing Lexi down and cornering her in the office where there was no one around to stop him from making a fool of himself?

If you refuse to take what is being offered then step aside and give me the girl.

No. Duncan shook his head as he leaned against the sink and glared at the reflection staring back at him, the silver eyes glowing beneath the fluorescent lights.

Come on, Duncan, the wolf cajoled, his voice wrapping around Duncan, tormenting him. *Let me out to play; I'll be good – better than good. The best Lexi ever had.*

His jaw tightened as the wolf continued to taunt him. *We're leaving her alone.*

You're a wolf, Duncan; embrace me and Lexi can be ours. The wolf let his words sink in, knowing they were having an effect on Duncan no matter how much he might try to deny it. *You know you want her and if you just give in, you can…."*

"No!" Duncan bellowed out loud, slamming his fist against the mirror and causing it to fracture. He stared at his broken image, ruthlessly ignoring the wolf.

Splashing cold water onto his face, he tried to drive both Lexi and the wolf out of his mind. She was driving him mad and his wolf wasn't helping, urging him to take the girl, damn the rules, damn the consequences. He was fighting against something he desperately wanted and he was tired of denying the attraction. But if he gave in the fucking wolf would win.

"There you are," Ashley's familiar voice called out. With the water dripping from his face, he looked up and in the broken mirror saw her standing in the door way to the bathroom, wearing a brilliant smile on her face and a black trench coat around her body.

"Ashley," he murmured, pushing his hands through his damp hair before straightening. Keeping his eyes on her in the reflection he didn't turn around to face her as he asked, "What are you doing here?"

"We had a lunch date planned, Duncan," she laughed lightly, untying the belt and letting the coat fall open to reveal a shimmery green merry widow with matching crotch-less panties. She was a fellow wolf and she exuded sex but his own wolf barely sat up to take notice, damning him for a fool a thousand times over. Dropping the coat to the ground, she rested an arm against the door jamb spreading her legs in invitation. "Or did you forget?"

Obviously he forgot if he took care of himself when he could have waited a few more minutes and had a warm, willing woman to screw. Except he knew he wouldn't have taken Ashley up on her offer – she wasn't who he wanted. Smiling at her, he turned around and leaned against the sink, "Of course I didn't forget. Unfortunately it has to be a quick lunch since there is so much more to do here than I originally thought."

"Oh," she said, crest-fallen, lowering her lashes but not before he saw the hurt in her eyes. What the hell was he doing chasing after a sex bomb, like a snake in heat, when he had a perfectly acceptable she-wolf on hand? "But I thought we could fornicate; my wolf is desperate for primal sex with another wolf, chiefly with an Alpha wolf."

His black heart actually went out to her as she looked up at him with her big, blue eyes, running her hands over her body hoping to entice him even as he remained unmoved. Of course, if Lexi was standing there wearing practically nothing, he doubted there would be a problem getting it back up. Just thinking about her was stirring things down below. "We will, Ash, just not today; I'm having difficulties with one of my writers."

"Ah," she nodded her head in understanding, stepping into the smaller room and pressing her body against his, draping her arms over his shoulders. Her red hair framed her beautiful face and he knew that he had kissed her lips at some point but he couldn't remember how they tasted; all he could taste was the honeyed warmth of Lexi's mouth. "Then perhaps you need release to help you deal with him."

"Her," he said, the image of Lexi looking at him with her gold and green eyes, her pulse racing in her throat as she tried to make him give in. One more word from her lips and he would have thrown all caution to the wind and taken her into his arms. In a last minute attempt to save himself, he begged her to release him from her spell and she froze. He still wasn't sure what it was that he said that caused her shuttered expression but it had hit him in the gut.

Frustration flared in Ashley's eyes before she simply smiled, "Then it's doubly important for you to lose yourself in my body for a few moments."

Even the promise of sex had been more with Lexi, a few hours compared to a few moments. An image of his body fused with Lexi's filled his head and his body responded. If he wanted any control over the situation, he was going to have to stop thinking about her. Or he was going to have to give in and hope to whatever gods may be listening that the mad attraction would burn itself out.

A small hand pressed against his burgeoning erection and he realized that he had closed his eyes when he was fantasizing about Lexi. Opening them, he saw Ashley smiling up at him, rubbing him through his pants in the manner with which she knew he liked. "See? I knew you'd want to make love to me."

"Ashley," he choked out, grabbing her wrists and trying to pry them from his body. Even knowing better, he wanted Lexi Darling. But Ashley was determined, straining against his hold to stroke him. "Ashley! As Alpha I demand you stop."

"You smell of sex, Duncan," she purred, pressing her nose against his chest and breathing deeply. She was panting as she twined her body around his, "It's driving me insane."

A knock at his door interrupted them as she continued trying to touch him and he continued trying to evade her. Scowling down at Ashley, he called out, "One moment, please."

Without giving them a moment, the door opened and Lexi stepped into his private offices looking like temptation incarnate and his body responded with an instant erection. He barely heard Ashley's approving gasp as her limbs went boneless and she fell against him. Color infused Lexi's cheeks as she saw Ashley pressed up against him, the scrap of material barely concealing her pale flesh. Lexi's eyes widened as they met his, the hazel-green eyes shimmering with hurt and anger and betrayal. But he hadn't done anything wrong.

Then why did it feel as if he were cheating on Lexi?

"Miss Darling," he said, his voice curt, professional as he gently but forcefully shoved Ashley away from him. Straightening his clothes, his hair, trying to act normal when he had a nearly naked wolf panting after him, a cock stand that was clearly visible, and the object of his lust staring at him with wounded pride, he asked, "What are you doing here?"

She cleared her throat, and she schooled her features to hide the emotions. Her eyes flitted away from his, taking in the discarded coat, Ashley's state of undress and his erection and her cheeks reddened further. Turning around, she started heading back out the way she came. "I, um, I came to apologize but I see now that it's not really necessary. Um, I'll just be leaving now; don't mind me."

"Lexi, wait," Duncan said, not wanting her to go away thinking he was an immoral bastard, ready to sleep with someone else after trying to seduce her. He bent down and grabbed Ashley's coat, draping it over her shoulders, keeping his eyes on Lexi. But then he glanced down and saw the intensity with which Ashley listened to the conversation, the way she looked between him and Lexi. That was a very unsettling feeling.

"It's all right," Lexi said, her eyes darting back and forth between him and Ashley. "I really need to get back to work. You see, I have a new boss and my job is still in question and I'm afraid I haven't made a very good first impression. But I intend to remedy that; after all, what is *lavish* without 'The Scene,' right?"

He squeezed his eyes shut, knowing that Ashley was going to say something about him firing the writer of the fluff column and hating the hurt he knew he would see in Lexi's eyes....

"You write 'The Scene?'" Ashley asked, excitement in her voice. Still nearly naked, she crossed the room, holding out her hand as she approached Lexi.

Uncertainty lined Lexi's features as she accepted the offered hand, "When Duncan told me he was buying this magazine I could hardly believe it, I'm such a huge fan. By the way, I'm Ashley Brown."

"Lexi Darling," Lexi replied, her features moving from confusion to something Duncan couldn't identify. Her eyes darted to Duncan, and he swore he saw a flash of weariness, before she looked back at Ashley. "I'll just let the two of you get back to… to whatever you were doing. Or about to do."

"We weren't doing anything," Ashley said, practically bouncing on her feet to be standing next to the writer of 'The Scene.' "Poor Duncan has a writer that he's having difficulties with and wasn't in to mood to mate with me."

"He wasn't in the mood for sex?" Lexi asked, a mischievous twinkle lighting her eyes as she glanced at him. Even the word sex sounded so much more… erotic when coming from Lexi's well-shaped mouth. The way her lips curved around the word, as if by saying sex she was having it. "How surprising, Mr. Tremain, all things considered."

"Yes, quite," he muttered, pressing his hand against the erection that Lexi caused. And by the spark in her eyes, she knew what she did to him.

Ashley looked closer at Lexi and narrowed her perceptive blue eyes, "Weren't you at the country club on Saturday? Only you had green hair at the time."

"It was mint," Lexi corrected cheekily. "And I'm sure I don't know what you're talking about."

"It *was* you," Ashley laughed, a full and throaty sound that exuded sex but Duncan had no interest in the wolf. "You were having lunch with the Rudnar women."

Lexi glanced at Duncan and he watched as she stiffened slightly at Ashley's words. "I was, um, interviewing them for a story I'm working on. Uh, influential members of society, or something."

"How well do you know them?" Ashley persisted and Lexi's eyes flew once more to Duncan, who was listening to the conversation with interest. The Rudnars could almost be considered American royalty; they were an influential family with their fingers in just about everything.

"How well do *you* know them?" Lexi reflected the question back.

"We're acquainted socially," Ashley said with an easy smile. "They're a lovely family, by the way."

"Th...." Lexi coughed, her cheeks reddening as she mumbled, "That's why I'm interviewing them."

"Oh, I look forward to reading that article," Ashley gushed. Grinning broadly and completely comfortable in her near nudity, she looped her arm through Lexi's as if they were now the best of friends, "Since Duncan is preoccupied, that leaves me free to spend my lunch hour with you."

Lexi's eyes widened in horror, "Um, I don't.... I mean, I like boys."

"What?" Ashley asked, confused. She glanced at Duncan as if he had the answer.

Duncan's lips curved upwards in a triumphant smile; he wasn't the only one with sex on the brain. "Lexi, it's just lunch. I'm sure Ashley just wants to pick your brain about your column."

Lexi looked at Ashley again, a little less horrified and slightly more embarrassed as she realized she jumped to the completely wrong conclusion. "Um, sure. Do you, you know, maybe want to change or something?"

"No problem; I have it covered." Ashley grinned, picking up a bag and disappearing into the bathroom, flashing her lithe body before she closed the door.

Lexi looked at him, the weariness apparent in her eyes and he anticipated the words before she said them, "Not up for sex?"

"I, uh, took care of the problem," he muttered, shifting his gaze briefly. But then he saw her blush and realized that she must have done the same thing. Lust roared through his body and his will to resist her was crumbling into dust. Fuck good intentions, fuck pride; let the wolf win so he could fuck Lexi. Smiling, he stepped closer to her, loving how her eyes widened and her pulse trebled. "Tell me, Lexi, did you think of me when you were touching yourself?"

Her eyes slid closed and she moistened her lower lip with her tongue. Softly, so softly, she said, "Yes."

"Did you imagined me touching you, stroking you?" he asked, his voice growing huskier and huskier as he spoke, as he imagined her with her legs spread, her fingers moving over her sex, her eyes hooded as she watched him watching her. "Have you imagined it, Lexi?"

A whimper arose from the back of her throat as she simply nodded. Opening her lids, she looked up at him with glazed eyes, silently pleading with him. Her lips trembled as she swallowed thickly. "Duncan, please."

"Please stop," he whispered, reaching out and running a finger over her lush lips. Her tongue darted out and touched the pad of his finger and his own eyes closed in ecstasy. "Or please continue."

"If you're serious about keeping me at a distance you have to stop," she pleaded. But then her mouth opened and he slid the tip of his finger into her hot mouth, making her eyes darken. Her lips wrapped around his finger and he nearly came when she sucked it into the heat of her mouth and let out a little moan of pleasure.

"You drive me insane," he murmured, feeling her tongue swirl around his finger, tasting him. Removing his hand, he bent his head until he could feel the heat of her mouth next to his. "I'm trying my damnedest to do the right thing but when I'm with you…."

The sound of the toilet flushing broke the spell and Lexi jumped away from him. With heightened color staining her cheeks, she fidgeted as she stood there, not quite meeting his eyes. "You keep telling me she's not but *is* she your girlfriend?"

He squeezed his eyes shut at the predictable question, unable to answer her because at the moment, all he could think about was Lexi. Who was still talking, "I mean, I've seen the two of you together, you know, and after catching the two of you just now, well, I assume she's your girlfriend."

"She's not," he answered curtly.

"But the two of you have slept together."

"Yes," he managed to say through clenched teeth. This was why he didn't get involved with humans; they didn't understand the needs wolves had, their society and rules. "But sex...."

"You'll sleep with her but you won't sleep with me?" she asked, her voice hurt.

"She doesn't work for me." He knew that that was a lame answer before the words were out of his mouth but he said them anyway.

"Then I quit." She crossed her arms beneath her gorgeous breasts, pressing them even higher and making his mouth water. Glaring up at him, she lifted her chin up and continued militantly, "And then we can fuck until our hearts' content."

"I won't let you quit," he growled, reaching out and touching air as she ducked her head. "We just have to make it through the next couple of weeks and then whatever madness or spell this is will be broken."

"Do you truly think it's a spell?" she asked carefully, her eyes watching him closely as if his answer were important.

He smiled at her and shook his head, "No; I just think there is a serious chemical attraction between us that defies description."

She shrugged her slender shoulders, "I can't seem to help myself. Even though I know it's... wrong. That this," she waved at the air between them. "Is wrong."

"I know," he said with a grim smile. "But I still want you."

Her lips curved upwards in a seductive smile and her eyes sparkled mischievously, "If you want to fuck me, you better hope to God that you're single. I don't sleep with other women's men."

"Then stop invading my dreams," he breathed, pressing a soft kiss on her lips and quickly stepping away. He watched as her hand touched the spot where his lips touched hers and smiled with satisfaction.

Her eyes lit dangerously, "I could say the same but then, I'm not the one with a girlfriend."

He smiled at her comeback, leaning back against his desk and watching her, just watching her. She truly was remarkable, especially when she was angry. "And I've told you, she's not my girlfriend."

Give in, his wolf whispered. *Look into those eyes and give in.*

He looked down as she gazed up at him with those jeweled eyes, unblinking and fully aware of his intentions as he lowered his head to hers, as he placed his mouth just over hers. As he took her breath into him and felt like he was almost home....

"Are we ready?" Ashley's bright voice interrupted him just as he was about to kiss Lexi. Both he and Lexi turned to face Ashley as she stepped out of the bathroom. She was dressed in a sedate, cream-colored suit belying her wolf nature and she looked like the daughter of a very rich banker; which she was, but she was also a wolf intent on having sex with Duncan.

Duncan's gaze drifted to Lexi, with her school-girl costume and her flushed cheeks, sun-kissed skin and humanity. One a man chooses for a mate, one a man enjoys passionately; long, hot, sweaty nights of arms and legs entwined, of bodies fused. Lexi was definitely the latter. Sexual bliss did not equal happiness, no matter how much his wolf might claim otherwise. The wolf wasn't the one who would have to live with her.

Except, he imagined a life with Lexi Darling would be incredible and satisfying in a million different ways.

Lexi looked back at Duncan and a guilty flush stole over her skin as she took a step away from him. Smoothing her palm over the short, black wig, her face red, she faced Ashley head on and told her, "Um, I don't think I can have lunch with you. Ever. I'm sorry."

With that, she bolted out of the office like the hounds of hell were on her heels instead of a horny wolf.

"The blond from the bar?" Ashley teased.

"Not a word," he said softly as he attempted to bring his raging libido back under control so he didn't charge after Lexi again, this time to finish what they started on Friday instead of telling her they couldn't.

"I think I'm going to go have a little chat with her." Ashley grinned, sashaying towards the door. "I think it might prove enlightening."

"Don't."

She paused at the door and looked at him, thrusting out her butt in a blatantly sexual invitation, "Then give me a reason to stay." When he didn't make a move or say anything, she shrugged her shoulders in resignation, "That's what I thought. I'll see you later, Duncan."

"Ashley…." He didn't have the heart to even try to keep her from Lexi.

You're either going to have to fire her or sell the magazine, his wolf snickered. *My esteemed master.*

Duncan squeezed his eyes shut and took several long, deep breaths; how had the day so quickly turned to shit? He woke up this morning ready to take on the world of publishing and now he was standing in the middle of his office suffering the lingering effects of a raging hard on, the girl he once planned on making his mate was chasing after the girl he couldn't get out of his system, and his wolf was being even more of a dick than usual.

If he had any interest in holding onto his sanity, he was going to have to deal with the Lexi situation. He was going to have to avoid her until he got this troubling lust under control.

Chapter 6

Lexi walked out of Duncan's office with her heart racing in her throat; the damn Siren was making her forget her good intentions. Even though the red head from the bar was in the bathroom, Lexi had still lured him into kissing her. She was going to have to do a better job of avoiding him if she planned on keeping him safe from her Siren's wiles.

"Hey, Lexi, hold up!" Ashley called out as she stepped out of Duncan's office. Lexi tried to ignore the summons but Ashley called out again," Lexi!"

Reluctantly, Lexi turned around to face the woman who had at one time shared Duncan's bed. She ignored the stab of jealousy at the thought and forced a smile, "I didn't know he was seeing anyone, otherwise…."

"What?" Ashley looked taken aback by the statement. "No, we're not dating... just the occasional fuck and that hasn't happened for too long."

"Because of Dima?" Lexi asked candidly. Before Ashley could answer, she added. "I never told Mr. Tremain if that's what you think."

Ashley laughed out loud, "Oh, Duncan knows and he is not happy with me but what can ya do? A girl has needs and he wasn't fulfilling them."

"If he was mine, I don't think I'd ever even look at another man, at least not for sex." Lexi shook her head, wishing her tongue wasn't so loose. "Forgive me."

With a grin, Ashley looped her arm through Lexi's and started walking over to the elevators. "I think you and I need to have a long conversation."

"I don't think that is a good idea," Lexi countered, trying to extricate herself from Ashley's grip but unable to do so; Ashley was surprisingly strong for such a delicate-looking woman. With a sigh, she gave in and let Ashley lead her wherever she may go.

"I think it is a fabulous idea," Ashley beamed, pushing the down button to summon the elevator and turning around to face Lexi. "I want to understand why Duncan is so interested in you."

"Great." Lexi was not looking forward to sitting across from Ashley for a single minute, let alone an entire lunch. What could she have to say to the woman who was sleeping with Dima when she had shared Duncan's bed? "Lead the way."

A few minutes later they were sitting outside the local bistro and Ashley was staring at her with an enigmatic smile on her lips. Forcing herself not to fidget, Lexi met Ashley's eyes and arched an eyebrow, "So, what's on your mind?"

"Are you, by any chance, related to the Rudnars?" she asked bluntly. Motioning with her hand towards Lexi's face she continued, "I see a similarity about your eyes and nose but mostly your mouth; they have a very distinctive mouth, don't they? A very sensual mouth. Now that I am looking, your mouth is definitely a Rudnar's."

"I guess it's a family trait," Lexi said with a light shrug of her shoulders, not coming right out to confirm or deny Ashley's question.

"Are you a cousin or something?" Ashley's eyes sparkled with discovery and she leaned closer, her strong citrusy scent filling Lexi's nose. "A long lost relation? It has to be something because you also have the Rudnar's breasts. A distant cousin?"

"Not exactly." Lexi couldn't quite meet Ashley's eyes. It was surprising in the nearly six years that she had been Lexi Darling no one had ever questioned her relationship with the Rudnars, never seeing the connection.

Ashley's eyes widened in her head and she fell back in her chair, her jaw dropping as she continued gaping at Lexi. "My God; you're the youngest daughter, aren't you? The recluse that has fallen off the map."

"What makes you think that?" she squirmed just a little in her seat, wondering how Ashley was able to see through the disguise so quickly when her family's closest friends couldn't.

"You are, aren't you? I knew it!" Ashley cried out in triumph, clapping her hands together. After a few moments, her smile faded and she looked at Lexi with curiosity, "Why do you refuse to be a Rudnar? It is a distinguished name for a very distinguished family."

Lexi snorted, "Look at me; I'm not exactly Rudnar material."

"I beg to differ; you simply express yourself differently," Ashley contradicted. With a dismissive sound, she grinned again, "But why Lexi Darling?"

This time Lexi's lips curved into a fond smile, "That has to do with my roommates."

"The bartender I enjoyed the other night?"

"Yes." There was something about the way Ashley spoke of Dima that bothered her but she couldn't quite figure out what; maybe it was her indifferent attitude towards her best friend. It was hard to feel bad for Dima because he was too cocky by half, breaking more than his share of hearts in his quest to score the perfect lay. Maybe he had met his perfect match in Ashley.

"You have to tell me the story." Putting her elbows on the table and resting her chin on her hands, Ashley looked like a little girl playing grown up, all bright eyed and eager to learn more.

"Well, when I first moved into their house, I was kind of shy and awkward," Lexi admitted, unable to keep her lips sealed. Almost against her will, she found she liked Ashley. "As my family is so fond of reminding me, I preferred books to parties and avoided everyone who came to the house for gatherings."

"That would be why nobody recognizes you; why it took me so long to put the two of you together." Ashley nodded sagely, stunning Lexi with her ability to match her with her mousier self at all. "Well, what happened?"

"Cole and Dima were determined to drag me out of my shell, by force if necessary." At Ashley's startled expression, she chuckled, "Not really by force. But they were always trying to get me to try something new and they would always say, 'Lexi, darling, why don't you try sushi,' or 'Lexi, darling, why don't you get your navel pierced,' or "Lexi, darling, let's go to the nude beach."

Ashley's eyes darkened and she leaned closer, "A nude beach?"

"It had been an eye opening experience for a naïve and sheltered eighteen year old girl." Lexi chuckled at the memory, thinking how good it felt to talk to someone about this. Her family would have been scandalized and Cole and Dima lived through it with her. But the woman sitting across from her was Ashley Brown, Duncan's occasional lover and her prospective rival. "Why am I telling you any of this?"

"Because I asked?" Ashley grinned, her teeth very white and her eyes very blue. "Besides, there is something very different about you and I find myself curious about the girl Duncan can't seem to shake."

"Are you planning on using any of this against me?" Lexi asked cautiously, experiencing a strange kinship with the woman. She didn't have a lot of female friends because girls generally saw her with Cole and Dima and hated her on principle. It might be kind of interesting to have a female friend, even one as inquisitive as Ashley. Even one who had slept with Duncan.

"Not at all," Ashley assured her. "If I wanted to have revenge, I wouldn't use gossip… I'd use my teeth."

Ashley snapped her teeth together and Lexi jumped back, startled. Pressing her hand over her racing heart, she laughed unsteadily, "That's not very reassuring."

"I like you, Lexi, so you don't have anything to worry about."

"Thanks?" Lexi picked up her glass and was dismayed to see that her hands shook slightly. Taking a sip of water, she set it back down and took a breath, "So, are you Duncan's girlfriend?"

"He's answered that question several times, Lexi," Ashley rebuked with a smile. "We have been lovers in the past; it is the way those in our… families do things. We prefer to know if we are sexually compatible before any… vows are exchanged."

"And are you?" Lexi asked casually as she swirled her straw around in her water, trying to act as if Ashley's answer wasn't all that important.

"He's very talented in that department and a girl could definitely do worse."

"You sound like there is a 'but.'" Did she sound too hopeful?

"Not at all," Ashley denied and then sighed, staring out across the street to the building that Duncan was still in. "If he were to choose me as his… wife I would be a very happy woman. But he has been losing interest in me even before you came along; I fear that his sights are on you now."

"Certainly not," Lexi protested even as her heart did a little jig in her chest at the thought. But it wasn't real; it was her Siren wrapping her net around him and dragging him to the shore where she could have her delightfully wicked way with him. "The thing between us is purely physical."

"And yet you escaped his clutches with your virginity intact." Ashley said so matter-of-factly Lexi was momentarily stunned speechless. "How was that even possible?"

"How could you possibly know something like that?"

Another enigmatic smile graced Ashley's lips, "I simply know and no, Duncan didn't tell me. Well?"

"I passed out and then slipped out in the middle of the night," she admitted, feeling the heat in her cheeks at the memory and at having admitted it to the red head.

"Interesting."

"In what way?"

"He must have realized it would be... challenging getting involved with someone like you." Ashley chuckled to herself, "Though it hasn't stopped him from fantasizing."

"In what conceivable way would it be challenging? I'm a sure thing." Unless Ashley knew about the Siren but, no, that didn't seem likely. Probably because Duncan was so straight-laced and sophisticated and Lexi wore vibrant wigs and racy clothes. And then the words echoed in her head and she slapped a hand over her mouth and felt her face go up in flames, "I can't believe I just said that to you of all people; I am so sorry."

Laughing, wiping an imaginary tear from her eye, Ashley explained, "Duncan is simply more than most people can handle."

Lexi couldn't argue with that since it was very true... and she wanted to handle all of him. He was the most compelling person of her acquaintance and she was unrelentingly drawn to him. "I could handle him."

Ashley looked at her for a few moments with a shrewd look in her eyes. Even when it became uncomfortable, Lexi continued to hold Ashley's blue eyes straight on. A small smile curved Ashley's lips and she murmured, "Yes, I believe you could. I knew I'd like you."

"Just so long as we're clear," Lexi cleared her throat, "You two are not together, right?"

"The rules are different in mine and Duncan's world, Lexi," Ashley explained carefully. "If he chooses you he is free to have you with no hard feelings on my side. In fact, I think I would respect him more if he had the balls to chase after you, damn the consequences."

"If he were mine I think I'd rip the eyeballs out of any girl who threatened to take him away from me," Lexi vowed, hearing the possessiveness in her words and damning the Siren bitch to hell for causing all of this.

Ashley threw her head back and laughed heartily, causing several heads to turn in their direction. Lexi could just imagine their thoughts: the society girl and the tramp. "You are a blood-thirsty little thing, aren't you?"

"Not at all," she instinctively denied then thought better considering. With brutal honesty, she admitted, "Apparently I have a blood-thirsty streak when it comes to Duncan, which is ridiculous – I barely know the man."

"Sometimes that's the way it works." Ashley relaxed back in her seat, resting her arms on the arm rests of the chair and smiling. "Maybe I should worry about Duncan; I don't think he has a clue about what's happening to him."

"I haven't cast a spell." Lexi sucked her lips between her teeth and bit down to stop her wayward tongue from wagging further.

"Even if you had it wouldn't matter," Ashley's eyes sparkled as she dropped that strange comment. "Now, tell me more about the nude beach; did Dima join you in the clothes optional adventure?"

"Of course," Lexi rolled her eyes at the thought of Dima; when didn't he prefer nudity over clothes? "He and Cole kidnapped me and took me to Cancun for three months my freshman year of college and then threw me to the sharks."

"'Lexi, darling, let's go to the nude beach,'" Ashley mimicked in a deep voice, laughing. "Lexi, darling, it's time to get naked."

"Exactly." The memory of that first morning came crashing back and she was a little dumb-struck by how cosseted she had been. Cole and Dima explained that they were on that particular beach to get her comfortable with her body. She had blushed like mad, especially when they dropped their pants and displayed their male parts in all their naked splendor. And they were glorious: hard, nineteen-year old male bodies....

It took her a little longer to feel comfortable enough to finally take off her swim suit. Eventually, it was exactly what Cole had promised; she had never felt freer than while she was on that beach completely bare. Everything was so much... more. The sun was warmer, the water was slicker; she was bolder. And it was a lesson well learned; she was absurdly comfortable with her body.

"It was nearly impossible to put clothes back on when it was time to come home," Lexi finished with a sentimental sigh.

"I think you've left some behind," Ashley teased and they shared a laugh. "And I am sure if Duncan had his way, you'd lose the rest of your clothes as well, preferably soon."

Despite the inherent awkwardness of having a conversation with Ashley, Lexi couldn't stop the image of a naked Duncan from filling her senses. His eyes would spark with desire as she ran her hands over the smooth, hard planes of his chest, down his ridged stomach to the erection that would stretch outwards to her, pulsing in anticipation. He would devour her and the thought sent a shiver of desire straight to her belly and she sighed in pleasure.

Ashley's eyes slid close for a moment and she took a deep breath. Letting it out slowly, her voice was rough as she whispered, "My word, you smell delicious; no wonder why Duncan is drawn to you."

Lexi was startled by Ashley's reaction and frowned, "That was random."

"Sorry, it's just that your scent when you think of Duncan...." Her words trailed off and she opened her eyes, smiling sheepishly, "It was unexpected and powerful, like sunshine and desire and bliss."

"That's... odd." But the words were flat; was that how she was controlling Duncan, with her scent? But how could she get rid of something that she had no control over. Maybe perfume... all of the women in her family wore some sort of floral scent, maybe she could try that. Maybe lavender or vanilla....

"He'd be able to smell you beneath artificial odors," Ashley interrupted her contemplations, grinning when Lexi looked at her in bewilderment. "Your face is very expressive, Lexi; it's an open book."

"Are you sure you aren't just a bit psychic?" she asked almost seriously. She glanced at her watch and saw that more time than she expected had passed and she stood up abruptly. Apologetically, she looked at Ashley, "As enjoyable as this has been – and it actually was – I really have to get back to the office. New boss and all that."

"Blow off work and spend the rest of the day shopping with me," Ashley said, coming to her feet and throwing some cash down on the table to cover the bill.

"I can't," Lexi actually regretted not being able to spend more time with the fascinating woman. "I don't think the boss would approve."

"Pshaw," Ashley said, dismissing Duncan with a wave and a smile. "I have the feeling that he would forgive you pretty much anything."

"I don't want to put him in the position where he will have to." Lexi shrugged her shoulders and gave a sheepish smile, "You see, I really do like my job and would rather keep it based on merit, not because I'm sleeping with the boss."

"If he didn't like your work he'd fire you even if he was sleeping with you." Ashley looped her arm through Lexi's once more and the two of them headed back to the office, Ashley's words reassuring in a strange way.

****

Lexi was staring out the window, as she had been on and off for three and a half hours since she returned from lunch with Ashley, when she was startled out of her reverie by the phone ringing. Smoothing her hand over the front of her blouse, her skirt, as if the person on the other line could see her, she picked it up, "Hello?"

"Miss Darling." Duncan's voice rumbled over the line and her body tightened in excitement and anticipation. "I was wondering if we could have a meeting in the conference room in five minutes… that is, if you're not busy."

She glanced around the office, at the papers on her desk that she hadn't looked over, the stack of messages she hadn't returned, the list of things to do that she hadn't done. "No, I'm not busy; I'll be there."

"Good," he heaved a sigh and she was sure he was going to say something else, but he simply hung up the phone.

Standing up, she straightened her clothes as much as possible, oddly nervous about coming face to face with the man who made her insane. Too nervous to sit still, she grabbed her bags and headed towards the conference room at once, eager to see him even if he was going to fire her.

Pushing through the door, her smile faltered when she saw Jeffrey sitting there, looking at her with warm, sympathetic eyes. Duncan wasn't there and she knew that he sent Jeffrey in his place to do his dirty work. "Will you make sure my severance pays goes to the usual place?'

"He's not firing you, Lexi," Jeffrey assured her, his eyes kind. "He simply asked me to sit in on this meeting for legal reasons."

"Does he think I'm going to sexually assault him?" she was astonished that a big, strong man like Duncan would need protection from her, even if her Siren was making it nearly impossible for him to resist her.

"Um, no," Jeffrey chuckled. "He's worried about his own behavior. Apparently…."

"That's enough, Jeffrey," Duncan said, striding through the door. Lexi's heart leapt in her chest and she couldn't stop the smile from forming as she looked up at the gorgeous man with his flawless black hair and his intense silver gaze. "I'm glad you could join us, Miss Darling. There is something we need to discuss before it gets out of hand."

"I'll try to tone it down," she said quickly.

"You're not the problem; I am." He ground his teeth together and his jaw tensed as he shifted uncomfortably. "I promised you a month to make your case for belonging at *lavish* and you will have that month but I seem to have a problem controlling myself around you so we have to set down some round rules to… protect you from unwanted advances."

"They're not unwanted," she interjected quietly but fervently, her words making the muscle in his cheek tic wildly. Then realization dawned and her eyes widened in horror, "Unless you're just trying to be kind and you don't want me."

He closed his eyes and released a long, troubled breath. "That's the problem, Le… Miss Darling; I cannot give you a fair chance if you keep tempting me. And I cannot allow outbursts like what happened at this morning's meeting to continue without reprisal."

"I *am* sorry about that," she said contritely, her heart fluttering madly in her chest. He was being so kind to her; after her behavior – both at the meeting and later on – he had every right to fire her and he was giving her another chance. She just hoped she didn't screw it up with rampaging lust and pheromones.

"I know you are," his gaze softened for a moment as he looked at her. Then he remembered who he was and what he was doing and his silver eyes became as impenetrable as any solid metal. "But the fact remains that I am your boss and certain standards of behavior are expected from both of us. For the foreseeable future it might be best if we attempt to keep our distance from one another; at least until we can get this… thing under control."

Lexi glanced at Jeffrey who offered a helpless shrug. It would probably be best to keep her distance from the man since she had no idea how the Siren spell worked. Maybe if they weren't in close proximity the spell would wear off and he would be able to get on with his life without her. Maybe her mom or aunt knew of a way to keep her from casting the spell again so Duncan could be free of her and her Siren. She would just have to learn to live with the long, slow burn of lusting after a man she couldn't have. Slowly, she met Duncan's eyes, "All right. I have an… assignment out of the office the next couple of days but I will figure out a schedule to limit our interactions as much as possible."

"The burden of responsibility isn't solely on your delectable shoulders, Le… Miss Darling," Duncan growled. "Give a copy of your schedule to my secretary and she will figure out the logistics. I just hope I can follow it."

She nodded her head and was going to leave but she got caught in Duncan's silver gaze and remained rooted to the floor, unable to move even if the building was about to collapse. His eyes darkened, the silver being swallowed by the black of his pupils as their gaze held. The temperature in the room was increasing rapidly because her body was melting and her skin was on fire. As she licked her lips with the tip of her tongue, he tracked the movement with his eyes. Breathing was becoming difficult as the air thickened and her clothes became too tight. Her fingers went to the top button of her shirt and Duncan sucked in a harsh breath as he watched....

"Is there anything else we need to discuss?" Jeffrey asked, standing up and brushing his hands together, washing them of the whole thing. Lexi turned her head and saw the flush spreading across the older man's cheeks but he didn't say anything about her behavior.

"There is one more thing," Duncan said, his voice rougher than usual. Turning her head, she once more found herself trapped in his gaze. "The Rudnars?"

"What about them?" she asked carefully, her heart picking up speed in her chest.

"Did they truly agree to an interview?"

"Uh huh?" her voice squeaked at the slight fib.

His mouth hardened into a shark's grin, "That would be an excellent coup; the Rudnars are notoriously tight-lipped. Congratulation, Miss Darling."

"Thank you?" she hated how her voice was so breathy when she was lying; he was going to figure it out that she wasn't being completely truthful if she kept talking.... But, maybe she could find out if what her sister said about them not mixing was true... "Um, the three daughters are exceptionally beautiful; did you ever consider taking one of them for a, um, lover?"

"The oldest daughter once showed an interest in me but it didn't last long." His eyes twinkling with genuine amusement, "Why this sudden interest in matching me with a Rudnar?"

"I'm trying to decide what type of woman you're interested in," she offered lamely. "Apparently the eldest Rudnar is not an option; what about the others?"

"Married women are off limits and from what I remember they are all married."

"The youngest one isn't...." Why was she still talking?

Duncan's brows pulled together in a slight frown as he considered her statement. "I suppose you're right but from what I understand she's not much for society. Now, if you could get an interview with her...."

Lexi made a strangled sound and bolted for the door before he could cajole her into interviewing herself.

Chapter 7 (Friday)

At exactly the right moment, Lexi glanced through the opened door of her office and was unable to prevent the smile from swallowing her face. Duncan – Mr. Tremain – was walking through the maze of cubicles and talking to the various employees. With the convention in a few hours, she didn't think the day could get any better and then Duncan appeared. Standing, she smoothed down the front of her copper robe dress and wriggled a bit to get the undergarments realigned.

She knew she would be seeing him, they worked in the same office, after all, but he had been conspicuously absent and she was growing worried that she wouldn't see him before the weekend. After all, it had been nearly a hundred hours since she last saw him. Glancing down at her watch – 3:17 pm – yep, almost a hundred hours. The only reason she had successfully stayed away from him for the past couple of days was for the simple fact she had driven six and a half hours to the Menominee River to go white water rafting and rock climbing with Cole. Not that she didn't think about Duncan at the most inappropriate moments; she almost went over because she was imagining what it would be like to take a shower with a naked Duncan and lost her grip on the rope. Thank God Cole had caught her before she fell in.

She had hoped that the exertion of the trip would have diminished her attraction to the captivating man but it had only grown. When she fell asleep the night before under the stars, exhausted from battling the rapids and then going for an extended hike, all she could think about was how nice it would be to curl up in Duncan's strong arms and sleep, knowing he was there. The disturbingly domestic image was made bearable by the hot and sexy dreams.

Had he not appeared, she was going to make up an excuse to accost him in his office. Luckily, the fates were smiling on her as she left the confines of her office to follow him. Wearing his dress shirt and tie without the jacket, her looked incredibly sexy. His sleeves were unbuttoned and rolled up, exposing his strong forearms, making Lexi long to see the rest of his arms. And then his chest, followed by his stomach and back; basically working all the way down his body until he was naked. And that was not a good thing to be thinking about when he made it clear that they were not going to engage in anything more intimate than chatter.

Having promised to play nice, she kept her distance as she watched him covertly, talking with her various coworkers as he discussed business with others. If she occasionally lost track of the conversation, she could blame Duncan for exuding so much charm and confidence and male sex pheromones. He fairly oozed sex appeal; she was surprised that more of the women in the office didn't simply follow him around. Of course, none of the other women were fatalistically drawn to the man, either. While they might appreciate his handsome face or his chiseled body, they seemed a little intimidated by his arrogance and self-confidence.

With a blinding flash of self-awareness, she realized she was acting like a shy and socially awkward high school girl who followed the captain of the football team in the hopes that he would turn around and see her and realize she was the one he had been waiting for all of his, admittedly brief, life. Or praying that he never looked because it would have been mortifying to be discovered spying on him. High school was a confusing time and she sympathized for every poor soul that had to suffer through it.

Laughing at her absurdity, she wandered to the break room to grab a cup of coffee and maybe she'd try getting out of there a little early. Even though the convention didn't officially start until five, she wanted to get there and get checked in as soon as possible. Grinning, she thought about her outfit beneath the copper dress and Duncan's reaction if he ever saw her in it. And then she wondered if he would even get the reference; he didn't seem the type to waste his time on pop culture.

*****

Duncan knew the moment Lexi stepped out of her office and he waited for her to cross the distance between them, leaping over any obstacle that was in her way, and talk to him in that sassy, sexy way of hers. The whole point of visiting that area today was to see her, since he knew she was back at work in her office. But, of course, he couldn't approach her directly since he explicitly stated they had to keep their distance.

But the little vixen just followed after him, keeping her distance as well, even as she sent flirtatious glances that he had to pretend to ignore. He continued talking to the various people on the floor, just enjoying being able to see her. And the moment she stopped following him he felt it in his gut; she simply wasn't there. Interrupting the man who was talking about his project, he excused himself to hunt her down, following the clean, spring breeze scent that was Lexi.

Prowling along the corridors, ignoring anyone who attempted to snag his attention, he tracked her down to the little break room, calmly pouring herself a cup of coffee. Clearing his throat, he rumbled, "Miss Darling, a word if you please."

"Sesquipedalian," she said, keeping her back towards him.

The strange response momentarily stunned him. "Pardon?"

Turning around, she leaned against the counter and grinned at him, "You asked for a word and I gave you on. It means 'many syllabled' and while it's exceedingly pretentious it is a lot of fun to say. *Sesquipedalian*; it tangles up the tongue and then just fall right off.

"Or perhaps you would prefer a different word?" she continued guilelessly and he was completely charmed by her. "*Tittle*, which is the little dot over *i*'s and *j*'s; or *ornithopter*, an aircraft that flies by flapping its wings; or *Tuatha De Danan Lora* or *Expecto Patronum*?"

"Now you're just making words up," he grinned, and realized he had missed talking to her.

Her eyes widened in her beautiful face and she looked innocent, until he saw the spark of mischief in those green and gold eyes. "They are all valid words or phrases, in books, in movies…."

"I don't spend a lot of time reading fantasy or watching movies…." He shook his head and tried to scowl but failed to turn his smile into a frown. "Miss Darling, you have made me forget why I came in here."

Artlessly, she stepped forward and handed him a cup of coffee before twisting around and grabbing a second cup; she had known he was coming. "Coffee break?"

Since he was pretty sure all rational thought fled the moment he met her, he took the cup without thinking. When his fingers brushed against hers sparks shot up his arm. He was lucky he didn't accidentally drop the cup.

"I wasn't sure how you take your coffee," she said, her voice a little unsteady as a pink stain of arousal colored her cheekbones becomingly. "So I made it like I take mine."

Glancing down, he saw that the coffee was suspiciously light but not wanting to offend the generous, if slightly crazy, woman, he took a sip. And grimaced at the sweetness, "Let me guess, a splash of coffee and a whole lot of sugar and cream?"

"Yep." She took a sip of her cream with a dash of coffee and closed her eyes in bliss as she gave a little hum of pleasure. When she opened her eyes, she smiled at him, "I make sure to use French vanilla creamer; it's better that way. Do you like?"

He shook his head and dumped the creamer pretending to be coffee into the sink before pouring himself a new cup. When he turned around, expecting her to be offended by his behavior, he found himself staring at her as she shook in silent laughter. When she noticed he was looking at her, she let the laughter out and he knew he had been had. He tried to sound stern but failed miserably as he informed the delectable Miss Darling, "I prefer black."

"I figured you would." She made an adorable face, scrunching up her nose, as she grimaced and handed him another cup of black coffee. "But it is so bitter."

"Black is perfect," he countered, taking a sip of the stronger brew, enjoying himself far more than he should. "I prefer sweetness in my desserts and women, not my coffee.

"I like my bitterness...." She paused and frowned as she thought a moment before smiling brightly, "I know! I like my men hot and my coffee sweet."

"Nice, Miss Darling," he grinned foolishly, feeling younger and more alive than he ever felt, even while running as a wolf. "I like my women creamy and my coffee strong."

"I like my men dark and dangerous and my coffee tepid," she purred. "So I can drink it without burning my tongue. What did you need to talk to me about?"

He laughed at her abrupt change of topic; it was so Lexi. "I wanted to yell at you for slacking off on the job but I can't bring myself to get mad when I seem to be slacking off as well."

"I like a man who takes responsibility and looks that good in a suit," she grinned, nodding her head towards his clothing. Her eyes sparkled as she looked up at his face, "I like a man better when he steps out of his suit."

Arching an eyebrow at her words, he asked, "Is that an invitation to get naked?"

"Only if you're willing...." She let the words hang out there and he was so tempted.

"I'm not willing," he lied.

She shrugged her shoulders and sighed, "Oh, well; it was worth a shot."

"You are a dangerous woman, Miss Darling," he muttered, sipping his coffee.

"I take that as a compliment, Mr. Tremain," she beamed and his heart skipped a beat.

"What's with the outfit?" he asked, noticing the relatively normal dress for the first time. It was a coppery dress that covered her body from neck to toe, leaving her slender arms bare except the spangling, swirly bracelet on her wrist. Her shoes were an odd looking pair of suede boot, not her usually sexy, strappy heels. He liked her hair, though; the front had a loose, romantic look about it as the whole mass was pulled back into a thick braid that hung down her back. The metal hair piece was a nice touch.

"I'm actually heading to the sci fi convention right after work," she admitted. "My roommates are picking me up and we're all dressing up; Dima is dressing up as Luke and Cole is going as Han and I am going to be Slave Leia." Scrunching her nose in that adorable way of hers, she added, "I thought my costume might be a little too distracting for the office."

Astonishment punched him in the gut and he grinned; what did Miss Darling consider too distracting for the office? "This I have got to see."

Grinning wickedly, she undid the frog clasps that held the front of the dress together and then let the silky material slide off her body to reveal a siren's body encased in a damned sexy metal bikini. A gauzy bit of maroon material twined about her legs and all of the blood in his body rushed to his penis. Without normal brain function, his coffee spilled down the front of his shirt, scalding his belly and bringing him painfully back to reality.

Flinging the mug down and plucking at the wet material, he swore, "Damn, that's hot."

"Mr. Tremain!" Lexi cried, reaching his side immediately and frantically unbuttoning his shirt. When it was opened, she pushed it off his shoulders then reached behind her to grab some paper towels, mopping up the rest of the liquid from his skin.

His breath caught in his throat as she diligently cleaned him up, the concern in her face slowly morphing to fascination as she realized she was cleaning his bare chest. The towels slipped from her fingers and her hand was pressed against his skin and his world narrowed until all that was left was Lexi Darling. As he stood there looking down at her, he tried to remember why he couldn't touch her but there was nothing there. Lifting his hand, he almost touched her but knew if he did, he wouldn't stop until she was out of her metal bikini. He had to satisfy himself with looking and not touching.

Her skin was kissed by the sun, a dusting of gold over smooth curves, and the metal bikini cupped around her perfect breasts. In that moment he hated the ornamental metal because it was touching what was meant to be his. As he watched, her hand and gaze slipped lower to the erection pressing against the front of his pant and he had to grind his teeth together to keep his hands to himself.

"It looks like you stained your slacks as well, Mr. Tremain," she said in a low, sexy, *aroused* voice. Falling to her knees in front of him, she gently pressed the towels against his penis, running her hand lightly over the length and driving him mad.

She looked up at him with those wide, hazel-green eyes and he imagined her unzipping his pants, sliding her hand inside and wrapping her fingers around his cock. In his mind, he saw her taking the length of his penis between her shiny red lips, sucking it into the depths of her hot mouth until he was mindless with pleasure. Grinding his teeth together, squeezing his hands into fists, he managed to drudge out, "That is not helping, Miss Darling."

Her eyes sparkled with knowing amusement as she continued to lightly run her hands along his erection, tormenting him and making him wish she would just take the damn thing out and let him fuck her mouth. "Miss Darling…."

The realization that they were in the middle of the break room, that they could be interrupted at any moment, gave him the strength to grab her beneath the arms and pull her to her feet. He was about to let her go but she wobbled so he tightened his grip to keep her steady, "Are you all right, Miss Darling?"

"Hmm?" she asked dreamily, visually feasting on his naked torso, his straining erection. Blinking, she came back to the moment and looked up at him, "I think you should be Han; I can imagine doing such wicked things to you…."

"Miss Darling!" he hissed, not needing any more temptation. If she kept it up, he was liable to go absolutely primal and take her where she stood, that provocative bikini the only barrier. He was sure the metal bottoms could be removed easily enough. "This isn't the time or place."

She heaved a sigh and glanced around the room, "Yes, I suppose your right." Bending down, she picked up the discarded dress and slipped it back on, hiding her glorious body from his view. "Besides, you don't sleep with your employees. Yeah, I got that. Plus, it would suck trying to get this outfit back on; metal is not forgiving and once free I'm sure my breasts would throw a fit if I threatened to bind them again."

In spite of his screaming hard on, he chuckled, "Miss Darling, I tremble in your presence."

Her smile was incongruously shy as she lightly ran her hand over his chest and started heading for the exit, "Have a nice weekend, Mr. Tremain. I'll see you on Monday."

She was leaving him? Spinning around, his damp shirt clutched in his hand, he had no choice but to watch her go. With another little smile, she disappeared, leaving him with a mammoth erection and a weekend of erotic images to look forward to. Stalking over to the sink, he turned on the water and stuck the ruined shirt beneath, needing to do something – anything – to get his lust under control. Thoughts of Lexi filled his head and he chuckled; she was a marvel.

And he absolutely, positively could not give in to animal lust.

It's more than that and you know it.

He clenched his jaw together. The only thing his wolf was good for was getting rid of his rampaging erection. *Go to hell.*

*****

Lexi walked back to her desk on wobbly legs, grateful for the absurd shoes that went with her outfit. Why did Duncan have to be so utterly charming? Or have a body that was simply breath taking? When she had rushed to rip his shirt off it was to prevent his skin from getting blistered by the hot coffee but as soon as she realized she was staring at his naked chest, she just wanted to touch it and the towels she was using magically disappeared.

His skin was scorching hot, and she didn't think it had anything to do with the coffee; he simply ran hotter than a mere human. The crisp black hair circling his nipples and then angling downwards to the waist band of his pants was sexy, neither too much to hide the skin or too little to give him an androgynous appearance. He was all man and she just wanted to bite him, take a little nibble of his flesh and....

Jeeze, she was turning into a cannibal, simply because Duncan Tremain was so scrumptious. And incredibly stubborn; most men would have taken her up on her offer but not Mr. Tremain. Strangely she was even more attracted to him because of it; there was definitely something to be said about the chase. It made his ultimate surrender that much more rewarding when he finally gave in.

Or she just found self-control incredibly sexy, even when it cost her endless, sleepless nights thinking about him. What would it be like to lose her virginity to him, what would sex be like with him once her virginity was long gone? And while her roommates might suspect she had a crush on someone, Duncan Tremain remained her tormenting and delicious secret. She supposed it was possible to talk to one of her sisters, probably Penelope, but that just seemed awkward. As much as she loved her family, she didn't share much of her life with them; when she was younger she had lived in her head and now that she was older... well, she had simply gotten into the habit of keeping to herself.

"Ready to go, Leia?" Cole asked, knocking on her door, wearing his white shirt and black vest. He golden hair was dyed dark brown for the occasion. "Dima's in the car waiting."

Startled, she realized she had spent the last hour of her day day-dreaming about Duncan. Standing up, she took a final glance around the office to see if she needed to bring anything home, then smiled at Cole. "Yep."

His brows pulled together, "Where's your costume?"

With a grin, she took off her dress. It was almost quitting time on a Friday afternoon; if they weren't already distracted, her outfit wasn't going to be a problem. Posing with a hand on her head and one on her hip, she modeled the bikini, "Well?"

Letting out a low wolf whistle, a slow smile spread across his face, "Very nice. The fans at the convention won't know what hit them."

As she was walking out the door, she felt Duncan's eyes on her and she paused, needing to see him before taking off for the weekend. Looking over her shoulder, she saw him leaning against the wall, his eyes burning into her as they moved over her body. In that moment he looked like a wolf, all predatory and dangerous, and it sent a jolt of electricity through her body. With a little wave, she forced herself to turn away and keep walking.

"Who's the suit?" Cole whispered.

"My new boss," she whispered back, her pulse pounding madly in her throat. She was so tempted to take another peak to see if he was still there but if he was, she wouldn't have made it out the door. And if he wasn't, she would have been sorely disappointed.

Chapter 8 (Thursday)

“Congratulations,” Duncan murmured late Thursday morning as he cornered Lexi between the copy room and her office, her arms loaded down with colorful pages. “In the nearly two weeks I've been here seventeen men have come up to me trying to convince me that you should keep your job; one of them was the guy who makes my coffee in the morning at the bistro across the street. How do you manage that?”

“Very carefully.” Lexi looked up at him, mentally rejoicing in the presence that was Duncan. Everything seemed more vibrant when he was around, like the world came into sharp focus and became hyper real. And she liked the butterflies and the irregular heartbeat he inspired, so she had no complaints, even if they only exchanged a word or two in passing, a glance from afar.

"I don't think my plan of keeping our distance is working." He glowered, "I know the moment you step into the building."

"You set the rules, Mr. Tremain... unless you are planning on breaking them?" she asked hopefully. He paused for a heartbeat before shaking his head *no*, making her huff in resignation. "Well, then, I am desperately trying to obey your absurd rules but you make it difficult. Now, if you will excuse me, I have a lot of… research to do for next month's article."

"What are you working on?" he asked, straining his neck to try and get a glimpse of what Lexi held in her hands.

Lexi frowned at his obvious attempts at snooping, hugging the pages to her chest. His woodsy, wild scent was seeping into her brain and doing wondrous things to her body. "Don't you have something more important to be doing right now? Like, oversee your empire, or whatever it is you do?"

"I do but I can't seem to stop myself from seeking you out; it's hell on days when I don't see you," he said, shaking his head and meeting her gaze, his silver eyes heating slightly as he looked at her. She reached up and touched the honey-blond bob she had on and didn't miss the slight frown that marred his forehead. "You're unlike anyone I've ever known and while I know I should keep my distance I can't seem to stop thinking about you, wondering what crazy outfit you'll show up in next, when I'll get to talk with you about things that shouldn't matter but become the most important things in the world because you and I are talking about them.

"It's insanity, Lexi."

His hot gaze drifted down to the outfit she wore and a low growl of appreciation rumbled from the back of his throat. She liked the soft pink dress that barely covered her ass with the matching pink heels. So what if the neckline was a little low; it showcased her breasts to their best advantage while still being suitable for the work place. And if Duncan lusted after her and looked at her with those hot, silver eyes....

When he looked at her with that burning hunger in his eyes and said such wonderful things, she felt like he could see into her soul and see all of her. Her heart was racing at the thought and it was suddenly much warmer in the corridor where they stood. In fact, her breathing had changed, becoming a little more... frayed. She needed to get away from him and this... thing he did to her.

"I'm trying to be good, Dun... Mr. Tremain, but you keep giving off mixed signals," she said curtly, trying to scoot past him and jumping from the swirl of pleasure that spiked her blood when her body brushed against his. She felt the charge all the way to her toes and she wanted to linger. But her panties were already damp and it would only take a word from him and she would be jumping him. Not good, especially since they were standing in the middle of a corridor used by all of the employees.

"Lexi," his voice whispered in her ear as she moved past him. She felt his fingers brush against her bare arm and her body shivered in response. "The signals aren't mixed; I want you more than my next breath but I cannot have you."

"Yes, you can," she whispered, clutching the papers even tighter, trying to stop the spontaneous combustion of her cells. Turning her head, she met his eyes, "Break your rules and I'm yours for the taking. Just break them, Duncan."

He laughed without humor, his eyes tormented. "Stop tempting me."

She decided it would be better to not say anything because the more time she spent near him, the more her resistance faltered, and she had no resistance to start with. Without even looking at him, she finished the journey to her office, closing the door behind her. Life had been so much easier when she was simply Lexi Darling, with her crazy outfits and her funky wigs, taking on the persona of a comic book character to embrace life. What was she going to do about Duncan, who was blurring the line between her created reality and her true self, to say nothing of her Siren-self?

Dropping the pages off on her desk, she sank into her chair. The sci fi convention the past weekend and her work load might not have been able to take her mind off Duncan but it did succeed in pushing all of her other concerns to the backburner, including the possibility that her Siren had improper power over

Duncan and it was all a fantasy.

She hadn't taken a moment to call her mother or aunt about what it meant to be a Siren, something she tried not to think about too often because it was depressing. It was one thing to believe Duncan was helplessly attracted to her because of something beyond his control but it was another to have it confirmed. Selfishly, she had just wanted to savor the flirtation for a little while longer before having it taken away.

Rubbing her forehead, she leaned forward, resting her elbows on the desk. It was time to call and have her hopes shattered before she spent any more restless nights fantasizing about him. Picking up the phone, she dialed the number, nervously tapping her finger nails against the desk as it rang and she waited.

"Hello?" came the wonderfully familiar voice, making Lexi smile.

"Say I believe you, that there's some truth to what you and mom sprang on me a few weeks ago," she spoke without any preliminary, jumping right to the heart of the matter.

"That you're a Siren?"

"Yeah, whatever," Lexi faltered a moment at her Aunt's calm response but soldiered on. "Tell me more – what does it even mean to be a Siren?"

"What do you know about Sirens?" Aunt Sophie asked carefully.

"Um, they were a trio of beautiful women who lured men – sailors – to their death with their hypnotic melodies," Lexi recited, remembering some of the mythology from her childhood. She lightly ran her fingers over the colorful brochures that sat on her desk. Maybe she should choose a destination and just go; maybe Cole or Dima would join her. Anything to get away from Duncan before she lured him to his death. God, being a Siren sucked.

"It was never the Siren's intention to lure men to their deaths," Sophie murmured. "And it wasn't their song that made men linger on the island until they died; it was the Sirens themselves."

"That is not very reassuring." Lexi paused, chewing on her lower lip as she tried to figure out how to put her fears into words and finding it difficult. "So, our lot in life is to kill men. Great."

Sophie laughed out loud, "Not at all, my dearest Lexi. We are the descendants of the Siren who fell in love."

"What difference does it make," Lexi lamented, tears welling in her eyes. "If we make men fall in love with us against their will?"

"We cannot make anyone fall in love against their will; only lust." Sophie cleared her throat and Lexi felt the heat blossom in her cheeks. "Men won't die of a little lust."

"But what if it is all consuming?" Lexi's voice came out as a whisper.

Sophie was quiet for a long moment before she asked in a hushed voice, "Is there someone specific?"

"There might be."

"Tell me about him."

"He's gorgeous, Sophie; all intense and powerful and so beautiful. I swear, in a previous life, he was a Viking, or a warlord, or something," Lexi said, feeling the heat trying to blossom in her body at the thought of his gaze, the intensity in his eyes. "He wants me but he doesn't want to want me and I want him so badly it hurts. What's wrong with me?"

"There's no spell, Alexandra," Sophie said firmly, kindly. "Unless you sang to him, which only… complicates matters; did you sing to him?"

"Nooo," Lexi said slowly, as her brain took a devious turn and tried to figure out a way to justify singing to Duncan to break through his rules, to make him want her as much as she wanted him. Ruthlessly, she pushed the intriguing idea out of her head, "I won't sing to him."

"Are you in love with him?"

Lexi scoffed at that, "Of course not; it's simply… lust; burning, soul consuming lust. And I am so afraid that the only reason he wants me is because of my own desire for him."

"Alexandra," her aunt's voice was amused. "It doesn't work that way. As long as you haven't sung to hum, you can assume it's real. Just be careful and don't fall in love with him if he isn't likely to return your feelings."

"Why?" Lexi asked slowly, bemused.

"Because a Siren whose love is unrequited tends to languish away," he aunt said theatrically. "Depending on the strength of the Siren, of course."

With sparkling eyes, Lexi chuckled at that, "That's so dramatic but no, I won't die of a broken heart, Sophie. But I might die from a lack of sex."

A shocked gasp echoed through the room and Lexi looked up, seeing the strangled expression of her office space-buddy. Covering the phone with her hand, she smiled, "Hey, Henry…."

"Kerry," he said.

"No, it's Lexi," she said. Uncovering the phone, she said, "Give me a moment, Soph; Henry just walked in."

"I meant," the guy said, shifting slightly. "My name is Kerry."

"Oh," Lexi frowned slightly. "I could have sworn your name was Henry."

His face was turning red again as he continued to stare at her with his gray eyes. With his overly long, strawberry blond hair and decent build, he was an attractive man who spent much of his time travelling to various locations around the globe and then writing up the reviews for the magazine. But he kept staring at her, his face getting redder and redder as she stared back.

Glancing down, Lexi saw that she had quite a bit a cleavage showing. With a careless shrug, she looked up and tilted her head to the side, "Can I help you with anything? Get you a glass of water? Call an ambulance?"

He let out a strangled sound and beads of sweat began forming on his forehead and his breathing was harsh. "I'm good," he squeaked, scrambling over to his desk, pulling out a drawer with such force it clattered to the floor. "I'm good."

"Okay," Lexi didn't sound certain but her aunt was on the other end of the line laughing. "Just so long as you're sure."

"Sing for me," Sophie said from the other end of the phone.

"Pardon me?" Lexi asked, her attention immediately back on the conversation with Sophie, Henry – or Kerry – forgotten as he continued to fumble with his desk

"The young man from earlier is still there," Sophie's voice filtered into Lexi's brain. "Correct?"

"Yes."

"Sing for me," Sophie repeated. "I want you to see something."

Lexi blinked slowly and reluctantly sang a few words of her favorite haunting ballad, her voice coming out sweet and pure with a strong underlayment of sensuality. A choked, garbled sound came from behind her and she spun around in her chair to see Kerry frantically doing… something, one hand on the front of his pants, the other digging through his desk. Damn, damn, damn. "Um, Kerry, what are you looking for?"

"Paper clips," he bit out.

"I want you to smile at him," Sophie instructed, the devil whispering in Lexi's ear. "Slow and sultry." When Lexi hesitated, her aunt hissed, "Do it."

Uncertain she was doing the right thing, she tilted her lips up into a seductive pout and watched as Kerry turned beet red, his hair matted to his head, and he let out a low groan. Lexi watched in horrified silence as a stain spread across the front of his pants. Grabbing a few tissues, she set her feet on the floor, stood up and walked around her desk, holding out her hand towards Kerry, "I am so sorry."

"This is so embarrassing," he mumbled, taking the tissues and blotting at his pants. Grumbling, he headed towards the door, rushing to be somewhere else.

"That was not helpful, Aunt Sophie," Lexi groused, her heart going out to the poor bastard. She looked at the art work on her back wall: some of Cole's earlier prints – to get the image of Kerry's stained pants out of her head.

There were three images from their time in Cancun, with one of her in profile looking like an ocean goddess in a colorful sarong and bikini top, her skin golden from the tropical rays, her hair hanging about her body. The other two were group shots of the three of them, splashing around in the cerulean blue ocean. She loved the pictures. She loved the memories behind the pictures. "What was the point in having me make a guy embarrass himself like that?"

"I wanted you to know what it is to be a Siren; now the young man is devoted to you," Sophie said casually, as if she hadn't just had Lexi enslave the poor bastard. "He will be summoned to your side whenever you smile at him."

Ah, so that was how Aggie did it. But that wasn't something she wanted to know. Ever. Frowning, she glowered, "I don't want mindless devotion, Aunt Sophie. I want to know what to do about Du… the reincarnated Viking."

"I hate to break it to you, Alexandra, dear," her aunt chuckled. "Without a song, it's just good, old-fashioned lust."

"I don't know if that makes me feel better or worse," Lexi groaned, picking at a piece of imaginary lint on her dress. "What good is being a Siren if I can have either mindless devotion or unrequited lust?"

"Because if you find your True Love," Sophie kept talking over Lexi's snort of disbelief. "You'll have magic."

"Okay," Lexi said sarcastically. It was hard enough believing in Sirens; there was no way she was going to believe True Love. Lust, absolutely, but love happened over time.

"Alexandra, your mother found it with your father." Sophie's voice was laced with melancholy. "She's a stronger Siren than I am and was lucky to have her True Love return her love. If she hadn't found your father she might have become a spinster."

"Does that mean you're a virgin?" Lexi was confused.

Sophie laughed, "Goodness no; I have enough of the Siren gene to lure men in but not enough to deny me the pleasure. Your mother found her True Love when she was in high school and they haven't been able to keep their hands off one another ever since."

"Is that why I have so many siblings?"

Sophie laughed, "You should watch them the next time you're home; they are always making excuses to check on something but in reality…."

"Oh, God," Lexi moaned, burying her face in her hand. "I do not want to hear this."

Sophie let out a gusty sigh, "The purer the Siren the stronger the reaction to her mate when he's found."

"I don't believe in One True Mate, or whatever you want to call it," Lexi said, shaking her head in denial. Pinching the bridge of her nose, she exhaled. Spinning around in her chair, she looked out at the world from ten stories up and swallowed painfully. "It's a great big world out there; the chances of finding a soul mate are astronomically against a person."

"Luckily, Fate has a way of working out; matching a Siren with her heart."

Lexi scoffed, "No, Fate has a way of fucking with you."

"That is true," Sophie almost reluctantly agreed. "There is no guarantee that the man chosen for you will return your love. In a way, I feel sorry for you, Alexandra."

"Oh, please," Lexi scoffed. "I can have sex with whomever I please."

"Then why are you still a virgin?"

"Because the man I want is being stubborn." Sophie burst out laughing as a reluctant smile played on Lexi's lips. "The Siren isn't all-powerful, Sophie; I can control her."

"It's not a matter of control, dear."

Lexi heard the door swing open and she rolled her eyes; the poor guy was back for more. She wondered how she should handle it; was there some sort of Siren protocol for dealing with men who were gluttons for punishment? Holding up a finger in a silent gesture to let him know she'd be with him in a moment, she said, "I've got to go."

"Alexandra," her aunt laughed. "Did Kerry return?"

"Yes," she answered, not bothering to turn around. Cupping her hand around her mouth and the mouthpiece, she asked, "What am I supposed to do with him now, since a song and a smile made him come; how do I get rid of him?"

"Miss Darling," a rich tenor said directly behind her desk, not two feet away. Glancing over her should she saw Duncan standing there, wearing his jacket and tie, looking very civilized. Judging by the amusement dancing in his eyes, he heard her words.

"Oh, shit," Lexi breathed, falling out of her chair as she dropped the phone and tried to stand up. Very classy, especially since her pink dress rode up slightly and she knew that she exposed her panties. Thank God there was a desk in the way; otherwise Duncan would have gotten an eyeful. Avoiding Mr. Tremain's eyes, she managed to right herself before she casually bent down and picked up the phone. "Listen, I've got to go."

"It wasn't Kerry, was it?" Sophie asked softly. "Lexi, I want you to be careful."

"I always am."

"No you're not," Sophie chuckled. "Is he looking at you now?"

"Yep," she said, lifting her eyes and meeting molten silver. Her breath caught in her throat, "And he looks pissed."

"He looks turned on," her aunt quickly surmised.

"Yep," Lexi nodded. "That, too. I've gotta go; talk to you later?"

"Of course."

"Bye, Sophie," Lexi said, hanging up the phone. Straightening a few papers on the desk, she took a moment to compose herself, fully aware of the intensity with which Duncan was watching her. Unable to bare the scrutiny any longer, she sighed and met his eyes, "Look, Kerry came in here while I was…."

"In more ways than one," he rasped, starting to walk around the desk towards her. She knew that look – wanted it and feared it – so she took off in the opposite direction. Keeping pace with his advance, she debated internally about what it was to be a Siren and if it was okay to let him catch her.

"Well, there is that," she admitted. She caught her lower lip, moving as he moved. "I sometimes have that effect on men."

"I've realized that," he practically growled. "You seem to be having that kind of effect on me."

She laughed in spite of herself, "I doubt you'd lose control like that. I mean, come on, have you ever come with just a look?

"Not yet but if you keep looking at me with those green and gold eyes of yours I might," he murmured harshly, his eyes darkening.

"Uh huh," she breathed huskily. Hormones were bouncing off the walls and crashing into one another. As long as she didn't sing then the lust was honest; she just had to figure out how to break through his shell to get to the hot, juicy center. She really needed to get out of there before she did something stupid, like rip her dress off and offer her body to this man. "Can you come now?"

He took a deep breath, his eyes closing briefly before he looked at her once more. "Not yet but right now, it wouldn't take much."

"Really?" she asked breathlessly, putting her hand over her chest. She wasn't surprised at how fast her heart was beating or how hot her skin was. She grinned up at him, "Does this mean you're going to break a few rules today?"

"Nope," he said simply, advancing once more. She didn't move.

She squeezed her thighs together to ease the ache that was building there; it only seemed to exacerbate the problem and she let out a little strangled sound of her own. It would be so easy to find the antidote in his arms but she wasn't going to do that. "If you're not going to play nicely than Go. Away."

"I intend to play very nicely," he rumbled, taking another step and prowling closer. And she realized that she hadn't countered the last three steps and he was within a hand's reach of grabbing her arm if he chose. "As I said earlier, I can't seem to go away. Are you wet?"

A pathetic whimper came from the back of her throat and she coughed to hide the fact that he was driving her mad and that she was very wet. "Why are you doing this?"

"You were talking about making a man come without physically touching him," his voice was rough and his eyes gleamed dangerously, the silver depths almost predatory in their intensity. "I was wondering if I can do the same thing since it won't be breaking any rules."

"I should hope not," she said frantically, clasping the edge of her desk with her hands as her knees turned to water. She was on the other side now, her back towards the door. "If you can make a guy come…."

"I want to make you come," he breathed, his lids heavy as he looked at her. "Lexi, let me make you come."

"If you touch me you'll be breaking your rules," she said, feeling the pressure building between her legs. God, if he would just leave, she could take care of it herself. In private. At this point, it wouldn't take much. "Besides, I'm sure you have more… pressing matters to deal with."

"None that I can think of right now," he murmured, putting his hand over hers, sending a jolt of electricity and awareness through her body. Stepping behind her, he pressed the lower half of his body against her and she was able to feel exactly how turned on he was. Her groin started buzzing in anticipation. "I want to…."

"No," she said before he could finish that statement. Unfortunately, her voice failed to convince her that she wanted him to stop. She squeezed her thighs tighter, feeling the edge of orgasm creeping closer. His fingers danced over her hand, coming to a rest on her stomach. Involuntarily, her eyes closed and her chest heaved with each breath she took. "I want you too much for you to be doing this to me; please, Duncan."

His hand skimmed over her stomach, stopping at the hem of her suddenly too-short dress. His fingers brushed the top of her thigh as he stood behind her. She could feel the heat and steel of his erection pressed against her back as he whispered in her ear, "Please stop or please continue?"

He asked her that before and she asked him to stop. And then proceeded to suck his finger into her mouth. Had Ashley not been in the other room dressing, she would have welcomed him into her body. Now, there was no outside distraction and if he was willing to bend the rules if not outright break them, who was she to refuse? His fingers were just a hair's breadth away from easing her suffering. "Touch me, Duncan."

"Lexi," he said, his fingers moving over the outside of her panties and she knew what he would feel: moisture and heat. And if he did that just a little harder, she'd fall apart. "You make me want to toss all of the rules away."

"Duncan," she breathed, her eyes closing as the tips of his fingers pressed against her. Her legs gave out and she was grateful when his arm came around her waist, supporting her weight, as his fingers pressed closer. His body radiated heat against her back and she arched into it, into his warmth.

"Let me do this," he whispered in her ear, his breath hot against her skin. Without waiting for an answer, he slid a hand over the top of her panties and against her skin. Parting the folds of her sex with two fingers, he slid a third into her, gathering wetness before rubbing her clit. Her body was rubber in his arms as he pushed her over the edge and she moaned when she came.

He changed the rhythm of his fingers, pushing deeper, circling slowly, pressing against her core. Within moments, her body was quaking with release and she was pushing against his hand to experience… everything. A low groan of pure pleasure escaped and she wasn't sure if it was her or him that made the sound.

"My God, Lexi, that was exquisite," he whispered, bringing his fingers up and tasting her orgasm. His eyes closed in ecstasy as his lips wrapped around his flesh. "Fuck the rules, Lexi; I want to bury myself in you… I want everything."

She made a sound, unable to form coherent words just yet. He still held her, but his free hand was fumbling with his zipper. In a few moments, she was going to be… Where? On her desk? She glanced at the top of her desk and realized that there was too much stuff and the noise would sound an alarm. Maybe the floor? That was hardly satisfying – she had no idea what was on the floor. Maybe up against the wall….

Suddenly she realized that he was no longer fumbling with his pants. Instead, he was breathing heavily, raggedly, his forehead pressed against her shoulder. And she knew he was struggling to regain control. "Lexi, what are you doing to me?"

"Nothing yet," she said softly, pressing her behind against his penis, hearing him groan.

He laughed harshly. "Then why do I have so little control around you?"

"You're still dressed," she said even as rational thought was trying to break through. She didn't want to be rational just yet; she wanted sex. "I'd say you have very good control."

"It's not good enough," he said hotly.

When she turned around to face him he was struggling to pull himself back from the edge, his nostrils flaring as his eyes burned through her. Desperate and mindless with lust, she hummed a few notes and watched as his eyes darkened. He stepped forward and cradled the back of her head in his palms as he bent his head, as his mouth hovered over hers, "Lexi."

"Duncan," she breathed, letting her hands stroke his ribs beneath his jacket and over his shirt. She was amazed at the lack of guilt she felt; if humming got her into his arms it would be worth it. Afterwards, once he returned to his senses, she would feel guilt, but now… Now she just wanted to feel his lips on hers. His skin was so hot beneath her fingers and she could just imagine how hot it would be against her skin. If she wanted to be entirely selfish, she would sing, bend him to her will until he was naked and….

The door burst open and they leapt apart as Kerry came bounding into the room, wearing a fresh pair of pants and carrying a steaming Styrofoam cup. Grinning and apparently oblivious to the discomfort of either Lexi or Duncan, he handed her the cup, "I brought you a cup of coffee, Miss Darling; is there anything else I can get for you before I head home for the day?"

"No," she laughed stiffly, her eyes drowning in tears of denied pleasure as she watched sanity descend on Duncan. The wildness disappeared beneath a suit of civility and she was disappointed to see it go. Taking the cup in one hand and running the other over her face, she murmured, "Thank you, Kerry."

"Mr. Tremain," he beamed, disappearing as quickly as he appeared, leaving a disaster in his wake.

Lexi looked up at Duncan and saw the familiar tic in his jaw and she knew he was angry with himself. But when he saw her eyes glistening, he stepped forward and tenderly brushed his thumbs over her cheeks, wiping the tears away. Bending his head, he pressed his forehead to hers, "I have to keep my distance from you, Lexi; if I don't I won't be able to forgive myself."

She offered him a watery smile, placing her hands over his, "I wish things were different."

"So do I," he breathed. Closing his eyes, he inhaled deeply, a soft, almost-purring, sound came from the back of his throat. "I lose my mind around you."

"I find mine."

His eyes darkened a moment before he pushed himself away from her. Straightening his tie, he spoke through clenched teeth, "Have this month's article on my desk by Thursday; I want to read it before you give it to the editor."

With that, he turned around and stalked out of her office, leaving her oddly fulfilled and strangely bereft. Her desire for him was stronger than ever.

*****

Duncan stormed down the hallway, Lexi's smell clinging to him and filling his senses until he was tempted to turn around and finish what he started. What she started, damn it. All that talk about making men come with a song and a smile and then that pink scrap of material pretending to be a dress and all of those damn pheromones crowding the room until all he could smell was Lexi. Lexi and her heat, Lexi and her sex, Lexi, just Lexi. He was definitely going mad.

No, it wasn't her fault. After he had seen her at the copy machine he had stalked back to his office to regroup, putting on the veneer of a civilized man. And then coming up with a flimsy excuse to track her down and ask her something, he didn't even remember what. She looked up at him with those green and gold eyes and he was lost. Even if he intended on not breaking his rules, his damn rules, he knew that he was going to break every last one. He was going to claim her in that office and then drag her back to his lair and keep her there.

Had that buffoon not burst into the office when he had.... He should be thanking the poor, hapless fool instead of consigning him to the depths of hell for interrupting.

Lexi was a temptation he could not indulge in, no matter how much he wanted her. And God, did he want her. A lot. He was never going to last another day in the same building with her, let alone several weeks, and as much as he hated to admit it, avoiding her was just not working. It would be a simple matter to deal with the magazine from one of his other offices; why was he torturing himself by remaining so close to Lexi?

Because she consumed him and he wanted to be near her, if only to experience the sweet torture of not allowing himself to touch. Because even as he tried to figure out the most efficient way to avoid temptation, his libido was figuring out ways to bump into it – hell, crash into it full force. He wanted her desperately.

Claim her,

"No," he said out loud, startling one of his employees. Squeezing his hands into fists as his wolf taunted him with something he could not have, he bit out, *She's a human; I'm a wolf. It would never work out.*

You're the Alpha, the wolf's seductive words whispered in his head. *The rules were made for you to break; claim her.*

No.

CLAIM HER!

The wolf's demanding roar startled him and he jumped. Glancing around the room, he noticed several sets of eyes staring at him. Scowling, he met each pair of eyes until their owners nervously went back to work and he prowled back to his office, ignoring the secretary as she tried to hand him some messages and slamming the door behind him. He didn't need this right now; he didn't need any of this. He had an erection that refused to go away and the scent of Lexi clinging to his fingers. If he didn't find some semblance of sanity soon he was going to succumb to madness; he was going to fight his wolf to claim her for his own.

Chapter 9 (Thursday/Friday)

The eighteen year old mouse followed the gorgeous lion as he pinned flyers up all over the quad, quietly taking them down as soon as he looked away. Alexandra was sure the gorgeous man was going to turn around and catch in the act of undoing all of his hard work but she had read the flyer and she desperately wanted to be the one who answered the ad. She hated living in the dorm; her parents had allowed her to attend the state university but they refused to allow her to have a roommate.

Well, she had decided to take matters into her own hands and when she overheard the two gorgeous guys from her photography class talk about taking on a third roommate, she had immediately perked up. For some reason, she was utterly fascinated by the bartender and the artist and learning that they wanted a roommate....

It was the perfect opportunity. As long as they didn't take one look at her and laugh her out of the house. As soon as she returned to her lonely dorm room that afternoon she had called the number and made an appointment to meet with them the next day.

Wearing a plain white t-shirt and a pair of blue jeans, hoping to look like an ordinary college coed, she stood on the front step and knocked on the door, nerves and excitement battling in her stomach. If they didn't answer, she was going to be sick all over the pot filled with dirt but no plant. When the door opened, her jaw dropped to her chest; the one with sandy blond hair was standing there wearing only a pair of boxers, rubbing his bare chest. His hair was standing on end and he looked as if he had just rolled out of bed. "Yeah?"

"I'm here about the room?" she squeaked, taking in the naked expanse of skin.

"Cole!" he called out, letting the door slide open the rest of the way while never taking his brown eyes off her, "You're victim is here!"

She took a step back, her eyes widening in her head, until the nearly naked man smiled, a warm friendly smile that dimpled. "Come on it; can I get you anything to drink? Soda? Gin?"

"Um, a glass of water would be great," she replied meekly, entering the masculine domain and leaving the safety of her world behind.

"It's odd but you're the only one who has shown any interest in rooming here," he said as he led her further away from the life she had known. Glancing over his shoulder, his eyes sparkled with amusement, "Why is that, I wonder?"

"I have no idea," she lied, offering a tentative smile to hide the fact that she was lying.

He chuckled, "I think some enterprising little mouse pilfered all of our flyers."

The other one bounded down the stairs at that moment, wearing a purple velvet smoking jacket and no pants. His golden brown hair hung loose around his face as he beamed down at her and clapped his hands together, "Our little thief. What a pleasure it is to make your acquaintance. Do you think I might have the flyers back?"

She felt the heat scalding her cheeks as she dug into her bag and pulled out the flyers, reluctantly handing them back to the men she had stolen them from. "I figured I'd save you the trouble of letting someone else move in only to discover they were not compatible."

"As if you're compatible?" Dima asked dubiously, glancing at her squeaky clean image. "With us? Sweetheart, you're as wholesome as apple pie."

Her cheeks flames hotter but she stood her ground, "Just because I don't chase after anything in a skirt doesn't mean I'm not compatible. In fact, it might do you some good to have someone like me to... to add balance, or something."

"Or maybe we could corrupt you instead." Dima said, waggling his eyebrows. Nudging Cole's shoulder, he leered at her, "We could share her...."

"Oh, please," she waved her hand through the air, pretending to be brave when her heart was pounding in her chest, begging her to shut up. "The two of you couldn't handle me."

Cole's laughter wrapped around her, embracing her in its warmth, "I think if anyone can make Dima a better person it would be you. But I'm afraid there's no hope for me."

"There's always hope," she said gently, patting him on the arm, not knowing at the time that he was teasing her. Or what form his teasing would take.

"I'm afraid not," he sighed, untying the sash of his smoking jacket and letting it fall to the ground until he stood before her, completely naked.

Her eyes widened impossibly in her head as she saw her first nude male and she didn't know where to look. In desperation, she looked at Dima, whose wicked grin was the only warning she had before he dropped his boxers and they both stood before her, naked as the day they were born but decidedly much more manly.

"I'm afraid we're both lost causes," Dima sighed regretfully, his brown eyes gleaming with challenge as he negligently leaned against the wall, arms crossed

over his chest, his legs spread and his... penis just hanging there.

Straightening her shoulders, ignoring the prickling heat of her burning face, she stood before them, "Well, if you want to see me naked, you're going to have to do a better job than that. Look at you two; you aren't at all happy to see me...."

Cole's arms were around her in an instant and he was hugging her, laughing heartily. "Can we keep her, Dima? Please? She's simply too precious."

A large palm brushed over her hair and was gone. When she looked over her shoulder, Dima was putting his boxers back on, a rueful smile on his face, "Yeah; we can keep her."

"I'm Alexandra."

"Hi, Lexi," Cole grinned, purposefully changing her name, giving her a new one. "I'm Cole and this idiot is Dima."

"Um, do you think you might put me down and get some clothes on?"

After several intense days of getting used to one another, they fell into a routine. She was disappointed to discover she very rarely saw her new roommates and life was pretty much the same as before but now she had her own bathroom and she had to cook her own breakfast. Cole and Dima went to class when they felt like it, if they felt like it, and usually stayed out until late at night. Or early in the morning, depending on when they stumbled home.

There were girls, and often Lexi would run into one in the morning, usually sneaking out of Dima's room. And occasionally from Cole's. She wasn't jealous of the girls that shared their beds because, oddly, she wasn't sexually attracted to them. But she was jealous of the time they spent with Dima and Cole, selfishly wanting them to spend time with her, to maybe help her out of the box she had built around herself.

Sighing, she looked around the empty kitchen and started singing one of her favorite songs, a depressing ballad about lost love and hopelessness. Her mother was so careful to make sure she never sang around strangers, even though she had a beautiful voice. And while Cole and Dima were no longer strangers she couldn't call them friends, either.

"What is the heavenly smell?" Cole asked, drifting into the kitchen while rubbing sleep from his red-rimmed eyes. He had barely gotten home and yet he was coming into the kitchen... Lexi could barely contain her smile.

"It's pancakes," she beamed. "Would you like some?"

"Absolutely," he said, sitting down at the table, looking nearly dead with exhaustion.

A moment later, Dima appeared, looking even worse than Cole, though Lexi wasn't sure how that was possible. He plopped onto the chair and propped his head up with his hand, "I was two seconds away from going to sleep when the most delicious smell wrapped itself around me and dragged me from my bed."

"Lexi is making pancakes," Cole answered. With a jaw-popping yawn, he garbled, "She's making some for me, too."

"Can I get in on the action?" Dima asked, his eyes so bleary she wondered how he was even awake but she was simply too excited to ask.

"Of course!"

After that, they started eating breakfast with her every day, no matter how exhausted they were. Within a few weeks, the three of them were inseparable. Before the year was over, they flew off to Cancun and changed the course of their stars.

Lexi bolted upright in her bed, a cold sweat breaking out across her forehead as she remembered how they become the friends they were today. "No, oh, please no."

She sang and they became her devoted slaves.

As hot tears burned tracks in her frozen cheeks, as her limbs shook, she blindly reached for her phone, not caring about the things she was knocking down in her desperation to make a phone call. Under her breath, she chanted, "No... no...no...."

After a few rings that seemed an eternity, her mother's sleep-heavy voice rasped, "Alexandra, what is it? What's wrong?"

"How do I release them?" her voice shook as her chest ached from the pressure of trying to hold itself together and not shatter. Her entire relationship with the two most important people in her life outside of her family was nothing more than a dream and now....

"What in the world are you talking about?" her mother asked. Lexi heard her shift and murmur something to her father. "Alexandra?"

"Cole and Dima." It hurt to say their names and she pressed a palm against her sternum as if that could contain the misery. "How do I release them, or whatever it is that Sirens do to let their victims go?"

Her mother took a long, deep breath and then slowly let it out; the delay was killing Lexi and she started to chew on her thumb nail before her mom finally asked, "What makes you think they've been... enchanted?"

"I sang, momma," she cried. "One day when I thought they were asleep I sang and that was the morning they welcomed me into their lives." She wasn't sure if her words were very clear since she was crying so hard; she just hoped her mother would understand enough to help her. "I love them too much to... to enslave them. How do I let them go?"

Her mother let out another long breath before she answered. "Kiss them and give them back what you think you've taken from them."

"How do I do that? How does one give back something intangible like acceptance? Friendship?" Lexi sniffed then choked back a sob. "Love?"

"Remember your time together," her mother explained, her voice soothing and calm, washing over Lexi and easing her pain somewhat. "And when you kiss them, give it all back – all of the memories, all of the laughter, the tears. All of the love."

Blinded by tears, she squeezed her eyes shut. Her heart was breaking at the thought of losing her two best friends in the universe but what choice did she have? "Will I remember?"

"Yes, sweetheart, it's the gift and the curse of the Siren." Her mother's empathy was nearly her undoing. "But, Lexi, you don't have to do this; they're happy, let it be."

"It's not real," she cried softly. "How can they be happy when it's not even real?"

"Sweetheart...."

Lexi hung up the phone and buried her head in the pillow, knowing everything she was going to be giving up. There were so many memories, so many good times... and bad. And for six years Cole and Dima were her world; how was she going to survive without them? Who was she going to lean on when the thing with Duncan blew up in her face?

The door to her room creaked up and Dima stuck his head in, "What's wrong, minx? You sound as if your heart is breaking."

She lifted her head and seeing Dima standing in the doorway, concern etched upon his handsome face, only made her cry harder. He rushed across the room and gathered her into his arms, rocking her and offering comfort without even knowing the reason why. Burying her face against his neck, she felt the bed shift and knew that Cole had joined them.

"Don't hate me," she pleaded, tears clogging her throat and making it nearly impossible to breathe. Pushing back, she looked at them with glossy eyes, "Please don't hate me."

"How could we ever hate you?" Dima asked softly, brushing his hands over her cheeks to try to stop the tears from falling. He was so tender, making it hurt even more to draw air into her oxygen-deprived lungs. She could only stare at him with red eyes, unable to talk past the lump in her throat.

Letting the memories of the past six years fill her, she framed Dima's face in her hands and placed her lips over his. Kissing him, she gave him back the memories as she desperately tried to memorize every moment of the present. When she finished, she pulled back and saw that his eyes were still closed, his expression blank.

Turning, she faced Cole, his dyed hair now sporting vibrant red spikes, his green eyes bewildered. "Forgive me."

"Whate...." He never finished the question before her mouth was over his and she was returning the memories to him.

Sitting back, she watched their blank expressions as tears continued to silently fall down her cheeks. They were quiet for so long as the spell worked its way backward and altered their memoires, erasing her from all of them. She was inconsolable as she drank in their faces, their familiar scent and missing them already. She would never get to hear them laugh again, never share a half gallon of ice cream with them, never get to try one of Dima's newest drink mixes for his club or pose for Cole's beautiful photos.

For years, she had assumed that she would end up married to either Cole or Dima; it hadn't mattered at the time because she knew the three of them would always be together. She would have given up her virginity on her wedding day to whichever unlucky bastard agreed to marry her. And then she probably would have slept with the other one just because the three of them did everything together.

They were the reason she didn't return to college; it wasn't what she wanted or needed at the time. Not wanting to live off her generous trust fund, they encouraged her to try everything and she did, first starting out small with various odd jobs. She tried a bit of everything, from waitressing (very short lived) to dog walking (lost her favorite pair of shoes to a Chihuahua) to selling books (loved the books, hated the hours.) But her favorite job was working for an up and coming designer.

Darnell Wu was half-black, half-Asian and pure genius; he used her as his model, creating her unique look and transforming her completely into Lexi Darling. Even after he ascended to unimaginable heights, he continued to design her wardrobe, from her every day wear to special occasions. She had been able to pay him back by writing him up in 'The Scene,' her current most favorite job.

Which was going to end in flames whichever way she looked at it.

Her misery was almost enough to make her forget about Duncan but when she remembered, her heart broke all over; she couldn't go through this again. She couldn't give her heart to another person only to have to take it back and leave nothing in return. But she didn't *have* to give her heart....

Sitting up a little straighter, she sniffed, wiping the tears from her eyes. She didn't love him, not like she loved Cole and Dima. If she sang for him, he would be hers for the taking and afterwards she'd be able to give it all back; she could have Duncan and he wouldn't be breaking any of his rules. Or rather, he wouldn't remember breaking any of his rules. She wasn't sure whether or not she would stay on at *lavish* afterwards but she could have Duncan and not make him compromise his damn rules. If she lost her best friends, nothing else really mattered.

She just wanted to see Cole and Dima one last time, to thank them even though they weren't going to know what she was thanking them for. Wiping the tears from her face, she climbed out of bed and went into the bathroom to splash cold water on her skin. Her reflection showed how many tears she had shed; her eyes were red-lined and puffy and her face was white. After Duncan, the fabulous Lexi Darling was going to fade away and all that was going to remain was Alexandra, a phoenix rising from the ashes of another life she left behind.

She was going to miss Lexi.

Pulling her hair back into a pony tail, she watched her reflection, hating the Siren that was ruining her life more than ever. The bitch took Cole and Dima away; she was going to lead Duncan astray and then cut him off as well. No wonder why Thea was such a biter woman, if she had to give up even half of what Lexi was giving up....

She would just have to try to not become bitter, to roll with the punches or whatever. Grab the balls and squeeze? No, that wasn't quite right but it seemed to suit her mood at the moment so she was going to go with it. Besides, squeezing balls might not be such a bad thing, as long as they were Duncan's and she got more than a quick don-t-blink-or-you'll-miss-it fuck out of the deal. She deserved a month, at least.

Dima stumbled into the bathroom, blinking his eyes at the bright light and Lexi grimaced; she hadn't thought this part through. How was she going to explain her presence in their bathroom when she was now a stranger to them?

A moment later, Cole was there, rubbing his eyes, "What a rush, Lexi; it's like I just relived every moment I've had with you and it was... it was simply incredible."

Her jaw dropped open like it had that first morning and her eyes flew to Dima. Scrubbing his hands through his hair, he grinned lazily, "Yeah, me too."

She looked from one tired but happy face to the other, not quite believing it. "You… remember?"

Cole shrugged his shoulders, a little confused by Lexi's odd behavior. "Of course we remember, at least I remember; I don't know about shithead over here."

"I remember," Dima mumbled through a yawn but Lexi didn't care how tired they were. She threw her an arm around each of them, hugging them as hard as she could. Their arms went around her waist and they were hugging her back, not understanding her need for the comfort but giving it none-the-less.

She loved them so much.

Chapter 10 (Saturday)

Overwhelming relief still made Lexi giddy nearly two days after believing she had lost her best friends. Instead of going to work on Friday, she had stayed home and the three of them had camped out on her bed eating popcorn and ice cream and drinking way too much as they reminisced about old times. She hadn't realized that Cole had known almost from the beginning that she had been following him and taking down the flyers almost as quick as he was putting them up. He said he originally planned on putting the flyers up all over campus until he had spied her and saw what she was doing. Then he decided to keep it to a smaller area to see how long he could go. He had gone through the entire stack.

They had laughed and cried and then laughed some more, at some point passing out on the bed, all curled around one another. It was a little awkward when she woke up from a dream involving a naked Duncan, some tanning oil, a mat and some creative poses. She wasn't sure if she moaned in her sleep or not but she woke up with two hard, male bodies wrapped around her. Luckily, both Cole and Dima were still asleep and she managed to wiggle her way out of the tangle of limbs, finding sanctuary in the bathroom where she took a shower to wash away the tears and emotions that had bled all over her.

She was grateful that her friendship with them was solid; otherwise she would have missed that night's grand premier of Cole's beautiful, almost erotic photographs, of which she posed for several. With their lives so entwined, she wasn't sure how they would have been able to forget her completely. Maybe she would have been a vague image, like a ghost, and while it was an interesting concept to think about she was extremely happy it wasn't a reality she had to live with. If the spell had worked, it would have been devastating to run into them at a function like this and have them look at her with no recognition in their eyes.

A shudder went through her at the near miss; it wasn't worth considering so she concentrated on the present. She was at a fantastic party celebrating Cole's photography and she was wearing Darnell Wu's latest creation.

Feeling like a character from a manga, Lexi knew her dress was truly a work of art in and of itself, covering her while giving the illusion of wearing hardly anything at all. It was a bunch of belts holding up a few scraps of fabric as leather straps crisscrossed her body, from over one shoulder to her waist, across her breasts, and over her hips, stopping mid-thigh and leaving her back almost bare while completely concealing her breasts. Adding to the post-apocalyptic look, her feet were encased in combat boots and her wig was deep, brown-red, flowing to her shoulders with short, chunky bangs. She wore just a little bit of mascara and brick red lipstick, making her lips look ripe and shiny.

As she sipped her champagne, she looked at the various photographs of men and women, all in their natural state. Each subject had been posed in such a way so that the photos were pure art, celebrating the beauty of the human form. The lighting emphasized certain body parts, keeping the rest in shadow; from a hand against a thigh, to the curve of a breast or the line of a hip. Cole's photos were breathtaking, which was why she had agreed to pose.

He had informed her that her photographs were going to be showcased, since he was so pleased with how the images turned out. She wasn't so sure since she had been painted with gold body paint and had felt faintly ridiculous when he was taking the pictures, as the gold kept getting everywhere. It had taken several days to get all of the paint off and for a long time she kept finding gold flecks in the most unexpected places.

As she moved to the next picture, the profile of Cole's sister when she was nine months pregnant, she started to feel that vaguely familiar heat in her belly. Casually, she looked over her shoulder and saw Duncan standing there, looking amazing in a charcoal gray suit, his black hair just as perfect as always. Ashley was with him looking absolutely stunning in an ankle-length, body hugging, black cocktail dress. Lexi realized that the two of them really made a striking couple, so elemental even in civilized dressing. Ashley caught her eye and gave her a knowing wink, before whispering something to Duncan.

But he was already staring at her, barely paying attention to any of the beautiful photographs lining the wall. Ashley looked at Lexi with a knowing grin and artlessly shrugged her shoulders. With a conspiratorial grin, Lexi discretely pointed across the room where Dima was getting a drink from the bar. Ashley followed the silent gesture and turned back with a brilliant smile before excusing herself from Duncan's side in pursuit of more carnal pleasures.

With a slight smile, Lexi took a step towards the man of her erotic dreams as he took a step towards her, a rueful grin on his too handsome face. A warm palm wrapped around her arm, stopping her in her tracks. She looked up to see Cole grinning down at her and she couldn't help but return the smile, despite his appearance preventing her from getting to Duncan.

"There you are, you little minx," Cole called out, kissing the air next to her cheek as he came to a stop in front of her. "You look fabulous, sweet; I love the look."

"Cole," she smiled, shifting her attention away from Duncan's penetrating gaze to her friend. He was dressed in a maroon ribbed-turtleneck with green and purple plaid slacks. And the scariest part was he actually made it work. His hair was spiky, making the red highlights stand out even more, and he wore two hoops in his left eyebrow piercing and God knows what in the piercings on the rest of his body.

He also wore more make up than Lexi, with heavily charcoal-lined eyes and mascara, though he didn't wear lipstick. Again, he pulled it off and still managed to look very male. It probably had something to do with the fact that he was nearly six feet of solid muscle and was too gorgeous and he had probably slept with a majority of the models he photographed. Or because she knew the man beneath the mask.

"Dima's right," he laughed, lightly touching the corner of her mouth. "You do drool."

"I do not," she protested, brushing her fingers over his as she ran her fingers over her lip to check. Cole laughed even harder making her scowl. Turning her head, she saw Dima and Ashley flirting with one another and she smiled, "Look at Dima; he's positively smitten."

Cole barely spared a glance at the couple, the sophisticated society girl and the handsome bartender. "He could find a willing woman at a wake."

Lexi's eyes sparkled with laughter as she snagged another glass of champagne, oddly nervous to have her photos unveiled with Duncan in such close proximity. Draining her second champagne and setting the glass down the tray of a passing waiter, she whispered, "I think I am going to sneak away and make my escape before you expose my pictures to the world; what was I thinking agreeing to be the model for your showcase?"

"That you love me and you know that the photos will be stunning," he grinned, his clear green eyes sparkling as he twined his fingers with hers. Bringing their hands up to his mouth, he kissed the tips of her fingers, and asked, "You haven't peaked, have you, minx?"

"I've been waiting for you." In truth, she hadn't had time to look at the pictures, otherwise she would have stolen a peak. Pressing her hand against her rebelling stomach, she did a quick scan for Duncan and sighed with relief as she spotted him near the back of the crowd. He was watching her but he was keeping his distance; he might have even been far enough away to not be able to identify the model.... "Just like I promised."

"Ready?" He slowly started making his way through the crowd, ignoring anyone who wanted to snag his attention; his focus was entirely on his art and on his muse.

"No." She inhaled and slowly let the breath out, trying to calm her trembling nerves; she was not ready to get up there and stand next to Cole as he opened the curtain on her naked, gold-painted body. "Let's just get this over with"

"They're phenomenal, Lexi; even more beautiful than I could have imagined," he said earnestly, attempting to reassure her when it wasn't the pictures she was worried about. "I was able to capture a bit of your inner siren and the results are simply magical."

Lexi's world shifted slightly beneath her feet at Cole's words. "Inner... Siren?"

"For lack of a better term," he said with an unrepentant shrug. "When I put all of the pictures up, the only thing that filtered through my dazzled mind was the fact that you were a Siren hence the title of this collection is *Siren Song*."

She looked at him with bewildered and slightly hurt eyes and he laughed, "Something so beautiful you know you are doomed if you follow yet you can't help it so you follow anyway."

Her stomach felt like it was lined with lead at Cole's words, but she laughed, the action almost painful. "That's me; a Siren luring all of the men to their destruction. I see how much you and Dima suffer with me in your lives. With you it's all 'Lexi, darling, I want to take pictures of you naked;' or 'Lexi, darling, I want to paint your naked body gold;' or my favorite, 'Lexi, darling, I want to exhibit your naked, gold-painted body to the world.' No, I take it back; I'm the one who has been led astray."

First one corner of his mouth quirked upwards and then the other; soon he was laughing at her, "You forget, Lexi, darling, that you followed me home."

She heaved a dramatic sigh as her eyes twinkled up at him, "And I have suffered for it ever since. I do love you, you know."

"I do know," Cole grinned, "Now let's give your adoring public something to talk about."

Lexi turned and she was staring out at a sea of faces, some familiar, many not. Pasting on a smile that gave no indication of the fear that was running through her brain and screaming at the top of its lungs, she felt Cole squeeze her hand in reassurance. Her sisters might love the spotlight but she still hated it, preferring the spotlight of a specific few. The only thing that made it bearable was the clothes she wore; the mask that gave her the freedom to be herself.

Cole released her hand and stepped in front of the burnished gold velvet curtain, addressing the gathering with a wide, friendly smile. "Welcome to my gallery and to my latest exhibit. I have been fortunate that most of my models were able to attend tonight, as many of you may be aware and as you can see, they are as gorgeous in real life as they are in print."

The crowd chuckled and clapped appreciatively as Cole pointed out each model and briefly introduced them by name and which nearly naked picture was theirs. When he got to Dima, everyone in the crowd turned around and caught him in a passionate embrace with the red head. Her body was entwined around his as he held her thigh around his waist, as he held the back of her head with a possessive hand. They remained completely oblivious of the attention as Cole chuckled, "And perhaps after tonight I will have a new model to photograph if my roommate can find it within himself to get his tongue out of her throat."

Lexi's smile faltered as her gaze shifted and collided head on with Duncan's; he hadn't even looked at his date kissing another man. His attention was entirely upon her, intense and searing. The fluttering nerves shifted gear into heated desire and she had to squeeze her legs together to stop herself from walking up to him and possessing his lips in a similarly passionate embrace. Since she made the decision to give his memories back when their affair was over, she had become even more eager to make him break his rules. And she could tell just by looking at him that he was on the verge of breaking them.

Letting her fingers drift over her collar bone, she gave him a heated look filled with unspoken promises. The air around him seemed to thicken and then condense into a ball of lust as his eyes flashed silver. He looked poised to pounce on her and the thought had her red lips curling into a sultry smile.

The eerie sound of silence brought her back to Earth and she turned to see that Cole had opened the curtain, exposing her to the world. There were at least a dozen pictures of her on the wall and she had to admit that Cole was right; they were phenomenal. In all of the pictures, the lighting against the gold body paint made her appear ethereal and incredibly sensual. From the indent of her waist, to the smooth planes of her stomach, the bend of her knees, the curve of her ass, her body glowed in golden rapture.

In most of the pictures her face was obscured, hidden within the shadows, but three of them showed her face. The first was a frontal view with most of her hair piled up on top of her head, except for a few strands that made her look like she had just had sex. She was sitting on the ground leaning back on one arm; the other elbow was resting over her bent knee, the arm folded back so her hand was covering the nipple of her exposed breast. A thin strand of her gilded hair danced down her shoulder, drawing attention to the naked breast. Her head was turned to the side as her eyes flirted with the camera, the viewer.

The second was taken from behind with Lexi looking over her shoulder, giving the viewer a come-hither look. Her back was bare as the strand of gilded hair dangled, making the picture seem even sexier. And then there was the picture in the middle of them all, a close up of her face, without the gold paint. The image stared back as if she had a secret, the curve of her lips and the sparkle in her eyes making her look as if she was laughing at the world.

A low, rumbling growl broke the silence. Startled, Lexi looked around and saw Duncan staring at her pictures, his teeth clamped together and that delicious tic working itself into a fine frenzy in his cheek. He turned his head and she gasped at the possessive glare deep within his eyes, much further back that the surface. Fury and lust warred within those silver depths as he continued to stare at her. But then he seemed to remember himself and the powerful emotions faded until all that was left was amusement and desire.

With a slight smile, she made her way through the crowd, ignoring all of those who called out her name. Coming to a stop in front of the most scrumptious man in the room, she ran the back of her fingers along the rocky hewn edge of his jaw, breathing deeply of the midnight woods smell that he emitted. It was even more potent with the memory of strong emotions coursing through his blood. "Well?"

Gesturing to the wall of images without taking his eyes from her face, he ground out in equal measures of annoyance and arousal, "Did you do this for another one of your fluff pieces?"

She laughed out loud, drawing her fingers over his firm lips, feeling the puff of hot air as he exhaled. "No, I did this to support my friend."

"Do you get naked whenever they ask?"

"It depends on why they're asking." Her hand moved over his cheek and she loved the heated silk of his shaven skin. With a delicate shrug of her shoulders, she twinkled at him, "You see, I have other career options to fall back on."

His jaw tensed until she thought he was going to break a tooth. Through clenched teeth, he seethed, "I don't want you to pose naked for other men; I don't want to share you."

Her hand moved across his temple and she brushed her fingers through the black strands of his hair, around the shell of his ear. "You're awfully possessive for someone you don't want."

His hand came over hers putting a halt to her explorations even as his gaze burned into hers, "Haven't we established that I do want you and that is the problem? Don't worry; I will figure out a way to get you out of my system, Miss

Darling. I'm just not sure I want to even though I know that I must."

"But until you do, why don't you give in – just a little?" she purred, twining her free hand around the back of his neck and plastering her body against his. Gazing up into his eyes, losing herself in the molten silver depths, she forgot her doubts, her concerns. And then his heated palm scalded the exposed skin of her midriff and she forgot the world existed outside of his eyes. Clearing her throat, she smiled brightly and stepped out of his arms, missing his heat almost immediately, "I think we should get something to drink, maybe some water."

After a moment he relaxed ever-so-slightly and offered his arm, which she gratefully took, considering how wobbly her legs became in the last few moments. "Anything Miss Darling wishes."

"Anything?' she asked hopefully, absurdly pleased by the slight smile that graced his hard face. "Or are you just teasing me again?"

"Miss Darling, I have the feeling that when you put your mind to something you don't let anything hold you back. "His voice held a certain admiration that thrilled her to her bone. He chuckled suddenly and she looked up at him, mesmerized by the flash of white teeth and golden skin. Mesmerized by Duncan. "Do you know that when I first walked into the gallery I felt an oddly familiar punch-gut sensation and I knew you were near?"

He reached up and tweaked her wig, "And as soon as I saw the Bordeaux-colored wig I knew I had found you, to say nothing of the highly impractical dress and larger-than-life charm. I would recognize you anywhere, Miss Darling, in any disguise."

She tilted her head down but was unable to wipe the silly grin from her face. If she wasn't careful, she might find more to like about Duncan than his too-die-for body and killer smile. "I doubt you would have recognized me when I was a teenager; I was horribly gawky, with a too-skinny body and boring, plain brown hair."

"You've filled out rather nicely," he commented, letting his eyes dip to her not very well concealed breasts before meeting her gaze. "Very nicely."

"You're not so bad yourself, Mr. Tremain," she teased, lightly bumping his hip with hers and missing because he was so much taller than her; she ended up hip-bumping his thigh. With a little giggle, she looked up at him, "I thought I was taller than that."

"When you wear five inch heels you are," he said matter-of-factly "In reality, I think you're about the same size as Ashley, maybe even a little shorter."

"Has anyone ever told you it's rude to talk about past lovers with new lovers?" she asked, sticking her lower lip out in a feigned pout.

Touching the full bottom lip with the tip of his finger, he asked, "Has anyone ever told you it's rude to pose naked for the world to see when your lover is a very jealous, very possessive beast?"

She laughed out loud at that; he wasn't a beast and he wasn't her lover; not yet. He grinned down at her, "You are utterly charming, Miss Darling, and I think that is far more dangerous than your provocative outfits and come-hither glances."

"You're going to make me blush, Mr. Tremain."

He cleared his throat and when she looked up at him, he looked faintly ill. "Uh, Miss Darling, I have to ask, where were you yesterday? Did my… behavior the day before keep you away?"

"What?" she was dumb-founded by his question and it took her a moment to get past the emotional near-disaster of Thursday night to remember Thursday afternoon. And when she did, a slow mile spread across her face, "Not at all, Mr. Tremain; I simply wish you'd stop playing games and give in to madness."

"Good," he said absently, a frown marring his brow. "I thought perhaps I went too far when I accosted you in your office…."

A laugh burbled out of her, "If only that were true; this wavering hesitation on your part is what is driving me insane. You tell me you want me but you refuse to take me when I am offering myself to you on a platter, with a lovely sugared rose garnish. A… touch is not enough to drive me away, Mr. Tremain, no matter how spectacular that touch is."

He stared at her for a moment as he brushed a strand of wine-colored hair from her face, "Lexi Darling, you are unlike anyone I have ever known."

"Is that a good thing or a bad thing?"

"I'm not sure yet." He shook his head and huffed an incredulous laugh, "There have been several occasions that I have come so close to tossing it all away and giving in but something always stops me. And afterwards I prowl in my den like a caged beast wondering when I will see you again, if I will be able to spend more than a moment with you."

"Fates like to fuck with you," she said, repeating the words she had told her aunt just a few days before. "If it were up to me, I would have stripped you as soon as we got to your hotel room; I would have tied you to the bed. In fact, if it were up to me, I think we'd still be there at this very moment."

"You are too bold – too brazen – by half and I find it sexy as hell." He rubbed his thumb over her lower lip, her flesh clinging to his, reluctant to let go, as his voice came out harsh and low, "If I were a different man, Lexi, I would...."

"If you were a different man I wouldn't want you." Her words came out softly as she touched her lips to his in a brief, whisper of a kiss. With her mouth against his, she met and held his eyes, "It's only a matter of time, Duncan; I can wait."

With that, she drifted away, leaving him to stare after her.

*****

Duncan sat in his study, nursing the brandy he poured himself an hour before. Having come so close to losing control again it was a struggle to regain the resolution to keep his hands off of Lexi Darling. But all he wanted to do was to claim her, to make her his, to enjoy her body over and over until the world ended.

After she had left him with that barely there kiss, he had strolled over to her pictures and lost himself in the green and gold eyes of the girl staring out at him in the middle of all of that gilded flesh. Of course he had seen and appreciated the artistic expressions of the other pictures of her; he was a man and Lexi was a very sexy woman; but it was the unadorned Lexi in the middle that ensnared him. He was sure he had seen more attractive women but when he stared at that image, with her sun-kissed skin and large hazel eyes, he couldn't think of anyone more magnificent than Lexi.

"Beautiful, isn't she?" her friend had asked, his vibrant outfit at odds with the tender expression he wore as he looked at Lexi's image.

"Exquisite," Duncan had breathed before he could think better of it. "How did you capture what is uniquely her?"

He chuckled, "This one was taken last year when we went to the Caribbean for our annual vacation; she was mugging for the camera... you know, making fishy faces and crossing her eyes, and I managed to catch the one of her laughing at herself. I think it's my favorite picture."

"Yes," Duncan agreed simply, sipping his champagne and staring at the image of the woman who had been tormenting him for eternity.

If it was only lust he would have been able to handle it; but there was something about the infuriating, delightful woman that made him want to be the uncivilized beast that lurked deep within his body. Even knowing how his wolf hungered for her, he wanted to claim her for his own. If he had to fight himself for her, he wasn't sure who would win.

He squeezed his hands into fists, needing to get a hold of this rampaging lust. This whole thing was not like him at all, he could not afford to be losing it like this. But she made him feel alive, so damn alive. And it wasn't just the fact that she was sexy – she was sexy as hell – she was... electrifying. He had never experienced anything like it before, lusting so violently after a woman, let alone a human, and wanting to release his wolf so he could give in to primal madness.

It had to be a disease.

Needing to find his sanity, he turned on the television, hoping to find something – anything – to distract him from his thoughts, his obsession. Grabbing the remote, he pressed a button and the television lowered from the ceiling, already on.

His eyes nearly bulged out of his head when he saw Lexi as he saw her the first time, in her blond wig, a seductress look in her eyes as she looked across the bar. A wave a jealous rage rushed through him until he realized it had been him she was looking at. Good God, the crew had videotaped the entire thing – and with two local celebrities engaging in such relatively scandalous behavior.... Of course they released the tapes; sex sold and Lexi was sex on steroids.

"It is quite apparent that *lavish* writer, Lexi Darling, enjoys what she does," the voice over said as the image of her laughing filled the screen. "Filmed on location, this footage shows the lengths Miss Darling goes to get her story. Sources say that this man," the television showed the two of them as they kissed, oblivious to the world around them, "is the new owner of *lavish* magazine and if his expression is any indication, things down there are bound to get interesting."

"Next on...." But Duncan had already clicked off the television and it was disappearing back into the ceiling.

He closed his eyes; the expression on Lexi's face as he held her in his arms was burned into his retinas: the pleasure, the desire. How was he supposed to resist that? Maybe he could get Lexi out of his system, get things back on track, and when his head was clear, he'd propose to Lexi and have....

His eyes shot open; even his thoughts were betraying him. He really needed to clear his head. Lexi was not what he needed in a wife, with her colorful wigs and her even more colorful clothes and her very humanness. He needed a wolf and there was only the most infinitesimal to be non-existent chance she could make the transition if he claimed her....

The thought of losing Lexi because she couldn't make the transition had his gut twisting in knots. He couldn't take the chance that she would be destroyed if he claimed her like his wolf wanted him to do. Hell, like he wanted to do. Damn it; he knew he was on the knife's edge and it wouldn't take more than a simple "*hello*" to push him over.

Grinding his molars together, he slammed the rest of his brandy down his throat, welcoming the liquid fire. She was driving him insane and if he didn't get her away from him he was going to explode or do something crazy and propose to her. Why couldn't he simply marry her, not attempt to transform her....

That was a dangerous thought; one that he couldn't quite ignore. Why couldn't he marry her? Because he knew that in a few years, a few months, he would forget himself, only for a moment, and bite her as he mounted her from behind; sink his teeth into her delicate skin and flood her blood with the wolf's venom. She would die writhing in agony because most humans couldn't make the transition. Hell, he didn't know of a single one; generally, wolves didn't mate with humans.

It's worth the risk, the wolf whispered.

He had to get her as far away from him as possible yet he couldn't fire her, not after he promised her a month. But he could make her quit. And then, maybe, he'd be able to get back his sanity. If he gave into temptation, he may never get it back and with each moment he spent with her, the more he didn't care that she was not what he wanted as a mate; she was becoming what he needed. He had to do something....

Sitting down in front of his computer, he composed the e-mail that would hopefully do the trick. Without a second thought, he pressed send, and prayed that it would work.

Chapter 11(Monday)

Hoping to make a more professional impression on the luscious Mr. Duncan Tremain while laying siege to his libido, Lexi got up much earlier than usual Monday morning, arriving at the office by eight. Thankfully Cole had to be downtown for an appointment and didn't mind leaving so much earlier than normal. She wore a conservative outfit, at least by her standards: a dark, pin stripe skirt that went all the way to her knees and a matching jacket. Of course, the skirt had a split up the back that stopped just below her butt and the jacket was very fitted over nothing but a lacy, electric blue bra. She wore a pair of stiletto mules and her brown hair was scraped back into a severe bun; no wigs today. Actually, her look was more like 'Dominatrix meets the work place.'

On the way in, she saw his roadster parked in his spot and she realized that she was going to have to get there a lot earlier if she really wanted to impress him. Fortunately, she didn't run into him as she made her way to her office, giving her a few moments to gather herself together and go over her game plan. Dropping her purse, she sat behind her desk and booted up her computer to check her e-mail.

Picking up the phone, she dialed her mother, something she tended to do at work to avoid getting into a long conversation. As soon as her mom answered, Lexi blurted, "Hey, mom, I have a quick question for you."

"Alexandra," her mom let out a long sigh. "You have the most impeccable timing; I was about to get my hair done."

"Why did Thea nearly suffer an apoplexy when the Tremains were mentioned?" she asked before her mom could say anything else. When Charisma didn't answer, Lexi thought she might have hung up the phone. "Mom?"

When her mom finally spoke, her voice was grave, "Alexandra; if you must know, you'll have to discuss it with Thea. Personally, I would advise caution when dealing with the Tremains; there is something dangerous, primal, about all of them."

A delicious shiver went down Lexi's spine and she smiled at the thought of Duncan, all dangerous and primal. Her voice was low, husky, when she breathed, "Yeah."

"Why are you asking about the Tremains? You usually aren't one for gossiping."

"Um, my boss is Duncan Tremain," Lexi said, omitting most of the truth.

"Don't get involved with him," her mother warned gravely. "Out of all of the Tremains, he is the most... amused by us. I think he secretly mocks up and I cannot abide being laughed at."

"I'm laughing at you right now, mom," Lexi teased. "And Duncan is too busy conquering the world to spare any thought on mythological creatures."

"I know you're laughing, Alexandra; you laugh at everything. But you're family so I'll allow it." Lexi heard the smile in her mother's voice and smiled in return. “Just think twice about getting involved with Duncan Tremain.”

“He’s my boss, mom,” Lexi interrupted before her mother could ask a question she didn’t want to answer. “I just want my writing to be given an honest shot because I think I might have influenced Jeffrey a little bit when I applied for the job, albeit unknowingly, since I didn’t freaking know about the Siren thing until recently and I’m worried I will do the same thing with Du… Mr. Tremain.”

“I am sorry I didn’t tell you sooner, my dear,” her mom apologized for the millionth time. "It's just...."

“Mom, I’m not mad,” Lexi chuckled, interrupting the excuses before they could start. “It’s just something I’m still figuring out.”

Charisma once again fell silent and Lexi chewed on her lip, knowing that her mother was working through the nuances of the entire conversation. As she waited for her mom to decide whether or not Lexi was flirting with danger, Lexi opened her email.

Her heart dropped when she saw one from him. Was he going to reiterate his ridiculous rules? She already knew them by heart; it didn’t change the fact that he was going to break them – but he wouldn’t necessarily remember. While she would prefer to leave him with his memories of her and whatever time they spent together, she knew that she would do anything she could to ease his torment if it grew too great. With a shaking hand, she clicked on it and began to read. Anger quickly replaced nerves and her nostrils flared as she pressed the print button.

“I’ve got to go, mom,” Lexi bit out.

“Are you… contemplating a relationship with Duncan Tremain?” she asked carefully.

“Yeah,” Lexi seethed. “Murder.”

Without a second thought, she hung up the phone and grabbed the printed e-mail, making her way to Duncan’s office. Marching up to his secretary’s desk, she took a deep breath to calm herself enough to smile, considering she was ready to strangle the man. That wasn’t Miss Reynolds’s fault. “Is Duncan in?”

The older woman looked up from her desk and met Lexi’s eyes, her face brightening as she smiled with affection. Lexi had always liked Miss Reynolds and hoped Mr. Tremain decided to keep the woman, who was fantastically organized and efficient. She kept things running smoothly even when deadlines made it feel like everything was on the verge of falling apart. "Mr. Tremain is not in his office at the moment; if you want to schedule a meeting, I'm sure…."

"Please," Lexi smiled beguilingly, knowing the woman was just doing her job; it wasn't her fault that her boss sucked. "Just tell me where he is?"

"The, uh, gym," Miss Reynolds hesitantly answered. "But, Lexi, you can't…."

Lexi didn't hear the rest as she turned on her heal and stormed back to the elevator, crossing her arms under her breasts and hoping that her temper managed to do what everything else couldn't: tone down this fascination with Duncan Tremain. God, if only it was that easy because even in her rage, she still wanted the man. Damn it.

Unconcerned with where she was going, she stormed through the door into the men's locker room, oblivious to the half-naked men frantically trying to cover themselves. She was seeing red because of Duncan Tremain, and she had to remind herself that he was her boss. He was insufferable. Gorgeous. Infuriating. Delectable. Arrogant.

Nearly naked.

Her knees trembled and she swallowed as she took in the expanse of his hard, masculine chest, the light dusting of dark hair over the brown discs of his nipples. He was ripped, his tightly compacted stomach muscles tensing as her gaze caressed them. Tilting her head back, she took in his damp skin and wet, slicked back hair; it was so black and so glossy. Drops of water glistened on his hardened jaw, across his supple lips…. A dry Duncan Tremain was mouthwatering; a wet Duncan Tremain was irresistible.

"Miss Darling," he ground out. When she met his eyes, she swore she was looking at storm clouds, roiling with barely leashed fury and passion. For a moment, her mind went completely blank as images of their bodies entwining filled her head, picturing all of that hard, wet skin moving over hers as his fingers tormented her breasts and his cock slowly eased into her swollen sex.... "What are you doing in here?"

Her fingers curled, crumbling the paper and bringing her back to the present. She quickly regained her righteous indignation and thrust her hand out. Plastering the paper against his damp, sculpted chest, she ignored the feel of his hot skin and glared at him. "You cut my words."

"Yes," he said simply, putting a hand on the knot of his towel, not doing anything to remove her hand. And did he just get closer, or was that just his aura expanding outwards and invading her senses?

Lexi glanced down and realized that he was going to take his towel off; that he was going to be naked in, like, two seconds. Her eyes shot to his and she saw the awareness in them. "I don't think you should be doing that in here."

He raised an eyebrow, and though he didn't move his hand, he didn't take the towel off, either. "This is the men's locker room."

"Yes," she agreed, feeling the warmth creep into her cheeks. She thought about taking a step back but somewhere along the way the idea was aborted and her feet remained firmly planted in place. Her fingers relaxed a bit, letting the piece of paper slip to the floor so no barriers were between her hand and his flesh. Her heart pirouetted in her chest and her tummy tingled as she pressed her palm against the slick dampness of his chest and felt his skin. It had been too long since she touched him and it was beyond intoxicating. "Yes, it is."

"You may want to consider leaving," he murmured, his voice pure seduction.

"Yes," she agreed. And again, neither one moved. She just continued to stare into his liquid silver eyes, losing herself in them. Yeah, she would give him her soul....

"Give me a few minutes and I will meet with you in my office; we'll discuss your word count then," he said, the storm raging in his eyes reeling her in until electricity moved along her spine, her skin. His eyes... they glowed with desire and possession.

"I don't think you'll do it," she rasped, her mouth absurdly dry as she continued to stand so close to an almost naked Duncan. As he arched his eyebrow, she swallowed and her heart trembled in her chest, "I don't think you'll drop the towel."

His lips curved upwards in a naughty smile and then the towel was gone, crumbled in a heap around their feet. Her eyes dipped down and then almost rolled back into her head as she took a moment to appreciate the exquisite beauty of his penis. Her hand drifted downwards, over his flat stomach, over the thin line of hair beneath his navel, downwards…. His fingers wrapped around her wrist, halting her downward journey and she looked up at him with dazed eyes, the butterflies dancing for joy and her skin on fire.

Projecting an image of calm and cool collectedness was difficult as she purred, "Very nice."

With a warm expression in his eyes, he lightly ran the fingers of his other hand over her temple, pushing a non-existent strand of hair behind her ear, "Give me fifteen minutes, Miss Darling." Leaning forward, he whispered in her ear, "We are not alone."

Jumping back, she felt foolish. She was standing in the men's locker room, for God's sake, practically melting at Duncan's feet and several men were staring at them and she realized she wasn't being professional at all. Well, she could do that; and she would. When she talked to him – in his office, with him dressed – she would be completely professional-ish. "Fifteen minutes."

"Fifteen minutes," he repeated, standing naked and proud. As much as she would have liked to stay and stare at him, standing there nude and glorious, she turned on her heel and walked back through the locker room. As comfortable as she was with her body, she wasn't prepared to engage in acts of public sex, no matter the temptation.

Besides, she was still angry at him for cutting her words.

*****

As he picked up the towel and finished drying off, Duncan took a few long, drawn-out breaths as Lexi walked away. Seeing her storm in here, her eyes blazing, was hell on his libido. He was painfully aware of his erection, and how stupid it had been to defy her expectations and drop the damn towel. She was so blatant in her attraction to him, desire of him, and as a wolf, he appreciated her boldness and vivacity. Even if she didn't taunt him with her words he would have known that she wanted him; he could see it in her eyes, feel it in her touch. But there was no way in hell he was going to attack her in the men's locker room with other men standing around. He wasn't a beast.

His wolf wouldn't have cared who was watching.

God, she was glorious! In everything she did, she did with her whole heart. Making love to her would be unlike anything he ever experienced before. Having sampled her briefly, he knew that much. It would be enough to change a man, make him forget what was important, forget his name, forget the reasons why he shouldn't. And it would be worth it – until she ended up writhing in agony as the wolf's venom coursed through her system because he forgot himself for one moment.

Damn it; he needed to get himself under control. He wasn't behaving rationally; in fact, he was acting no better than his wolf, willing to rut without any concern of civility. He could control himself around Lexi; she wasn't a Siren, luring men to their downfalls, their deaths. She was just an intoxicating woman that stirred his basest passions. Hell, if he kept panting after her, he would be luring her to her death. He shouldn't sink any deeper.

Of course, if he were absolutely honest with himself, he would admit that he already had. If she had just been a sexy woman, he could have given in to lust and fucked her before letting her go. But she had to go and make him like her.

Just once, his wolf whispered. *Take her just once and end the madness.*

No, because once would never be enough. He was going to accept her resignation and never surrender; he was already too twisted up inside and he did not like the feeling, the spiraling out of control, of losing control to the wolf inside of him.

"That Lexi Darling is a real piece of work," someone to his left said. Duncan turned his head and saw one of the copy editors standing there, staring at the door where Lexi disappeared. Letting out a low whistle, he continued, "I'd fuck her, though."

"Excuse me?" Duncan asked, his voice full of disdain that this man should dare talk about Lexi. He didn't like the guy's look, with his slicked back white-blond hair, ice-cold blue eyes; the guy was a malignant tumor on a cockroach's ass.

The guy sneered, apparently unaware of the grave he was digging for himself. "Uh, Miss Darling. She comes in here like it's her God-given right, wearing those… outfits. I swear, she just asks for it."

Duncan's nostrils flared, his chest tightened, and his hands curled into fists; if the jerk said one more word, he was going to end up in the ER needing surgery to remove his head from his rectum. Turning back to his locker, Duncan threw the towel down, needing to get dressed in order to make the meeting with Lexi. He didn't need to hear some jackass talk crap about her.

"I can see she has the same effect on you," the guy continued.

Duncan turned his head and caught the guy staring at his erection, which had barely gone down, even with the idiot blathering on. He wanted to wrap his hand around the idiot's throat and squeeze until there wasn't a drop of life left. Breathing heavily, it took a moment to get the violent thought out of his head.

Gritting his teeth together, Duncan grabbed his pants and pulled them on, not bothering with his briefs. Dressing as quick as possible, he needed to get the hell out of there before he committed manslaughter. If the guy kept talking, his wolf was going to rise to the surface and rip the bastard's throat out.

Pausing, he took a deep breath to get the fury under control; the last thing he needed was to turn into a wolf in the middle of the locker room and slaughter an idiot. Damn it; he hadn't been this out of control since he was a boy barreling through puberty. How the hell did Lexi get so much power over him in such a short time that he was willing to become a savage to protect her?

The oblivious fool with a death wish chuckled to himself, "The other day, she came in wearing some sort of school girl uniform; I swear, I had some x-rated fantasies for a week."

Hearing this other guy, even if this other guy was slime, admitting his own lascivious thoughts regarding Lexi strengthened his resolve. He couldn't get any more involved with her; he didn't need to be all twisted up inside. Tying his tie, he closed the locker, turning his back on the asshole. With a grim expression, he left the locker room behind, grateful for the encounter with the lecherous ass since it managed to reinforce his decision to keep Lexi at a safe distance. Say, Antarctica.

He just wasn't sure who he was trying to keep safe.

*****

Mrs. Reynolds kept throwing friendly smiles her way, but Lexi was not in any state of mind to chat; her thoughts were warring between desire and annoyance. She leaned against the outer door to Duncan's office, arms crossed beneath her breasts, lust and indignation fortifying her resolve. She could control her lust long enough to yell at Duncan and then he better be ready to pay because after that performance in the locker room.... She had to fan herself to keep from burning up.

He finally appeared looking even more powerful – even more warrior-like – then he looked in the locker room. The dark suit only emphasized his incredible build; unless that was just Lexi remembering what he looked like underneath all of those clothes. A rush of heat tore through her body at the thought and she had to consciously remember to not groan out loud. God, he was just so damn sexy.

His spine was rigid, almost to the point of breaking, as he stopped at his secretary's desk, not looking at her, and asked for his messages. Lexi wondered what would happen if she ran her fingers along his back, if he would arch into it like a cat or if he would claw at her. She wasn't going to risk touching him; if she touched him, she'd be the one liable to arch like a cat.

"Miss Darling," his voice interrupted her thoughts and she straightened. He held out his hand for her to precede him into his office, careful not to touch her as she passed, his expression grim and reserved. She wanted to see him lose control so she added a little swing to her step as she walked past him.

Yeah, that worked until the door closed and she was alone in the office with this paragon of masculine virility, this warrior, and she realized that more often than not fire burned and consumed everything in its path. Sucking in a deep lungful of breath, she watched as he made his way around his desk and sat down in his chair, looking every inch the powerful warlord who could determine whether or not she lived or died. Whether he would choose her to be in his harem.

The image of her in a slave girl's costume awaiting her master's pleasure detonated in her brain and she could almost feel the flimsy material that hid nothing from his silver perusal. She would kneel before him, looking up at him with kohl-lined eyes, as she reverently pull his thick cock from his silky harem pants, holding his gaze as she took him into her mouth and….

"Ahem," he cleared his throat, dragging her thoughts away from wearing a slave girl costume and pleasuring her lord. Shaking her head, she looked at him and saw that he was once again the impassive businessman. Good, that was good; keep things strictly professional between them. "You had a problem with my decision to cut your words?"

Straightening the lines of her jacket, lifting her chin with indignation, she stared down at him, trying not to imagine him in his harem pants. "I just got them increased and now they are even lower then when I started. I thought you said you would at least give my column a chance before you axed it and you're doing everything in your power to guarantee its demise."

Haughtily, he raised that arrogant eyebrow and folded his hands beneath his chin as he coolly studied her. "I am giving your column a chance and if you can't write an effective column with the words I've given you then perhaps you don't belong at this magazine."

"From the very beginning you have been the one who has tried to get rid of me," she shot back, her heart beating frantically in her chest as she watched him just sit there looking so damn impervious, so goddamn sexy and wanting him even while fighting with him. She wanted him to get angry; she wanted to see beneath the calm, collected exterior to the warlord beneath. "If you're that determined to keep your rules then fuck it; I give up. Keep your damn rules; I'll find someone who chases me. And what is your problem with my column?"

"Your column does not belong with this magazine," he said simply. "It's simply gossip."

"Have you even read anything I've written?" she demanded to know, already knowing his answer. If he had read it, he would know it wasn't a gossip column; it was an adventure column with interesting conversations from the people taking the adventures with her. "Of course not; you think that just because I take a different approach to showing *lavish* lifestyles that they do not count. But that's like saying having sex in a garden is not suitable because it's sex in a garden. Well, I'll have you know that sometimes the thought of making love in the great outdoors holds far greater appeal to me than the same old, boring bed routine."

Oh, God, why was she talking about having sex at all? Didn't she just say she was giving up on him? And why was he just sitting there not responding while her body was getting primed for earth-shattering sex? So, of course, she had no choice but to push him further, to break through that iron control.

"You are just trying to get me to quit and I understand your reasons," her words were filled with passion as she paced back and forth in front of his desk, unable to look at him as she got everything off her chest. "I know that you want me – almost as much as I want you – but you don't want to want me. Fine, you're probably right; the attraction between us is so intense, so overwhelming, that if we did finally succumb to the madness it would probably be a huge let down.

"I mean, you're all show and no play," she continued, stopping in front of the desk and looking down at him. His expression was stony but that irresistible muscle was pulsing ruthlessly in his jaw so she knew he was listening. "That's probably why you keep leading me on and then slamming the door in my face when I get too close to breaking through your control. You simply don't want to live up to my expectations and let me tell you, they are sky high."

Walking around his desk, she stood directly in front of him, trying to make her point. From up close, she noticed the slight flush along his cheek bones, the sweat beading on his brow, the strain of keeping his expression neutral. It wasn't exactly what she was looking for, but it was a start. Leaning her butt against the edge of his desk, she looked down at him, "You're probably a bread and butter lover, aren't you?"

She saw his jaw tighten and so she pushed on, "Does your lover just lie there on the bed while you move in her just so, making as little disorder as possible?" Reaching forward, she ran her hands through the thick mass of his black hair, mussing it up. It was like running her hands through raw silk: thick and heavy and so luxurious. She wanted to keep her hands threaded through his mane but forced her hands back to her side. "I bet you don't even take your suit off – there's just no point in wasting time undressing completely; it wouldn't be..." She sneered, "Efficient."

"Lexi," he growled.

She looked down and her heart leapt in her chest when she saw the hunger in the liquid silver of his eyes. It thrilled her and scared her at the same time. She was so going to get burned and she was relishing the blisters she would get. "I suppose you might remove your tie," she said thoughtfully, tapping her finger against her chin. "Though having your airway constricted does increase the pleasure and since you'd be in such a rush, leaving the tie on might make more sense; more bang for the buck, one might say."

"Lexi," he repeated, his voice dark and sensual. Slowly, he stood up and she noticed that he wasn't unaffected at all: his pants were straining against his huge erection. As she watched, he pulled the tails of his shirt out and began unbuttoning it, slowly revealing a span of golden skin as it opened. He loosened the tie and lifted it off his head, answering her tie question. Shrugging out of his shirt, he repeated, "Lexi."

She looked back up, their eyes met and she forgot how to breathe. "What?"

"Shut up," he murmured, bending his head and capturing her lips in a soul-searing kiss. Automatically, she wrapped her arms around his neck and plastered her body against his, relishing the feel of his hard muscles and heat. She heard a low moan and wasn't sure if it was coming from her or from him.

His hands undid the three buttons holding her jacket together and when he lifted his head her breath caught in her throat as he ravished her with his silver eyes. His hungry gaze dipped to her breasts, encased in a lacy, blue bra. Pushing the jacket off her arms, letting it fall to the desk, he reached behind her and unclasped her bra. Her breasts spilled into his hands and the heat of his touch burned any remnants of her rational mind away. As he took a rosy nipple into his mouth, she inhaled sharply in acute pleasure, threading her fingers through his hair to hold him in place.

As he manipulated her nipples with his tongue, his fingers, she ran her hands over his broad shoulders, down his muscled chest, across the front of his flat, sculpted stomach. With trembling fingers, she unfastened his pants, releasing his straining erection, only momentarily surprised to discover he wasn't wearing underwear. Before she could contemplate that fact, she wrapped her hands around his penis, stroking the hot, silken length. This time, she knew that he was the one who growled.

Hearing the zipper of her skirt being unzipped, she felt it slither down her legs to the ground, exposing the matching blue panties. Duncan kissed a path from her sexually sensitized breasts, across her collar bone, along her throat, until he caught her lips once more, groaning into her mouth as his hand slid between her legs. Strong, masculine fingers probed the moist, feminine heat and her body softened, accepting the pleasurable invasion. In savage desperation, he tore the scrap of lace from her body, sucking her tongue into his mouth as she gasped.

Throwing her head back, desperate for air, Lexi moaned as Duncan pressed first one finger and then another into her, making her tremble. She had to hold onto his arms to remain standing since her bones had disappeared with her rational mind. As he watched her face with gleaming metallic eyes, he slowly withdrew his fingers and then thrust them back in several times, priming her already-primed body and drawing out her feminine lubrication. Dragging his fingers along the swollen folds of her sex, he rubbed the moisture around her swollen clitoris, eliciting another moan from her.

He stopped and Lexi frowned until she realized he was grabbing a condom from his back pocket. Smiling sultrily up at him as he slid the condom onto his raging erection, she asked, “Are you always prepared?”

He muttered something about recently stocking up and she almost laughed but then he was kissing her again, his fingers wrapping around her thigh and hoisting her leg up so his cock was poised at the entrance to her body. She sighed into his mouth, “Hurry, Duncan. I want to feel you inside of me.”

Hungrily, his silver eyes gleamed as he watched her expression; gone was the civilized veneer, in its place was the wolf, the Primal Male, desperate to claim his mate. His nostrils flared as he continued watching her face, nudging his cock against her, finding the entrance of her sex. A low growl came from the back of his throat as he pulled her body flush against his and thrust fully into her.

There was a moment of discomfort, barely there and then just as quickly gone, and then a glorious wholeness as he filled her completely. Lifting her other boneless limb, she wrapped her legs around his waist as her back arched, pressing her all the way onto the length of his erection. It was the most exquisite sensation she had ever felt and she never wanted the feeling to end even as her body begged for more.

Using his hands, his thighs, his body, he set a relentless rhythm, driving her to the point of desperation and her nails dug into his shoulders, drawing blood, fueling the lust-crazed frenzy between them. His teeth skimmed across her throat until he was sucking her throbbing pulse, marking her as she marked him, pumping into her over and over until her body tightened and felt like it was going to snap.

She was barely aware of the cool desk against her burning skin as he set her down and then urged her backwards, his hips pummeling against her thighs as he continued to thrust in and out of her. Straightening, he looked down at her with that primal gaze and an orgasm tore through her body, leaving her breathless as he continued to pump, making her breasts bounce in the same rhythm.

"It's too much," she gasped, as he slowed his rhythm and went deeper.

His lips curved into a dark smile, his eyes, his silver eyes, glowed. But he didn't speak, instead, one of his hands curled around her breast, the other reached between their bodies and rubbed against her swollen clit, making her back arch off the desk as lightning coursed through her body and set her nerves on fire. Making her scream.

His mouth found a nipple and suckled – hard, adding unbearable pleasure to her already tortured body. Her fingers once more twisted in his hair and convulsed erratically; she was desperate for something to hold onto as she shattered into a million pieces.

His hips pummeled her, his penis stroking her insides, closer and closer to release. Her breathes came with increasing gasps and high pitches of air intake, driving him further and further. As her body stiffened, as her inner muscles flexed around him, he came, filling the condom with his seed, filling her ears with a dull roar.

Spent, he collapsed onto her, breathing heavily. Wrapping her arms around his glistening back, she caressed his shuddering muscles, needing to touch him. Little aftershocks were making their way through her body and Lexi sighed happily, "I knew it would be incredible."

He stiffened slightly but he didn't move and his voice was rough but without conviction as he rasped, "It shouldn't have happened."

"It was inevitable," she sighed, not wanting to let him go, loving the weight of his body on hers – in hers. Knowing she didn't want the moment to end, she still let him go, not surprised when he straightened and stepped away from her exhausted body. Removing the condom and then tugging his pants back up, he brushed his hair back into place and regained his control. If it weren't so depressing, it would have been absolutely mesmerizing, watching her warrior replacing his mask of civility.

"This was a mistake," he said gruffly, grabbing her bra and suit jacket and tossing them to her. Duncan's gaze lowered to the glistening curls between her thighs and she felt the desire start to build again. But then he was squeezing his eyes shut and turning away from her. "I apologize, Miss Darling."

Frowning, she put her bra back on, then her coat and her skirt. Sitting on the edge of his desk, she watched him as he paced back and forth, coming to terms with what they just did. "Don't you dare apologize, Duncan Tremain; don't you dare!"

He turned around and faced her and she was taken aback by the desolation in his eyes. "There are things you don't know about me, Lexi; things that would terrify you."

Standing, she closed the distance between them and cupped his cheek in her palm, tilting her head back much further since her shoes had been lost somewhere along the way. "We all have secrets, Duncan; don't think yours are any worse than anyone else's."

His hand covered hers and he closed his eyes as he rubbed his cheek against her palm. But when he looked at her, the despair was still there and her heart ached for him. "Lexi, you are a temptation I cannot afford; if I hurt you…."

His big body shuddered and she stepped even closer to show him that she wasn't afraid of him, until her breasts pressed against his chest and her other arm was wrapped around his waist. "You could never hurt me."

In that moment, she loved him with her whole heart and that thought made the air in her lungs coalesce, making it thick and cold and impossible to breathe. It wasn't love, it was just sex; explosive, brain-melting sex. It couldn't be love because it would be false; without the allure of the Siren, he wouldn't love her in return. Of course it wasn't love.

Abruptly pulling away from him, she began to search for her panties, remembering that in their haste to mate, Duncan tore them off. With her thoughts roiling, she blurted, "It's just sex."

His eyes hardened as if her words wounded him but he simply nodded, "Of course."

"I need to get back to work," she said. Pasting a smile on her frozen face, she teased, "I don't want the boss to fire me for sleeping around on the job."

Gazing at her with the eyes of the damned, he ground out, "This can't happen again."

"I can't make that promise," she whispered, slipping on her heels and walking over to the door. As her hands wrapped around the doorknob, she paused and without glancing at him murmured, "At least read some of my work, Mr. Tremain, you might be pleasantly surprised."

*****

He watched as she walked out the door, thoughts and recriminations racing a million miles per hour as his wolf sighed his contentment. At least he had made it past *hello*, not that she ever said hello. But when she started talking about sex and expectations, he had lost it, attacking her like the savage beast that lurked within him.

When she was around, he was not himself; not only did he fail to get her to hand in her resignation, he had failed to keep his paws off her. It didn't matter that it had been the most explosive, most satisfying sex of his life, he shouldn't have given in.

If you don't want her, let me have her, my master and slave, his wolf said, its voice drowsy with sexual repletion. *She was delicious and I want her again.*

Duncan closed his eyes in self-disgust; his beast had never participated in his sexual encounters before; he had been able to control the beast, keep him caged. As long as it was allowed to run with the wolves and rut with Ashley on occasion, the beast behaved, abiding by the rules Duncan had set down all of those years ago. Unless he could figure out a way to keep his wolf caged when Lexi was near, he couldn't afford to be around her. Her presence made him do things – want things – which he couldn't, shouldn't, want.

Sitting down at the computer, he addressed another email to her. He wasn't going to apologize again; he couldn't, he wasn't sorry. Typing the quick message, he reread it and prayed he had the strength to resist tracking her down and absconding with her, taking her back to his lair to savor whenever he pleased.

Miss Darling:

I think it would be best if I keep my distance from you; whenever I am around you, I forget myself. Please continue your work on 'The Scene;' if you need to communicate with me, please feel free to email me. I will try to keep my distance.

D. Tremain.

Clicking send, he leaned back in his chair and stared out the window at the world beyond, still feeling the lingering effects of being inside Lexi's body. It had been the height of stupidity to lose control in such a spectacular fashion but he couldn't regret it; he just had to figure out a way to get her out of his system so that he no longer craved her more than the air he needed to breathe.

Chapter 12 (Saturday)

Duncan swung the club, sending the golf ball flying through the air, grateful that they were on the final hole. It was difficult trying to concentrate on his game when memories of having sex with Lexi kept replaying themselves in his head, Lexi's seductive scent, her mindless moans; the way her body welcomed him.... It had been nearly a week and she still invaded his thoughts. Swearing about the distance his ball went, or rather, the lack of distance, Duncan waited for his brother, Senator Philip Carson, to swing.

"What's up with you today?" Philip asked, lining up his shot, glancing at the hole and then adjusting his grip. "You're eight above par and that never happens. With your wolf vision, you should be well below."

"Nothing's up," Duncan clipped out, tightening his jaw and watching his older brother with a dark scowl. Despite the nearly ten year age difference and having two different fathers, the two men were surprisingly close. Because Philip's father had been a human there had never been a question of whether or not he would be the Alpha and so he decided to take the world of politics by storm instead. Philip had the power and intelligence of a wolf but he did not shift and being a half-breed gave him the strength to persevere against almost any obstacle, including the dog-eat-shit world of politics. "Take your damn shot."

Philip chuckled, "Yes, sir."

"There's a woman," Duncan blurted, unable to keep the words to himself. As his brother paused and looked at him, waiting for more, Duncan sighed, "She's unlike anything I've ever known, Phil; she drives me insane and I think I like it."

"Then what's the problem?" he asked, swinging and sending the little white ball soaring. Smiling when he saw it land next to the hole, he turned to Duncan, "Well?"

"She's human."

"Ah, I see." And he did. As the product of a human-wolf relationship, he was in the very unique position of understanding, perhaps one of the only two people to understand. "Have you talked to mom about this yet?"

"Are you crazy?" Duncan huffed a laugh at the thought. "She would freak out and I wouldn't hear the end of it. Besides, I've already told Le... the girl that we can't be together."

"Why don't you just enjoy her for the moment?" Philip asked with bewilderment as they moved closer to the hole. "You've had human lovers before."

"I've had one human lover, Philip," Duncan clarified. "And it was a disaster. No, this girl is... she is dangerous. I lose control around her and she makes me want things...."

"Are you taking measures to prevent pregnancy?" Phil asked casually even though Duncan knew how important the answer was to him.

"Of course," Duncan assured him, seeing his brother's shoulders relax slightly.

"But I would get her pregnant in a heartbeat if it meant I could keep her."

Philip ground to a halt and stared at him in dismay, "You know what happened to my father, Duncan; don't even joke about such a thing."

"Forgive me," Duncan murmured, letting the matter drop; he wasn't going to burden Philip with his demons because the story of Philip's father had been used as a cautionary tale for as long as he could remember: the dangers of falling in love with a human.

When she had been very young, Isabel, their mother, had fallen madly in love with a human and she had told him about her nature and he still loved her. Miraculously she fell pregnant with his child, with Philip, and they foolishly believed Philip Senior was destined to be her mate, that he would survive, and she had bit him.

At first everything seemed to be okay and they were overjoyed, since they were going to be bringing a little half-human, half-wolf into the world. And they were going to be able to raise the little cub together, as wolves. But then, within a day everything had changed and it all started when he came down with a fever that burned out of control. Within a few hours, the pain overtook him until he was clawing at his skin to make it stop. The venom had killed him quickly after that, leaving their mom pregnant and alone.

Devastated by her loss and overwhelmed with guilt and grief, she had returned to the pack only to be mocked and shunned for daring to fall in love with a human, for having the audacity to bring a half-breed abomination into their midst. She was an omega wolf and they rest of the pack never let her forget.

Until the day the Alpha returned home from an extended hunt and took one look at the shattered woman and knew that she was meant to be his. It had taken a lot of time for her to deal with her loss and heartbreak but Julian had been patient, giving her what she needed, the time to heal, while always being a presence in her life. He had been a father to Philip from the moment the child was born, even when Isabel wanted nothing to do with the Alpha.

Eventually, she realized that she while she would always love Philip Senior, she madly and passionately loved Julian, that he had returned her love a thousand fold. Nine months after he finally claimed her, Duncan was born, the first of many children they were to have.

Philip and Duncan walked the rest of the green in silence, each lost in their own thoughts. In the end, Philip managed to just make par on the course, making Duncan's ten above that much worse. As a wolf, his score shouldn't have been that dismal and Duncan couldn't help but shake his head. Laughing as they entered the dining room of the club house, Philip clapped his brother on the back, "Rounds are finally on you. Are you sure there isn't anything else eating you up?"

The image of Lexi's lips taking the length of his erection into her mouth flashed into Duncan's head and his body responded immediately and painfully. Almost allowing the groan to escape, Duncan managed to covertly adjust while sitting down on the veranda.

"There's nothing else. No, wait; I take that back." He glared at his Philip, though the amusement in his voice ruined the effect, "You announced your decision to run for president to a gossip columnist?"

"You're talking about Lexi Darling?" Philip asked, leaning back and sipping the water the efficient waiter placed in front of him. At Duncan's grunted yes, he smiled, "Yeah, I seem to recall mentioning it to her when she fried my brain with that luscious body of hers."

Duncan ground his molars for a moment, as jealous rage rampaged through him. Trying to act as if his brain wasn't going to explode, he asked, "Doesn't it bother you that your presidential plans were announced so… imprudently?"

"Don't you own *lavish* now?" Philip asked, crunching an ice cube, an amused look on his face as he studied his younger brother.

"That's not the point," Duncan bit out, trying to get his thoughts away from wrapping his hands around his brother's throat for daring to ogle the body of the woman he lusted after. It would be in very poor form to murder him when he loved him. "If you wanted to announce it in the magazine, why didn't you choose a more… respectable column?"

The corner of Philips lips curved upwards in a crooked smile, "Have you ever seen Miss Darling in a bikini? I swear that woman has the body of a goddess."

He had to agree; it was a body made to be worshiped, by tongues and teeth if necessary. Looking away, Duncan was startled by Philip's raucous laughter, "My God, Duncan, you're actually blushing. I take it you've met the exceptional Lexi Darling."

"I have," Duncan admitted, still not quite meeting Philip's eyes, wondering if his brother was going to put two and two together and figure out why the conversation was making him so uncomfortable. He busied himself with drinking his water. "She's very… unique."

"Yeah," Philip agreed, the one word making Duncan's description sound woefully lacking. "When she called for an interview I had no idea who she was even though I recognized the name because my wife reads her column all the time. I agreed to answer a few of her questions over the phone and I was impressed as hell by her intelligence, her enthusiasm."

"I'm sure that's not all that impressed you," Duncan grunted.

Philip's smile widened, "I admit, when she adjusted her bikini top, I nearly split the seam in my trunks even though I'm a happily mated wolf, but I digress. I had no idea what she looked like during my interview – and I had no intention of announcing anything. But somehow she had discovered I like to wind surf and asked if I'd like to do a quick, informal follow-up, something that would make it more… interesting."

"I see," Duncan grumbled, tightening his grip on his glass until he was sure it was going to shatter. Forcing his hand to relax, he concentrated on breathing and not smashing his fist into his brother's face.

"Did you even read the article?" Philip asked, sitting forwards in his chair. "Lexi is someone I would like to have on my team."

"I bet you would," Duncan actually snorted.

Philip laughed outright at his younger brother's obvious irritation. "Tell me then, if you're so smart, what do you make of the girl?"

"Disturbing," Duncan answered without thinking, making Philip laugh even harder than before. He glared at Philip. "What?"

"She's gotten to you," he smirked matter-of-factly. "She had that effect on me as well."

"So you've lost control and fucked her, too, huh?" Duncan asked, acid eating away at his stomach. It didn't matter how much he loved his brother, he was going to slam his fist into Philip's smug face....

"WHAT?!" Philip nearly fell out of his chair, his eyes widening in disbelief, in shock. "You... slept with her? Wow, Duncan, you don't do casual sex; you're practically a monk with the number of women you've been with. What's the number? Four? Five?"

"There was nothing casual about it," Duncan huffed out, surprising himself with his frankness. Knowing that Philip hadn't slept with Lexi left Duncan feeling rather charitable towards his older brother. Of course Philip hadn't slept with Lexi; he was completely devoted to his wife Stacey. More importantly, he was a happily mated wolf; he couldn't sleep with Lexi even if he wanted to; and if he wanted to, Duncan was going to.... With a wry smile, he added, "Besides, I've learned quality trumps quantity every time. What I lack in numbers I make up for in performance. Even the human I bedded walked away happy."

Philip threw his head back and laughed, "You are so full of it, Duncan; I'm surprised you allowed yourself to be lured to the dark side. And with a girl that exudes sex." He let out a low whistle, "Ashley is going to be furious."

"I don't know about that; Ashley adores her." Seeing the expression of horror on his brother's face, not quite understanding it, Duncan paused, "Don't look at me like that."

"I can't believe you would introduce your girlfriend, your prospective mate, to your mistress," Philip shook his head.

"Ashley is not nor has she ever been my girlfriend," Duncan ground out, irritated with his brother's assumptions, knowing that the entire pack had the same assumptions.

"But, under the full moon, the two of you…."

"She was the only one I could tolerate and you know what the wolf is like when the moon is full." Even if Philip didn't shift, he still felt the driving, animalistic need to fuck beneath the full moon. Duncan didn't know why he was making excuses; it was his life and Ashley was not his girlfriend. He didn't owe her or Philip an explanation.

"Wow, I never thought I'd see the day where you would let your beast take over completely," he let out a low whistle, leaning back in his chair as he stared at Duncan in awe. "Did you lose your mind, Duncan? Go insane? What?"

"There may have been some madness involved," Duncan admitted, downplaying the extent of their combustible attraction. "I don't know; there's just something about her.

"I agree," Philip said, still a little stunned over his brother's behavior. A low growl came from the back of Duncan's throat and Philip held up his hands and chuckled, "Whoa, there, Duncan, I'm just agreeing with you. After all, she got me to announce my plans in a gossip column and she made Duncan Tremain lose his infamous iron-control. What does your wolf think about Lexi?"

"He won't shut up about her," Duncan shook his head; hell, he was jealous of his own bloody wolf. Looking out across the manicured lawns, he admitted something that he had never told another person, "I haven't bonded with my wolf, Philip; and yet when she's near me I can feel him straining against the leash to get to her."

When Philip didn't say anything, Duncan turned his head and saw that his brother was staring at him with his jaw hanging to his chest, his eyes wide in astonishment. "How is that even possible, Duncan?"

"I don't know," he shook his head as he thought about Lexi's effect on him and on the wolf. "He wants her as badly as I do…."

"Not that, you idiot,' Philip growled, his gray eyes glowing with the wolf that was inside. "How can you be the Alpha of the Prentiss clan, the Alpha prime of ours, and yet you haven't bonded with your wolf?!"

"No, I haven't," Duncan said through clenched teeth, grateful that the veranda was empty. "You may want to keep your voice down, Philip; I don't think the country is ready to have a wolf for their next president."

"But you run with the wolves on the nights of the full moon," Philip blurted, still stuck on Duncan's admission, disregarding the fact that they were in a public place, albeit one completely void of patrons other than themselves. "You rut in your wolf form."

"And afterwards I regain control," Duncan said calmly. "It is a bargain we have, he and I. But that is not the point, he's struggling to break free and I cannot allow that."

"I think you're problems are much bigger than that," Philip shook his head in confusion. "You talk to him, you transform into him; how can you not be bonded?"

Duncan sighed, knowing he just didn't have time to explain his choices to his brother, or how he was able to be the Alpha when, technically, he shouldn't be. It wasn't his fault that he was powerful enough to control not one but two clans, at least when his father needed to get away, without being bonded with his wolf. Glancing at his watch, he stood up, "Look, I've got to go; I'm meeting Ashley for dinner and…."

"I thought you said she wasn't your girlfriend."

"She's not; it's something to do with the pack." Throwing some cash down on the table, he faced his brother; "I'd appreciate it if you didn't mention this conversation to anyone; it could make things… problematic."

"Of course not," Philip said quickly as he came to his feet. Holding out his hand, "You're my brother."

Duncan accepted the hand and the two men shook. When he met his brother's eyes, he saw sympathy and concern; there was no condemnation and he appreciated that more than Philip could ever possibly know. "Thank you."

"Take care, little brother," Philip said softly, concern underlying the amusement. "You wouldn't want your empire taken down by a mere human."

Duncan smiled slightly, knowing that he was going to have to read Lexi's work since her e-mails had proven to be vastly entertaining, making him chuckle when he should have been serious. He had been putting it off because he knew he couldn't afford to see Lexi's depths; she was already creating havoc in his life and it was tearing him up inside. Any more havoc was damn near going to destroy the hold he had over the wolf and if that happened.... He wasn't sure what would happen if the wolf got free.

Let's find out, shall we, Duncan?

*****

At an upscale restaurant that evening, Lexi sat with Cole, across the table from Ashley and Dima, who were so madly in love – at least deeply in lust – it was absurd. Dima and Cole were wearing tight, black leather pants; Dima in a white t-shirt that stretched across his broad shoulders, delineating his muscled chest, and Cole in some sort of artsy-fartsy poet's shirt. He still looked entirely too-masculine, despite the ruffles. Of course, with the front gaping open, the laces loosely tied, he resembled a model on the front of a romance novel.

Ashley was also sporting a pair of leather pants, pairing them with a cropped t-shirt that showcased her flat stomach and intricate tattoo on her lower back. Her red hair was loose and her makeup minimal but she glowed. Rounding out the group, Lexi wore an almost-Renaissance get-up: a flowing, white shirt beneath a tight, low-cut bodice of black brocade that pushed her breasts up. Of course, she had on the requisite leather pants as well, with stiletto boots. Her elaborate wig was black, the hair piled on her head in braids and curls, almost haphazard in manner, with a few more braids woven throughout; it was very gothic. Any other quartet would have looked ridiculous; together they looked purely amazing.

"I just want to thank you for coming with us this evening," Ashley gushed, leaning into Dima's embrace as her brilliant smile lit the room. "I have been so nervous about this and having the two of you here with us has calmed my nerves so much."

"Of course," Lexi said with a smile, finding Ashley's enthusiasm contagious despite her confusion over Duncan. Despite her attempts at engaging him with her e-mails, his responses invariably were very polite and distant; he wasn't biting at any of the lures she was sending out. But whenever she happened to see him at the office he would be watching her with the silver predator eyes of his, devouring her from across the room. Once she made the mistake of turning towards him; he had disappeared faster than ice in the desert and she had chuckled at that.

Glancing at the couple across from her, she couldn't help but smile; they looked so happy. It was strange to see Dima completely head over heels for a girl but it was good; he deserved all of the happiness in the world. Lexi was just a little concerned that perhaps she had held him back all of these years since he didn't get serious with Ashley until after she kissed him good-bye. And while it was a good thing that he was moving on with his life, she knew she was going to miss their time together. Of course, she was moving on with her life, as well; she just wasn't sure in which direction she was moving.

She glanced at Cole out of the corner of her eyes and wondered if he had been held back, too. Neither of them acted like they hated her; in fact, they didn't act any differently towards her at all. They hugged her and kissed her with abandon, continued to eat breakfast with her, and generally escorted her wherever she wished to go; then why did she feel different?

"So," Ashley's voice interrupted her contemplations and Lexi smiled as Ashley leaned closer, her eyes sparkling with humor and curiosity. "Now that you've finally done it, do you mind me asking if Duncan was everything you'd hoped he'd be?"

Both Cole and Dima stilled, staring at her with volatile expressions. Cole's voice was deadly even as he turned to her and asked, "Would you care to explain to me what she means?"

"Oops," Ashley giggled, her face bright red, making her red all over. She also happened to be one of the lucky few who looked really good all in red. "Was I not supposed to say anything?"

"I wasn't keeping it a secret," Lexi protested, even though it was obvious that she had been. With a negligent shrug, she grinned at her roommates, "It simply happened and now I've moved on; we've both moved on."

"Lexi," Dima's voice was low in warning. "Why didn't you tell us?"

"Because we have all been so busy this past week," she finally said, making up an excuse on the fly. "When has there been time?"

"At any point in the morning when I've driven you to work?" Cole suggested.

"In the evenings when I come home from the club for a few hours to have dinner and gear up for the night?" Dima added, his molars grinding together as he stared at her.

"Oops," she grinned sheepishly, hoping to diffuse the tension, knowing that they would find some time in the near future to sit her down and have a long, long conversation. "If it makes you feel any better it was only the one time. He has been avoiding me ever since."

Ashley's brows pulled together into a frown, "That doesn't sound like the Duncan I know; he doesn't sleep around and he doesn't avoid anything."

"Let's just drop it," Lexi said, her cheeks hurting from the blinding smile she pasted onto her face. "Why don't you tell us who we're meeting?"

Dima flushed as Ashley's eyes widened, as she looked between Dima and Lexi. "I though you knew; Dima was supposed to tell you."

"I thought it would be a nice surprise," he muttered. "I didn't know about the other thing or I wouldn't have done it."

Lexi's stomach twisted in on itself, knowing the answer but needing to hear it from Ashley. "Who are we meeting?"

"Duncan Tremain," she answered softly, sympathy in her pretty blue eyes.

Lexi stood up abruptly, "I've got to go."

Cole chuckled as he stood up at a more leisurely pace, "It seems Duncan isn't the only one doing the avoidance thing. Come on, Lexi, I'll take you home."

Bending, she gave both Ashley and Dima a hug goodbye at the same time, not bothering to ask why they needed to meet Duncan in the first place. "Have a lovely night, you two; I am so sorry I can't stay."

*****

Duncan walked into the restaurant at eight o'clock, as per Ashley's request as a member of his pack. He wasn't positive what she wanted but he was fairly certain it had something to do with the bartender she had been banging for the last couple of weeks. The bartender who was Lexi's best friend and roommate. The bartender Lexi had probably slept with at some point in her life. He was going to kill the bartender.

He came to an abrupt stop when he saw who was sitting with Ashley at their table. Lexi. Taking a step to the side, he hid behind a column, just to observe her, to see if this attraction worked when she wasn't looking at him. As he looked at her, his muscles tightened and his blood burned within. It took less than half a second to realize that it was just as powerful. God, he'd never get enough of her; a hundred lifetimes wouldn't be enough.

Almost as if sensing him, Lexi's head lifted and a slight frown crinkled her precious forehead as she looked around. He held his breath as her gaze slowly moved towards him, as if she could see him behind the stone column where he was hiding. But he wasn't hiding; he just wanted to watch her, perhaps take a moment to get his body under some semblance of control. Of course, control was in excessively short supply whenever Lexi Darling was around.

Just as he was about to step out from behind the pillar, Lexi and one of her… friends - the artist - stood up and the control Duncan managed to achieve vanished. Her legs were encased in supple leather, her breasts were spilling over the top of some sort of tight vest; her wig was artistically arranged, emphasizing her uniqueness and her femininity. God, she was glorious!

She bent forward to give Ashley a hug and her ass – good God her heart-shaped ass! was accentuated by the stretch of black leather. He had to manually adjust to ease the tension of his erection against his too-tight pants. There was no way in Hell he was going to let Lexi know the effect she had on him and if that meant he stayed behind the pillar until she was gone so be it.

It was a fine line between cowardice and self-preservation, one Duncan Tremain never had to tread before. Damn. Lexi Darling was twisting him up inside and there was nothing he could do – wanted to do – to stop it.

As the pair passed his hiding spot she turned her head and their eyes met. Her lips parted in surprise, even as her eyes darkened in awareness. Powerless to resist, they each took a step towards one another. Her companion wrapped his hand around her upper arm, stopping both of them. Duncan watched as she looked up at the artist and they spoke without words.

Her body tensed and she turned away from where he stood and he knew that she was not going to come back to him. Disappointment roared through his blood – she was his, damn it! But then she looked back at him and he could see the longing in her gorgeous hazel-green eyes, as well as the resignation. On a sigh, she turned and let her keeper lead her out of the restaurant.

Duncan watched her go, momentarily forgetting why he was in the restaurant and not going after her. But then it all came back and he inwardly winced. He had to deal with Ashley and her lover; a man who had known Lexi intimately. Straightening his jacket, he took a breath and joined her at the table, sitting in the seat just evacuated by Lexi in her tight leather pants.

"Ashley," he smiled. God, he could still smell Lexi, the subtle scent that was pure seduction; pure Lexi. Having to force himself to not get lost in the elusive scent, he asked, "How are you tonight?"

"Anxious," she murmured, offering him a wry smile as she twined her fingers with the blond man sitting next to her. "I want to introduce someone to you."

"The bartended from *Skin*," Duncan ground out, feeling an animalistic rage that the man existed. Surprisingly, his wolf was unnaturally quiet.

"Lexi's obsession," the man bit out with just as much venom.

After a moment of uncomfortable silence as the two men sized each other up, Ashley smiled brilliantly, "Duncan, I'd like to formally introduce you to Dima, who has not slept with Lexi by the way. Dima, this is my…."

Ashley's words trailed off and she looked to him for help. Knowing that Dima hadn't slept with Lexi eased Duncan's tension and he decided the bartender could live. As long as he kept his hands off Lexi. "Advisor."

"Friend," Ashley corrected with a warm smile. "Duncan, I would formerly like to ask for permission to discuss our nature with Dima."

"Do you think it wise?" Duncan asked, watching Dima's bewildered expression as the man glanced back and forth between the two wolves.

Ashley looked at Dima with her heart in her eyes and smiled even more brilliantly than before, "I do."

Duncan bowed his head, "Then you have my permission; you may welcome him to our community."

"What the fuck?" Dima growled, pushing out of his seat and looking at Duncan with anger. "Who died and made you the fucking king?"

"Ashley?" Duncan arched his eyebrow as he continued staring dispassionately at Dima.

Ashley put a restraining hand on Dima and pulled him effortlessly back to his seat. At his dumbfounded realization that she had so easily handled him, she said softly, "Duncan is the Alpha of my pack, well, the son of the Alpha, Dima. I needed his permission to tell you what I am if we are to get serious."

The color drained from the man's face and Duncan almost felt sorry for him. Standing up, he exchanged a glance with Ashley and then left the bar, needing to run. Seeing Lexi, being so close to her when it had been almost a week since he had ravaged her, was destroying even the illusion of self-control. Loosening his tie as he headed into a dark alley, he glanced around to see if anyone was looking.

Behave yourself, he warned.

As you wish, my most noble and stoic lord.

The wolf didn't wait for Duncan to strip before he changed form, tearing the expensive suit to shreds as bones shifted and muscles realigned themselves. Relishing the night air against his muzzle, the feel of his legs as they moved in perfect harmony, the wolf ran. It was good to be a wolf.

Chapter 13 (Friday)

Having successfully avoided Duncan for almost two weeks, except that little blink of an eye instant at the restaurant the week before, Lexi was appreciating the man's mind even more from dealing with him through e-mails, text messages, and memos. At first, his emails had been very business-like, very professional but sometime after Saturday he flirted back and the texts turned into the electronic version of their verbal banter, digital foreplay. The last exchange still made her chuckle.

Are you out of the hotel yet?

Yes; I moved into my house a few days ago but I will always have fond memories of the room where I almost had you the first time.

Aw, Duncan; you could have had me if you had only woken me up.

But you looked so peaceful sleeping there.

You just wanted to horde all of the little chocolate that the housekeeping staff leaves on the guests' pillows.

You know me so well. I miss those little personal touches.

If you give me the key to your house I'll leave a little something on your pillow every morning. You won't even have to unwrap me.

There was a long wait before he replied late Thursday afternoon. **You're killing me here, Lexi. Since I was out of the office today; what crazy outfit am I missing?**

She had described the outfit in loving detail, from the crimson-colored wig to the fuchsia colored body suit, right down to the five inch heels. **I was a sight to behold.**

You're always a sight to behold. What color are your panties?

What panties?

You've officially killed me; good night, Lexi. I'll see you tomorrow.

Good night, Duncan.

Knowing that today she was going to see him, she wore a dress in the form of a tailored blouse, lengthened almost to her knees. It flared out slightly at her waist, buttoning all the way down the front. Her wig was chin-length and baby blond, and her shoes were four-inch strappy things that accentuated her calf muscles. Of course, dressing properly negated getting to work on time, despite Cole's efforts of breaking inner-city speed records.

Wobbling only a bit on the heels as she rushed through the atrium to the elevator bay, she saw her possible salvation just ahead: an elevator with doors just shutting. If she caught this one, she'd barely be late at all. It was strangely reminiscent of the first day Duncan started there. "Hold the elevator, please!"

A hand shot out, a hand she'd recognize from anywhere. As the doors slid open, she saw Duncan standing there looking sexy as hell in his black suit, his legs spread in self-assured, alpha-male dominance. Her heart tripped over itself to get to him, though her rationale brain said it would be a bad idea to just run and jump into his arms. Twelve days, dozens of e-mails and texts, and she was crazily infatuated with him.

So she smiled radiantly, put a little extra swing in her step and walked towards him, watching how his eyes never wavered from hers. How they darkened, even though he didn't look at her body in its form-fitting dress. When she stepped into the elevator, she realized it was probably a good thing she didn't fling herself at him; there were three, no four, other riders.

Smiling at the people she just noticed, she turned and took her place next to Duncan, her heart racing in her chest, her blood boiling through her veins. Her soul sighed in relief at once again being near him, as if she was finally home. "Mr. Tremain."

"Miss Darling," he said, his voice low and so inadvertently seductive, her knees trembled. God, just imagine if he tried to seduce her!

Unintentionally, or perhaps slightly intentionally, she brushed an arm against his and even that minor contact shot tingles through her. He was staring straight ahead and she thought he was ignoring her but then his fingers brushed against hers and she smiled. Her body was vibrating with excitement, with being near him again. He was a drug and she was finally getting some after a too-long absence. With a covert glance, she saw that his erection was straining against the front of his pants and her smile widened.

"Not a word, Miss Darling," he whispered darkly, softly, so only she could hear it over the annoying music.

She looked up and saw the laughter in his silver eyes, "I wouldn't dream of it. Well, actually, I would and I have. But I won't say anything."

The familiar low growl rumbled from the back of his throat and it just made her burn hotter. Lowering her lashes, she whispered, "That is so sexy."

"Miss Darling," he warned again.

As the elevator passed each floor, the other passengers departed and Lexi's skin began to hum even louder with excitement. Finally, the final intruder, er passenger, got off a floor before Lexi's and Duncan's. Turning her head, she looked up at him and every cell in her body throbbed; his look was dark and heated and full of promise. She fell backwards, weakened by all of the latent sensual promises coming from him. Her back hit the wall and she stopped, unable and unwilling to go any further.

"Lexi," he rasped, his heated silver eyes boring into her, and she knew what he was asking.

"Yes," she whispered, drowning in silver flames.

The corner of his mouth curved upwards in a seductive smile as he reached his hand out and pushed the stop button between floors. He kept moving until he stood directly in front of her and she smiled up at him, "Hey, there."

"Hey," he murmured.

"I've missed you," she admitted breathlessly.

"I've missed you, too," he whispered, bending his head and softly kissing her mouth. His hands went to her waist, his fingers curling into her flesh. He stopped kissing her, swallowing thickly as he rested his forehead against hers, "If we do this there has to be some rules."

She tried not to but a hearty laugh came out, making Duncan smile reluctantly as well. "You and your damned rules, Duncan. Okay, lay them on me."

"One, I cannot marry your."

"I'm not looking for marriage."

"Two, this cannot interfere with work."

"Only if you can keep your hands to yourself when we're at the office."

"And finally, it can only last a few days; a week at most."

"Why?" she asked, concentrating on unbuttoning his shirt to get to all of that glorious skin.

His fingers played with the ends of her wig as he admitted, "I don't want to get addicted to you and I don't want to fall in love with you. Or you with me."

"Too late," she breathed, standing up on her toes and running her tongue along his neck, tasting the familiar and wonderful midnight woodsy taste of Duncan. "I'm already addicted."

"Lexi," he breathed, sealing his lips over hers, filling her mouth with his tongue.

She whimpered softly in pleasure of once again feeling his mouth on hers. Grabbing his shirt, she pulled it from his pants and spread it open, slipping her hands against his stomach to feel the heat of his skin, his masculine chest.

A hum of appreciation came from the back of her throat as she leaned forward and ran her tongue over his hard nipple. He tasted of wildness and midnight runs, of warrior, of Duncan. Scraping her teeth over the pebbled flesh, she ran her fingers over his muscled stomach, inundating her senses with the taste, the smell, the touch of Duncan. If only she could crawl into his skin and live inside of him.

"Don't move," he whispered against her ear, his breath hot against her skin.

She stood still as he groaned, fisting his hands briefly before he quickly unbuttoned her dress. His hands trembled slightly as he pealed the shirt-dress open, revealing her body. His breath caught in his throat as his eyes roamed over her curves: breasts encased in gold lace, her hips in teeny, tiny gold bikinis. And garters that held up silk hose on long, slender legs bound in mile-high slave sandals. "I wore them for you."

"I appreciate it," he growled, falling to his knees in front of her, pressing his face against her sex, breathing deeply. Holding her hip, he pressed a reverent kiss on the damp curls before looking up at her and spoke in a gravelly voice, "You don't know what you do to me, Lexi."

Her entire body shivered from the heat she saw in his eyes, the heat of his breath against her skin, and her heart skipped a beat or two in her chest. She ran her fingers along his hair line, cupping his jaw in her hand. "It's what you do to me."

He made a gruff sound as he untied the delicate strings holding the scraps of her panties together. Tucking the lacy bit into his pocket, he ran his hand up her leg, hooking her knee over his shoulder, opening her to his perusal. Then he buried his face between her thighs, breathing deeply and nuzzling her sex. She moaned at the first swipe of his tongue; her fingers twisted in his silky black hair. Her legs felt like rubber and without his strong hands holding her up, she would have melted. As it was, she only knew bliss from the mouth of her lover.

He suckled her clit into his mouth, gently biting it before soothing the slight pain with his tongue. Two, thick fingers were pushed into her sex and she swore she could see stars dancing around Duncan's head. Over and over he tortured her until pleasure welled up and exploded outwards and her fingers convulsed in his hair as she came.

She was desperate to feel him in her and, dropping her leg to the ground, urged him to his feet. In a move that would have taken years to perfect, he stood, releasing his erection and pushing his pants down his thighs. At the last moment, he slipped on a condom. Grabbing her hips, he thrust into her, growling as he sank into her swollen and wet sex.

Lexi's back arched as Duncan filled her, re-igniting the fading embers of the orgasm he just gave her. Crying out, she wrapped her arms around his neck, her legs around his hips. His head was pressed against her throat as he thrust into her, his breathing ragged and harsh and wonderful.

Over and over, for mindless eternities, he pumped in and out, keeping her on the razor's edge of orgasm until he pushed her over. She held him even tighter as his body stiffened and he grunted his release. Kissing his damp temple, she let her love wash over him as they stood there panting in the after math.

"You drive me insane, woman," he growled, gently easing his body from hers. He frowned when he removed the condom, not sure where to put it. With a grimace, he held it in his hand, needing to dispose of it discreetly.

Looking up at him, she cupped his face, feeling the smooth plane of his closely-shaved jaw. "You…."

The elevator lurched and they jumped apart at the same moment, hastily pulling themselves together before the elevator doors opened and they were discovered. Lexi looked around the small, enclosed space, nearing panic. "Where are my panties?"

Looking around, Duncan shrugged his broad shoulders, "I don't see them."

She frowned as she fastened the last button of her dress. Patting her wig, she made a face, half-smile half-grimace. “I seem to lose my panties around you.”

“I wish you’d lose the wigs,” he murmured, looking at the short, blond bob framing her beautiful face. He finished tucking his shirt in, looking as if he didn’t just have the most mind-blowing sex of the century. Why that should perturb Lexi, she didn’t know. While he looked just as put together as ever, she was pretty sure everyone was going to be able to tell she just had some pretty fantastic sex. All they would have to do was take one look at her and they would know.

Cocking her head to the side, she asked, “You don’t like my wigs?”

"I prefer you." He reached out and brushed his fingertips along her jaw, but before he could say more, the doors opened and they returned to the real world. Clearing his throat, he stepped back and held out his arm for her to precede him, “After you, Miss Darling.”

Slightly disconcerted, she got out of the elevator before him. After a few steps, she turned around to ask him something, maybe to just look at him, but he was already walking away, his back towards her, one hand in his pocket. His other hand was in a tight fist. And she smiled.

She was going to have to make a quick stop at the bathroom before heading to her office; she smelled like sex and Duncan and she wanted to adjust her clothes, just to make sure she didn’t look completely ravaged.

*****

Duncan paced back and forth in his office, feeling like a caged wolf. He should have followed his first instinct and not read her work but that wouldn’t have been fair to her. After her first e-mail, which had had him laughing in spite of himself, he knew she had a gift for bringing her stories to vibrant, vivid life.. He had no choice but to read everything she wrote, which meant finding all of the back issues of his new magazine.

Now, having read all of her columns, including the latest one featuring her new photo and write up of Cole Christian’s photography, he was impressed. Very impressed. It was not what he expected – *she* was not what he expected. Her writing was informative but didn't take itself too seriously, as if the events everyone felt were crucial were, in fact, secondary to the art of truly living. They even shared many of the same values, though they expressed them differently; she took a much more festive approach to life. He found himself laughing out loud on several occasions, imagining Lexi so clearly, so perfectly, in her crazy outfits existing out loud, embracing life, freedom, joy and occasionally sorrow.

Her stories had such depths and every now and then he got the feeling that Lexi was... lonely; that she loved deeply but was terrified of not being loved in return. But that was ridiculous; everyone loved her.

Everyone.

Over the course of twelve days, she managed to burrow her way into his head and she was all he could think about. She was addictive and he found that intermittent e-mails or texts, or even her full length columns, were not enough. He wanted the girl and last night when things had gotten heated during their text exchange he knew that he was going to be hunting her down as soon as he got to the office. Of course Lexi managed to even turn those tables on him, stepping onto his elevator and smelling like Lexi and spring time and desire.

He had planned on keeping a professional detachment from her until they had a more private setting but then she bumped up against him on the elevator and he found his fingers tangling with hers.... He didn't even last the morning of being in her presence. She intrigued him like nothing had ever done before, and having made love to her – twice – he was definitely infatuated. His wolf was infatuated. It would have been better had he been able to avoid her like he had been doing since he almost ran into her at the restaurant.

How could he let her continue working at the magazine when she so completely and utterly destroyed his self-control? But how could he let her go? Granted, after he wrapped up what he was doing, which was learning the ins and outs of the magazine to run it more efficiently, he wasn't planning on working full time out of the *lavish* offices. He had plenty of places he could run his empire. But knowing that Lexi would be here, in this building, he wouldn't be able to keep himself away.

His wolf wouldn't let him stay away and that was worrisome; the beast was straining even harder against the constraints they had agreed upon all of those years ago. *Are you still afraid of losing yourself, fearless one?*

Duncan's hands squeezed into fists as his wolf whispered in his head. *I'm afraid of being trapped in my own body, watching as you destroy the world and not being able to do anything to stop you.*

Give me the girl and you can have the world.

Duncan laughed without humor, falling back into his chair and staring at the blank monitor, seeing his silver eyes glowing. The wolf was gaining strength; Duncan could feel the chains breaking and he knew that there would come a time he was going to have to confront the beast. Again. Closing his eyes, he tried to shut out the sound of the wolf's voice, but the whispered words only grew louder.

With her I wouldn't need to see the world burn to feel alive. Give me the girl.

She's not mine to give or take.

Then let me have a taste, the wolf demanded relentlessly. *Give me a nibble and I will be your devoted servant once more.*

No; she's mine until the end.

At least I would have shared, the wolf complained with a huff. *But I'll let you have your way for now because it is only a matter of time before you bond with me and the girl will be ours.*

Duncan sighed wearily, pressing his fingers into his eyes and rubbing until the black dots turned white. If he allowed the wolf to go free, if he bonded with it, he could claim Lexi and not give a damn that he might hurt her in the end. As painful as he knew it would be to lose her, to destroy her, he would take her for the simple fact that he wanted her. As a wolf, he wouldn't worry about the consequences, the fall out; he would have Lexi and that would be all that mattered.

Until she was lying on the ground in searing agony, crying red tears and sweating red blood, because he bit her. God, he couldn't bear that; he would control the wolf for a few weeks more. After Lexi was safe and far, far away from him and the wolf, he would deal with the beast head on,

He would continue to exist on the line, keeping Lexi safe as he devoured her whole.

*****

The rest of the day was spent putting out fires and dealing with the everyday business of running his small kingdom. Even though he was able to get his work done, his thoughts were always occupied by Lexi; the way her mind worked, how she fought with him, how she melted into him; the clothes she wore, the way she looked without the clothes she wore. Looking at his watch he realized that it was almost five; almost time to call it a week.

He had to see her, now, before she left for the weekend. Without giving himself time to change his mind, not that he would, he left the relative safety of his office. He barely paid attention to any of the other writers and what not as he made his way through the maze to her office, so intent he was on getting to her. Damn it, he was putting his finger on the knot while she tied the bow. And instead of being annoyed about it, he found himself hoping the bow was straight.

Pushing the door open, prepared for just about anything, he wasn't prepared for what he saw. Her back was towards him as she leaned over her desk, her dress rising up the back of her thighs threatening to reveal her lack of panties. His heart thudded painfully in his chest and his body blazed with lust. She was tapping her foot, and he realized that she was listening to music through head phones.

She was unaware of his presence.

Carefully closing the door so it didn't slam shut and alert her to his presence, he slowly turned the lock to keep everyone out. Between holding his breath and losing his blood as it rushed to his penis, he was feeling slightly faint. And very horny. He knew what was beneath that dress – or what wasn't beneath it – and he wanted it.

As he moved closer to her, he opened his pants, releasing his erection. Even though he took her in the elevator just a few hours before, his penis was dark plum red, just as desperate as the rest of his body to be in her. He ran his fist along the length and had to swallow a groan as he grabbed a condom from his packet and tore it open, quickly suiting up. How he longed to feel her flesh to flesh.

Unable to resist, he pressed his erection against the crevice of her butt as his hands gripped her thighs. She jumped, grabbing the headphones and yanking them off her head. He held her in place as she fought to turn around, whispering in her ear, "Relax, it's me."

Her entire body sighed as she relaxed into him, "Duncan; you scared me."

"I'm sorry," he murmured, running his tongue along her neck and smiling when she mewed in pleasure. His hands slid around her legs until they touched her most intimate flesh and he was rewarded with another mew. "I couldn't resist."

Lexi turned her head, seeking his mouth as he slid a finger into the quickly swelling folds of her sex. When he brushed a particularly sensitive spot, her back arched, pushing her against his hand and she moaned. He broke the kiss, keeping his lips next to her ear and he whispered, "You're already wet."

"I haven't stopped thinking about you all day," she admitted guilelessly, not caring that she was handing him her heart and her secrets. He pumped a finger into her wet depths and she gasped, closing her eyes in pleasure. "I had to listen to my music to concentrate."

"Did it work?" he asked, rubbing his erection against her, feelings so much more exquisite since it was Lexi's body he was dry humping.

"N…no," her breath caught as his fingers moved in her. Her head dropped forward and her breathing was ragged, "I've been walking around all day without my panties on and every draft of air against my bare skin made me think about you, about the elevator."

He closed his eyes and took a long breath, trying to savor the pleasurable torment of waiting just a little bit longer. It didn't work. On a ragged groan, he nudged her legs apart and pressed the tip of his erection against the entrance to her body. "Are you ready for me?"

"More than," she breathed, bending forward as he moved over her and into her, surrounding her with his heat, his presence. "Oh, God."

Her muscles clenched around him; blistering, feminine heat. Lexi. Resting his cheek against her back, he slowly pumped his hips, every nerve in his penis buzzing, so close to the edge. "I don't think I can last very long."

She didn't answer in words. Instead little mewls of bliss came from her throat, her soul. Her head fell forward even further as her elbows collapsed, giving Duncan an even deeper, more penetrating access. He grabbed her hips, holding her as he pounded into her, pushing her to the edge; driving himself insane.

"Duncan!" she cried out and he was finished. His seed pulsed through his cock, shredding the last of his control. She was addictive and he feared he was addicted.

He collapsed against her, their breathing coming fast and hard – and in unison. Pressing a kiss to the middle of her back, he smiled, "I want you to come home with me."

Where the hell did that idea come from? Duncan had no idea. Still, he didn't want to take the words back; he wanted her in his huge bed. He wanted to make love to her with absolutely no clothes on. He wanted to spend days with her, completely naked, to see her in the morning, to have her in his house. Pressing a kiss to her temple, he murmured, "I want you to spend the weekend with me."

"Wouldn't that be breaking your rules?" Lexi teased, feeling relaxed and energized all at the same time. She wiggled her bottom a bit and he had to bite back a moan.

"Not at all," he said gruffly, pushing himself up slightly and running his palm down her spine. She arched her back and his penis leapt back to life. He eased out of her hot body before he could take her again; before his seed spilled over the edges and impregnated her. "We have a limited amount of time to be together and I plan on making the most of it. Are you in?"

She rolled over and looked up at him with those gold-green eyes sparkling,

"Oh, yeah. I'm definitely in."

"This is insanity," he groaned, sensation shooting through his groin as he pulled his pants together. "I just had you and I want you again. I don't think I'll ever get enough of you."

Drawing her hand over her face, she let out a little hum as she smiled lazily, "This weekend we'll have to make love without our clothes on, at least once."

He chuckled gruffly, her words mirroring his thoughts almost perfectly. "I'm not sure I'm going to let you get dressed at all once I have your clothes off; at least not until we have to return to the real world. I think I would kill anyone who saw you naked."

She chuckled, her eyes dancing with laughter, "Then you'll have to kill everyone who has seen my photos."

"Those were taken before I met you," he growled, sliding a hand up her stomach and covering her breast. Her breath hitched in her throat as she held his gaze, "If necessary I will buy every image that exists and send out a team of psychics to erase the memories of any who had the pleasure of seeing them."

Her laugh was warm and wonderful and he realized he would say or do anything to hear her laugh. "Maybe it wouldn't be so bad if you had Cole take your pictures, too. But then I think I would have to gouge the eyes out of any woman who dared look at them."

He chuckled, "I can't wait to get you back to my house and get you naked."

"I'm hoping you're planning on joining me in the no-clothes option this weekend," she purred, standing up and smoothing her palms over her dress, pushing the skirt back down over her naked bottom.

"I'll give the staff the weekend off," he smiled. "So we will have privacy."

"Who will feed us?" she asked, lowering her lashes as she ran her hands over his shoulders, sending reawakened desire coursing through his body. Coyly, she looked back up to him as she rested her chin against his chest. "Or are we not going to worry about food?"

His eyes closed and he groaned. "I'll take care of it. Trust me."

"I do," she murmured solemnly, holding his gaze.

Duncan's heart stilled in his chest at the trust she placed in him, so honest and unfettered. Who was this girl? Clearing his throat, holding her hips in his hands, he asked, "Do you want to follow me in your car?"

"I don't have a car," she admitted. "I usually catch a ride with Dima or Cole or I take the bus or a cab."

"You don't drive?" he sounded incredulous.

She laughed, "I drive, I just prefer not to in the morning. I mean, have you ever tried driving in four inch stilettos? It's not exactly easy, especially when you're barely awake."

"So, we take my car?" he asked, still holding her.

"Unless you want to give me your address and have me call a cab," she smiled, her eyes sparkling with laughter. "Or I could call Dima or Cole and have one of them drop me off, sort of like an adult version of a slumber party."

"Lexi?"

"Yes, Duncan?" she grinned up at him.

"Shut up," he grinned back, lowering his head and kissing her fast and hard. Before the kiss could go any further, Duncan stepped back, and took a moment to catch his breath. "We'll take my car."

"Brilliant idea," she smiled.

Chapter 14 (Friday Night)

Lexi lay in Duncan's arms, their bodies still slick from their frenzied lovemaking upon getting to his house, located a half hour outside of the city limits on a huge wooded lot. She barely had time to register the magnificence of her surroundings before Duncan had his lips on her and he was leading her to a sitting room with a chaise. Then she was naked and writhing on the soft couch with Duncan between her thighs, furiously thrusting away. As soon as they exploded, he rolled over so that her boneless body was sprawled over his and he discarded the used condom.

She still had her wig on.

She idly drew circles on his chest, feeling out-of-breath and blissful. "Wow."

He grunted, his chest rumbling against her chest as he tightened his grip around her shoulders, pulling her even closer to his spent body. Kissing the top of her head he let out a wince, "I want to see you without the wigs, Lexi; I want to make love to *you*, damn it."

She chuckled as she reluctantly pushed herself away from his lovely, hard body and straddled his thighs. Taking a moment to appreciate his masculine beauty, she exhaled softly: his muscles gleamed in the low light and he smelled of sex. Reaching up, thrusting out her breasts, she removed the pins from her hair and then removed the wig. Scrubbing her hands through the strands of her hair as it fell limply down to the middle of her back, she shrugged her shoulders in apology, "My hair's a little flat from the wig."

He sat up, snaking one arm around her waist as he reached up with the other to run his fingers through the tangled mess. As he studied the boring brown hair his expression was reverential and his words appreciative as he whispered, "It's beautiful."

"Now I know you're lying because I know how my hair looks after it has been pinned up under a wig all day," she laughed. The amusement faded as he held her gaze, sincerity and desire making the silver shine.

His muscles flexed as he ran his hand over her scalp, his other hand up her spine. She was held immobile by the intensity of his expression as his eyes moved over her face, making her blood surge through her veins. His silver gaze caressed her and she swore that she could feel it in her soul. Her body trembled as he continued to consume her without words. "Duncan."

"You make me want to be stronger," he rasped, the silver of his eyes glowing as they met hers. "So I can have you and keep you safe."

Cupping his face in her hands, she shook her head and smiled softly, "You're a warrior, Duncan, always plotting your next conquest or preparing for battle. Let me be your strength when you're with me; let me be your port in the storm."

His eyes closed and he inhaled deeply as his other arm wrapped around her and he pulled her closer, resting his cheek against her breast. "You're a siren."

She stiffened at his words and her mouth felt like ash, "What do you mean?"

"You tempt me like no other," he whispered, kissing the skin over her heart, kissing a trail over her chest to her neck, where he feasted and made her lose her mind. "You're a goddess that offers cool water to a weary traveler; you're an angel that offers shelter in the wilderness."

His words brought tears to her eyes and as she closed them a tear managed to slip out. Resting her cheek against the cool black silk of his hair, she whispered, "You're not supposed to make me fall in love with you, Duncan. It's only temporary, remember?"

"I think it will be all right to fall in love a little bit," he rasped, his breath hot against the damp skin of her throat. "For a little while."

Pushing herself up, not comfortable with the emotional intimacy that felt too close to love, she kissed him lightly on the lips and stared deeply into his wonderful silver eyes. Brushing her lips over his cheeks, feeling the stubble of new growth, as his hands moved over her naked body, caressing her waist, her hips, she continued kissing him. Needing to establish some emotional distance from what she was feeling, she looked at him through lowered lashes and purred, "Duncan, I burn for you; I want to see you lose control completely."

"I'm not an animal without control," he eyes flashed as his lips pressed together in a thin line. Pushing her hair away from her face, he smiled reluctantly at her sultry expression, "Except, perhaps, around you."

"I'm an animal around you, Duncan," she hummed, pushing him backwards and down onto the chaise. Running her foot along his calf, enjoying the feel of his crisp hairs against her toes, she dug her fingers into the hard muscles of his chest and his eyes blazed with lust. His body was so solid beneath hers, reinforcing her impression of him being a warrior in a past life; in this life. But he didn't smell of sweat and horses; he usually smelled of clean male. Now, well now he smelled of sex and she didn't want to think, only feel. "A horny beast."

That got a reluctant smile from him and her breath caught in her throat at how handsome he was when he smiled. There was simply nothing better than a naked, smiling Duncan. His breath hitched in his throat as she pressed her hot and wet sex against his hardening cock. "Lexi."

Her smile was sultry and playful all at once, "Am I to be alone in this madness, then?"

"Hell, no," he breathed, cradling her face in his hands and kissing her as he rolled her beneath him, until her soft body was covered by his much harder one. He was so dominant, always wanting to be in control. One of these times she was going to be in control. When she put her hand over the lips that were about to kiss her, frustration and bewilderment colored his eyes and he asked, "What is it?"

She was quiet, contemplative, for a long moment, chewing on her lower lip as she deliberated back and forth in her head. Finally, she looked at him from beneath her long lashes, feeling a little foolish. "I'm clean and I was wondering if maybe you'd want to do it without a condom?"

"I've never made love without a condom," he murmured, almost to himself. Wiping his hand over his face, he put the finger of his other hand beneath her chin tilted her head up. Holding her eyes, he rasped, "Are you sure?"

"I'm on the Pill," she said, smiling slightly with amusement.

Enchanted by that smile, he smiled, "What is it?"

"I went to the gynecologist the afternoon after that first meeting, when I found out you were going to be my new boss," she laughed softly, turning her head and kissing his palm, leaving out the part about being a virgin until she met him. "I wanted to be prepared because I knew we would end up here; I just want you to know that I'm clean."

His smile widened and her heart lurched in her chest. "As am I,"

"So… yes?" she asked hopefully, as if there was any doubt as to what his answer would be. She caught her lower lip between her teeth and looked at him….

"Hell yes," he rumbled, bending his head and capturing her lips in an explosive kiss. He entered her slowly, reverently, as she wrapped her legs around his waist. Feeling her flesh embrace his cock without any barriers was Heaven. Being with Duncan was Heaven.

Even if it was only temporary.

*****

Lexi blinked her eyes open and found herself staring into the most beautiful silver eyes above a black muzzle that was filled with lots and lots of sharp, white fangs. She blinked again and the dog didn't disappear. And she realized her fingers were curled into the thick fur, making her smile; she hadn't known Duncan had a dog, and such a lovely one, too. "Hey, there, handsome; where did you come from?"

In response, the dog licked her nose, making her cringe and laugh in equal measures. Wrapping her arms around the dog's thick neck, she briefly wondered where Duncan had wandered off to but she was already falling back to sleep. With a big yawn, she rubbed her face against the warm fur, "I like you, too. But I'm not going to give you a tongue bath."

With another wide yawn, she snuggled further against the dog, feeling its slick tongue against her neck as he licked her. She fell asleep with a smile on her face, feeling strangely safe with the massive black dog.

*****

Lexi woke up when the sun hit her eyes. Blinking, she looked over and saw Duncan's big, hard body sprawled across the bed. Rolling over, she plastered her body against his, resting her cheek against his shoulder blades and smiling with contentment.

"Hmm, Lexi blanket; perfect," Duncan's sleep gravelly voice murmured as he grabbed her arm and pulled her over his body until she was lying in front of him.

She giggled as she curled up against his chest and tangled her fingers in the dark hair that grew there. "You didn't tell me you have a dog; what's his name?"

He peeled his eyelids apart and looked at her oddly, "What are you talking about?"

"Last night I woke up and there was a gigantic dog on the bed with me."

Letting his eyes drift back shut, he chuckled, "Sweetheart, I'm pretty sure you were dreaming; I don't have a dog, big or otherwise."

"But I was sure…."

His arm slid around her waist and pulled her harder against his body as he kissed her forehead with his eyes still closed, "It was just a dream."

Relaxing, she rubbed her face against his chest and smiled, "I suppose you're right. It's just strange, is all; I mean, he had your eyes."

"That's because I'm a wolf, Lexi," he said with such a deadpan voice that she jerked her head back and looked at him. As she continued to stare at him, the corners of his lips curved upwards in a sexy smile, "And I want to devour you whole, my pretty little vixen."

She laughed at his ridiculousness, loving this less-serious side of him as much as she adored his all-too-serious nature. "I have a red cloak."

He chuckled, tightening his hold in a hug, "But are you foolish enough to go traipsing through the woods to get to grandma's house?"

"If I knew you were lying in wait?" she tilted her head back and grinned at him. "Hell, yeah."

When the laughter slowly eased away, he kissed the top of her head, "I want to take you out, Lexi; and when I say I want to take you out I mean that I want to take *you* out, no wigs or crazy outfits, just you, just Lexi."

She smiled to herself, his words filling her with a warm glow. "Where do you plan on taking me?"

"There's this bar that some friends of mine run," he said, his voice surprisingly gruff for what he was saying. Clearing his throat, he added, "It's about an hour away but they brew their own beer and make the best cheeseburgers this side of paradise."

"It sounds wonderful," she murmured, pressing a light kiss against his chest, over his heart. She loved listening to the strong, steady rhythm; it made her feel cherished and safe. "But the only outfit I have has gone missing somewhere in this mammoth house of your and even if I could find it it is probably wrinkled beyond compare."

"You and my sister Jillian are about the same size," he murmured, his hand gently stroking her arm. "She has a closet-full of clothes here for emergencies."

Lexi giggled, "You've lived here only a couple of weeks and your sister already has a stash of clothes?"

"You don't know my sister," he grinned, his voice warm with affection.

In that moment, Lexi realized that she wanted to meet his sister; she wanted to meet all of his relatives; she wanted to learn everything there was to know about Duncan Tremain. And she knew that it was impossible while he insisted on keeping it brief and she held any Siren-sway over him. Resting her head once more against his chest, she sighed with contentment and a little bit of melancholy, "Are you sure we can't break your rule about having this be only temporary?"

"I have too many secrets and if I were to keep you I'd have to tell them to you," Duncan answered slowly. When she tilted her head back to look at him, he was observing her, waiting to see what her reaction would be. "They'd make you run the other way."

"You've mentioned secrets before, Duncan," she murmured, reaching up and running her fingers over his firm lips. "And I understand. I think we keep secrets from those we love, or hope to love, because we don't want to disappoint them or hurt them or risk losing their love. It's terrifying opening yourself up to ridicule, especially by those you love, isn't it? If you need to keep your secrets, I won't make you tell me."

"You humble me, Lexi," he breathed, placing a gentle kiss on her forehead. "Maybe someday, if I get it together, I will tell you and we can have forever."

"Maybe you won't want forever if I tell you some of my secrets," she grinned, needing to lighten the mood. Her heart was too engaged and she didn't want to think about it, about her feelings for this incredible man. She didn't even know if his feelings were real since she had hummed a few bars near the beginning of their acquaintance and all of his talk about love and forever actually hurt a little.

"What are your secrets, Lexi?" he asked with an amused grin.

Sitting up next to him, ignoring the way his eyes dipped to her naked breasts, ignoring the erection that was nudging her thigh, she grinned, "Well, I used to be kinda shy."

He reached up and cupped her cheek, brushing his thumb over her full lower lip, and she could see the disbelief in his eyes. "I find that hard to believe."

"No, it's true," she insisted, widening her eyes as if that would help make her point. "Before I moved in with Cole and Dima, I was a social misfit." She didn't miss the way he cringed when she mentioned her two roommates by name, the flare of jealousy in his silver eyes. Deliberately ignoring the danger, she continued, "They insisted on pulling me out of my cocoon and embracing who I am. Of course, my family thought I was sleeping with both of them and pretended to accept the relationship but I knew they were uncomfortable about it. I let them believe what they wanted to believe because I liked the notoriety and until recently I never told them the truth."

"And what would that be?" he asked through gritted teeth.

Leaning forward until her breasts were cushioned against his chest, until her hands were on either side of his head, she whispered, "I've never slept with either of them."

The breath he had been holding whooshed from him and he huffed a laugh, "I knew about the bartender but I didn't know that about the artist."

She smiled slightly, "You did not know about Dima."

"Ashley told me when she introduced us last week."

Cocking her head to the side, she frowned, "Isn't it a little weird for your former lover to be introducing you to her current lover?"

"You would think so," he said. But he didn't expand, just brushed her tangled hair out of her face. He seemed to be fascinated by her natural hair, insisting on brushing it after their late late shower the night before. Before he used the strands of damp hair in a seduction that required another, even later shower.

"You're not going to explain are you?"

Grinning, he shook his head no. making him look young and carefree. It was a good look. "I'd rather hear more about your secrets."

"That's not terribly fair, you know," she sighed, laying back down and snuggling up against his chest. Being in his arms was like coming home and she knew it couldn't last and she wondered what his secrets were that kept him from giving their relationship more than a few days, a week at most.

"Life's not terribly fair, you know," he replied, sadness darkening his voice. Brushing her hair behind her ear, he cupped the back of her head and tilted her head back until she was looking into his eyes. "So confess your sins and let me offer absolution."

"You're right," she said softly, her eyes sparkling with mischief. "Where do I even begin? There are just so many sins to choose from...."

He growled and before she could tell him she was teasing, she was on her back and he was showing her how easily he could forgive her as he got very intimate with her body.

Chapter 15 (Saturday)

Duncan's sister might have been the same height as Lexi but she obviously wasn't as well endowed; the tight t-shirt lovingly stretched over Lexi's breasts in a way that had Duncan re-thinking his desire to take her to the bar he owned and his pack managed for him. When he had acquired the pack at fifteen he had taken some of his trust fund money and bought the run down establishment until he could figure out what else to do with the rag tag pack of seventeen hungry and half-wild wolves.

Their previous Alpha had done a piss poor job of protecting them, keeping them under his tyrannical thumb, keeping them hungry and broken and giving them just enough to keep them loyal, to ensure his own power. After Duncan became the

Alpha they respected him but they weren't comfortable with the world Duncan moved in. Not knowing what else to do, he bought bar for them, which they affectionately named *The Black Wolf*.

Within a few months, once they had realized they were capable of running the place, they had turned the bar around, adding a few dinner items and eventually a full menu and brewing their own beer: Foolish Moon Pale Ale, Lunatics Wheat, Howling Wolf Stout, Lonely Wolf Bitter, and so on to his favorite, the Black Wolf Dark, created especially for him by his loving pack.

That nightmare of almost eighteen years ago became one of the best things to have happened to him. It led to his involvement in business and manufacturing, which lead to untold wealth. And indirectly to Lexi, who looked too damn sexy in the simple t-shirt and blue jeans. When she looked up at him, an oddly nervous smile on her face, his breath caught in his throat.

He wanted to keep her forever.

Pushing the dangerous thought deep, deep down, he pushed the doors open and ushered her inside, oddly nervous himself. But he needn't have worried: as she looked around, the slightly anxious smile melted into one of genuine appreciation, "Duncan, I love it! How did you ever discover such a perfect gem?'

He looked around at the bar, trying to see it through her eyes. It was old fashioned, reminiscent to the old pubs in England, with wooden paneling and low lighting. There was a second floor as well that opened to the main floor below. It was cozy and comfortable, a place people went to meet up with their friends and hang out. When he had been younger, before he went away to pursue a lucrative business opportunity, Duncan had spent plenty of time there. He realized he had missed the place and while he had kept tabs on his pack, it was good to see them.

Really good. They were thriving, the original members glowing with health and vitality, their mates and children happy and energetic.

"Duncan!" Marissa called out, stepping out from behind the bar, still impossibly attractive at thirty-five as she had been at seventeen. Because wolves age at a different rate, she looked to be in her twenties, still very blond and very curvy. Out of the original pack, she was the only one who had remained unwed, since it was her mate that had been eliminated. She had been fourteen when the bastard took her as his mate and she had no desire to lose the independence that she relished. "It's good to have you back, stranger."

Her slender arms wrapped around him in a warm, welcoming hug and tears stung the back of his eyes; he had forgotten how much he loved this pack that had accidentally made him an Alpha as a teenager. Returning the hug, he whispered, "It's good to be back."

"Had I known you were coming I would have put the call out," she gently rebuked, stepping back and looking up at him with her old soul eyes. When he had been fifteen, she had seemed so much older and wiser than he even though she had only been two years older. And she still tried to mother him, despite the fact that he was twice her size and fiercely independent. "The pups would love to see you."

Turning her head, her smile faltered for a moment as she realized Lexi was a human. Keeping her eye on Lexi, her lips forced upwards in a tight grin, she asked, "And who is this?"

"Hi," Lexi beamed, sticking her hand out and pumping Marissa's hand when the she-wolf offered it. "I'm Lexi Darling, but you can call me Lexi; I work with Duncan at his new magazine."

Marissa looked at Lexi then she looked at Duncan and arched a perfect blond eyebrow. "I didn't realize Duncan was sleeping with his employees now."

Lexi burbled with laughter, "Well, it took a lot of effort on my part but I finally wore him down. This bar is fantastic, by the way. Duncan says you brew your own beer and you make the world's best cheeseburger; I'm dying to see if he's right but judging by the smell, I'd have to say he wasn't lying."

Slightly taken aback by the girl, Marissa looked like she was ready to try to make an escape. While the bar was open to the public, most humans were slightly uneasy around so many wolves and those that did venture in tended to keep to their own kind. Lexi's enthusiasm made Duncan adore her that much more. With a grin, he wrapped his arm around Lexi's waist, "We'll take a couple of cheeseburgers and two bottles of the Black Wolf Dark."

"Ooh, that sounds delicious," Lexi enthused, following Duncan over to a booth, her eyes absorbing everything, sparkling with admiration and making him feel a thousand feet tall. Sitting down, she slid into the seat next to him, not giving him any space. Not that he was complaining; if he could, he would have pulled her closer. "Do you know if they sell their brews? I would love to get some for my family; my brothers would absolutely die for this place." Pressing a kiss just beneath his jaw, she whispered, "Thank you for bringing me her; it's... it's just fantastic."

"Thank you," he said gruffly, his cheeks turning faintly red.

That wonderful burble of laughter came from Lexi again and when he looked at her, she was smiling at him, "It's your bar, isn't it?"

His smile was a little guilty but very proud, "Guilty as charged. It is mine but my p... friends run it completely."

She laughed again, "We have more in common than you think, then."

"In what way?"

"I co-signed the loan so Dima could open his bar, well, nightclub; whatever." She chuckled, shaking her head in self-mockery. "I will probably have to put a qualifier in my piece when I write it up even though I have absolutely nothing to do with it. I even refuse to work there." Looking around the bar once more, she sighed, "I think I would work here, though; it is so comfortable. I could imagine hanging out here, drinking beer, chatting with friends; I just love it, Duncan."

That stupid emotion welled in his chest again but he continued to ignore it. "Later on we can go to the back room and shoot some pool or throw some darts?"

"Really?" she beamed. "I'll have you know that I am an abysmal pool player. I figure out all of the geometry and line up my shot but somewhere between me pulling back the cue stick and pushing it forward to strike the ball I lose it and either send the ball flying off the table or barely moving it at all. It is not pretty but I do enjoy playing."

He was about to reply when an irritatingly familiar brunette slid into the booth across from them, a mischievous smile on her lips, "I recognize that shirt; isn't that my shirt, Duncan? Would you care to explain to me how it ended up on another woman?"

Before Duncan could answer, Lexi was out of her seat and sliding into the booth next to the newcomer. Duncan had to chuckle at the look of horror on the brunette's face as Lexi gave her a fierce hug, "You must be Jillian. I am so glad you had some clothes at Duncan's house otherwise I would have had to go out in public naked and there are laws against that you know. I'm Lexi, by the way; Lexi Darling. I work…."

"She's sleeping with me," Duncan interrupted before Lexi could tell that preposterous truth again. Jillian's eyes widened even further but Lexi chuckled like he knew she would. "Jillian, this is my date. Be nice."

"When am I not nice?" Jillian pouted, her expression easing as she examined the situation more closely and realized Lexi wasn't a threat. "But mom will want to hear about this."

"Let it rest, puppy," Duncan murmured good-naturedly, glancing up and seeing Marissa motioning for him to join her. Excusing himself, he walked over to the stunning blond, not entirely comfortable leaving Lexi with his sister, who would pelt her with questions. "What is it?"

"Most of the pack has shown up," she said, a sly smile on her face letting him know that she sent the call out that he was there. "We were hoping you'd go running with us; nothing too far, just a quickie and then I'll bring out your food and you and your, ahem, date, can enjoy your time together."

"Watch yourself, Marissa," he warned softly, glancing over his shoulder at Lexi and catching her staring at him with a soft, dreamy expression that made his heart skip a beat or two.

"But she's a human," Marissa hissed, her eyes narrowing dangerously. Despite having Duncan as her Alpha, knowing his family history, she was still very weary of wolf-human relationships. She could deal with the occasional human that came into the bar or even the occasional fuck but she didn't like the idea of wolves taking a human for anything more than some sport.

He sighed, "Don't worry, Mar; I don't plan on taking a human for a mate."

"So she's strictly casual?" Marissa asked, her voice laced with doubt.

"It's all she can be," was his telling reply. "Let me go excuse myself and then we can run."

She let the matter drop but he knew she wouldn't let it rest for long. Of course, he would come in next week and let her know that he had let Lexi go; that would appease her and she wouldn't have to worry.

"Hey, you," Lexi murmured, standing up and wrapping her arms around his waist as she gave him a warm hug. "Is everything all right?"

"Of course," he fudged. "Um, I'm going to take care of some… personal business while I'm here but it won't take long and while you're waiting you can play a game of pool with Jillian."

She chuckled, "Okay, but hurry back."

Going up on her toes, pressing her luscious body against his, she gave him a reason to hurry. And as he walked away, he had to adjust his erection, wondering if he was ever going to get enough of the intoxicating Lexi. Walking out the back, he saw the pack gathered, some already in their wolf forms, others stripping down. All of them turned when he appeared, the smiles on their faces genuine and warm as they greeted him.

Marissa stepped out of the shadows already naked but still in her human form. She had a spectacular body, curvy and sexy; but Duncan preferred Lexi by far. With a wry smile at his thoughts, he stripped off his clothes, his cock sticking straight out from his body from Lexi's kiss. He jumped when Marissa wrapped her hand around his penis and whispered in his ear, "Lose the human; we'll find a place in the woods and mate as wolves."

He chuckled, prying her fingers off his penis knowing she didn't mean anything by it; she was just trying to establish her position in the pack. "I'm sorry, my dear, but this erection is for Lexi. Now, let's run."

With a sigh, she shifted into the gorgeous blond wolf he knew so well. As the others shifted, he let the wolf out, feeling him relish the opportunity to run. His bones shifted, his vision changed, and then he was on his four paws, panting and eager to begin. With a series of barks, the pack was off, crashing through the wooded area and being wolves.

*****

"Duncan's never brought a date here before," Jillian said as she chalked the end of her pool cue. "He must really like you."

"It's just really great sex," Lexi teased, her belly still buzzing with arousal. When Duncan had put on a black t-shirt and a pair of blue jeans that cupped his hard ass, Lexi just about came right then and there. He looked amazing in a suit, all sexy and powerful; but in jeans and a t-shirt.... He was sinfully yummy, like hot fudge melted all over a hot brownie, topped with whipped cream and a maraschino cherry. "You cannot imagine the things he can do with his tongue."

"Ew," Jillian groaned, her amber eyes dancing with laughter. "I do not want to hear about my brother's sex life."

Lexi really liked Jillian; the girl was comfortable in her own skin and was blunt, which Lexi appreciated. She much preferred honesty over pretentiousness. And she absolutely loved Duncan's bar; it was what Duncan was beneath the stern, business-suit exterior: warm, comfortable, dependable, safe. And of course, gorgeous, but that pretty much described Duncan in whatever guise he wore. "Do you come here often?"

She couldn't imagine her family every stepping foot in Dima's bar; even if they knew she had co-signed the loan. And as much as she loved Dima and adored his nightclub, she much preferred the old world charm of Duncan's place. *Skin* was for flashy people looking to be in the spotlight and while Lexi was flashy, she still wasn't interested in being the center of attention. Except for Duncan. She felt comfortable in her own skin at *The Black Wolf*, which reminded her about the dream she had had the night before. Maybe it hadn't been a dog at all but a wolf.

That would actually make a lot more sense.

"I come here every chance I get," Jillian said enthusiastically. "All of us come here to hang out so I always know that somebody will be here to play with."

"I'm more used to *Skin*," Lexi admitted. "That's where my roommate works and I tend to spend any free Friday or Saturday evening there."

"Ooh, I love that place." Taking her shot, Jillian fanned her face for dramatic effect, "They have the sexiest bartenders in the city. In fact, one of my best friends is sleeping with one; she says that it's the best sex she's ever had and she's been with Duncan."

"Are you talking about Ashley?" Lexi had to squash the little green monster that tried to raise its head at the mention of Ashley sleeping with Duncan. She knew that, had known it from the very beginning; she shouldn't be jealous of something that was in the past.

"Oh my God!" Jillian cried out, drawing the attention of several patrons. Pointing her finger at Lexi, disbelief and delight on her face, she exclaimed, "You're the blond!"

Lexi actually felt the heat creep into her cheeks, but why she should be embarrassed she had no idea; it's not like she slept with him that night. And even if she had, it wouldn't have mattered. "You were there that night?"

"We were expecting to hang with Ashley and Duncan that night," she explained. "Except he bailed on us and went home with the blond – with you. Wow, this is kind of cool."

Knowing that Duncan chose her over his friends should have made her feel bad; it didn't. But she felt a little bit bad for not feeling bad at all. Curious in spite of her lack of guilt, she asked, "How did Ashley end up going home with Dima?"

"How do you know who she went home with?"

"I got home as she was leaving," Lexi gave a flippant shrug of her shoulders. As Jillian continued to stare at her, she added, "Dima's one of my roommates."

It took a moment to sink in but when it did, Jillian giggled, the sound charming and sensual. In fact, now that she took a moment to think about it –and

Duncan wasn't around to mess up her senses – Lexi realized almost everyone in the bar exuded an almost animal sensuality, magnetism. And yet they had all been deferential to Duncan, with the exception of his sister, who was a normal sibling pain in the butt. It was fascinating.

"Shortly after you left the bartender came up with a tray of shots," Jillian chuckled. "He sat the tray down and then he sat down right next to Ashley and started flirting like mad, not caring that there was a group of us there. When Marsters cleared his throat, the guy, uh, Dima, simply motioned towards the shots and, without taking his eyes off Ash, said, "Drink up, I'm busy." I think that was the moment Ashley decided to sleep with him though she let him buy the table drinks for the rest of the night. It was a good night."

Lexi chuckled at Dima's antics; it was just like him, single-minded and determined. "It was certainly a good night for Dima and Ashley."

"Oh, yeah," Jillian chuckled, gossiping about Ashley's night with Dima.

After nearly forty-five minutes of mindless chatter and pool playing where Lexi sank a total of two balls, Duncan appeared, looking disheveled and wind-blown but also happy and relaxed. Spying her, he walked over to her, his gait looser and more fluid. And as he wrapped his arms around her, his scent wrapped itself around her, too: the clean, crisp freshness of night. Pressing her nose against the curve of his neck and closing her eyes, she inhaled deeply, wishing she could bottle the scent so she could take it out whenever she wanted to simply breathe it in.

"You smell absolutely sinful; I want to eat you up," she purred, her body responding to the wind-blown, wild smell of Duncan. Out of the corner of her eye, she saw Marissa step back inside, buttoning up the last two buttons of her shirt and patting down her hair. When the blond spied Duncan, she gave him a sultry smile and Lexi felt jealously eating her bones. Stiffening, trying to remain unaffected because her time with Duncan wasn't supposed to mean anything, she stepped back and asked in what she hoped was a light, nonchalant voice, "So, did you play a game of strip poker? Did you both lose or something?"

He gently nudged her chin up with his fingers until she met his laughing silver eyes, “We raced, Lexi; a whole pack of us. Look.”

Glancing over her shoulder, she saw ten or twelve others saunter in, just as disheveled as Duncan had been, if not more so. Confused, she looked up at him, “Do you run naked?”

He chuckled and pulled her into a powerful hug, until the steady rhythm of his heart worked its magic and she sighed. Relaxing against him, her arms slipped around his waist and she returned the hug.

He never answered the question.

Chapter 16

Wearing one of Duncan's robes late Sunday night, Lexi rummaged through his state-of-the-art kitchen, searching for something to eat. Even though tomorrow was Monday, they had agreed to one more night. Since their time together was so short they figured they should steal one more day and one more night. Being with Duncan was amazing, even the time spent together when they weren't making love. He had her laughing so hard she thought her stomach would burst; and then he would feed her ice cream and get more ice cream on her breasts than in her mouth, which he proceeded to clean with his tongue. It was a very messy Sunday.

They showered and then climbed back into the bed, exhausted after a day of being together and he made love to her, slowly and wholeheartedly. After yet another explosive orgasm – one of many over the too-short, very gratifying weekend – she fell asleep on top of him with the feel of his warm hands rubbing her back.

But that was hours ago and she woke up starving. Climbing out of bed without waking Duncan was surprisingly easy; he was apparently a very sound sleeper. Just like every other aspect of his life, he slept hard. And if she weren't so darn hungry, she would have enjoyed watching him sleep; he looked younger, less troubled, but every bit as sexy. Like the hotel, she felt his eyes on her but the rumble of a snore convinced her he was still asleep.

His kitchen was packed with so much food, which was good because during their time together, he ate. A lot. She was amazed that he was so fit, considering the vast quantities of food he could put away. He said that he had an extremely high metabolism and she believed him; there wasn't a spare ounce of fat anywhere on his hard, lean body. Pulling a cupboard open she glanced inside to find a breakfast bar or something; just something light to quiet the ravenous beast in her belly.

Without finding anything, she closed the cupboard and nearly had a heart attack when she saw Duncan standing there, nude and with a rampant erection, his arms crossed over his chest as his eyes glittered in the darkness. He had been so silent she hadn't even known he was there. Pressing her hand over her racing heart, she laughed, "Holy crap, you scared me; I didn't even know you were there. Are you hungry?"

"Always," he growled, his eyes moving over her body, smiling slightly as he saw her nipples stiffen beneath his regard. Meeting her eyes once more, he rasped, "Wanna play a game, Lexi?"

This was a new side of Duncan she hadn't seen before; darker and more primal. Her stomach quaked and she found that she liked this new Duncan. "Yes."

He moved then, slowly, predatorily, stopping in front of her and putting his hands on the tie around her waist. His silver gaze glowed as he loosened the tie and then slowly pushed the robe from her body until it pooled on the floor. "You are so beautiful, Lexi… Alexandra."

She inhaled sharply at the use of her given name; she hadn't known how sexy it would sound when growled in Duncan's voice. Her belly tightened in anticipation and her thighs grew damp. She held her breath as he took her hand in his and led her through the house to the living area that looked out over his vast backyard. He never took his eyes from her and she was damned if she could have torn her eyes from his. Trusting him to lead her through the darkness, she followed.

Pushing the French doors open, he stepped outside, pulling her with him. The moon was nearly full, bathing the world in its soft light and making it easy to see. Duncan's voice rumbled through her skin as he commanded, "Run."

Startled, a little confused, she looked up at him and met those wild, silver eyes. "Run?"

"Run," he repeated. Reaching out, he drew his hand over her breast, cupping the heavy weight in his palm as he brushed his thumb over the hard tip. "Run and I'll catch you."

A slow smile curved her lips as she understood the game he was playing; her body was burning for his possession and she knew the sex was going to be primitive and hot. Without a word, she took off at a dead run towards the heavily wooded area, naked and barefoot and utterly free. When she didn't hear anything, she slowed down and glanced over her shoulder to see if he was following.

He was standing where she had left him, rubbing his thumb over his bottom lip; his eyes glowing even from this distance. He was so preternaturally still she wasn't sure he was fully awake. But then she looked down and she saw his thick cock sticking straight out from his hard belly and she knew that he was giving her a head start to make it even more thrilling.

With a soft sound of delight, she sped back up, feeling the cool night air against her overheated skin, caressing her bouncing breasts, her damp sex. Keeping to the grassy path, not knowing what creatures were watching her mad dash through the woods, she laughed out loud. She was so damned aroused she could barely think straight.

The sounds of the night added to the adrenalin pumping through her system;

the crickets chirping, an owl hooting, and the wind softly blowing through the trees, rustling the leaves. Light from the nearly full moon filtered through the trees, giving her enough light to see the path. The woods at midnight smelled like Duncan.

Then she stumbled out onto a meadow bathed in moonlight and she had to take a moment to appreciate the beauty; the grass was silver and the trees were shadows. Inhaling deeply through her nostrils, she breathed in the scent of grass and woods and Duncan. Spinning, she gasped as his large form came barreling out of the woods straight at her. His arms were around her waist and she was flying backwards when he spun and landed on his shoulder, cushioning the fall with his body. She landed on top of him with a hard exhalation of air.

Laughing breathlessly, she looked down into Duncan's handsome face; the tightness of his features as he looked up at her with predatory hunger was exhilarating. Brushing the wild black hair off his face she asked, "Now that you've caught me, what are you going to do with me?"

He simply smiled and in a move so quick it took her breath away, she was on her hands and knees and he was behind her, surrounding her with his body and his heat. The grass was soft against her knees as she looked over her shoulder, a little startled by the hunger on his face. She tried to turn around but he held her still with a heavy hand on the small of her back. "Duncan?"

He clasped her around the waist with his large hands as he bent forward, rubbing his cheek over her back, "Hands and knees, Lexi. I'm going to steal your soul."

The heat of his body disappeared for a moment and when something warm slid between the crevice of her bottom she jerked. His large hand ran down her spine as he leaned over her, "Shh; it'll be all right."

"I've never…."

"I know," he growled. "You came to me a virgin; of course you've never."

She swallowed, not knowing how he knew or why he didn't say anything before. Glancing over her shoulder, she inhaled sharply as she saw him rubbing something onto his larger than normal cock with his hand, making it glisten in the moonlight. She had no idea what it was or where it came from as fear and anticipation raged through her body; she wasn't sure she wanted this. But then he lifted his head and her protest caught in her throat at the stark craving gleaming in his eyes. "Relax, Lexi; let me claim you."

Her lips parted as he rubbed his slick cock over the curve of her bottom, her nerve endings screaming in fear. In excitement. Grabbing her hips to hold her steady, he slowly pushed into her, easing past the tight muscles. Fire raced outwards, burning her up as he pushed forward. "Relax."

With her neck aching from the awkward position, she faced forward, putting her head down as he claimed her inch by slow, decadent inch. When he was buried deep within her, his body came over hers once more, dominating her completely. His breath was hot in her ear as he growled. "You have the most delicious body, Alexandra."

A little squeak came from the back of her throat and beads of perspiration broke out across her forehead as he slowly moved in her, slowly in; slowly out, stealing what was left of her mind. The heat of his body was blistering and she knew she was never going to survive such dark pleasure. With one hand holding her in place, the other roamed over her body, touching her wherever he could reach: her thighs, her belly, her breasts. As he cupped a breast in his hand, as he captured a nipple between his fingers, sharp teeth sank into the curve of her shoulder and she screamed as ecstasy bombs detonated throughout her body, filling her with pleasure and taking everything.

Her arms trembled, gave out, and she fell forward onto her elbows, sending him even deeper into her body. Inhaling sharply, he paused for just a moment before he pulled his teeth from her neck and clasped her hips with both hands, pounding into her until her world was destroyed and nothing was left of her.

"You're mine," he growled savagely as his body stiffened and she felt the heat of his orgasm deep, deep within her body. It set off another round of explosions and she came again.

When he released her, she collapsed onto the ground, barely having enough strength to push herself over and look up at the man who dominated her so completely. The crushed grass emitted a deliciously green scent and the gentle breeze cooled her overheated skin. She didn't know if her heart would ever beat normally again and she was pretty sure all of her muscles were now jelly. "Wow."

Tenderly, he scooped her boneless body up in his arms and stood up. Her arms automatically went around his neck as he carried her back to the house in silence. His silver eyes continued to glow as he held her gaze, never wavering even as he took the stairs up to the bedroom. She was too overcome with emotion, with pleasure, to speak; she simply wanted to stay in his arms forever. But she knew that she couldn't; tomorrow they would go back to work and a few days after that it would be over. And she was going to let him go knowing that it wasn't real, at least for him.

"My lovely, little Siren," he rumbled as he gently lay her down on the bed, brushing the strand of hair from her face. His gaze was tender as he caressed her face and whispered, "You've claimed my soul, Alexandra; will you be able to give it back?'

In horrified silence, she simply stared at him.

"Never mind, my delectable sweet; I know you will do what you think is right," he chuckled, climbing into bed next to her, wrapping his body around hers and keeping her close. "And forgive me for letting you go; I'm a fool."

*****

Still reeling from the experience in the woods, Lexi left Duncan sleeping on the bed when she woke up early Monday morning. Her thoughts were still all over the place about what happened; that had been a much darker, more dangerous side of Duncan than she had been prepared for and it terrified her how much it intrigued her, aroused her. He had thoroughly claimed her body and she still felt the imprint of him.

Her fingers went to the bite mark on her shoulder and she smiled slightly; that was definitely unexpected and so damn erotic that memories of her orgasm still made her shudder. He had been so possessive, so primal, and it had delighted her more than she cared to admit.

Grabbing a bowl of strawberries and some heavy cream, she closed the fridge door and set the ingredients down on the counter. Searching through his cabinets, she found sugar and vanilla and the hand held mixer. "Perfect."

Her stomach rumbled so she grabbed a strawberry to tide her over until her masterpiece was finished. Humming to herself, she went about whipping the cream, adding the sugar and vanilla as required. Dipping her finger in the bowl, she was about to taste it when strong fingers wrapped around her wrist and brought her hand to another mouth. Soft lips enveloped her finger and her body melted. Looking over her shoulder, she smiled at Duncan, "Well?"

"Mmm," he murmured appreciatively. His hair was damp and his sleeper pants hung low on his hips; he must have taken a quick shower before coming downstairs and joining her in the kitchen. "You taste wonderful."

Smiling, she took a strawberry and dragged it through the cream before feeding it to Duncan. His lips wrapped around her fingers as he ate the fruit and she had to remind herself that it was Monday morning and they didn't have all day to spend in bed. "And this? Is it good?"

"It could be better," he murmured huskily, betraying nothing regarding their midnight rendezvous in the woods. Maybe he was embarrassed by how primitive he behaved; she wouldn't push it until he was ready to talk about what had happened.

"More sugar?" Lexi frowned, trying to concentrate on the conversation instead of imagining him throwing her over his shoulder and carrying her back to bed where he would do even more wicked things to her all-too-willing body. She was pretty sure she added the right amount; maybe he had a sweet tooth for his whipped cream, not just desserts, though one would never know by looking at him, all sinew and hardness.

His lips curled up into a wicked grin, "Something like that."

Without another word, he loosened her lash, opening the lapels of the robe and letting it fall to the floor. Sucking in his breath, his eyes darkened at the sight of her body. Grabbing her around the waist, he hoisted her up onto the counter and stepped between the spread legs. Using his fingers, he scooped up some of the cream and painted her breasts, her nipples.

The cool cream felt even colder on her overheated body, but it felt so good. Her pulse raced as she watched the intensity in Duncan's face as he concentrated on painting her skin. And then his hot mouth closed around her nipple and the contrast of hot skin, cold cream, and even hotter mouth almost made Lexi come right then and there. Her eyes rolled back and she moaned.

"Much better," he rasped, flicking his tongue over her pebbled flesh, over her soft breasts. While suckling her other nipple, he scooped some more cream out, spreading it lower, across her abdomen, over her most intimate flesh. She sucked in a breath as his fingers pushed cold cream into her sex and she felt him smile against her breast.

"Don't eat it all," she breathed as his mouth moved lower. "I want to return the… oh, God, Duncan!"

His tongue swirled through the cream and into her body. Unable to control her response, her body arched off the table, pressing her clit harder against his mouth. His tongue probed her, licking the cream up until she was a quivering mess. Her orgasm was swift and powerful. It took her a moment to catch her breath and when she did, she looked at him with a sinful smile, "My turn."

Sliding off the counter, Lexi pushed Duncan's pants down his long legs. Grabbing the bowl of cream and the strawberries, she went to her knees so her face was right next to his thick erection and she blushed, remembering how he had taken her the night before. His clean, musky smell filled her senses as she looked up at him with smile, "You're so beautiful."

Watching her hand as she smeared cream over his erection, Lexi memorized the feel of the hard length; the heat, the strength. She wanted to remember every moment she had with him so she would be able to savor them at some point in the future. It would take a few weeks – months – to be able to look back on this time with him without hurting but it was worth it; he was worth it. He flung his head back as she took the hot, hard length of him into her mouth, swirling her tongue around the velvet head.

His hips jerked and he twined his fingers in her hair, holding her in place as she took him deeper, savoring the musky, woodsy taste of him. She wrapped her hand around the base of his penis as she concentrated on the head. His fingers convulsed, the movement inadvertently pulling her hair, and her body responded, her breasts swelling, her belly tightening. His involuntary groans were music to her ears as his cock nudged the back of her mouth. The movement made her moan, opening her throat to his full possession of her mouth. She concentrated on breathing through her nostrils, breathing in the scent of Duncan, as he fucked her throat.

"Lexi, I'm going to come," he warned, and she curled a hand around his testicles, gently rolling them as his fingers twisted into fists, jerking handfuls of her hair. Too soon, or not soon enough, he exploded into her mouth, and she felt every pulse of his release as it went on forever.

Lexi reveled in the power to make him lose control, in the feel of his orgasm in her mouth. Lapping up every drop of semen, she licked her lips and looked up at him, a satisfied smile on her lips, "Hmmm."

He opened his eyes and when their eyes connected she felt herself drowning. Tenderly, he brushed his thumb along her lower lip, still glistening with his release. And as he smiled down at her, passion and sadness in his eyes, her heart trembled and she couldn't quite catch her breath. She knew before he even said the words that he was letting her go. "Duncan."

He groaned, grabbing her arms and dragging her to her feet. His arms were around her and he was holding onto her as if he never meant to let her go. But she knew that was what he was going to do. "Before I say anything I want you to know that I love your writing, Lexi; *lavish* is better for having you on the staff but I can't... I can't do this any longer."

"Are you firing me?" she asked lightly, her heart pulsing madly in her throat, choking her.

He shook his head, "No; I want you to stay at *lavish* but I have to work at the offices for the next two weeks so I can wrap up everything I have been working on to pass off to the manager I hired. I am begging you to take a two week vacation at my expense."

"That's all right," she managed, forcing her lips into a smile when her face felt like cracking. "You don't have to pay for anything; I'll take care of it."

"God, I don't want to let you go."

"Then why...."

"I can't change who or what I am, Lexi," he rasped, his voice rough with emotion. "If I hold onto you any longer I will destroy you and I couldn't bear the thought of hurting you."

"You don't know," she protested, thoughts racing a million miles an hour in her head. She would risk it, if it meant being with him and depending on his answer..... Slowly, she met his eyes, "Do you love me?"

His silver eyes burned with torment and his jaw tightened but he didn't answer and she knew that he didn't love her. She couldn't hold onto him; she had to let him go. Cupping his chin in her hand, she whispered, "It's okay; I never expected you to."

"I could love you, Lexi; so easily," he ground out, his eyes burning brighter. "And if I hold you in my arms for five more minutes I won't be able to let you go."

"Then hold me in your arms, Duncan, and never let me go." She laughed sadly when he looked at her with stoic resolution. Cupping his beloved cheek in her hand, she whispered, "Otherwise we need to go our separate ways before we reach the point where we can't."

His hand covered hers and he turned his head, pressing a desperate kiss to her palm, "I wish things were different; I wish I was a different man."

"What did I tell you about being a different man, Duncan?" she asked lightly, her heart breaking as she realized that she would never see affection for her burning from his eyes after she said goodbye. Her breath caught in her chest but she ruthlessly pushed it down. "I wouldn't want you if you were anyone else."

His lips curved upwards in some semblance of a smile but his eyes were still bleak. "So this is it."

"This is it," she nodded and took a deep breath as she let the memories of their too brief of time together fill her thoughts. Licking her lips, she was going to confess all of her secrets, since he wasn't going to remember her anyway. "One last secret, Duncan; I'm a Rudnar."

As his eyes widened in surprise and shock, she smiled wryly, "Alexandra Rudnar, the youngest daughter you wanted me to interview." She laughed but it was a pathetic and hollow sound. Taking an even deeper breath, she held his eyes, "I'm also a Siren and I am so, so sorry."

Standing up on her toes, she pressed her lips against his and squeezed her eyes shut as she let her love and memories return to him. His hard chest pressed against her breasts and she wanted to take it back but she didn't, kissing him until there was nothing left. With a cry, she wrenched herself away from him and looked up into his stunned face. Gently laying her fingers over his lips, she whispered, "I love you."

With one last look, she gathered up the robe and slipped it onto her body. She would call Cole and have him take her to the offices so she could pack up her stuff; it would simply be too difficult to continue working at *lavish* and seeing nothing behind his eyes when he looked at her. As she headed towards the front door, she found her dress and her purse along the way and laughed sadly.

Every moment with him had been worth it.

Chapter 17 (Monday)

When she got into the car nearly an hour later and two miles from Duncan's house, Cole took one look at her and wrapped his arm around her shoulder, holding her like that as they drove home. He didn't ask why she was wearing the dress she had worn on Friday morning, nor did he ask what had happened to the wig, he simply held her as he drove. When they got home, she offered a few words to let him know that she was quitting and today was her last day. And while she showered he typed up her resignation and found some boxes.

With Cole by her side, Lexi entered the *lavish* offices for the last time. It was hell trying to stay awake because she was just plain exhausted, physically, emotionally, and mentally. She would have blamed it on having a sex-filled weekend but she knew that it was her aching heart that was draining her. Or possibly the flu, since her forehead was burning up. Getting sick on top of getting dumped was just great. At least she wouldn't have to worry about calling in sick in the morning.

Wearing a silky shirt that had a front but really no back, being as it was held together by a few ties, Lexi maneuvered her way through the cubicles to her office. Instructing her best friend on what to pack, she took her final article and her letter of resignation up to Duncan's office, signing her name as 'The Writer of The Scene.' She smiled at his assistant, ignoring the way the room wobbled. "Hi, Miss Reynolds; can I leave these here with you? They're for Duncan... Mr. Tremain."

"Certainly, Miss Darling," the older lady said with a soft smile. When she looked up and saw Lexi, she gasped, coming to her feet and pressing her cool palm against Lexi's blazing forehead, "My goodness, child, you're burning up! Why aren't you at home getting some rest?"

Lexi's smile felt force and she was a little short of breath, "I will be going home as soon as I've packed up my things."

"You're quitting?" Ms. Reynolds looked even more horrified by that announcement than by Lexi's flushed cheeks. "But... why?"

"It's time to move on," she said easily, lifting her shoulders in a casual shrug that she didn't mean. "I've decided to try my hand at cliff diving. That or macramé, I'm not sure."

Miss Reynolds chuckled as Lexi knew she would. The older woman pulled Lexi into a soft, motherly hug, smelling of peppermint and office paper. "Take care of yourself, Lexi, and don't be a stranger."

"Okay," Lexi murmured, returning the hug with affection. Setting the folder down on the desk, she rested her hand there a moment longer to steady the world that was suddenly spinning too fast. When she was stable, she straightened and forced a smile to her bloodless lips. "Make sure Mr. Tremain gets this."

With that, Lexi made her way back to her office, hoping to get the hell out of there before she passed out; she really was feeling ill. Pressing her hand against her forehead, she was shocked at how hot her skin was. She wanted to put off the inevitable as long as possible, severing her last tie to Duncan, but she also wanted to get home and crash.

Not paying attention, she almost ran into Mason Jones, one of the last people she ever wanted to run into, especially in a completely deserted hallway. She stumbled back a step as he smiled cruelly down at her, "Hey, Lexi."

"Hi, Mason," she returned with a grimace, not in the mood to deal with him. She took a step to go around him, but he didn't move. In fact, he seemed to take a step closer to her, making her apprehension sky rocket. "Excuse me, please."

"I don't think so," he murmured, grabbing her hips and grinding his pelvis against her. "I think that I will keep you."

She pushed against his chest and glared at him, "Let go, Mason."

"Come on, babe," he taunted, refusing to let her go. His cold blue eyes stared down at her with malicious intent as he ran his hands over her bare back, his smooth palms nauseating her. His breath invaded her nostrils and she turned her head as he tried to kiss her. "Without your killer shoes on, you're the perfect height for me and everyone knows you're easy; hell, you're only wearing half your damn shirt. C'mon, Lexi; I can make you scream."

His behavior made something snap and without quite knowing how it happened, her hand was around his throat, her nails digging into the soft flesh and she was… growling. If she didn't smell the acrid scent of pee as he pissed himself she would have torn his throat out with her bare hand and the thought made her tremble. Pulling her nails out of his flesh, she continued to hold her hand around his throat and her voice came out in a snarl as she glared at him, "I said to let go, you fucking moron."

His eyes widened even further in his miserable face as he wrapped his fingers around her wrist, either to keep her hand from pulling away, taking his throat with it, or to hold himself up. "I'm sorry, Miss Darling. God, I'm so sorry. Let me go, please."

She snorted, pushing him away and noticing the five half-moon marks on his neck, little droplets of blood trickling out, as he crumbled to the ground. Shaking her head in disgust, she started to walk back to her office, throwing her leg out and kicking him in the shin as she passed him, "Bastard."

Wiping the back of her hand against her moist forehead, she didn't give the sniveling imbecile another thought. Stepping through the door to her office, she got a little thrill of watching Cole pack her stuff, his shirt straining against his taut muscles as he hefted a full box onto the desk. His red highlights were now purple, a bright and vibrant purple, and when he turned around and saw her he griped, "How the hell did you manage to amass so much shit?"

She gave him a crooked smile, ignoring the fact that there were two of him standing and glaring at her. "A lot of gifts from businesses I wrote about and a lot of gifts from businesses wanting me to write about them. It adds up."

He grumbled good-naturedly as he struggled to carry the box out the door. As soon as he left, she sagged against her desk and focused on not fainting. She had never felt so ill in her life, it was like her stomach was boiling, all rumbly and hot. Crawling into bed and pulling the covers over her head, not thinking about Duncan, not remembering Duncan, sounded like Heaven.

"Miss Darling," Kerry said coming into the room with a bright smile on his face, reminding her there was still one person under her spell. "I saw you come in so I ran out and got you a cup coffee. Here."

He was so damn eager to please and she just wanted to go home. Accepting the hot drink, she smiled kindly, "Thank you, Kerry. I want to give you something since I am leaving."

"You're leaving?" he looked crestfallen, his smile disappearing instantly. "Was it something I said? Something I did? Or didn't do?"

"No," she shook her head, her smile gentler as she struggled to bring forth her memories of him. She was just so tired.... Crooking her little finger, she purred, "Come here."

He did so eagerly, only grabbing her elbow when she took a step forward and stumbled. "Miss Darling, are you okay?"

"Of course," she lied. Grabbing the front of his shirt, she pulled him down and placed her lips over his, kissing him before he could say anything else. She just hoped that whatever she had wasn't contagious because poor Kerry didn't deserve to get sick when she was freeing him.

Releasing him, she fell back against the desk, thankful that it was there to hold her up; her muscles had turned to putty and she was pretty sure her insides were liquefying. If she had been able to, she would have left when Kerry was stunned but she couldn't seem to move.

When he opened his eyes, he blinked a few times and then looked around the office, startling when he saw her standing there. Smiling warmly, cautiously, he held out his hand, "Hi, I'm Kerry."

"Lexi," she laughed, taking his hand and shaking it. "It's a pleasure to meet you."

"You, too," he grinned, boyishly handsome and oblivious to the things she made him do. She still felt a little guilty, even though it hadn't been her fault entirely. His brow pulled together in a frown as he looked at her and she was afraid he was remembering. But he simply put the back of his hand on her forehead, "Um, you look really sick. Are you sure you should be here?"

"I'm just waiting for my ride to come back and get me," she murmured softly, focusing on the Kerry that was attached to the wonderfully cool hand pressing against her forehead. She glanced up as Cole walked through the door, a smile lighting her face, "And there he is."

Cole's smile disappeared as he stepped forward and caught her in his arms as she passed out.

*****

Lexi blinked her eyes open and saw Cole sitting at the side of her bed, concern darkening his eyes as he looked at her. It took her a moment to figure out why she wasn't curled up in Duncan's arms on his bed, and when she did she grimaced.

How could she have fainted at work? How embarrassing; had Cole not been there.... Reaching out, she smiled as he took her hand in his own, "So, you took me to the hospital?"

"You passed out, Lexi," he scolded her gently, kissing her knuckles in relief. "The doctor says you're going to be okay but she has you on a full spectrum antibiotic; your white blood cell count was extremely high."

"I haven't been here too long, have I?" she asked, wishing she could call Duncan up and ask if she could come over; she wanted to curl up in his arms and have him hold her. But of course she couldn't. She should stop thinking about him; it was over. He didn't know her anymore.

"Nah, only a few hours." He chuckled, brushing a strand of damp hair from her face. "The doctor said that as soon as you woke up you should be good to go; just so long as you pick up the prescription at the pharmacy and rest."

"Ugh," she groaned with a smile. It was easier to pretend she was all right as long as she kept on smiling; the moment she forgot to smile, the pain would come rushing back in and she would drown. All she had to do was get through the day, the moment. "All this for a little fever."

"It was a fever of 105," his voice was rough. "The doctor was surprised by how fast your temperature went down when she administered the antibiotics. She said that it usually doesn't work that quickly but in your case she was happy that it did. I was surprised they were letting you go but she had the lab re-run your blood and everything was back to normal."

Swinging her legs over the side of the bed, desperate to get out of the hospital, she paused a moment as the room continued to spin. Chuckling to herself, she smiled up at Cole. "That was a rush but I don't want to experience it again. Get me out of here."

"Lexi," he looked at her with his clear green eyes and she stilled. "The doctor noticed a... bite mark on the curve of your neck; what exactly happened this weekend?"

She looked at him for a moment, blinked, and then laughed as her fingers went to the area Duncan bit. Despite her misery over losing him, she would always have the memories from that night and for that she was grateful. "If I told you it would make you blush, Cole."

"I don't blush easily," he said smugly.

She grinned, wagging her eyebrows at him, "This would make you blush."

He smiled but concern still marred his expression, "At first the doctor thought that perhaps the bite had something to do with your fever but there was no redness or swelling around it. She thought maybe perhaps a dog might have bitten you and was prepared to order up a course of rabies shots."

Lexi shuddered at the thought, knowing that the treatment for rabies was not something to be taken lightly. "It wasn't a dog that bit me, Cole."

Cocking his head to the side he looked at her in confusion until realization dawned and his eyes widened with fascination. Lowering his voice, he leaned in, "That uptight prick in the suit bit you? Kinky."

"You have no idea," she whispered back. Stretching, arching her back, she groaned as her tight muscles pulled pleasurably, "I feel unbelievably good right now. And starving. Do you think we could pick up a couple of steaks on the way home?"

"You haven't been released yet," he chuckled, helping her to her feet since it was obvious she was determined to get going. "Besides, the doctor wants to check you out once more before releasing you to me; otherwise she will insist on calling your mom."

Working a few more kinks out of her back, she looked at him with a slight frown, "You didn't call up my parents, did you? You know I don't like to worry them."

"I was prepared to if the fever didn't come down," he admitted. "But no; I didn't. I did call Dima and he said he would be here in a few minutes which is right about...." Glancing at his watch, he grinned as Dima rushed into the room with Ashley hard on his heel. "Now."

"Lexi," Dima panted, pulling her into a tight hug. "When Cole called and told me you had fainted I thought the world had stopped spinning; thank God you're all right."

Lexi awkwardly patted him on the back since her arms were plastered to her sides. "I had a slight fever and they put me on some antibiotics; no big."

Ashley's nostrils flared slightly as she took a deep breath and looked around the room in confusion. When her gaze landed on Lexi, she paused, blinking a few times. Coming closer, she tilted her head to the side in an inquisitive manner, "Antibiotics you say?"

When Lexi nodded, Ashley asked, "You weren't, by any chance, bit recently, were you?"

Lexi and Cole exchanged a look before they both burst out laughing, "I was but it wasn't the bite that made me sick; it was something else."

"Interesting," Ashley murmured, contemplating something. Her gaze darted to Dima and a slow smile curled her lips, "Very interesting."

"As soon as I am released from this sterile prison Cole and I are going to pick up some steaks," Lexi grinned, ignoring the dull ache where her heart used to be. "Do you think you two might want to join us?"

"Honey, when it comes to steak, I will be there with bells on," Ashley grinned, her eyes dancing with intense joy that seemed oddly out of place in the hospital.

*****

As soon as she finished the last bite of her monstrous steak, Lexi wiped her mouth off with the napkin and then leaned back in her chair, "My God, has meat every tasted so delicious?"

"Do you really want me to answer that?" Ashley asked with a sparkle in her blue eyes, making the small group chuckle.

"No, we really don't," Dima groaned, throwing his napkin down. Putting his arm around Ashley's shoulders, the pair also leaned back and Dima put his hand over his stomach as he looked at Lexi with a glimmer of laughter in his eyes, "I have never seen you eat so much in my life; have you turned into a carnivore?"

"It's the hospital food," she said with a completely straight face. It was easy to pretend everything was okay when one was surrounded by good friends. "You know how bland that stuff tastes. If it weren't for the promise of real food after I got out I would never have made it."

"You were there for a few hours," Cole grumbled, throwing his napkin at her. "And most of that time you spent asleep."

"I know," Lexi groaned dramatically, putting the back of her hand against her forehead and tilting her head back in a languishing pose, "I nearly perished."

Cole abruptly stood up and tackled her around the waist, sending her and the chair backwards until she was looking up at the ceiling and laughing as Cole lay next to her. But he wasn't laughing; his eyes blackened as he growled, "Don't ever do that to me again, Lexi; never again."

"I'm so sorry," she whispered, her lips curled up into a smile as her eyes watered. If her smile faltered for even a moment she wouldn't be able to hold back the waterworks and so she held that smile in place even when she apologized to Cole. "I don't even know what happened; one moment I was fine and the next the room was spinning. It happened so fast."

"Why are you smiling?" His teeth were clamped together in a wounded grimace as he glared at her with hurt eyes.

"If I stop smiling I'll die, Cole," she said as a tear slipped down her cheek. "Give me a few days and I'll be able to go out without a smile plastered on my face."

He brushed the tear away, glancing at Dima and Ashley who were staring at them in confusion. Clearing his throat, he stood up and then pulled her to her feet, pulled her into a hug. Softly, he asked, "Do you want me to send the love birds home?"

"No," she smiled softly at Dima and Ashley. "I think it's nice that people can fall in love and be happy."

"Hey!" Ashley beamed, standing up and pulling Dima to his feet. "We should go to a karaoke bar and get up on the stage and sing."

"No," Lexi said firmly, not about to have a repeat of what happened in Cancun. How horrible would it be to be in a roomful of people making out when the only person she wanted to kiss was.... She looked around the intimate setting and tears not so unexpectedly welled up in her eyes. When the others tried to offer their comfort, she laughed humorlessly, trying to stop the tears from coming. She drenched three tissues as she laughed and cried, "I am so sorry about this; I don't know why I'm crying so hard."

Cole pulled her into a hug and she let him, accepting the comfort he offered because she needed it. "I think you should get a change of scenery, Lexi. Just to get you over this hump."

"I think you're right." She didn't care where she went, she just wanted to go away for a few days and clear her head. It was ridiculous to be upset over something when she knew from the very beginning that this was how it was going to end, how it had to end. And if she had the chance to do it all again, she would make the exact same decisions. She just had to get over her aching heart and get on with her life. She was Lexi Darling and she was a Siren; life couldn't possibly be any cooler than that.

And as soon as her heart thawed out she would be sure to remember that.

Chapter 18 (Thursday)

Lexi was resting under the sun out on the lounge chair in the back yard of her Aunt Cassandra's large, beach front mansion, complete with a pool. A week and a half ago she had arrived on her aunt's doorstep with a normal wardrobe, a lot to think about and not a single wig. Aunt Cassie made sure there were plenty of things for them to do, though Lexi was happy just hanging out at the house, on the beach. It had been a relaxing holiday and she was fully recovered from whatever flu bug had knocked her out. Her heart, on the other hand, was still a little battered but she knew she was going to be okay.

Although the dreams that were keeping her awake at night were… odd. She dreamt she was a wolf, running through the woods with the gorgeous black wolf with Duncan's eyes chasing her; it was a mating run. In her dreams, she could see the world as if through a wolf's eyes; smell things that were long gone; hear things that were far, far away.

And when the black Duncan-wolf caught her, they made love as wolves, his teeth holding her by the scruff of her neck as he mounted her from behind. But then their bodies would transform and they made love as humans, face to face. While she was dreaming it made perfect sense that she would be a wolf one moment and a human the next; it was in the morning that she realized there was something seriously wrong with her brain. It wouldn't have been so bad if she didn't crave meat so damn much: she wanted meat at every meal, bacon, pork chops, ribs, steak, chicken wings.... And everything smelled so much stronger than before. It wasn't natural and there had been several times that her aunt looked at her with perplexed amusement.

"Hey, you," Cassie's voice broke through her reverie. With her ash blond hair, she didn't look like her sisters. At least, not until you got close and saw her hazel eyes and full mouth; then she was definitely related to Charisma and Sophie. Carrying a tray with two glasses of ice cold lemonade, she smiled down at her niece. "You might want to consider heading in soon; you've been out here for a while."

"SPF 30," Lexi grinned, gratefully accepting the cool beverage. A drop of moisture spilled onto her nearly bare breast and she shivered, enjoying the chill against her skin on the hot afternoon. Taking a long drink, she smiled, "Thank you."

Cassie lay back on the other chair, closing her eyes. Just as Lexi was beginning to think that her aunt just wanted to bathe in the sun, Cassie took a sip of her lemonade and murmured, "I remember you when you were a little girl."

"Please," Lexi cringed, the image of her mousy self flashing in her head.

Cassie smiled. "You were such a serious, imaginative little thing, creating all of these stories in your head. You were also very charming, once you warmed up."

Lexi made a face, "I don't remember it that way at all."

"It's true," Cassie insisted. "It's why they thought you weren't a Siren, or enough of one, to warrant bothering you with the truth."

"I know," Lexi grimaced, torn between the desire to have been told and the wish she never knew at all. If she didn't know she was mesmerizing Duncan, she would still be with him because she wouldn't have accepted his decision to end things. She would have pushed and pushed until he accepted she was a part of his life and eventually he would have told her all of his secrets. She had spent a lot of time contemplating what his huge secret could be and came up with a variety of options, from premeditated murder of a potential rival to being occasionally gay. Whatever it was, she doubted there was anything big enough to make her hate him. And she couldn't imagine him outright killing anyone. Or being gay.

"We didn't know you'd be a late bloomer," Cassie continued. "Or the most… vibrant Siren there's been in several generations."

Lexi chuckled, "My plumage is safely at home; this vacation is strictly a non-wig vacation."

"That's not what I mean and I think you know that," Cassie grumbled, smiling in spite of herself. "It's… well, I think our worries did not come to fruition and for that I am grateful."

"Mom and Aunt Sophie were awfully concerned about true love and whatnot but it's all a bunch of bull," Lexi chuckled, taking a sip of the sweet lemonade. "According to them I should be languishing at the bottom of the sea and other than missing Duncan an obscene amount I feel fantastic. Better than fantastic."

"You fell in love?" Cassie's voice held dismay.

"No, of course not," Lexi shook her head, denying any feeling she had for Duncan. "Of course I didn't fall in love. Remember? I'd be languishing at the bottom of the sea if I had."

"When you arrived on my doorstep you were a wreck." Cassie said considerately, watching Lexi closely.

"I was on strong antibiotics for an unknown infection," Lexi returned calmly as her heart started pumping twice as fast as it had been beating before. "Besides, it doesn't matter if I fell in love, and I am not saying I did, because he didn't return my feelings, that is if I had any, and I kissed him good-bye."

"And he let you go?" Cassie's brows drew together in a thoughtful frown.

"I'm here aren't I?" Lexi chuckle sounded forced even to her own ears. Clearing her throat, she added, "I'm just a regular Siren, like my sisters; just a late bloomer, like you said."

"You're not like your sisters," Cassandra said softly. "You're more like me or your mother but even that isn't a fair comparison since you are so much more of a Siren than either of us."

Everything within Lexi stilled, her thoughts, her heart, "What do you mean?"

"I fell in love once, the only man to hold my heart and share my bed... well, until a few months ago," Cassandra said softly, blushing and looking out over the pool, not seeing the present. "But he didn't love me in return. Unlike other, um, lesser Sirens, the unrequited love nearly destroyed me. If it weren't for Sophie and Charisma, I think I would have 'languished at the bottom of the sea,' as you say. It took years for me to recover and I'm still missing pieces of my heart. Hell, I just recently started having sex again."

Lexi didn't want to hear about her aunt's sex life but she listened, fascinated despite the uncomfortable topic. Cassandra chuckled to herself, "I missed sex but I just couldn't find it in me to... make love without love. Your Aunt Sophie, on the other hand, can sleep with anything on two legs and enjoy every moment of it. She just draws them in, enjoys them, and then sends them on their way with a kiss and a pat on their ass. I have been lucky to fall in love again, though not nearly as deep as before."

Cassie's gaze flashed to the man standing off to the side; a gorgeous creature with olive brown skin, long, bluish-black hair and black eyes. Marco was twenty six and Cassie's man-of-affairs; at least that was what Lexi believed until that moment. Clearing her throat, her voice was a little garbled, Lexi said, "He's a good looking man but I don't know what it has to do with me since I didn't fall in love with Duncan, or whatever, and I'm not languishing."

"Maybe you're a new breed of Siren," Cassie grinned mischievously. Nodding her head, she added, "Maybe you can love as passionately and deeply as me and enjoy sex as much as your Aunt Sophie. Wouldn't it be nice to have more than one Grand Love Affair?"

"Okay," Lexi said wryly, sipping the lemonade through her straw and becoming peripherally aware of the gorgeous Marco standing next to her. She jumped when his shadow came over her, making the lemonade splash over the edge of the glass and onto her stomach. Setting the glass down on the ground, she wiped her stomach and grimaced; she had been enjoying that. Oh, well; she'd just grab some more when she had enough sun.

"Shall we try a little experiment?" Cassie grinned. Without waiting for Lexi to accept or decline, she smiled up at Marco, using her Siren charm, "Sweetie, give my niece one of your… special massages."

"Cass, I don't think…." She yelped as warm hands grabbed her ankles and slowly started massaging her legs. Her eyes closed in pleasure as he worked muscles she hadn't realized had been so tight; maybe a massage wouldn't be so bad. Relaxing back in her chair, she groaned as he got a particularly sore muscle. Keeping her eyes closed, she grinned, "See? I can handle this."

"Marco?"

Hot breath moved over her thigh as blunt fingers started tugging at her bikinis bottoms. Between one heartbeat and the next, Lexi was out of the chair and Marco was on his back with Lexi's claws at his throat. Her voice was feral as she growled, "Don't touch me; you are not allowed to touch me."

His eyes widened impossibly in his handsome face and she was pretty sure he pissed himself; she seemed to be having that effect on men lately. Clearing her throat, she slowly released him and stepped back and offered a remorseful grimace, "Wow, I am so sorry about that; I have no idea where that came from; I'm not sure what came over me."

With a whimper, he scampered over to Cassandra's side, whose own eyes were as large as saucers as she stared at Lexi in horror. "What in the name of all that is holy was that?"

"I'm not sure," Lexi admitted. She licked her lips and then a caught her lower lip between her teeth, awkwardly sitting back down on the chaise, her feet firmly planted on the ground as she stared straight ahead. "It wasn't the first time it happened; the day after I kissed Duncan good-bye I had a similar reaction to a dick in the office. He pissed himself, too."

Cassandra was quiet, pensive, for a long time, her palm on Marco's head, comforting him. "Is your… Duncan human?"

"Of course he is," Lexi scoffed, her heart picking up speed once again as she paused. A lack of humanity could be a viable secret – and it would explain so much. "At least, I think he is. I mean, what else could he possibly be?"

"Sweetheart," Cassandra said kindly, considering her lover was cowering in fear at her side. "You're a Siren; maybe there are other things out there we don't know about."

"Well, whatever," Lexi frowned, waving her hand through the air, her thoughts coalescing on the possibility that Duncan was more than he seemed. It was kind of an exhilarating thought, except she had kissed him goodbye and would never be given the chance to discover just what Duncan Tremain could be.

"I'm so sorry for causing you all of this trouble, Lexi," Cassandra said solemnly, standing up and taking Marco into her arms. Holding the much bigger man, comforting him and protecting him from the vicious Lexi, she added, "But when I mentioned what I saw to Sophie and Charisma, I didn't know they never told you."

"It's not your fault," Lexi said absently, Duncan wasn't human…. "I'm okay with being a Siren and I think I would rather know than not, all things considered."

If Duncan wasn't human, what could he be and how could she possibly find out? The curiosity was going to drive her mad. Would it be considered bad form to reintroduce herself into his life, make sure to keep her humming to herself, and maybe make him fall in love this time? Enough to get him to trust her with his secret, with what he was?

Cassie whispered softly, "You should go back inside, love."

"After a quick dip." Shifting off her seat, Lexi adjusted her bikini bottoms as she sauntered over to the pool. A swim would help her think; if nothing else it would get the sticky lemonade off her stomach. Diving off the diving board, she swam through the cool water, feeling it surround her, embrace her.

If he wasn't human, that would change everything.

She had spent enough time sitting around and moping; she was going to pack her bag and fly back home, storm the office and demand… an… introduction. Shit. She was going to have to come up with a better plan.

*****

Duncan sat in front of his computer, the glow of his desk lamp the only light in the other-wise dark room. For almost two weeks he had worked non-stop, not allowing any thoughts non-work related filter into his head. Tomorrow was his last day at the *lavish* offices and he would be able to move on, get on with the rest of his life. It didn't matter if he was shattered inside; he was still an Alpha, still in charge.

Rubbing his eyes, he leaned back in his chair, deliberately not thinking about any tempestuous vixen. He was going to offer her a pay raise when she did return, via a memo, of course. Her column had breathed new life into the magazine and he hadn't even realized. All he had known was *lavish* was an excellent investment; an established magazine that seemed to be increasing its sales in the harsh climate. It wasn't until after he looked over the figures and compared them to her arrival that he realized she was the reason why.

He had been an idiot, about a great many things.

Giving himself permission to indulge himself for five minutes, he closed his eyes and pictured her as she had looked in the kitchen the Monday he let her go. Her hazel-green eyes sparkled as she went to her knees and, after unzipping his pants, she eased his erection out and slowly stroked the rigid length took. Taking his cock into her hot, wet mouth, she looked so sexy and he could still feel the pleasure as she took his cock deeper and deeper.

Mechanically, Duncan freed his erection from the bindings of his pants, stroking the hard flesh as he continued picturing Lexi on her knees, pleasuring him with her lips and tongue. Sensation had shot up his penis, into the base of his spine and he hadn't known if he would be able to remain standing. And then the wicked little minx started playing with his testicles and his brain exploded. She had looked so self-satisfied after she brought him to his knees.

He concentrated on her expression as she wiped the excess semen from her lips and stuck the finger into her mouth, the sheer seductiveness of it. Straining, desperate for release, he fucked his palm imagining it was her tender touch.

I love you, his wolf whispered in Lexi's voice and his body tightened as an orgasm tore through him. The wolf snickered as Duncan fell forward in the chair to clean up the mess, angry with himself and angry with the wolf.

"I had no choice but to let her go," he said out loud to the empty room. Tucking his cock back into his pants, he scowled even more as he realized he hadn't even had an erection for the past two weeks. He could try to convince himself it was because he had been working so hard but he knew that was a lie. He hadn't allowed himself even a moment to think about Lexi and the moment he did.... "Fuck."

Almost violently, he powered up his computer; he was going to check his email one last time and then he was going to get out of there for the night. If his suspicions were correct he was going to find a way to kill the fucking wolf who was destroying his life.

Taking a few breaths to calm down, he half expected to see something from Lexi, now that he allowed himself to think about her. His heart leapt in his chest when he saw the subject line titled "Lexi Darling," and with a trembling hand, he clicked on it.

Mr. Tremain-

What would you like me to do with Miss Darling's final paycheck? She left no forwarding instructions and she has not returned any of the messages I have left for her.

-Mrs. Reynolds

Duncan flew out of his chair and opening the door to his office with such force it slammed against the wall. Mrs. Reynolds jumped, spinning around in her desk to face him with wide eyes, "Can I, er, help you, Mr. Tremain?"

"Lexi Darling quit?" he asked through clenched teeth, the veins on his neck popping out until he felt like his head was going to explode.

"I gave you her resignation letter and final column almost two weeks ago," she calmly explained as she pushed her chair a little further away from him. "It was in a folder marked 'Lexi Darling.'"

That would explain why he hadn't seen it; he refused to allow her into his thoughts and so he had ruthlessly denied anything having to do with her. "Get her back. Now."

"Um, she hasn't been returning my calls," she repeated the words from her email. "Her roommates tell me that she is on indefinite vacation and will forward any messages to her but they couldn't make any promises that she would return them."

Duncan's fingers squeezed into a tight fist and he wanted to punch a hole through something, preferably his wolf's mangy ass. "I want her address, her phone number, the Rudnar's phone number…."

"Why do you want the Rudnar's phone number?" Mrs. Reynolds asked slowly even as she wrote down the items he had rattled off.

Duncan froze as a hazy memory came ripping through his head. *"One last secret, Duncan; I'm a Rudnar; Alexandra Rudnar, the youngest daughter you wanted me to interview." She laughed but it was so full of sadness he couldn't fathom it coming from her. "I'm also a Siren and I am so, so sorry." Standing up on her toes, she pressed her lips against his, "I love you."*

Slowly he looked at his secretary, "She loves me."

"Well, of course she does," the woman scoffed. "Anyone with two eyes could see it. Miss Darling was a flirt but she never actively pursued anyone until you came along." She chuckled at her memories, "That little girl was tenacious; it's no wonder she quit when you broke up with her."

"What makes you think I was the one doing the breaking?" he asked, aghast at his behavior yet powerless to stop. He needed to know everything about Lexi – about Alexandra.

"Pshaw," Mrs. Reynolds rolled her eyes. "As if that girl would do the breaking. I swear men are so oblivious."

"Mrs. Reynolds," Duncan murmured firmly. "I'd like to remind you that I sign your paychecks. Now if you please, find me the information I requested because as you may have realized, I am not oblivious any longer."

She beamed up at him and then frowned, "Um, Mr. Tremain, you have... something on your shirt. You may want to take care of that."

Duncan looked down and swore when he saw the viscous fluid on the front of his shirt; it was obvious to anyone with eyes what it was. Acting like it wasn't there, he nodded his head in his secretary's direction, "Very well. Now, about those phone numbers...."

He disappeared back into his den to the sound of Mrs. Reynolds's laughter. Swearing yet again, he tore the shirt from his body and threw it across the room. Irritated, he put on a clean shirt as he made a mental list of things he needed to accomplish: kill the wolf, learn everything he could about Sirens, pay a visit to Ashley, find Lexi. And as he let thoughts of Lexi fill his head, he felt the familiar rush of sensation as his penis thickened and grew and he amended his list: discover anything about Sirens; his brother had dated a Siren, he might know something. Otherwise he could hunt down one of the Rudnar women and pry the information from them. Then, once he knew something, he'd pay a visit to Ashley and then he'd kill the wolf.

And then there would be nothing preventing him from hunting Lexi down and claiming her for his own; the wolf couldn't have her.

*****

Ashley had just stepped out of the shower when there was a furious knocking at her front door. Wrapping a towel around her body, she left the humid heat of the bathroom and answered it, surprised to see her Alpha standing there looking worse for the wear. His cropped black hair was slightly longer than usual and standing on end; his silver eyes were red-rimmed, his clothes were wrinkled and he looked like death. “You look like hell, Duncan.”

Without a word, he clasped her head and smashed his mouth against hers in the least finessed kiss he had ever given her. There was desperation in his kiss as he thrust his tongue into her mouth and tugged at the towel. As the towel fell, he guided her backwards against the wall, his lips growing more desperate and frantic with each heartbeat.

Grabbing her wrist, he guided her hand to the front of his pants, holding it over the flaccid penis as he frantically humped her palm, his hips thrusting almost violently. He growled against her lips, “Tell me she isn’t my mate.”

Trailing kisses along her neck, cupping a breast in his hand, he rasped, “Tell me.”

Before she could tell him what he wanted to hear, his face was pressed against the curve of her neck and his arms were wrapped around her damp and naked body. He pulled her into him and held on to her as if he were a man drowning and he had nothing else to hold onto. Awkwardly, she patted the shuddering back, “Duncan, what is it?”

“My wolf claimed her,” his voice shook with strong emotion. “My fucking wolf claimed a Siren for a mate; she's mine and he claimed her!”

Ashley gasped; how could Duncan be surprised by his wolf’s actions? Weren’t they bonded? “I see; does Lexi know she’s your mate?”

“No,” he ground out, abruptly letting her go and stepping away from her. His cheeks colored as he saw her standing there, naked. Shrugging out of his coat, he handed it to her as he turned around, giving her some privacy which was ridiculous since he had seen her naked plenty of times. Dragging his fingers through his wildly messy hair, he spat, “She probably thinks I don’t remember her because in her fucking selflessness she gave me the Siren’s good-bye kiss.”

“What’s that?” Ashley asked, clumsily putting the proffered jacket on, breathing in the wild, musky scent of Duncan and loving it, even though she was in a relationship and unexpectedly madly in love with the man.

“A Siren can return a person’s memories, or rather, erase a person’s memories, with a kiss,” he bit out, pacing relentlessly back and forth across Ashley’s carpet. “In their fucked up heads, it’s their way of letting a person go and I suppose it is kinder than simply banishing them but, damn it, she kissed me good-bye.”

“How do you know this?” Fascinated by Duncan’s aberrant behavior, she sat down on the edge of the seat and continued watching him wear a path in her floor.

“I’m an Alpha,” he said simply, arrogantly, not quite meeting her eyes. “It is my business to know these things.”

“Why would she kiss you good-bye?” she asked slowly, her mind struggling to catch up to everything her Alpha was dumping on her.

He snorted, “Sirens believe in love and all of that nonsense.”

“And you don’t love her.” It was a statement but Duncan didn’t know how to respond to it. He already liked Lexi; she had a quick mind and a thousand watt smile that fried his brain, but love? She was… Lexi; it had been easy to say the words to her when he had thought their time together was limited but he didn’t *love* her, not in a sunshine and roses and rainbows way; his feelings for her were far too tempestuous. In time he supposed he could love her but it didn’t matter because she was his mate; he really had no choice.

The fucking wolf took that away from him when he claimed her.

“If she’s your mate, why didn’t you know?” Ashley’s simple question interrupted his musings before he could reach a satisfactory answer because when he was with Lexi the only organ doing any thinking was his dick.

“Because I didn’t allow myself the luxury of thinking about her,” he muttered through tight lips. "Because I hadn't realized it had been two weeks since I've had an erection until the moment I thought about her. Because she's mine, not his; he shouldn't have claimed her."

Ashley bit her lips to prevent a giggle but it didn't help; a burble of laughter escaped and she looked at Duncan with sympathy, "Poor Duncan; two weeks without an erection is a lifetime for a wolf."

"Only if the wolf is unmated," he grumbled.

"So, what happens now?"

The question was deceptively hard to answer because he didn't know if Sirens had the same physiology as humans, if they work react as negatively as humans did to the wolf's venom. Or would they have a worse reaction? Once, his brother had come close to taking a Siren for a wife but then Stacey had come along and the Siren married some other poor sap.

Since Lexi was his mate, whether he wished it or not, he would discover a way to keep her safe. Otherwise he would never have sex again, which was, quite frankly, the most depressing thought he had ever had. Of the two extremes: sex with Lexi or sex never again, he knew which one he preferred. But first he had to find Lexi. And if she didn't love him, despite Mrs. Reynolds's belief that she did, he hoped that in time she may grow fond of him. He'd keep her so sexually sated she wouldn't be able to even think about leaving him. Also, he could try wining and dining her, or whatever it took to win her heart. Maybe he would take her tandem jumping from an airplane; that seemed like something she'd appreciate.

"Look, if you see her or her roommates, let her know I'm looking for her," he sighed in resignation; he was a mated wolf. "And, um, I'm sorry about..." he motioned with his hand to her state of undress. "All of this. Thank you, Ashley."

"No problem," she said with a soft smile, watching him as he let himself out of her house.

The door to her bedroom opened and Dima was standing there with a dark scowl on her gorgeous face. Crossing his arms over his scrumptiously naked chest, he glared at her, "You were going to let that prick fuck you just because he wanted to prove something to himself?"

Absurdly pleased by the acid jealousy eating away at him, she shrugged her slender shoulders and stood up, letting Duncan's coat slide to the floor and not caring about the wrinkles. Running her hands over Dima's muscled chest, she purred, "It wouldn't have been the first time, love; he is, after all, the Alpha, or he will be."

A low growl emanated from the back of his throat as he picked her up and threw her over his shoulder, "You're mine, Ash; you bit me and made me a wolf and you're fucking mine."

She squealed her delight, knowing that eventually, she was going to have to tell the pack, tell Duncan, the secret to a successful human transition. Powerful antibiotics. They were only needed to get them over the hump and then everything seemed to go smoothly. It was such a simple solution that nobody had considered because wolves never got sick. And because so few attempts were made at converting humans. Dima had been a wolf for almost two weeks and the transition had been painless. "Take me to bed, my lover."

"Your mate."

Her eyes lit up at the words and what they implied. "Really? You'll claim me?"

"Hell, Ash, I should have done it as soon as you turned me," he growled.

"Are you ever going to tell your roommates about us? About you?"

"When Lexi comes clean about being a Siren," he said, kicking the door shut behind him. Tossing Ashley onto the bed, he said, "When she admits to being in love with a wolf."

Flinging himself onto the bed so that he covered Ashley's body with his own, he growled, "After I've fucked you fifty ways from Sunday and you scream my name and howl at the moon then I might think about it."

Chapter 19 (Saturday)

Uncomfortable with knocking on the Rudnar's door and demanding to know where the youngest Rudnar daughter was, Duncan decided to track her down through her roommates. His first stop had been to *Skin*, since Dima was a member of his pack now. Despite the early hour, both Dima and Ashley were inside, Dima's arm firmly around Ashley as he glared at the Alpha.

"You're not going to try to fuck my mate again," Dima growled and Duncan had to give him credit for his foolish bravery for standing up to the Alpha. "I claimed her after you left last night with your limp dick between your legs."

Okay, there was a line between foolish bravery and just plain dumb foolishness; Dima had taken a giant leap over it. But Duncan didn't come to put the new puppy in his place.... Narrowing his eyes, he looked at Dima, letting his wolf out for a moment to confirm his suspicion. "When did that happen?"

With furious rage, Dima bit out, "I was there at the apartment...."

Duncan turned his burning eyes on Ashley, "When did you turn him?"

"About two weeks ago," Ashley replied meekly, though her eyes were defiant.

"Are you insane?" he asked, his tone deceptively soft. "If you had killed him it would have devastated Lexi."

"It was a chance I was willing to take," Dima said boldly, putting his arm around Ashley. "To be with Ashley I would risk anything."

Duncan laughed without humor and shook his head, "You're a fool. But I didn't come here to discuss your... recklessness; I want to know where Lexi is."

Dima smiled cruelly, "I don't have to tell you that."

"You're a member of my pack," Duncan reminded him firmly. "Your loyalty is to me."

"My loyalty is to her," Dima retorted. "But I'll be sure to let her know you're looking for her. By the way, does she know what you are?"

Duncan ground his molars together; the puppy's loyalty to Lexi was admirable but it made his life that much more difficult. Looking at Ashley, he bit out, "Keep an eye on your new dog; make sure he doesn't leave a mess on the carpet."

With that, he stormed out of the bar and decided to make his way to the other roommate's haunt: Cole's studio, hoping to extract the information he needed from the artist.

Within a few minutes, Duncan stood in the studio looking at some of Cole's more recent work. The set of incredibly erotic body photos of Lexi caught his attention and he stopped to stare at the woman who had captured his imagination. With the artful arrangement of limbs, what could have been pornographic was art; exquisite in their lines and illumination. Cole truly was a talented artist, even if Lexi's photos had jealousy eating at Duncan's stomach and hunger burning his gut. His cock responded with eagerness, despite the fact that Lexi wasn't near.

"They're my favorite photos, too," a familiar voice murmured behind him.

Without turning around, Duncan knew that it was Cole. "They're beautiful."

"I have a beautiful subject to work with." Duncan could hear the smile in the other man's voice. "Lexi is... well, Lexi. But, of course, you know that."

"I do," Duncan murmured, turning his head and looking at Cole in his vibrant orange shirt, unbuttoned to reveal his naked chest. Duncan cleared his throat and looked back at the pictures, "Where is she?"

Cole actually chuckled, "She's where she needs to be."

"What the hell is that supposed to mean?" Duncan snarled, turning around and glaring at the man.

Cole's smile widened, infuriating Duncan to no end; this man knew where she was and he wasn't going to tell him. "Mr. Tremain, I'm sure you understand; my loyalties are to her, not you."

"Just tell me where she is, damn it."

"I can't do that, not until I know you're worthy of her and, quite honestly, you'll never be worthy," Cole grinned, obviously enjoying having all of the power.

Duncan's molars ground together and his nostrils flared; he just wanted to find Lexi, to hold her in his arms once more. To breathe her in. "I simply want to know where I can find her."

"I'm afraid I'm not at liberty to tell you," Cole said, almost apologetically. "However, I am willing to... trade."

Duncan did not particularly care for the way Cole was looking at him; as if seeing him naked and imagining the possibilities. Glaring at the other man, he ground out, "What kind of trade?"

Cole bit back a laugh at the guarded expression on Duncan's face; the man should be concerned. But what Cole did, he did for Lexi. "I'll throw you a bone if you let me photograph you."

"What's the catch?" Duncan asked skeptically.

"Isn't it obvious?" Cole grinned, nodding his head towards his photos. "I want you naked."

Duncan closed his eyes and swallowed. He wasn't uncomfortable with his body, but posing nude was not something he ever considered doing. And the fact that he was even entertaining the idea proved just how tied up he was. He could almost hear his wolf laughing at him. "What guarantee do I have that the information you give me will be… useful?"

"None," Cole beamed. "However, it's something Lexi wants and since you seem so eager to find her, I figure any scrap of information would be… desirable."

"Fine," Duncan agreed through clenched teeth since Cole said those magic words *It's something Lexi wants*. Duncan knew he would do anything for her, even pose naked for her best friend. But he didn't have to be happy about it. "When do you want to do it?"

"Right now," Cole laughed, already heading towards the studio. Talking over his shoulder, assuming (correctly) that Duncan was following him, he said, "I've been dying to take your picture; your lines are just incredible."

"Great," Duncan grumbled, not sounding very happy about it, which made Cole laugh even harder.

Surprisingly, or perhaps not, Cole was a complete professional and Duncan was impressed with the man's ability to see beauty in what appeared to be ordinary muscles and sinew. Within moments of the first picture being taken, Duncan was more or less comfortable. Well, as comfortable as possible considering he was naked in front of another man taking pictures. He just kept reminding himself that it was for Lexi and that the man on the other side of the camera did this for a living. And his private parts were carefully concealed.

"There," Cole said calmly, putting his equipment away afterwards; nearly an hour later. "That wasn't so bad, was it?"

"Fuck you," Duncan growled, buttoning his shirt back up. Of course, Cole laughed. With a sigh, Duncan smiled, too, "It wasn't the end of the world."

"You are a photographer's dream," Cole grinned.

"Aren't you forgetting something?" Duncan asked as Cole went about his business. When Cole lifted his head and cocked his head to the side in feigned confusion, Duncan's raised an eyebrow, "Our bargain?"

"I haven't forgotten," Cole grinned, disappearing into another room for a long moment before coming back with a large portfolio. Handing it to Duncan, he shrugged his shoulders, the orange shirt gaping open. "Here."

Cautiously he took it from Cole, asking, "What's this?"

"An early wedding present."

Carefully, Duncan opened it and his breath caught in his throat. Inside was a series of photos of Lexi – Alexandra – looking beautiful, a balm to his broken soul. The color pictures showed her with her big, hazel-green eyes and long, gleaming brown hair, wearing a simple dress and looking so damn young and innocent. Only her eyes spoke of wisdom beyond her years: an old soul that he hadn't seen before because she hid it behind laughter and sensuality. Duncan's heart squeezed in his chest and he had to swallow a few times before he was able to speak. "Thank you."

Cole put a hand on Duncan's shoulder in a show of support, "Good luck, my friend."

He tried to tell himself that it wasn't love but he knew he would be lying. He had loved her almost from the very beginning and he hadn't known. But his wolf had.

Fuck; he was going to have to deal with the bastard once and for all if he had any hope of being with Lexi. Of being whole.

*****

Duncan sat in the darkened study, the glass of bourbon untouched as he willed the confrontation with the wolf. One of the wolf's sense memories filtered into his head, the pure scent of Lexi before he so thoughtlessly took her in his office.

She was a virgin. His clenched his hands into fists even though he knew he hadn't hurt her their first time. His jaw clamped together; he wouldn't have done anything differently had he known. He had been too lost in rapture to think.

She tames me, his wolf whispered. *She makes it so I am able to breathe and I claimed her*

I am aware of that. Duncan's fingers ached but he couldn't unclench his fist.

She's mine, the wolf continued relentlessly. Ruthlessly. *Accept me and she can be ours.*

I will not share.

We're more bonded than you care to believe. The wolf was merciless as he whispered ceaselessly in Duncan's head. *Remember, Duncan; remember what happened eighteen years ago that scared you and embrace your fear.*

Closing his eyes, Duncan relaxed his body and let the memories wash over him, through him; memories he hadn't allowed himself to remember....

Duncan reveled in the freedom of being a wolf and at fifteen he was the youngest member of the pack who could transform at will, going from human to wolf and back again whenever he pleased, between one heartbeat and the next. The best was running through the woods at night, his senses open to the exotic nocturnal world surrounding him.

A tantalizing scent made him freeze: a she-wolf bitch in heat. Without a second thought, he instinctively took off after the she-wolf, frantic to mark her, take her. Catching up to her, he bit the ruff of her neck and started to mount her when the reality crashed into Duncan.

He was fifteen years old; he didn't want his first time having sex to be with an animal. Hell, he didn't want any of his sexual experiences to be with an animal. With every ounce of his strength, he wrestled the horny wolf off the she-wolf, battling against a superior adversary. But he had desperation and fury on his side and after a brief battle that lasted an eternity he got the wolf under control.

Panting, exhausted, he returned to his human form and limped over to a fallen tree. Collapsing against the wood, he leaned against the bark, welcoming the bite of wood against his naked flesh. He had almost lost his virginity to a she-wolf.

A shudder wracked his young body as he covered his face with his hands; the wolf was strong, dominant and demanding. How could he remain who he was if he bonded with the wolf and the wolf proved to be stronger? He would lose who it was to be Duncan.

"What's this?" a gravelly voice sneered as a wolf took human form. An enormous man stood before Duncan, his naked body so much larger than his own, his cold blue eyes gleaming in the darkness. "Are you lost, little lamb?"

Duncan managed to get his exhausted body back on its feet. Pushing his shoulders back and thrusting his chest out, he glared at the unexpected intruder, "This is my land; you are trespassing and I ask that you leave."

"Do you?" the man sneered, his eyes growing brighter as they drifted over Duncan. He let out a low whistle and three more scraggly wolves appeared and Duncan knew that they were shifters even though they didn't shift. "Look what we have here, my pack; a tasty little morsel who thinks we are trespassing."

Duncan could feel the wolf growing within him but he tried to suppress it, not wanting to feel that loss of control again. He held his chin high and when he spoke, his voice didn't quaver at all, "This is the property of the Tremain Alpha; it would be unwise to cross him."

The three wolves cowered but the man threw his head back and laughed in derision, "The all-mighty Tremain? The man is a fool who mates the disgraceful whore who consorted with humans, the whore who gave birth to a half-breed bastard; a wolf who can't even shift to his true form. I spit on the Tremain name."

Fury welled up in Duncan's chest as the strange wolf lambasted his beloved mother, his older brother Philip. As the man continued to taunt him with insults to his family, Duncan lost it, unleashing the wolf, barely noticing that the other man had taken on his wolf form as well. The battle was ferocious and the sounds of a wolf yelping and bones snapping filled the night air as Duncan tore the other wolf apart.

Panting, he slowly came back to himself, returning to human form and looking around at the carnage, realizing what he had done, what his wolf had done. Frightened by his actions, he looked at the three wolves, waiting for them to attack, almost wishing they would. But the three wolves shifted, revealing two women and a man, their naked bodies thin from hunger, their eyes hollow.

"Alpha," one of the women said, but she wasn't looking at the dead wolf, who

had reverted to his human form in death. She was looking at him, at Duncan, her expression one of awe and respect. Going down to her knees she tilted her head to the side in a show of submission and the other two followed suit. Bewildered, Duncan mechanically did what he had seen his father do a thousand times before: he kneeled before them and put his teeth against each throat in turn, accepting them into his pack.

But he was fifteen years old; how the hell could he possibly be the Alpha?

Duncan slowly opened his eyes, remembering the first member of his pack: Marissa. She had offered herself to him that very night but he had been too exhausted in body and mind to give her his virginity. He had been out of his depths when he became an Alpha at fifteen and he had had no choice but to grow up quickly. And what had been meant to be a temporary solution became a popular bar for Shifters and non-Shifters alike.

His wolf had never pushed him again, even agreeing to the ridiculous rules Duncan had set down.

Go back a little further, Duncan, his wolf whispered, pouring salt into his raw wounds. *Remember the first time you shifted; remember* my *memories.*

Closing his eyes, Duncan concentrated, trying to remember that first time, the excitement, the fear. His family was hosting a large gathering and there had been so many people there. Under normal circumstances, Duncan enjoyed himself in such social situations, but that day he had been restless, feverish, as if he no longer belonged in his own skin.

He remembered being annoyed with Philip for flirting with a girl who was too young for him, a girl not much older than Duncan's own fifteen years. Yes, the girl was gorgeous and wildly flirtatious but Philip should know better.

You're not concentrating, the wolf interrupted, nudging his memory a little further. *Do you remember going to the woods to escape?*

"Yes," Duncan's voice shattered the silence, startling him and almost taking him out of the memory.

Duncan! Think!

As soon as Duncan had entered the woods, he began to pace, faster and faster as his blood began to boil and he knew - he knew - what was happening. His father had explained it but mere words could not match the rush of changing. And as he closed his eyes, he willed the transformation.

It had happened so quickly and he hadn't remembered to undress before shifting....

"The memory is fuzzy," Duncan admitted, trying to remember past the torn clothes hanging from his hairy, four-legged body.

My memories, Duncan, the wolf encouraged. *Remember my memories.*

Squeezing his eyes shut, Duncan focused on the feel of shredded material, of being on four legs. Eventually, the memory became clearer as he padded through the woods, absorbing all of the new sights and scents and sounds through his new wolf senses.

For hours he explored the woods, newly born into the wolf world and exulting in his new form. But when a pang of hunger ripped through his stomach he wasn't sure what to do. He still had human thoughts and the idea of tracking down game and eating it raw did not appeal to him; he preferred his meat cooked.

Lifting his snout into the air, he inhaled deeply, hoping to discover an alternative to raw rabbit or raw deer. There! About fifty feet away, someone had left out a peanut butter sandwich. His father or mother must have figured out what had happened and put the food out for him to find when he was ready.

Running, loving how his body moved, how his four legs worked in perfect unison to propel him forward, he came upon a little girl leaning against a tree. She was absorbed in a book while an uneaten sandwich sat next to her on the ground. He didn't want to expose himself to a human, even a child, but he desperately wanted that sandwich.

Stealthily, he crept forward, his eyes on the food. Just as he was about to snag the treat with his teeth, the sandwich disappeared. Irritated, he looked up to see the little girl staring at him with wide, green and gold eyes, the sandwich in her little fingers. He could tear the food from her fingers and run....

"Would you like a bite?" the little human asked, tearing off a piece of the sandwich and tentatively holding it out to him.

Warily, he took the bite, scarfing it down in one swallow and making the girl giggle as she tore off another, bigger piece. She fed him until the food was gone and then looked at him with regret, "I wish I had more to give you but mama only agreed to let me bring one sandwich. She thinks I'll return to the party when I get hungry enough."

Drawn to the sweet, oddly mature, voice, he curled up and lay down beside her, his ears twitching as the wind blew. Her little fingers sank into his fur, petting him, hugging him. "Oh, I do love you. I wish I could have a dog...."

He yipped in protest at being called a dog but she ignored it and continued, "But Thea is allergic so mama says we can't have one. But I think Thea is lying because I saw her playing with a dog this afternoon and she didn't sneeze at all."

The little girl chattered on and on and he was enchanted, wanting to protect her and keep her safe from all harm. As her little arms wrapped around his neck and her cheek pressed against his throat, he vowed to be her guardian.

Closing his eyes, he had fallen asleep.

"Who...." Duncan started to ask but the wolf interrupted. *Remember what happened next.*

"I found her!" his father's voice broke through his sleep-fogged head and Duncan startled awake, disoriented and lost. A little girl was lying next to him and for a moment he thought his wolf had killed her. But she made a little snuffling sound in her sleep and rolled over and he sighed as relief washed through him.

And then he realized he was wearing the tattered remains of the clothes he had been wearing and there wasn't a lot of coverage. Scrambling to his feet, he turned and crashed into his father, who was laughing. "I changed, father."

"I know," Julian had grinned, pride shining in his eyes as beamed at Duncan. "Was it everything you hoped?"

Duncan couldn't prevent the smile from stretching his face as he remembered the exhilaration of shifting, of being a wolf. Words could not describe what it was like, but his father would know that. "It was... incredible."

His father clapped him on the back, "Why don't you shift while I get little Alex inside; her parents are sick with worry. As soon as they're gone, I'll join you on a run through the woods. I want to show you our world."

Duncan and his father shared a smile as Duncan dropped to the ground, shifting before he landed. Taking off into the woods, forgetting all about the little girl, he ran.

"My, God," Duncan breathed, slowly opening his eyes, half-expecting to see the woods that had come alive to him that night. But it was the darkened study, reminding him he was still human; that he had partially bonded with his wolf and had ended things before it could be completed. He remembered the little girl.... "You claimed her back then."

If I could I would smack you upside you head for even thinking something so stupid, the wolf growled. *Of course I didn't claim her back then, you moron. But it has been your stubbornness that has caused no ends to my annoyances and grief. She's ours, Duncan; she has always been ours and while* you *didn't remember the little girl, I never forgot.*

Duncan was still trying to reconcile his past with his present; with his future. His wolf had respected his wishes, until Lexi came back into their lives. But how could he keep her if his very presence put her in danger? She....

Do shut up, Duncan, the wolf growled. *I will keep her safe, I promise.*

But....

I didn't expect to love her as an adult, the wolf admitted. *To want her, but the moment she came back into our lives I knew we would claim her. I promise she will be all right.*

"You cannot make that promise," Duncan ground out. "If I forget myself, you'll bite her and then we will both lose her. We'll lose everything."

Don't you understand? The wolf's voice was rough, passionate, as he spoke. *I am not separate from you; I* am *you. And you are me. Accept me. Embrace me, accept my gifts and live up to your full potential; embrace who you are, Duncan;*

you are a wolf. You are the Alpha; you have always been the Alpha. And Alexandra is our mate; we will not hurt her.

Yes, Duncan murmured, feeling the influx of power as he finally became utterly one with the wolf. The wolf's essence filled him and instead of overpowering him, it complimented him. With his eyes opened, he saw the room sharpen, brighten around him; the scents became stronger, the sounds clearer. The dam in his chest burst open and flooded him with what he was always meant to be; what he always was.

He was the Alpha.

And Lexi was his mate.

Finally.

Shut up. But this time, Duncan said the rejoinder with a smile.

*****

Lexi lugged her bag inside, wondering how she ended up with so much more stuff than when she had left; she didn't remember shopping all that much. Her time spent with Aunt Cassandra had been illuminating and she understood why she remained a virgin until Duncan came along and she was so eager to be rid of her virginity. Apparently Sirens of their magnitude were only tempted by the man who would win their heart, which Lexi thought was ridiculous and complete bullshit. It wasn't fair that the man she was destined to spend the rest of her life with was chosen for her by the Fates or whatever; it didn't matter if the man chosen for her was Duncan, whom she adored. Whom she had kissed goodbye.

With a grunt, she turned on the lights, wondering where her roommates were. She probably could have called Dima or Cole from the airport but she needed just a little bit more time to figure out what to say to them. Having spent the entire flight trying to figure out what to say should have been the first clue that a forty-five minute ride from the airport wasn't going to help much. How was she going to tell the two most important men in her life that she was a Siren, or that she was apparently sexually attracted to only one man? The two of them were going to look at her and then laugh at her.

It would be a good sound to hear, if only she knew where they were. Well, it was fairly late; they were probably at *Skin*. Maybe after she got her bag upstairs, she'd get dressed up and join them there. After all, it had been almost three weeks since she donned a wig; it might be kind of fun to see what was happening at the club.

Or maybe she'd pull on a pair of jeans, pull her hair back in a ponytail and drive out to Duncan's bar. Maybe she'd run into him and be able to strike up a conversation. Maybe convince him to take her home and to his bed since she no longer worked for him and he wouldn't be able to use that excuse. No matter how much time it took, she would work her way beneath his skin until he realized he loved her. And if he never loved her, at least she'd have a few more months with him.

Hopefully it wouldn't take thirty years to desire sex again. No wonder why her aunt had been dotty; it must have been difficult to go that long without sex. The Siren's gift truly could be a curse if that were the case: loving one man and not being able to have him and thus not being able to have anyone. A shudder went through Lexi as she pushed the door to her bedroom open, wondering how the Fates could be so cruel as to choose a mate and then deny love.

Her thoughts circled around and around with Duncan standing in the middle. Duncan… possibly the only man she'd ever have sex with.

Maybe she should call Cole's cell and ask him to come home, maybe see if it were possible to have sex with someone not Duncan. Or she could call Dima but the bar was probably insanely busy and he wouldn't be able to get away. Not that she was going to call either of them up and ask them to have sex with her; it was simply an option to see if it was possible.

Even if the idea held zero appeal.

If Duncan wanted to have nothing to do with her after she re-introduced herself she might consider the Cole and/or Dima option. Hell, if Duncan couldn't love her, she'd fake it because she was not going to go the rest of her life without sex, even if she had to fall in love with someone not her Soul Mate. Besides, what did the Fates know? Maybe they weren't so cruel as to offer only one; or maybe they were exceedingly cruel to offer just one.

Turning on the lights, she shook her head and smiled wryly; that just seemed....

Her thoughts ended abruptly as she saw the pictures of Duncan on her wall, the pictures of a naked Duncan on her wall. The bag slipped from her fingers and landed with a thump next to her feet, her jaw falling nearly as far. Duncan. Naked. And on her wall.

Of course she recognized Cole's hand in the artistry of capturing the essence of Duncan, she just wondered how on earth her newly promoted to favorite roommate had accomplished such a feat. Maybe blackmail, though Lexi couldn't figure out what dirt Cole could possibly have on Duncan that would get Duncan to strip off his clothes and get his picture taken. It didn't matter; his pictures were on her wall.

Walking over to the first, her breath caught in her throat as the light backlit Duncan's muscled form, the curve off his butt, the sleekness of his back. Running her hand over the achingly familiar lines, Lexi could almost feel his flesh beneath her fingers and her body responded as if he were real, as if he were there. The next picture was from the front, his body twisted in such a way to hide the more interesting parts of his anatomy but revealing his strength, his sheer masculinity. Flashing, silver eyes stared out at her from his beloved face and she had to squeeze her eyes closed for a moment to regain control of her emotions.

Taking her time, she examined a few more photos that highlighted different parts of his body: his ridged stomach, the sharp hips, his long limbs, his elegant back. And then she froze in front of the close up of his face, the harsh planes made even more stunning by the beautiful silver eyes. If she stared long enough, she would fall into the picture and never be apart from the man again. If she stared long enough, she could believe in fairy tales and happily ever after and True Love.

Tearing her gaze away from the mesmerizing image, she saw something out of the corner of her eye and jumped. Realizing it was only Cole standing in the doorway, his arms crossed over his chest as he watched her with an enigmatic smile, she laughed. Placing her hand over her racing heart, she crossed the distance between them, walking into his arms, "You scared me Cole; I didn't think anyone was home.'

"I've been standing here for the last twenty minutes as you stared at my latest masterpieces," he chuckled, kissing the top of her head. "I was thinking about using them in my next show."

"Don't you dare, Cole," Lexi growled, stepping back and glaring at him with flashing green and gold hazel eyes. "If anyone else sees those photos I will rip their eyeballs out."

Cole laughed harder at the vehemence in her voice, draping an arm around her shoulder and guiding her over to the bed. "Don't worry, my sweet; I promised Mr. Tremain that the pictures were for a strictly private viewing. How was your trip?"

"It was good," Lexi murmured, wanting to get back to talking about Duncan but not knowing how to do so without appearing rude. "Aunt Cassie gave me a lot to think about and I'm glad I went."

"By the expression on your face when I came in I would say you are still mooning over the delectable Duncan Tremain," Cole teased, giving her a lead in but in a way that made it seem like she was still mooning over him. Which she wasn't.

Okay, she was.

But Cole was here and it was the perfect opportunity to prove her aunt wrong; she could have sex with someone not Duncan. After all, she loved Cole and she knew that Cole loved her since the goodbye kiss didn't work on him.... Catching her lower lip between her teeth, she looked up at him, "Cole?"

"Yes, my sweet Lexi?" he asked, grinning.

"Will you have sex with me?" she asked bluntly, her fingers going to the hem of her t-shirt.

He made a strange strangled sound and color flooded his cheeks as he stared at her aghast, "Lexi, I think you may have had too much sun. You're asking me to have sex with you? Why now, after all of this time?"

"Well," she hesitated to explain. But Cole had seen her at her worst, recently in fact when she passed out at the office, and he knew everything there was to know about her; she could trust him with anything. She did trust him. "It turns out the women in my family are descendants of Sirens and apparently I'm one of the breeds of Sirens that can have only one mate... er, sex partner. But I kind of want to prove that theory wrong. So, you wanna have sex?"

That same strangled choking sound came again and his face was even brighter red, "Lexi, as much as I love you and would love to share your bed, I don't think I can have sex with you."

Throwing caution to the wind, she whipped the t-shirt off her body. Standing up, she undid the buttons of her blue jeans and slid them off her legs until she wore only her lacy peach bikinis and matching bra. "I'm a Siren, Cole; a mythological creature that lures men to their death with their beauty and sensuality. Don't you want to be a part of a myth?"

"I don't want to die," he said gruffly, his voice thick with desire as he came to his feet and took his shirt off. As his eyes roamed down her nearly naked body, he added, "But in this case, I think it would be worth it."

Stepping forward, he took her into his arms until the warmth of his body pressed against hers. Sinking his fingers into her hair, he held the back of her head as he slowly lowered his lips to hers. And all Lexi felt was the absurd need to laugh. Biting her lips, she watched as he brought his mouth down over hers, expertly kissing her with the skills of a modern day Casanova.

And she felt nothing except the overwhelming belief that it was wrong to be kissing Cole when her heart belonged to another. His tongue stroked over hers and while she could appreciate his technique, she was detached and her evaluation was clinical.

As soon as he realized she wasn't kissing him back, he leaned his forehead against hers and sighed loudly, "Not feeling it, Lexi?"

"Um, you're a very good kisser," she said softly, licking her lips and tasting Cole there. She wanted the taste of Duncan to be on her lips. "But I think I am a one-man woman."

He let her go and sat down hard on her bed, laughing at her, "I have seen you in less, Lexi, but right now you are the sexiest damn woman I have ever seen. If I didn't like the bastard, I would want to kill him."

Chapter 20 (Saturday, a week later)

Lexi walked along the balcony around the edge of the ballroom in her parent's palatial estate. There were already so many people there, all eager to be a part of Senator Carson's bid to take the White House by storm. The idea of spending two years on the campaign trail, of grueling schedules, speeches, baby kissing, whatever else politicians did, sent a shiver of the utmost dread through Lexi. She was grateful she had no political ambitions what-so-ever. She much preferred to change the world in her own way; wearing marvelous clothes was just an added bonus. And as long as she held the spotlight of one good man, of Duncan, she didn't need fame.

Her red silk dress felt like heaven over her body, slithery with a mindless will of its own. The two slits on either side allowed her to walk with ease and showed off the patterned leggings she had on underneath. Her shoes were minor works of art, elegant in their deceptive simplicity: red, silk-wrapped four inch soles. Deciding against a wig, her brown hair was artfully arranged in a style vaguely similar to a Geisha's, including the porcelain sticks. Completing her look was her make-up, again a nod to the Geisha, though she did not powder her face. Her lips were glossy red and her eye liner exaggerated the lines of her almond-shaped eyes.

Flattening a hand against her quivering stomach, she wished the butterflies would take a break. Both Cole and Dima said they would swing by later and while she waited for them Lexi had hoped to be able to spend some time with her parents, just to know that love sometimes did conquer all. Unfortunately, they were both engrossed in conversations whenever she saw them, though they did smile at her, happy she showed up. Of course, they didn't know the reason why she even hesitated to begin with; and if she had her way, they would never find out. Her mom didn't need to know that she was so foolish as to fall in love with someone and then kiss him good-bye before he could fall in love with her.

Maybe luck was with her and Duncan wasn't going to be there and she could put off the re-introduction for a few more days, not knowing if she'd be able to bare the lack of recognition in his silver eyes that had once burned so hotly for her. After all, why would he be at Senator Carson's party? Sure, he was a rich business tycoon, but maybe their politics didn't mesh and Senator Carson wasn't the man Duncan wanted for the job. Yeah, and that was wishful thinking on her part; according to her mother, the Tremains were very big supporters of Senator Carson. In fact, there seemed to be some sort of connection between them, though Lexi wasn't entirely sure what, exactly, the connection was.

Why didn't she pay more attention when her mother talked about these sorts of things with her friends? Even when she was in high school she avoided the social parties her parents hosted, preferring to stay in her room doing just about anything else. In a strange turn, it was highly probable that Duncan Tremain was a regular guest at Casa Rudnar. That thought brought a wry smile to Lexi's face; at one point, she might have met him had she not hidden herself away in her room whenever her parents had people over. She wondered if she would have had the same exhilarating, unruly, devouring reaction to him if she met him while she was a mouse.

Probably; but would she have been bold enough to pursue him as relentlessly as she did as Lexi? It hardly mattered, since she hadn't met him before and even if she had she probably would have been beneath his notice, both as a mouse and a teenager.

Putting her hands against the railing, she watched the people below, looking so dignified and stunning in their tuxes and evening gowns. Her mother was so beautiful in her cream chiffon dress, her hair styled in a French twist; classic pearls encircling her throat. Her father was as handsome as ever, wearing an expensive tuxedo with a cravat instead of the usual bow tie. She smiled at the two of them as they effortlessly talked to their friends and guests.

Her brothers and sisters were all there with their spouses, all sophisticated and beautiful, mixing effortlessly with the politicians, the local celebrities, the media. Just the thought of being down there and talking with all of those superficial people had her skin breaking out in hives; if she didn't have her disguise on, she would have died of stage fright long ago.

"Look at all the beautiful people," Thea said as she sidled up next to Lexi at the railing. With a glass of champagne in her hand, she pointed at the group below, "Do you think they know how their every thought, every whim, is fabricated by powers beyond their control?"

Lexi looked at her oldest sister, seeing the fine lines around her hard eyes, the desolation within their depths. "You're not talking about the Siren's allure are you?"

Thea bit out a bitter laugh, "If only Sirens were as powerful as the puppet masters pulling the strings of these fools; no, they're all driven by fame, power."

Lexi smiled slightly. "Don't you crave fame?"

"I crave love," Thea whispered, her voice broke, her hard eyes on the husband that gazed up at her with absolute adoration.

"Your husband loves you to distraction," Lexi said softly.

With a cruel laugh, Thea shook her head no. Her eyes were bleak as she met Lexi's gaze, "He doesn't love me, Alexandra; he doesn't even exist. How can a man exist when his will is not his own?"

"I thought we couldn't control anyone," Lexi whispered, feeling queasy at the thought of how much she could have hurt Duncan had she not let him go. "Only... nudge."

"If a man is weak enough he can be controlled by any woman," Thea sneered. "And Richard is simply Richard; a fool too stupid to realize he's no longer a man."

Turning her head, she looked at Lexi, "Don't ever marry a man you can control, Alexandra; it eats away at your soul until there's nothing left but hatred and bitterness."

"Why did you?"

Thea shook her head and her eyes glistened with tears she'd never let fall, "When I was eighteen I fell madly in love with an slightly older man that was completely immune to the Siren's allure and I thought he loved me in return. I let him do things to me...."

Her voice trailed off and she took a moment to gather her composure once more and Lexi's mind flitted to her weekend with Duncan; her run in the woods.... When Thea spoke, her voice was hard, brittle, and Lexi winced. "I gave him three years of my life, knowing that he was The One. And on the night he was supposed to take me to dinner and ask me to marry him he showed up with a hangdog expression, begging me to forgive him.

"He had fallen in love with some tart he met at a conference he had attended the week before," Thea scowled. "And now we get to stand around and cheer him on as he announces his decision to take the White House by storm. Here's to you, Senator Scumbag."

Thea toasted the air and then swallowed the rest of her champagne in one gulp. With a smile that was closer to a sneer, she summoned a waiter and grabbed two more glasses, handing one to Lexi, "Hold this for me."

Lexi openly gaped at her sister; she hadn't known her sister had had her heart broken and empathy swelled in her chest. She reached out an arm to offer something – a hug, support – but Thea batted it away, glaring at her through narrowed eyes, "Don't you dare pity me, Alexandra."

"I don't," Lexi said meekly, letting her arm drop to her side and standing in silence next to her sister, uncomfortable and bleeding for her.

Thea let out another bitter laugh, "I had hoped to snag his brother's attention just to make the bastard jealous but even then Duncan was beyond my touch. Now that he's back, I'm glad I missed that opportunity; Mr. Tremain is not an easy man to deal with."

Lexi choked and then quickly drank the champagne meant for her sister. When Thea looked at her strangely, she pasted a smile on her face, "Excuse me; something must have gone down the wrong pipe."

"Isn't he your boss at that magazine you dabble in?" Thea asked curiously.

"He is, I mean, he was," Lexi said quickly, feeling the heat building in her cheeks. "I quit."

Thea snorted, nodding her head in agreement, "I'd quit, too, if I had that man breathing down my neck day in and day out."

Lexi's knees went a little wobbly at the thought of Duncan breathing down her neck and she grabbed onto the railing to steady herself. She had finally come to a place of peace, she didn't need any reminders of what was hers for only a moment of time. Luckily, Thea was oblivious to her discomfort and continued on, "After Philip left I decided I would never again let another man have that kind of power over me."

"So you went to the other extreme and married Richard." Lexi looked out over the crowd and saw Thea's handsome husband smiling up at his wife, devotion shining in his soft blue eyes.

"If a man is captured by the Siren's song, Alexandra, he doesn't die. No, it is far worse and far crueler. Look at Richard; I can treat him like a dog and like a dumb dog he comes crawling back, begging for more," she sneered, drinking deeply of the champagne as she glared down at the poor man. "I could fuck the pool boy in front of him and he wouldn't bat an eye. It disgusts me; he disgusts me. For eleven years…."

"Then let him go," Lexi said quietly, passionately. Looking out over the crowd, her brain short-circuited for a moment as she saw Duncan walking in, looking a little less civilized than before. Her fingers curled around the railing to keep her from flying into his arms and kissing him until he remembered her. She couldn't do that to him; she didn't even know if it was possible. Instead, she would have to take things slowly, since he would be meeting her for the first time and have no memories of their time together. It was going to be really difficult but she'd manage, especially if it meant getting Duncan back. Clearing her throat, ignoring the temptation that was Duncan, she faced her sister, "Let him go, Thea."

"We have eleven years together, Alexandra," Thea laughed darkly, her face miserable. "And two children; how do I let that go?"

Lexi shook her head; she didn't have an easy answer. Her eyes drifted back to Duncan and her heart wanted to rip itself to shreds. Would she have enslaved him for eleven years? Kept him as her pet until nothing remained and she ended up despising him as Thea despised Richard? She couldn't fathom ever hating him but she also gave him up. She pressed her hand against her stomach, against the butterflies that wept.

Thea gasped and when Lexi turned her head and looked at her, Thea spoke in a scandalized whisper, "My God, you love him."

"I don't know what you're talking about," Lexi said dispassionately, pressing her hand harder against the butterflies that were going to fly up and out of her throat and accuse her of lying at any moment.

Thea slowly turned her head in the direction of Duncan and Lexi struggled not to look, keeping her posture loose and her expression blank. "You're in love with Duncan Tremain."

"I don't know how you can say that." Her voice hardly quavered at all. "He doesn't even know who I am."

Thea's eyes widened as they flew back to Lexi, "You kissed him good-bye?"

"What choice did I have, Thea?" Lexi asked softly, no longer able to lie. "He didn't want me, not really; and the only reason he was with me was because I hummed."

Thea pressed her lips together and Lexi could see she was struggling not to laugh but her eyes danced. It perturbed Lexi to see her sister laugh at her after she had opened up and finally exposed her heart. Crossing her arms beneath her breasts, Lexi glared at Thea, "I'm glad you think it's funny because I have bled for almost three weeks trying to get over him. And now I get to pretend that I've never met him before when Philip introduces us…."

Lexi slapped a hand over her mouth, realizing that Philip had been her sister's former lover. The world she moved in was small and treacherous and she feared she had just stepped in a landmine, "I swear, Thea, I didn't know about you and the Senator when I did that interview."

"Shut up, Lexi," Thea said, but the words lacked heat. "Of course you didn't know; you were a child with your nose buried in your books; I'm surprised you even knew you had any siblings. And as far as Duncan Tremain goes, I doubt your kiss was much of a deterrent."

Cocking her head to the side, she asked, "What makes you say that?"

But then she felt it, the heated gaze burning into her skin. Slowly, letting her arms fall to her side, she turned her head and saw the fire burning in his silver eyes. He didn't look like a man who had forgotten anything. Quite the opposite, he looked like a man who had never forgotten a thing in his life and had relived his memories of their time together until he knew them by heart. The air of danger, intoxicating and potent, surrounding him was even more powerful than before and Lexi's attraction to him exploded exponentially.

His black hair was again perfectly cut; if ever-so-slightly uncivilized, and the tux emphasized his broad shoulders and long legs. She had thought he looked good in a suit, but, holy hell! he was overwhelming in a tux. The warrior cleaned up really, really well.

Out of the corner of her mouth, she whispered, "He said he didn't love me and I kissed him good-bye; he doesn't remember our time together, only the… lust he feels when he sees me."

"Haven't you figured it out by now?" Thea asked, amusement and bitterness making her voice rough. "The members of that family are immune to Siren allure; if he wanted you before it was of his own volition and nothing you did could have influenced him. And Lexi? You can't control that particular man simply by humming."

With that, she finished off her champagne and headed towards the stairs with a little extra sway in her steps. Lexi watched her go, her final words working through her dazed brain, rearranging what she thought she knew into something new and wonderful.

Duncan wanted her of his own free will.

And then her joy sank and despair gripped her and shook her senseless. What if her sister was wrong and the kiss worked in erasing his memories of their strange courtship? After all, she *had* kissed him good-bye before giving him a chance to fall in love. Unless he was truly was immune to her good-bye kisses. If he remembered….

She couldn't stop the smile from forming as she turned her head to find him but he wasn't there. The smile withered and died as another possibility occurred to her: he remembered and was adamant on keeping his distance. Or worse, disgusted that she was the mousy youngest daughter of the Rudnar family. Or equally worse, he thought she was insane because she claimed to be a Siren. Of course, if he wasn't human, than he'd have no right to hold her Siren-ness against her, unless his supernatural species abhorred Sirens….

Lexi was thinking in circles and she wasn't going to learn anything until she tracked him down and confronted him directly. She just had no idea where he had gone. She scanned the room, her eyes falling on Ashley, looking as elegant as ever in a black sheath dress, her hair perfect without a wayward strand to mess it up. She was smiling broadly at someone, her hand sparkling with a huge, glittering diamond ring. With her stomach clenching, Lexi forced herself to look at the man Ashley was talking to, afraid of what she was going to see.

Duncan, looking so devastatingly gorgeous her knees weakened and she had to tighten her hold on the railing before she melted to the floor. He was smiling down at Ashley, obviously unaffected by Lexi's absence over the last couple of weeks. She had been wrong to hope; Duncan didn't miss her, not if that ring on Ashley's finger was any indication. She wondered if he rushed out and proposed the next day or if he waited a week. Bastard. Obviously he forgot….

At that moment, Duncan turned his head and when she looked into his eyes, even from this distance, she forgot everything but him. He narrowed his eyes as he looked at her, a wolf scenting his prey, but was he going to devour her or tear her to pieces? He bent his head to say something to Ashley who in turn looked up and saw Lexi standing there.

"Oh, shit," Lexi breathed, not sure what to make of Ashley's smile. Turning, she resumed walking along the balcony, hoping she'd be able to avoid Duncan for the rest of the party. Hell, for the rest of her life. If he was engaged, she didn't want to have anything to do with him; as powerful as her attraction to him was, she was not going to poach on some other woman's husband, especially Ashley. She briefly thought about Dima, since he had seemed really attracted to Ashley, but he hadn't said anything when she talked to him on the phone the last couple of weeks.

Suddenly, the air inside was too hot, too stifling; the house was too small. She couldn't handle being in the same building as him. Her emotions were already raw but then to see him with Ashley…. At least before, even if he hadn't remembered her, there had been hope that she could wrangle her way back into his life. Now, it didn't matter if he remembered or not….

Pushing through the doors to the deck, she exited the house. Without thinking where she was going or what she was doing, she hurriedly made her way down the steps to get to the immaculately landscaped grounds. The pool house was just ahead and she'd be able to take a moment and collect her thoughts, figure out a way to face Duncan without having her heart rip itself from her chest and chase after him when he was engaged to another woman.

Fury seethed through her at the thought of Duncan with anyone not her and she was sorely tempted to march back inside and tear him from Ashley's arm, to viciously suggest the red head find her own mate, and then punish him for daring to look at another woman. But she wasn't an animal and Duncan was free to make his own mistakes. She just needed to get her bewildering jealous and possessive instincts under control and once Cole and Dima arrived the three of them could put in a brief appearance and get the hell out of there. She'd explain everything to Mother in a few years when she was able to look back on this entire episode and laugh.

"Alexandra!" Duncan's voice broke through her raging thoughts, making her walk faster. Damn it, why did she insist on wearing shoes that made running all but impossible? On today of all days, why did she insist on making escape so difficult? And how the hell did he follow her so quickly? Obviously he must have exited the house on the ground floor, after seeing which way she fled.

"Stupid," Lexi chided herself, quickening her pace, practically feeling Duncan right on top of her. His hand wrapped around her upper arm and the spark of electricity nearly burned her. With a cry of alarm, she came to a stop. If he didn't let her go she was liable to claw his eyeballs out for engaging himself to Ashley. And then kissing him until he was all better. Of course, she wasn't sure how she would replace his eyes. And where the hell did this violent streak come from? It was not natural. In a low growl, she breathed, "Let go, Duncan."

"Where the hell have you been?" he asked in a quietly furious voice. He didn't pull her to him, but he didn't let go, either. "I have been looking everywhere for you and no one would betray your hideout."

"I wasn't hiding, Duncan," she bit out. "I kissed you goodbye; I was simply… resting."

"About that kiss," he growled and her knees went week. "It doesn't work on a wolf."

She swallowed against the lump in her throat, “And I suppose Ashley is your mate?”

“I tell you that I’m a wolf and you’re worried that Ashley is my mate?” he chuckled and she wanted to scream. Softly, his breath moving seductively over her ear, he whispered, "Turn around and look at me, Lexi.”

Slowly, she turned around and drank in the sight of Duncan. Up close, she could see the slight darkening under his beautiful silver eyes, the relief in those eyes. Joy mixed with confusion as she looked at him, seeing the hunger in his gaze, the wildness. She had seen the wildness before, when she had woken up with a wolf in her bed. She should have figured it out; of course he was a wolf. Of course he was. Her brows knit together as she continued to drink in the sight of him. “Do you turn into a wolf only when the moon is full?”

"When I was a teenager I could change whenever I pleased but then I shut the wolf out and could only change when the moon was full. I still had to change when the moon was full." The corners of his mouth drew up into a wide smile at the question. “Now that the wolf and I have bonded I can turn into a wolf any time I want. But Lexi….”

His eyes became tormented as he looked at her and his mouth tightened into a firm line, “I gave you up because I couldn’t bear the thought of hurting you, destroying you, and I know at some point I would have lost control and bit you.”

“Duncan,” she tried to interrupt but he put a finger over her mouth so he could finish.

Swallowing, he vowed, “I swear on my life that I will keep you safe; if I have to chain myself up to keep the wolf from biting you I will live in chains.”

“Duncan,” the word was muffled since his hand was still over her mouth.

His expression became fierce as he glared past her, “Before I bonded with him, the wolf acted on his own volition and claimed you as his mate. I want you to know that if you don’t wish to be mated to a wolf, to me, I will let you go.”

“But how can the wolf be mated to me if you’re engaged to Ashley?”

The smile he gave her was dazzling, “I’m not engaged to Ashley.”

He stepped closer to her and she could feel the heat from his body washing over hers. As he moved closer, dangerously closer, as his breath fanned out over her face, filling her lungs with his scent, she whispered, "But I saw the ring."

Reaching into his pocket, he pulled out a blue velvet box. With one hand, he popped it open, revealing a three-carat solitaire diamond set in a simple, platinum band. Somehow, his hand that was restraining her was around her waist and he was holding her, and she reveled in it. His voice was low, seductive, as he asked, "This ring?"

Without taking it, she focused on his molten silver eyes and not the lips she wanted to kiss. "I don't understand; I saw the ring on Ashley's finger."

"Did it never occur to you that she was engaged to someone else?" he asked with a half-smile, tightening his hold on her, wrapping his other arm around her, the box still in his hand.

"Well, no," she admitted, pressing her palms against his chest and feeling the steady rhythm of his heart. He was looking at her as if he was a dying man and she was his Heaven; the way she felt about him. "I can't imagine anyone choosing someone else over you."

"She's not engaged to me," he smiled, rubbing his free hand up and down her back, and she was grateful to be in his arms once again. "Do you really think I'd ask you to marry me if I was already engaged?"

Her breath caught in her throat as the significance of the diamond in his hand began to sink in. "You're truly asking me to marry you? But, why?"

"Don't you know?" he murmured, bending his head and placing a soft kiss on the corner of her mouth.

"No?" But she did know, it was all there in his stormy eyes, in his desperate hold.

"I love you," he said hoarsely, sincerely and everything within Lexi ground to a halt. She had to remind herself to breath. "I love you, Lexi. From the first moment I saw you I've loved you. You make me want to howl at the moon and run naked in the streets, and not while I'm a wolf," he teased, smiling down at her.

Getting down on his knees, he looked up at her, "Marry me."

Unable to have her warrior lowering himself to anyone, Lexi fell to her knees as well. Reaching up and cupping his beloved face in her hands, she had to know, "Are you only asking me because your wolf claimed me?"

"No; the wolf made me see what was right in front of my face; I love you," he assured her huskily, claiming her mouth with his in a searing kiss. Holding her in place with one hand, he told her without words how much he wanted her, letting his tongue caress her lips until she opened for him. Realizing he was a hair's breadth away from losing complete control, he pulled back. Both were breathing heavily as he drew her attention back to the ring. "Marry me, Lexi; Tell me you'll marry me."

She hesitated, catching her lower lip between her teeth as she looked up at him through lowered lashes, her eyes sparkling mischievously. "There's something I should tell you first."

"I don't care what it is, Lexi," he growled, framing her face in his hands and staring deeply into her eyes, showing her the wolf; showing her his soul. "I cannot exist without you."

"The wolf already bit me," she said. Her hand automatically went to the long faded bite, a slight smile playing at her lips at the memory. She always smiled at the memory of that night. "I thought it was you – I mean, it *was* you – but it was the wolf and...."

He closed his eyes and after a moment he whispered roughly, "I remember. He had kept that memory back but I remember. Oh, God, that was... that had been incredible." Swallowing thickly, his eyes opened and she was drowning in silver fire as his mouth crashed down over hers and he consumed her whole.

"Duncan," she gasped, reluctantly pulling her mouth away from his. "Does this mean I can turn into a wolf, too?"

Breathing heavily, nearly panting, his eyes glowed as he slowly nodded, "You are a wolf, Lexi; in time, you'll be able to shift but it takes practice."

"How?" her eyes sparkled with excitement and anticipation.

"You just... imagine it," he said, trying to explain something that was impossible to describe. "And simply let it happen."

Closing her eyes, she started to shimmer, feeling the cells in her body begin to boil, her skin begin to tighten. Duncan's hand was on her arm and when she opened her eyes, he had an amused smile, "Not here, my love. but I think you'll manage."

She beamed at him and he couldn't resist snatching her back into his arms and kissing her madly. The little Siren was going to be a glorious wolf. And she was his. "Marry me," he beseeched ardently against her lips. "Goddamnit, Lexi; Marry me."

"Yes," she rasped, trying to catch her breath as Duncan possessed her completely. "Yes, yes, a thousand times yes."

As he continued to kiss her, he somehow managed to pull the ring out of the box and slip it onto her left ring finger; it fit perfectly. Tossing the box over his shoulder, he wrapped his arms around her and plundered her mouth once more. "God, Lexi, I love you."

"I love you," she breathed as his lips claimed her once again. Without any thought beyond the feel of being in his arms once more, she fell back against the ground, taking him with her, connected by their mouths. Duncan's body moved over hers as his hand slid to her waist, as her hands slipped beneath his jacket. As he trailed kissed along her jaw, her throat, as tears of joy shined in her eyes, she whispered, "I love you, I love you, I love you."

"Alexandra!" her mother's shocked voice interrupted their reunion. "What on earth are you doing? Duncan Tremain? What have you done to my daughter?"

Duncan lifted his head, still a bit foggy from kissing Lexi, and he looked at the woman standing over them, at her equally astonished husband; at three gorgeous Sirens and their equally handsome spouses, the three Rudnar sons and their partners; at various children; at his oldest brother Philip, at Philip's wife Stacey; at Ashley and Dima and Cole. With a low growl, he stood up and helped Lexi to her feet, keeping a tight hold around her waist. Glaring at his brother, he asked evenly, "Was it necessary to invite the whole party to our engagement?"

"You're… engaged?" Charisma asked, her expression bewildered as she looked at her youngest daughter. "Is he The One?"

Lexi closed her eyes and nodded, "I thought I was being selfless and I kissed him good-bye."

Her mom and sisters all gasped but Duncan's tightened his hold on her shoulders, pulling her closer to his hard body until his scent, the wild woods smell stronger now that he had fully bonded with his wolf washed over her. "But I love her and it didn't work."

Penelope squealed, stepping forward and embracing her sister, "I am so happy for you! I knew you were destined for great happiness, Lexi; I simply knew it!! When are you getting married? What about kids? Are you planning on starting a family right away or…."

"Penny, dear," her husband said, gently wrapping his arm around her shoulders and pulling her away from the newly engaged couple. "Let's give them some space to breathe."

Lexi smiled and then her gaze landed on Ashley and Dima and her smile widened. Without a word, the pair stepped forward and while Ashley and Lexi hugged, Dima and Duncan shook hands. Then Dima turned to Lexi with a sheepish smile and took her into his arms. Softly, he murmured, "So, I guess this means you'll be an Alpha female."

Astonished, Lexi drew her head back and looked at her best friend, truly looked at him; he was a wolf, "What?"

"About that," Duncan said uncomfortably, wrapping his arm around Lexi and pulling her back to his side. The possessive, dominant streak was oddly arousing. "I'm the Alpha of the pack that manages *The Black Wolf;* I hope that won't be a problem."

She chuckled and shook her head, too overwhelmed to speak; *The Black Wolf,* it made so much sense. As everyone continued to talk animatedly around her, Lexi exchanged a troubled look with Thea, who looked miserable and resigned. As Thea glanced at her husband, Lexi knew that Thea wasn't going to let him go. Shaking her head in sorrow for her sister, for Richard, she knew there was nothing she could do but hope; Thea would have to make that choice.

Finally, her gaze went to Cole, whose highlights were now lime green. He wore a powder blue tuxedo and he was so comfortable in his skin that he made the look work. His eyes sparkled as he stepped forward and took her into his arms. "I love you, Lexi. I wish you all of the happiness in the world, my sweet."

"Thank you," she choked out, tears welling in her eyes. "I wish the same for you."

Stepping back, she took Duncan's hand in her own and smiled at him, her eyes teary with an onslaught of emotion, "Are you sure you still want to marry me?"

"You're the love of my life, Lexi Darling-Alexandra Rudnar," Duncan said, his voice warm with love and affection. "My life will be a barren wasteland without you in it; you damn well better believe I want to marry you."

She smiled at the unmistakable shimmer of love in his eyes. Duncan Tremain was going to be her husband. A huge bubble of joy exploded in her body and she laughed, wrapping her arms around him and hugging him with all of the love in her heart and soul. "I love you, Duncan."

Epilogue

The Scene by Lexi Tremain

It was the wedding of the year: the marriage of Alexandra Rudnar, AKA Lexi Darling, to Duncan Tremain. The ceremony took place on the bride and groom's stunning estate and the happy couple was surrounded by all of their friends and loved ones. Though the bride tried to convince him to wear a kilt, the groom still managed to look quite dashing in his black tuxedo. Beneath the three-button jacket, he wore a burgundy vest, a burgundy Windsor band tie and a white wing collar shirt.

The bride wore an unusual, one-of-a-kind wedding dress designed by the immensely talented Darnell Wu. It was made of a white, gossamer material shot through with silver thread. The bodice lovingly embraced her torso and flared out slightly at her hips, ending mid-calf. Instead of a veil, she opted to wear fairy wings; large, iridescent fairy wings. She wore her hair in a complicated up-do with strands of crystals woven through it. There were no wigs in sight. Her make-up was artfully applied, with intricate scroll work around her eyes in soft colors while her lips were painted a glossy rose. As she stood beneath the sun with the love of her life, she sparkled.

She wore no shoes.

The weather had been absolutely perfect, as if the Fates themselves smiled upon the union. The sun glowed brilliantly in the blue sky as puffs of white clouds lazily drifted along; the slight breeze teased the guests with the subtle scent of wild flowers. Birds sang from the trees and danced in the skies overhead but the only thing the bride could see was the man who stood in front of her, promising to love her for all eternity.

After the vows were spoken and the couple was pronounced husband and wife, the guests were invited to dance on the makeshift stage while enjoying the spectacular brews from *The Black Wolf* bar. As evening fell and day gave way to night, lights twinkled from thousands of little fairy lights strung throughout the trees. And as the moon rose overhead, the song of a hundred wolves filled the sweet-smelling air.

Addendum: The couple is expecting their first child in six months; a honeymoon baby who is already loved beyond reason.

*****

"Duncan, will I grow two more sets of breasts?" Lexi asked, standing naked in front of the mirror as she examined her body, trying to see if there were any changes yet.

Chuckling, he came up behind her and cupped her breasts in his warm hands, making her hiss in pleasure. That was something that had changed; her breasts, her nipples, were extraordinarily sensitive. "No, my love, just two perfect breasts, just the same as when you shift into your beautiful wolf form."

Pressing a hand over her flat stomach, she met Duncan's eyes in the reflection, melting a little when she saw the love that shone so brightly. Even though he had bonded with his wolf he was still Duncan, only enhanced, and she loved him so damn much it hurt sometimes. The sex was phenomenal but it was in the silence that she knew her love was real: being held by him, talking quietly with him, arguing with him and then making up; all of the little things that added texture to their lives. He was her perfect mate.

Sex as a wolf was... it was everything the night in the moonlit woods had been, only more. But she preferred making love with Duncan, face to face. She loved looking into his eyes as he whispered words of passion and made love to her body, her soul. Their wolves were there, too, adding spice to their already hot sex.

And she loved his wolf, who guided her into her new world; taking her by the paw until she was ready to run on her own and then running by her side. When they went running as wolves, they were frequently joined by Ashley and Dima. And by Cole, who was enjoying the notoriety of being a single wolf who used to be human. He hadn't wanted to be left behind, preferring to be transformed into a wolf so he could remain with his best friends, even though he had been terrified.

He was a gorgeous, golden wolf and all of the she-wolves loved him....

Narrowing her eyes slightly, trying to determine if her stomach was a little bit bigger, she asked, "Now, you're sure I'll only have one little cub, right?"

"Maybe two," Duncan teased, kissing the curve of her neck and sending a buzz of aching need down her spine. His palms dropped to her stomach, covering the baby that nestled within as he murmured, "Wolves have a slightly higher chance of twins but I'm more concerned at the possibility of daughters; a Siren-wolf will storm the world and take no prisoners."

She grinned, rubbing her butt against his erection, "Did you know pregnancy makes me extremely horny?"

"I am aware of that," he said calmly, his eyes glowing in arousal. His cock leapt in anticipation as she spun in his arms and draped her arms around his neck. As her full breasts pressed against his chest, he growled, "Do you want me or do you want to run in the woods?"

"I want both," she purred, slipping out of his arms and taking off down the stairs and out the back door, not bothering to dress or shift. She knew he would be on her in a heartbeat and she looked forward to making love to Duncan in the Great Outdoors.

He was her Duncan and she loved him. All of him.

###

CPSIA information can be obtained at www.ICGtesting.com
Printed in the USA
LVOW131938191212

312463LV00001B/94/P